Mary Howitt, Margaret Howitt

# Mary Howitt

An Autobiography

Mary Howitt, Margaret Howitt

**Mary Howitt**
*An Autobiography*

ISBN/EAN: 9783337010867

Printed in Europe, USA, Canada, Australia, Japan

Cover: Foto ©Raphael Reischuk / pixelio.de

More available books at **www.hansebooks.com**

# MARY HOWITT

## An Autobiography

EDITED BY HER DAUGHTER

## MARGARET HOWITT

" Confide to God that thou hast from Him ; oh thou soul weary of wandering !  Confide to the Truth, that which is from the Truth within thee, and thou shalt lose nothing."

ST. AUGUSTINE

*IN TWO VOLUMES*

VOL. I.

LONDON
WM. ISBISTER LIMITED
15 & 16 TAVISTOCK STREET COVENT GARDEN
1889

# PREFACE.

How this autobiography gradually grew into shape can best be told in my mother's own words, drawn from the correspondence of half a lifetime.

In 1843 she thus addresses her elder sister, Anna :—

"Many tenderly endearing incidents came crowding into my mind of our young life in Uttoxeter, especially connected with thy unselfish, amiable, sweet spirit, which seems to me without a shade. Thou and I had been for years, nay, all our girlhood, *one*; we had no thought or feeling unshared. There are little incidents which have occurred in my life, such as a look, a changing colour, nay, even a sigh, that will remain in my mind for ever. It is especially so as regards thee and those times. I remember so much, which, I dare say, thou hast forgotten, but which draws my heart, as by the most powerful attraction, to thee. How I shall like to talk over these things with thee !"

Endowed with a retentive memory, deep-rooted affections, and poetic feeling, my mother delighted to speak of the Past with her children. We, in our turn, were always asking this, that, and the other question, when incidents especially charmed and interested us. She had,



*b*

in a little juvenile work belonging to her "Tales for the People and their Children," and entitled "My Own Story," given us some details of her childhood. But as the autobiographical sketch ceased when she was ten, it did not suffice us. It seemed to us like a beautiful idyllic romance to hear of the two tender, poetical, enthusiastic sisters, Anna and Mary, as maidens on the banks of the Dove.

The very restricted, silent, almost conventual life which they led, even their quaint, plain attire, had a charm of original purity about it, with a vernal freshness and fragrance as of primroses and cowslips. We were always wanting a great deal more information of a girlhood distinguished by a keen love of Nature, an insatiable hungering and thirsting after poetry and books, and an undercurrent of artistic impulse and vitality. We wished that all her graphic descriptions could be connected together in one clear, consecutive narrative.

In the summer of 1868, much, therefore, to our satisfaction, she wrote a chronicle of her parentage and early life, which, when completed, she read to our aunt Anna, receiving from her additional information and useful suggestions. Then the memoirs remained in abeyance until after my father's decease in the spring of 1879, when her mind became once more steeped in recollections, especially of her husband's life and character.

Speaking of William Howitt—whose name and her own are, to use the simile of an American author, indissolubly wedded in English literature—she says :—

"His birthplace, Heanor, was an obscure and rural

nook linked to the outer world by the carrier's cart, retaining many traces of feudal rudeness, and filled with a motley assemblage of eccentric, undisciplined, but often very humorous individuals, whose odd sayings and doings amused my husband throughout his life. Indeed, the scenes and characters of his secluded youth produced upon him the same permanent fascination as those of mine had done in my case, and which imparts a biographical rather than inventive quality to our works of fiction.

"The bold, happy lad to whom Nature had been nurse, guide, and guardian never had his brain dwarfed by excessive study, and gradually amassed a vast stock of learning. As a young man, when the use of tobacco was not carried to the present excess, he for a short time accepted that indulgence, but perceiving the power it might gain over him, and resolving never to become the slave of any enjoyment, he speedily and entirely relinquished it. He never accustomed himself to the use of wine or spirits, or the habit, either for pleasure or labour, of turning night into day.

"He was through the whole of his literary career a steady, industrious worker. He faithfully fulfilled every engagement in the accomplishment of task-work; and maintained with equal exactitude his regular relaxation and refreshment, and that simply of fresh air and exercise. Thus preserving a sound mind in a sound body, he reached his eighty-seventh year without the failure of any mental or physical faculty.

"He traversed much of Great Britain on foot, principally to gather up personal knowledge for his 'Rural Life in England,' his 'Visits to Remarkable Places,' and his 'Homes and Haunts of the Poets.' He was very conscientious in never describing as known to him what he himself had never visited. Hence he became familiar with the character of England, its scenery and its people as existing half a century ago. He had immense sympathy and an infinite fund of humour; wherever, therefore, he paused for a night, or sat to rest by the wayside with peasant people, he left behind him a memory that long survived."

In August 1879 my mother, then recently become a widow, and physically suffering from the shock of her bereavement, writes from Dietenheim, her summer home in the Tyrol, to her elder daughter, Anna Mary :—

"I sit in my upper chamber with the door open to the balcony, the awning up, and a pleasant, gentle breeze refreshing me, as if an angel softly wafted an air-fan. I watch the shadows of the swallows flitting over the sun-lighted awning, but the birds I see not, excepting such as fly past more distantly and leave no shadows. Through the iron railings of the balcony I see the pleasant landscape, and the people busy in their rye-harvest, the crops of which they are bringing home. How delightful it is !—a quiet life, which the Heavenly Father permits, and which is so sweetened by the remembrance of all my dear departed ones.

"Then, in memory, I go back with you to the old times. I do not think I have forgotten any incident. I walk again amid the crocuses of the Nottingham meadows, by the full, flowing, placid Trent; wander with you under the old, yet ever-new, elm-trees of Clifton Grove. We visit once more Hardwick Hall, Annesley, and Thrumpton. We sit down as of yore in the friendly basket-maker's cottage at Wilford. All this morning and yesterday I have been occupied with the Past, not, however, so much yours as pre-eminently mine, making in thought a little harmonious narrative of a still un-written chapter of my youth."

To the same.

"*Dietenheim, September* 13, 1879.—What a most beau-tiful, accurate, and appreciative article on your beloved father's works is that in the July number of the *Edin-burgh Review*, under the heading 'Rural England!' I wonder who the writer is. I think some one living in one of the south-eastern counties, from the familiar re-ferences to the country features and incidents of such a locality."

"*September* 18, 1879.—I read, write, and take quiet little strolls. Yesterday I gathered the last flowers of the trollius, the golden ball, as we called it when we were children. It was a favourite of your father's. He always brought in the first and the last. When I saw them again, they touched my heart very deeply. I gathered all I could find, and shall keep them as long as they look the least fresh, for the sake of those blessed days, which I did not value as I should have done. If one could only give to each day a stamp of that tender, imperishable love which springs up in one's heart when one can no longer pour it out in deeds of service. What would I not give now for a little walk, even on the dullest road, with that true, old companion, with whom I can never more wander on earth!

"How sorry I am you destroyed that copy-book full of your early sketches done at Nottingham! There was in it your father standing on the parlour-hearth, with its fine lofty mantelshelf. There was, too, old William Theobald, the Quaker Swedenborgian, once baker at Ackworth School, sitting in his antiquated drab suit, at some meal in the kitchen—a splendid sketch. What a pity it is that precious book is gone!"

"*Meran, February* 1880.—Your aunt Anna is getting me all the information possible about our father's family. She is searching, for the purpose, through old Monthly Meeting books, which have been lent her. I cannot tell you how kind and helpful she is. She never seems to feel it a trouble to be bothered by me."

"*December* 21, 1880.—I had quite forgotten many of my poems and tales, and have begun, when in the humour, to read them. It is just like perusing the works of some one else, so completely had they passed out of my mind. I had in earlier days such a constant, enduring sense of the struggle for life in my soul or in my brain, that I had not time, I regret to say, to elaborate my work, or to dwell upon it with any fondness and lingering. I am, therefore, quite thankful when I come upon any really good sentiment or bit of simple, true religion."

Towards the close of 1884 she writes to a friend:—

"My dear married daughter, Anna Mary, came to see us at Meran the beginning of May. It was nearly three years since we had met, and I thought it would probably be our last meeting on earth, I naturally supposing I should be the first summoned hence. She came to Meran at the time of roses, bringing with her a collection of drawings and sketches, which she had earlier made of her parents' 'Homes and Haunts.' She began at once to make sketches of our present surroundings, with a sense of their being needed. Towards the end of June we left for Dietenheim. There too she made many drawings and sketches, as she had always done on her visits to us, for the character of the place was kindred to her spirit. In July the weather was intensely hot. On the night of the 19th a violent gale suddenly came up from the north. The icy wind seemed to pierce her. She complained of sore throat, which rapidly developed into diphtheria; and on the night of July 23rd she passed away. Now the sketches so thoughtfully and lovingly made by her will illustrate the 'Reminiscences,' which I have promised the Editor of *Good Words* to write for that periodical. It seems strange to me, after my long rest from all literary labour, and now devoid of all authorly ambition, to be thus engaged. I shall, however, have Margaret's co-operation."

To her friend, Mrs. Gaunt, she says, later, December 27, 1885 :—

"It is very gratifying to us to find that you read those 'Reminiscences' with interest, for we desire that they who have known and loved us in former days should do so. I say *we*, because Margaret helps me. I drew up, some years ago, the original autobiography of my youth; and all that follows, being of later date, has to be filled in, and to receive its life-touches, so to speak, from the old family letters, of which we have many hundreds; being all great letter-writers, and, at the same time, fond of describing people and things as well as places. These letters, therefore, are regular chronicles of long-past days, and naturally furnish the groundwork and the incidents of the narrative, which is, as you may believe, interesting, and often somewhat sorrowful. But the canvas on which our pictures are drawn is of necessity so circumscribed, that we are often disheartened by being compelled to omit many portions which are interesting and curious, and even valuable, as being bits of real life. However, these are only 'Reminiscences;' and some time or other, if people like them, much fuller pictures may be given."

The desire being generally expressed for these brief "Reminiscences" to be expanded and amplified, my mother commenced gradually making the needful preparations. I read to her letters for the purpose of selection; she also wrote down, under the name of "Gathered-up Fragments," past events as they might occur to her, and which her amanuensis had to incorporate in the narrative. This occupation, though slowly, was nevertheless steadily pursued to within a few weeks of her death, and when the framework was sufficiently completed for the autobiographic character to be maintained throughout.

By the kindness of various correspondents and intimate friends placing her letters to them at her daughter's disposal, the work has been much enriched, and finally brought to a close. It is hoped in her spirit. Had she been spared to superintend the publication, the only possible difference in this Life might have been a preference given in the selection of letters to those more pointedly bearing allusions to literary pursuits and to the characters and doings of her children—in the maternal eyes those dearer selves, for whose good she counted every labour light and the greatest sacrifice easy. Death, the revealer, seemed, however, to permit the choice rather to be given to such as conveyed a special insight into her character, and some indication of those seeds of love and joy which, in her onward course, she was ever sowing in the hearts of the oppressed and the sorrowful.

MARGARET HOWITT.

# CONTENTS.

## CHAPTER I.

### *PARENTAGE AND DESCENT.*

### 1758–1796.



## CHAPTER II.

### *EARLY DAYS AT UTTOXETER.*

### 1796–1809.

# CONTENTS.

## CHAPTER III.

### *GIRLHOOD.*

#### 1809–1821.



## CHAPTER IV.

### *MY HUSBAND'S NARRATIVE.*

#### 1792–1821.



## CHAPTER V.

### *FIRST YEARS OF MARRIED LIFE.*

#### 1821–1824.

# CHAPTER VI.

## *IN NOTTINGHAM.*

### 1824–1830.



# CHAPTER VII.

## *IN NOTTINGHAM—(continued).*

### 1830–1836.

## CHAPTER VIII.

### AT ESHER.

#### 1836–1840.



## CHAPTER IX.

### IN GERMANY.

#### 1840–1843.

# LIST OF ILLUSTRATIONS.

# MARY HOWITT.

## CHAPTER I.

### PARENTAGE AND DESCENT.

#### 1758–1796.

I CAN best commence my narrative with a few particulars respecting my father and his family. He, Samuel Botham, was descended from a long line of farmers, who had lived for centuries in primitive simplicity on their property, Apsford, situated in the bleak northern part of Staffordshire, known as the Moorlands. It was a wild, solitary district, remote from towns, and only half cultivated, with wide stretches of brown moors, where the undisturbed peewits wailed through the long summer day. Solitary houses miles apart stood here and there. Villages were far distant from each other. There was little church-going, and education was at the lowest ebb.

The town of Leek, in itself a primitive place, might be called the capital of this wild district. It was the resort of the rude farmers on the occasion of fairs and markets. Strange brutal crimes occurred from time to time, the report of which came like a creeping horror to the lower country. Sordid, penurious habits prevailed; the hoarding of money was considered a great virtue.

The Bothams of Apsford, who had accepted the teach-

ing of George Fox, might be preserved by their principles
from the coarser habits and ruder tastes of their neighbours, but refined or learned they certainly were not.
The sons, walking in the footsteps of their fathers, cultivated the soil; the daughters attended to the house and
dairy, as their mothers had done before them. They
rode on good horses, saddled and pillioned, to meeting at
Leek on First-day mornings, and were a well-to-do, orderly
set of people.

Now and then a son or daughter married "out of the
Society," as it was termed, and so split off like a branch
from the family tree, with a great crash of displeasure
from the parents, and "disownment," as it was called,
from the Monthly Meeting. In the ancient records of
the Staffordshire Monthly Meeting, preserved by the
Friends of Leek, they appear, however, to have been
generally satisfactory members, living up to the old
standard of integrity of their ancestress, Mary Botham,
who, a widow at the head of the house in the days of
Quaker persecution, was imprisoned in Stafford jail
for refusing to pay tithes. In Besse's "Sufferings of
Friends" Mary Botham is also mentioned as set in the
stocks and put into jail in Bedfordshire, leading to the
supposition that she travelled in the ministry.

Years glided uneventfully on, generation followed
generation, until 1745, when the rumour that "the
Scotch rebels were. coming" filled the scattered inhabitants of the Moorlands with terror. Even the quiet
Friend, John Botham, of Apsford, might have prepared to
fight; one thing is certain, he hurried wife and children
out of the way, and buried his money and valuables.
But there was no need of fighting, hardly of fear. The
Scotch soldiers, Highlanders who came to that secluded

spot, only demanded food.   They sliced the big round cheeses and toasted them on their claymores at the kitchen fire.   James Botham, the youngest son of the house, then a lad of ten or twelve, and who died at the age of eighty-nine, watched them thus employed, and talked of it to the last.   I remember as a child being one of his most eager listeners.

John Botham, like another King Lear, divided his property during his lifetime amongst his children, three sons and two daughters.   But his eldest son, another John, although he received the comfortable old home-stead as his portion, being naturally of a roaming, sociable disposition, removed in the year 1750, at the age of twenty-six, to Uttoxeter, in the more southern part of the county.   A small but long-established company of Friends, chiefly consisting of the two families Shipley and Summerland, resided there.   William Shipley's sister, Rebecca Summerland, a comely, well-endowed widow between thirty and forty, living in a house of her own, may have been from the first an attraction to the new-comer from the Moorlands.

She had married young, and had at the time of which I speak two sons, remarkably tall and stout youths, both amply provided for, and quite ready to be their own masters.   Many men had looked upon the widow as a desirable wife, but she had declined all proposals, until wooed and won by John Botham, six years her junior. She became his wife in 1755, and handed over to him her malting business.

Their first son was born in 1756, and called James; their second, Samuel, in 1758, and he was my father.

Here I may mention a favourite playmate of Samuel's childhood, his first cousin, Ann Shipley, two years his junior.  In after years she and another first cousin, Morris Shipley, fell in love with each other; and as the rules of the Society to which they belonged did not allow of first cousins marrying, they set off to Gretna Green, and returned man and wife, to the great scandal of the Friends, by whom they were disowned, but afterwards reinstated in membership.  Emigrating to the United States, they became progenitors of the important banking firm of that name.  She died in 1843, in the ninety-fourth year of her age, and in the full use of her faculties.  My youngest sister Emma, then residing in America, had called on her, and been most kindly received.

My grandmother's second marriage brought her much disquietude.  It was an enduring displeasure to her grown-up sons, and made a considerable breach in the hitherto united meeting.  I use here the phraseology of Friends, " meeting " in this sense being equivalent to church or religious body.  She speedily discovered, moreover, that her husband had no faculty for regular business. He was an amateur doctor, with a turn for occult sciences, and later on for animal magnetism—a system of cure by means of " sympathetic affection " between the sick person and the operator, introduced by Father Hehl, a Jesuit at Vienna, about 1774.  For this purpose my grandfather used Perkins's metallic tractors—two small pointed bars of brass and steel, which being drawn over the diseased parts of the body were supposed to give relief through the agency of electricity or magnetism.  He also prepared snuffs and vegetable medicines.  His roving sociableness, combined with a love of nature, caused him to spend much time amongst friends and acquaintances up and down the country.  His accredited healing powers, his grave and scriptural way of talking, his position in the Society of

Friends, he having been an acknowledged minister from about his twenty-fourth year, the interest he took in mowing, reaping, and other agricultural pursuits, perhaps in remembrance of his early years at Apsford, made him welcome in many a village, farmhouse, and Quaker's parlour, whilst he on his part cast aside his wife's anxieties and all needful forethought for the future of their two sons.

Rebecca Botham, therefore, took upon herself the entire management of affairs. She sent the lads to the best reputed Friends' school of that time, kept by Joseph Crosfield at Hartshill, in Warwickshire. Later on she provided handsome apprenticeship fees, and decided their callings in life. It was then a principle with Friends, that their sons, of whatever rank by birth, must be educated to follow some useful trade or profession. Law was forbidden to them, and but few, strange to say, were educated for the practice of medicine, although the art of healing appears peculiarly consonant with their humane and benevolent sentiments.

She placed James with a merchant, the father of a schoolfellow with whom he had formed a strong friendship, and who dwelt in Lancaster; at that time a place of greater maritime and commercial importance than Liverpool. She apprenticed Samuel to William Fairbank of Sheffield, one of the most noted land-surveyors, whether amongst Friends or others.

Unfortunately the ever-prudent and affectionate mother died in 1771, in the first year of the apprenticeship of her youngest son. Probably about the year 1784 or 1785 the young land-surveyor returned to Uttoxeter to establish himself there in his profession. On his so doing he made an appalling discovery. His father had mortgaged the greater part of his wife's property, and a considerable portion of the income that remained was needful to pay the interest.

The ill-will with which the elder half-brothers regarded their mother's second marriage was increased by these after circumstances. They considered that they had not only been robbed of their birthright, but that it had been squandered by their stepfather.

It was a joyless beginning of life to my father. He was, however, young, and endowed with much of his mother's spirit and determination. He sold some of the less valuable property to free the rest, and took up his abode with his father in a humble tenement belonging to them in Carter Street. It consisted on the ground-floor of a whitewashed parlour, with a kitchen at the back. There was in the sitting-room a broad fireplace in a porch-like recess, but without a mantelpiece, and he, wishing to give a little ornamentation or finish to the bald piece of masonry, painted a series of graduated or interlaced lines in grey and black to represent a cornice. It was sure to be accurately and effectively done, as he possessed considerable skill in this sort of delineation. It, however, displeased his father, who, with his rigid notions, considered it indulging the lust of the eye.

Nothing more of the kind was attempted. Indeed my father would soon be too much occupied by his profession to have time for home decoration, being employed to enclose the Heath, an extent of common land to the north of the town; the appointment fell like a gift of God's providence into his hands. This and other professional earnings, together with the aid of his brother James, who had settled in Liverpool as a broker in West Indian produce, gradually enabled him to redeem the mortgaged estate.   Yet even this praiseworthy success was clouded by the death of his brother, who was carried off by fever only six weeks after his marriage, in 1787, to a young Friend, Rebecca Topper.   In due course of time a posthumous daughter was born, who was likewise called Rebecca.   The widow removed with her parents to Chelmsford, where she later married a Friend named John Marriage; her daughter likewise becoming subsequently the wife of another member of the same family.

My father seldom spoke of the sorrowful commencement of his career.   On one occasion he related, however, what, in a moment of weakness and failing trust in God, he had been tempted to do.   In those days a popular belief in the occult power of so-called witches prevailed. The most noted of the period and locality was Witch Hatton, who lived in the high Moorlands, from where his father came.   To her he went in the darkest time of his perplexity, when he could see no possible means of rescuing his father's affairs from their terrible entanglement. He did not reveal to us, his daughters, what the witch had said or done.   He simply told us, with a shuddering emotion, "he had left the house with deep self-abasement, inasmuch as he saw that he had been in the abyss of evil."

About the same period he took the liveliest interest in the first outbreak of the French Revolution, in the supposition that it would lead to the release of the Christian world from "the fetters of Popery," as he termed it. He and two of his acquaintances in Uttoxeter, William Warner, a young lawyer, and Thomas Hart, a young man of fortune, afterwards a banker, joined in the same newspapers and met regularly for the discussion of events which might usher in the second coming of

Christ and the dawn of a new day of human brotherhood. His Quaker principles, however, made him scruple at many deeds and utterances over which his associates rejoiced. He began to perceive that something more abhorrent than even Popery was evolved in the vaunted liberty and equality. By degrees his two associates came to regard him as a renegade, and withdrew their intimacy, but not their personal regard. They themselves remained firm friends. As married men they resided near each other, and their wives and children were on the best terms; and when death carried off the lawyer, the banker, true to a last request, walked once a year over Warner's grave, that he lying below might know that he was not forgotten by his oldest friend.

In the threatening aspect of public affairs, English landowners appear to have become anxious about the amount of acres in their possession, and my father found constant employment. On one occasion, a dispute having arisen regarding the measurement of an estate, which he was called in to adjust, the rival surveyor, on seeing the methodical way in which he set to work, withdrew the very first day, on the plea that it was no use measuring land as if it were gold.

The extreme accuracy of my father's work was, however, appreciated by proprietors, and consequently many large estates in Staffordshire, Shropshire, and even in South Wales were measured by him. His long sojourns in Shropshire brought him intimately acquainted with the Friends at Coalbrookdale, who had a warm regard for him. Here, perhaps, his interest in iron-forges had its beginning, and in South Wales many opportunities for speculation were offered him, which had their fascination, though not always answering his hopes.

He was a man of a singularly spiritual turn of mind, holding with entire sincerity the Quaker doctrine of the indwelling influence of the Holy Spirit. He sought its guidance with the simplicity and faith of a child ; and when disappointment and loss came, received them submissively as a needful discipline, and steadily persevering in his own legitimate calling, gave thanks in the silence of his spirit for the training which the Divine Teacher had vouchsafed.

To quote one instance which he sometimes related. He had become a shareholder, probably with the Bishtons, two brothers of Shifnal, in some coalfields in Carmarthenshire, the coal being stacked at a wharf they had at Kidwelly. Early in the spring he went thither to see how affairs were going on. All seemed prospering, with immense stacks of coal ready to be shipped away as orders came in. It was a satisfactory review, and he anticipated with pleasure the profits that would ensue. The weather was fine, and he went to bed at his lodgings near the shore. He comfortably fell asleep, then almost immediately awoke with a deep depression of mind, a solemn sense of adversity and tribulation. A heavy spiritual burden had fallen upon him. Outwardly all was still, with a sort of deep, dead hush that seemed portentous. It was impossible to sleep. Anon the wind rose, and the voice of the sea came up moaning and roaring like an irresistible force of destruction. He heard the people of the house astir, and the next moment a knocking upon his door and a voice bidding him rise, for the sea was in the town. Hastily dressing, he rushed out. The roaring, foaming waters had entered the street, and the poor distracted inhabitants were seeking to save their possessions. He joined his help to others, snatched up terrified children and carried them off to a place of safety, and led frightened horses and cattle out of danger; gave them all the aid in his power as his bounden duty, believing the whole time that this terrible visitation was sent specially to him.  He knew that all those valuable stacks of coal by the shore, which had so lately been his pride, were washed away.  " Let them go," was the answer of his submissive spirit.  The sea swept through the town with hungry violence, demolishing many houses and causing general ruin and dismay.

The wholesale calamity made his own individual loss seem small.  But the solemn and sorrowful experience of that night was never wholly effaced from his mind, and it was an event of which he was averse to speak.

About the year 1791 he was employed by Lord Talbot to survey his estates in Glamorganshire, and he remained in that county some years, pursuing his profession, and still connected with iron and coal works.  Now and then in his later years he would relate incidents of his life at this time, which probably was far from unpleasant.  Once, whilst engaged on an estate that lay remote from town or village, he was located in a farmhouse.  The family consisted of the father, mother, and two daughters, stout young women, who took upon themselves the management of the farm; so that if anything went wrong with the cattle in the evening, they would start up from their female employment and make all right, whilst their father sat quite still.  The girls, at the same time, were fond of reading, and not without general intelligence.

One event that occurred during his stay with them my father mentioned with a peculiar unction.  The grandmother, who dwelt at some distance, was taken ill, and the mother went to attend upon her.  When sitting, therefore, one evening in the chimney-corner, the young women spinning and our father reading to himself, there being no shutter to the window or even curtains, and the night dark, the sudden fluttering of a bird outside was heard upon the glass. My father remarked that the light through the uncurtained window had attracted the belated little creature.

"Oh no," said the girls, who had suddenly assumed a grave and sorrowful countenance; "it is the sign that never fails in our family. Poor old grandmother is dead."

According to their expectations, the news came the following day that she had died on the preceding evening.

When engaged, in 1795, on Lord Talbot's estate at Margam he attended the Firstday Meeting of Friends at Neath, and met at the hospitable table of Evan Rees Ann Wood, a convinced Friend, on a visit to Evan's wife, Elizabeth.

They saw each other frequently, and became well acquainted. On one occasion, at dinner, she suddenly learnt his regard for her by the peculiar manner in which he asked, "Wilt thou take some nuts, Ann Wood?"

She took them, saying, "I am very fond of nuts."

"That is extraordinary," he replied, "for so am I."

There was in those parts an aged ministering Friend of so saintly a character as to be regarded in the light of a prophet. One Firstday morning, after they had both been present at meeting, this minister drew her aside and said, "If Samuel Botham make thee an offer of marriage thou must by no means refuse him."

Accordingly he was before long her accepted suitor. In the year 1796, on the sixth day of twelfth month, they took each other for man and wife, after the prescribed simple form, "in the fear of God and in the presence of that assembly." They were married in the Friends' Meeting-house at Swansea, where the bride's mother lived, in order to be near her favourite married daughter and son-in-law. These relatives, members of the Church of England, were present at the Quaker marriage, and subscribed their names to the certificate—"Jemima Wood, Thomas Sylvester, Dorothy Sylvester." In the same certificate the bridegroom is stated to be an ironmaster, so that he must at that time have considered the iron-works with which he was connected as likely to become the established business of his life. He was thirty-eight and she thirty-two.

My mother was attired in a cloth habit, which was thought suitable for the long journey she was to commence on the wedding-day. She travelled with her husband post into a remote and unknown land, and as they journeyed onward the weather grew colder and drearier day by day. They were to set up house in the old home where he had been born, and his father was to live with them.

But now let me give some account of the Quaker bride before she arrives at Uttoxeter and is introduced to her new connections. She was the granddaughter of the much-abused patentee of Irish coinage, William Wood, who, as the Rev. David Agnew states in his "Memoirs of Protestant Exiles from France," was fourth in descent from François Dubois, who with his wife and only son fled after the Massacre of St. Bartholomew, in 1572, to Shrewsbury, where he founded a ribbon manufactory. By 1609 his descendants had anglicised their name to Wood. Removing to Wolverhampton, they purchased coal-mines there and built iron-forges, some of which remain in operation to the present day.  In 1671, during the reign of Charles II., my great-grandfather, William Wood, was born, and became a noted iron and copper founder.

In the reign of George I. the deficiency of copper coin in Ireland was so great that for pence small coins called "raps" and bits of cardboard of nominal value were in circulation.  The Government determined, therefore, to remove this pressing want by supplying Ireland with a much better copper coinage than it had ever before possessed.

William Wood, yielding to the corrupt usage of the day, gave a bribe to the Duchess of Kendal, the King's mistress, to procure him the contract.  It was granted him by the Whig Ministry in 1722–23, and he issued farthings and halfpence to the value of £108,000, superior in beauty and value to those of England. "They were," says Leake, "undoubtedly the best copper coin ever made for Ireland," and Ruding confirms the statement in his "Annals of Coinage."  Dean Swift, however, desirous of avenging himself on Sir Robert Walpole and the Whigs for the defeat and disgrace of his great patrons, Oxford and Bolingbroke, availed himself of this opportunity to vent his spleen against the new coinage and inflame the Irish against the Ministers, who had made the mistake of ordering it without consulting the Irish Privy Council and the Lord Lieutenant.  He audaciously asserted that the English were intending to enrich a stranger at the expense of the whole of Ireland, and amongst other ballads and lampoons, excited the people by the lines :—

> "The halfpence are coming, the nation's undoing,
>   There is an end of your ploughing and baking and brewing,
>   In that you must all go to rack and to ruin."

He next anonymously issued a series of papers entitled "The Drapier's Letters," supposed to be written by a poor but independent-spirited draper, who did not mean to be ruined without a good hearty outcry. He thus worked up the nation to the pitch of rebellion.

In the midst of the ferment Lord Carteret, the new Lord Lieutenant, landed in Ireland. He issued a proclamation against "The Drapier's Letters," offered a reward of £300 for the discovery of the author, and caused Harding, the printer of them, to be arrested.

But the Grand Jury threw out the bill against him, and a second jury, so far from entertaining the charge, made a presentment, drawn up by Swift himself, against all persons who should, by fraud or otherwise, impose Wood's halfpence upon the public.

It was in vain that the Government published the official report of Sir Isaac Newton, then Master of the Mint, who tested the new coinage in 1724, and pronounced that, in weight, goodness, and fineness, it rather exceeded than fell short of the conditions of the patent; in vain that it declared no one was compelled to take the money unless he liked. The excitable population, Catholics and Protestants, Whigs and Tories, rich and poor, would not receive it. Wood's effigy was dragged through the streets of Dublin and burned, whilst the portrait of Dean Swift, as the saviour of Ireland, was engraved, placed on signs, woven in handkerchiefs, and struck on medals. The Ministry, having no alternative, withdrew Wood's patent.

The Dean had branded the unfortunate patentee in "The Drapier's Letters" as "a hardware man and tinker; his copper was brass, himself was a Woodlouse." He was in reality very wealthy, lived in a fine place at

Wolverhampton called The Deanery, a venerable building, at present used as the Conservative Club, and surrounded by a small deer-park, now built over. He held at the time of the patent, as we learn from " Anderson's Commerce," vol. iii. p. 124, a lease of all the iron-mines in England in thirty-nine counties. He was proprietor of seven iron and copper works, and carried on a very considerable manufacture for the preparation of metals.

By his wife Margaret, daughter of Richard Molyneux of Wetton Hall, Staffordshire, he had fifteen children. Two died young, but thirteen handsome sons and daughters grew up, and are reported to have made a fine appearance when seen together in church.

After the withdrawal of the patent Wood appealed to Sir Robert Walpole for compensation, stating that he had six sons. The Minister said, " Send your sons to me, Mr. Wood, and I will provide for them."

" Do me justice, Sir Robert," he replied, " and I will provide for them myself."

As an indemnification for his losses £3000 per annum was granted him for a term of years.

Wood later wrote a remarkable work on the advantages of Free Trade, which he dedicated to George II. It may be presumed that he died in 1744, from the entry, " William Wood 44 d," extant in an old Prayer-book that belonged to his eldest daughter, Mary, and which, containing other family dates, is in the possession of her descendants. ,

His extensive mines and forges were inherited by some of his sons. William, the eldest, had the Falcon Iron Foundry at Bermondsey, and cast the iron railings round St. Paul's Churchyard.

Charles, the fourth son and my grandfather, was born

in 1702. He was appointed when quite young Assay-master in Jamaica, a lucrative post, as the gold, which at that period came to England from the Spanish Main, was taken there to be tested. The office was given him by Sir Robert Walpole as further compensation for the losses which the family had sustained by the withdrawal of the Irish patent. Former Assay-masters had returned home rich, but being a man of high principle, he never soiled his hand or conscience by bribe or perquisite, and after thirty years of service in the island he came back in moderate circumstances, having merely amassed great scientific knowledge, especially about metals.

On December 13, 1750, William Brownrigg, M.D., F.R.S. (through William Watson, F.R.S.), presented to the Royal Society in London specimens of platinum, a new metal hitherto unknown in Europe, and stated in an accompanying memoir :—" This semi-metal was first presented to me about nine years ago by Mr. Charles Wood, a skilful and inquisitive metallurgist, who met with it in Jamaica, whither it had been brought from Carthagena, in New Spain."

My grandfather, who was thus the introducer of the extremely useful metal, platinum, became the brother-in-law of this learned Dr. Brownrigg, who, descended from an ancient Cumberland family of position, dwelt at his estate, Ormathwaite Hall, in that county. Charles Wood returned from the West Indies a widower, and married in Ireland Dr. Brownrigg's youngest sister, Jemima, a lively, fascinating lady. She too had been in Jamaica, and was the widow of an Irishman, Mr. Lyndon, the captain of the *Dolphin*, a slave-ship. She had one son living, named Roger; another son, Charles, had been lost at sea. Two branches of the Brownrigg family had settled in Ireland about 1700, and Brownriggs, Annesleys, and Lyndons had married and intermarried.

My grandfather Wood built Lowmill ironworks near Whitehaven. There his six children by his second marriage were born. From Cumberland he removed to South Wales, and became active in establishing the important Cyfarthfa ironworks near Merthyr Tydvil. A great impetus had been given to the iron trade at this period by the application of a discovery, made as early as 1619 by Lord Dudley, that the ore could be smelted by the use of pit-coal. In 1740 the system was first introduced at Coalbrookdale, and led to the establishment of extensive ironworks in various parts of the kingdom; amongst others those at Merthyr Tydvil, where Mr. Anthony Bacon became lessee of a considerable tract of land, and began the first smelting furnace at Cyfarthfa in 1755.

My mother, who was Charles Wood's youngest child, and taken almost an infant to Cyfarthfa, often spoke of Mr. Bacon. She well remembered another individual intimately associated with the undertaking, old Mr. Crawshay, whom she described as a large, stout man, deeply pitted with small-pox. He laid the foundation of his immense wealth by buying up old cannon on the Continent, which were recast at the works. And as Mr. Bacon contracted with Government during the American War to supply the several arsenals with cannon, the casting of cannon became an important trade at Cyfarthfa.

Her earliest recollection dated from 1768, when she was four. Every one at Merthyr was talking about Wilkes and Liberty, more especially as Alderman Wilkes had, equally with Mr. Anthony Bacon, represented Aylesbury in Parliament. Although threatened with outlawry, he had just been elected for the county of Middlesex; an

act followed by riots in London that convulsed the whole
land.    Little Ann Wood, a bright, inquisitive child,
anxious to know the meaning of Wilkes and Liberty,
turned for explanation to Peggy Jones, a good-tempered,
cheerful young woman, the best ironer in the place, and
therefore employed to get up the cambric frills of Mr.
Wood's shirts.

Peggy knew all about Wilkes and Liberty: "He was
a very nice gentleman, who had lodged three weeks at
her aunt's.    He had at parting given her aunt a nice silk
gown; Miss Ann should have a piece of it to make herself a housewife."

Little Ann, delighted to be the bearer of such important news, hastened to impart it to the family.    It
was received with a peal of laughter that abashed the
poor child.    She learnt later that Wilkes and Liberty,
in this instance, meant a strolling-player, who, unable to
pay his landlady, had discharged the debt with an old
silk gown.

For her father she always retained the deepest love
and veneration.    He likewise regarded her with intense
affection, and chose to have the child with him in his
private room, where he spent much time apart from the
rest of the family, to whom pleasure was the object of
life.    Surrounded by his books, he read to her, heard her
read, and taught her pieces of poetry, of which he was
extremely fond; and when the sound of laughter, singing,
and dancing reached them from a distant part of the
house, would clasp her to his heart and even silently
shed tears.

Seated on a low stool at his knee, she learnt his
opinions on public events.    He awakened within her a
deep detestation of slavery, the horrors of which he had

witnessed in Jamaica, where, possessing sufficient knowledge of medicine, he had compounded healing ointments for the wounded slaves. His wife and elder children could never see the unchristian spirit and atrocity of slavery; nor did they feel any sympathy with his views, when, on the breaking out of the American War, he sided with those whom they deemed rebels. He taught Ann that the citizens of the United States rose to assert their rights as men in the resistance of tyranny, and inspired her with such admiration for Washington, that he ever remained her ideal hero and patriot.

After my grandfather's death, which occurred when my mother was still a child, the family continued to reside at Cyfarthfa, Roger Lyndon and his half-brother, William Wood, being engaged in the works. The eldest daughter, Mary, adopted by her childless uncle, Brownrigg, had remained in Cumberland. She was distinguished for her good looks, and had many admirers, amongst others young Mr. William Wilberforce. She did not, however, encourage the addresses of the future renowned philanthropist, from the notion that " she could do better for herself," and ended in accepting a clerical suitor, the Rev. Thomas Wilkinson, vicar of Thetford, Norfolk.

The next daughter, Dorothy, who had been educated at Monmouth Castle, a fashionable ladies' school, possessed a vivacity and love of amusement which endeared her to her mother. The thoughtful Ann, who had lost her best friend and protector, occupied a painfully isolated position at home, and she resolved to become independent by taking a situation.

Kind friends approved of her determination ; amongst them the wife of Dr. Samuel Glasse, rector of Hanwell, one of the chaplains to George III., and who kept a celebrated school for young gentlemen of position.    Ann thus being recommended to Dr. Horne, the noted commentator on the Psalms, then Dean of Canterbury, later Bishop of Norwich, she was engaged by his wife to take charge of their children.    Lady Abergavenny and her mother, who were acquainted with the Woods and sympathised with Ann most thoroughly, sent her a handsome lilac silk gown and other pretty and useful articles of female attire before she went to Canterbury.    She always retained a grateful remembrance of the amiability and kindness of the Dean, whose poem on autumn—

"See the leaves around us falling,"

had, from this circumstance, a peculiar interest for my sister and me as children.    The Dean's daughters, however, did no credit to their excellent parents, they were proud and imperious; she could not govern them, and was consequently dismissed.

She then accepted the invitation of her cousin, William Wood, and his wife to stay with them at Hammersmith. He was a gentleman of good fortune, who had inherited the money of their uncle Francis, the Nabob.    This was the second son of the patentee, a remarkably handsome man, whose marriage with a daughter of Lord Dudley and Ward was prevented either by her death or his being sent to India.    After living many years at Surat he returned home an elderly man, with much money and treasure and the rank of a colonel, but was commonly called the Nabob, and retained the beauty of his youth, although his hair had become of a venerable whiteness. He occupied a house on the Mall at Hammersmith, with a red brick summer-house overlooking the Thames, and lived on his capital, asserting that he should leave the residue to his greatest enemy, as it must bring a curse with it, having been unrighteously gained. He died suddenly at the age of eighty-three, and the only curse it brought to his heir was a very worrying lawsuit. William Wood was a skilful amateur artist, who devoted himself to copying the works of his favourite Murillo. He was very intimate with the Alsatian landscape-painter, Loutherbourg, who likewise lived at Hammersmith. Opie, also a frequent guest at his house, requested the young visitor from South Wales to sit to him for a Magdalene. This, to the later regret of her daughters, she declined to do, always silencing our lamentations by, "Oh no! I could not be painted as a Magdalene; anything but that."

Her aunt, Isabella Wood, the wife of Mr. John Cox, of the Horse-Shoe Brewery, Bloomsbury, had been dead some years, and her kind-hearted cousin Margaret kept the opulent brewer's house. Her younger cousin Bella, a handsome, dashing, self-indulgent girl, who used a bottle of lavender water daily, was the father's favourite. He restricted her in nothing, except in marrying a soldier, an Irishman, or a Papist.

On one occasion Ann Wood consented to accompany Bella Cox to a fashionable fortune-teller then making a great stir in London. They went in a coach, sufficiently disguised to prevent recognition, and on reaching the sibyl's dwelling were ushered into a mysterious chamber. The walls were draped with sable hangings; on a centre-table, covered with a dark cloth, lay a white wand; and from beneath the table issued, as if it had been the familiar spirit of the place, a large black cat. The door of an inner room slowly opened, and a tall woman of a grave, almost severe aspect, attired in black velvet, entered, and without a word fixed her eyes steadily and penetratingly on them.

According to agreement, my mother first presented her hand. This the sibyl taking in hers, examined carefully, then said in measured accents, "You will not marry your present lover. You will change your religion and marry another."

On Bella Cox next coming forward the woman took her hand, and immediately raising her eyes from it, demanded sternly, "Where is your wedding-ring?" She then added solemnly, "You have done the worst day's work you ever did. You will repent it as long as you live."

These terrible words, which closed the interview, proved only too true. Bella had privately married an Irish officer, who was a Catholic. After the fact was revealed to her father he is said never to have smiled again. She lived with her husband for a few years, but finally was obliged to leave him.

The lover to whom my mother's fancy turned in those days was probably Robert Wilson, a young lieutenant, who had been sent, as it seemed to her, by Providence to save her from the danger of some street mob in which she suddenly found herself involved. He accompanied her back to the Coxes', and was greatly liked by them. He continued his visits and paying her his addresses; they finally parted with the understanding they were to meet again. Some years later, when she had become a Friend and was staying with the Foxes of Falmouth, he, then Captain Wilson, called upon her to renew his suit. She refused to see him for conscience' sake, her friend Sarah Fox doing so in her stead.

We must not overlook a little episode belonging to

the period of my mother's visit to London, and connected with another first cousin, Catherine Martin. She was a daughter of John Wood, the third son of the patentee, who lived in great splendour at Wednesbury, where he had inherited ironworks from his father. Catherine, wife of a purser in the navy, and conspicuous for her beauty and impulsive, violent temper, having quarrelled with her excellent sister, Dorothea Fryer, at whose house in Staffordshire she was staying, suddenly set off to London on a visit to her great-uncle, the Rev. John Plymley, prebend of the Collegiate Church at Wolverhampton and chaplain of Morden College, Blackheath. She journeyed by the ordinary mode of conveyance, the Gee-Ho, a large stage-waggon drawn by a team of six horses, and which, driven merely by day, took a week from Wolverhampton to the Cock and Bell, Smithfield.

Arrived in London, Catherine proceeded on foot to Blackheath; there, night having come on and losing her way, she was suddenly accosted by a horseman with, "Now, my pretty girl, where are you going?" Pleased by his gallant address, she begged him to direct her to Morden College. He assured her that she was fortunate in having met with him instead of one of his company, and inducing her to mount before him, rode across the heath to the pile of buildings which had been erected by Sir Christopher Wren for decayed merchants, the recipients of Sir John Morden's bounty. Assisting her to alight, he rang the bell, then remounted his steed and galloped away, but not before the alarmed official who had answered the summons had exclaimed, "Heavens! Dick Turpin on Black Bess." My mother always said, "Dick Turpin;" another version in the family runs, "Captain Smith."

Catherine Martin died at an advanced age. Her portrait still exists, painted by Edward Bird, R.A., a native of Wolverhampton, at the time he was japanning at Turton's Hall, formerly the residence of the Levesons, who were woolstaplers, and ancestors of the present Duke of Sutherland.

Catherine's sister, Dorothea, a pious, sensible, and clever woman, was the mother of Richard Fryer, a man of great independence of mind. He held the patentee's principles of free trade, was the first Liberal member for Wolverhampton, and noted before the days of Cobden and Bright for his persistent advocacy of the abolition of the Corn-Laws, making him ridiculed and almost persecuted in the House for many years as "the man of one idea." His great ability and force of character are inherited by a surviving daughter.

My mother spent some pleasant months at the Glasses'; and whilst she became the especial protector of the fags, took a deep interest in all the pupils, amongst whom she was wont to mention the Earl of Drogheda. His mother, "the ever-weeping Drogheda," was so styled, I believe, from her abiding grief at the loss of her husband and stepson by drowning when crossing from England to Ireland.

She met at the Glasses', amongst other celebrities, Dr. Samuel Johnson once or twice; and Miss Burney frequently, and used to relate how much people were afraid of her, from the idea that she would put them in a book.

My sister and I, as children, were much impressed by the following narrative:—Dr. Glasse's son George, who became a clergyman, was acquainted at college with a dissolute set of young men, who turned religion into ridicule, and aimed to extract as much so-called pleasure out of life as possible.

On one occasion a member of the group entered the room where the rest were assembled, with an unusually depressed countenance. All rallied him upon his gravity, and demanded the cause. He explained that on the preceding night he dreamed he was breathing stifling, oppressive air in a large gloomy hall, which was densely thronged with undergraduates, their gowns wrapped round them, and their countenances indicative of suffering and extreme dejection. Inquiring where he was, "This is Hell!" replied a melancholy young man, unfolding his gown and revealing in his breast a transparent heart as of crystal, in which burned a fierce flame.

"Good God!" he exclaimed, appalled by the sight. "Cannot I escape from this place?"

"You have a chance for nine days," answered the gloomy figure, folding his arms within his gown and concealing his burning heart.

The undergraduate awoke full of horror, and, in order to dispel the strong and painful impression, sought the society of his friends. They laughed at his disordered fancy, drank deep, and persuaded him to spend the ensuing nine days with them in especial gaiety.

On the ninth day, however, whether from the natural effects of excessive debauch or in solemn fulfilment of the warning, he suddenly died, an event which produced a strong and salutary effect upon some of his comrades, who began from that day an amended life.

Dr. Glasse procured for my mother the post of companion to Mrs. Barnardiston, a wealthy old lady of a very sociable disposition, although enfeebled by paralysis. She entertained judges, generals, and admirals, with their womankind, at her town house near Turnham Green. These guests regarded my mother as little better than a servant, and often showed it. But on accompanying Mrs. Barnardiston to Weston, her seat in Northamptonshire, she met with much kindness from the neighbouring aristocracy and gentry. Old Lady Dryden especially treated her with marked favour. There was constant visiting between Weston and Canons-Ashby, the splendid home of the poet Dryden's family, and where his youngest son, Sir Erasmus, had lived and died. A trifling incident, however, somewhat destroyed my mother's enjoyment of dining at Lady Dryden's, for whilst Mrs. Barnardiston's butler, who had accompanied them, stood behind his mistress's chair, the postillion was stationed behind that of Miss Wood. My mother requested that she might be relieved of his attendance, but was told it could not be dispensed with. We can picture the three ladies solemnly waited on by a retinue of servants in the vast dining-hall of Canons-Ashby, which is thirty feet long by twenty wide. Of Weston, too, a vivid image rises before my mind, probably from some description heard in my childhood, as an ancient mansion with deep mullioned windows, square towers, a stone terrace and balustrade— standing on a slight elevation, surrounded by a wide park and woods.

Towards the end of the summer spent in Northamptonshire my mother was recalled to South Wales, as her sister Dorothy was about to be married and to live at Swansea, and she must replace her at home.

Her solitary position in her own family, combined with an ardent craving for spiritual light and rest, had led her during her travels to inquire into the Catholic faith. She had come in contact with an abbess, and contemplated entering her community, but was deterred from taking the step by a young nun, who told her " all was not peace in a convent."

In South Wales, still searching for light and assurance, she yielded to an earlier influence.  She had, as a child, attended with her father a public meeting held by a ministering Friend in Merthyr, and although she could never afterwards recollect the preacher's words, they had, in a vague but indelible manner, appealed to her inner nature.  Her mother, discovering that she possessed a secret drawing to Friends, told her that her father had left it as a dying request, that if any of their children showed an inclination to join that body she should not oppose it, as he had himself adopted its religious opinions. Full of gratitude to her mother for this communication, Ann Wood sought and obtained membership.

It is noteworthy that Samuel, the youngest son of the patentee, had also become a Friend.  By so doing he must have removed himself from the family cognisance, as we knew nothing of him until my sister Anna traced out his history from the records of the Society.  We thus learnt that he had been a man of good property, residing at Milnthorpe, Westmoreland, where he died in 1800, at the age of ninety-one.  About two years ago I had the pleasure of receiving a letter from a Catholic lady, the granddaughter of his only daughter Margaret, recognising our kinship ; a fact that had become known to her by the mention of my great-uncle the Nabob in " Wood Leighton," the first work of imagination that I wrote.

My grandmother, deciding to reside near her favourite married daughter, soon found she could dispense with the society of Ann, more especially as the latter had united herself to a sect with which she had nothing in common.

My mother, therefore, was at liberty to associate with her own people, and her life became most consonant to her tastes.

She resided chiefly at Falmouth, on the most agreeable terms of truly *friendly* intercourse with the distinguished family of the Foxes; and with Peter and Anna Price, a handsome couple of a grand patriarchal type, but comparatively young. Her dearest friend was Anna Price's relative, Kitty Tregelles, a sensible, lively young woman, to whom she felt as a sister. Whether she had her own hired apartments, or whether she had a home with some of these Friends, I know not; merely that she lived in the midst of these kind and superior people.

She always reverted with peculiar pleasure to her life in Cornwall. It was a time of repose to her, spiritually and mentally; whilst her natural love of the poetical and picturesque was fostered by the many grand, beautiful legends connected with the wild rocky shores, the seaport towns, and also by the old-fashioned primitive life and simple habits of the people.

She likewise treasured most happy memories of Neath, where dwelt her staunch and valued friends, Evan and Elizabeth Rees, under whose roof, in 1795, she met the faithful partner of her future life, as already narrated.

# CHAPTER II.



*EARLY DAYS AT UTTOXETER.*

*1796–1809.*

My father took his bride to an unpretending, roomy, old-fashioned house. We see the back of this home of my unmarried life reproduced on the next page, not exactly as it was in those days, when, instead of the present greenhouse, a large porch adorned with a sundial screened the garden-door. In the quaint, pleasant garden grew no modern species of pine, but hollies and arbor-vitæ, with a line of old Scotch firs down one side. This garden, sloping to the south, was separated by a low wall and iron palisades from a meadow through which ran a cheerful stream, and it was crossed by a small wooden bridge that led into beautiful hilly fields belonging to my father. The house, built in the shape of an L, enclosed to the front a court, divided from the street by iron palisades, and paved with white and brown pebbles in a geometric pattern. At one time three poplars grew in the court, but were cut down from their falling leaves giving trouble.

A parlour and bedroom, reached by a separate staircase, looked to the street, and were appropriated to my grandfather. The domestic offices filled the middle space. On the garden side lay the common and best parlours, with comfortable chambers above them. This portion of the dwelling was reserved for my parents.

The arrangement of the home life would have been excellent had the father-in-law been a different character. His peculiar temper, ignorance of life outside his narrow circle, and inability to allow of dissimilarity of habits and

THE HOME AT UTTOXETER.

opinions, made him undervalue a daughter-in-law from a great distance, who had chiefly lived among people of the world, and who after joining the Society had become accustomed to the more polished usages of the Friends in Cornwall and South Wales.

She came as an alien amongst her husband's kindred; for the little intercourse between the different parts of England made people meet almost as foreigners. Her cast of mind, manners, speech, the tone of her voice, even the style of her plain dress, were different from theirs. She was considered by the half-brothers, who remained irreconcilable, and their sons and daughters-in-law, to be "high," and was nicknamed by them "The Duchess." She found, however, a sympathiser in the wife of her husband's cousin, John Shipley, a native of Kendal, whose comeliness substantiated the popular toast of the day, "A Kendal woman." Ann Shipley had herself endured sufficient loneliness of heart to enter into the feelings of the new-comer.

The one really unfortunate circumstance in my mother's relationship to her father-in-law was her nervous sensibility to strong odours, which brought on intense headaches that affected her eyesight. His occupation of drying and pulverising herbs, by which the house was often filled with pungent smells and impalpable stinging dust, was not only offensive to her, but productive of intense pain. The old herb-doctor, who could not induce her to try his headache-snuff, was obdurate, and made no attempt to abate the nuisance.

In September 1797 a little daughter was born, the naming of whom was for some time a serious difficulty. The father wished her to be called Ann, after her mother; his wife demurred, not choosing there to be an old Ann and a young Ann in the family. The grandfather almost insisted on Rebecca, or Becky, as he called it, after the deceased grandmother. The parents would not acquiesce, and the grandfather made it almost a quarrel. Fortunately just then came Ann Alexander from York, on a religious visit to Friends' families in the county of Stafford, and when staying in Uttoxeter took great interest in the mother and her first-born child. A sort of compromise, therefore, was made, and the child called Ann-a, which implied a compliment to Ann Alexander. The father was pleased to have the dear mother's name given to the little daughter, and the mother indulged her affectionate remembrance of her beloved friend Anna Price; though she kept this sentiment in her own heart.

In 1798 Samuel and Ann Botham went to Coleford, in the Forest of Dean, to commence a new chapter of life, trusting, with the Divine blessing—it was thus that they spoke of their Heavenly Father—it would be the beginning of a prosperous career; and they took with them the lovely little Anna, who, in the quaint, demure costume of her parents' sect, looked like an infant saint, whilst her attendant, a grave young Quakeress, resembled a nun.

Of the time spent at Coleford I will quote from a memorandum by my mother. She writes :—

"After I had been married about a year my husband received a proposal from his partners, the Brothers Bishton, to exchange his shares in the very advantageous iron-forges in which they were concerned for a principal share in some ironworks in Gloucestershire. He had already rejected the proposal when it was again renewed. Being naturally of a confiding disposition, incapable of taking any unfair advantage, and never suspecting others, especially his old friends, of being less upright than himself, he at length fell in with their scheme, and we removed to Coleford, in the Forest of Dean. I may say that from the time we left Uttoxeter everything went ill with us. All the money which my husband could command he embarked in this affair; and when he wrote to his partners for an advance of money, as much on their account as his own, they held back on the plea of not being prepared.

"The winter of 1798–9 set in with unusual severity. Deep snows fell, which were succeeded by such heavy rains that the brooks rose like rivers, flooding the new works. In one night, so to speak, we saw our money swept away. Nothing could be more gloomy than our prospects, and it was our belief that the longer we stayed the worse matters would get. Some Friends who came there at that time on a religious visit said that 'we were not at home.' Truly we felt that we were not so. Nothing could be done with the Brothers Bishton. They seemed to care neither for the ruin of the new works nor the risk my husband would run by their recommencement.

"It was at this time, when our fortunes were quite at the lowest, a period of distress and great anxiety, that our second daughter Mary * was born, the twelfth of Third Month 1799. Ruin almost stared us in the face. My husband was desponding, and nothing but a firm reliance on Providence supported me. I, however, never lost faith to believe that He who careth for the sparrows would in His own time open a way for us, and guide us where we ought to go.

"To add to the darkness of this time, I may mention that there were some amongst my husband's relations who, having heard of our troubles and disappointments, wrote to him, insinuating that 'his proud wife had brought this cross upon him ; that if he had been satisfied

---

* I remember as a child our parents speaking of the peculiar significance of my sister's name and my own ; she was Anna, in Hebrew Grace, and the Lord at the time of her birth had been gracious to them. I was Marah, or bitterness, coming at a season of sore trouble and anxiety.

to remain single, none of these calamities would have fallen to his lot.' This was a great sorrow to me, because I not only knew it to be most untrue, but because I feared it might sour his temper. However, my mind remained fixed on our Heavenly Father, and He did not fail us.

"One morning my husband came into my room, and desiring the nurse to leave it, I perceived an unusual cheerfulness and composure in his countenance and a greater kindness in his voice, as, turning to the bed, he thus addressed me :—' Ann, thou wast always averse to my entering into this partnership. If I had followed thy advice I should have steered clear of this trouble and loss. But as it has come upon us, it behoves us to bear up as best we can. I have had this night a dream in which I have seen the course which we must pursue. I thought I was mounted on a very small white horse, so small that my feet nearly touched the ground, and that I was in the market-place of Coleford. I thought that I whipped and spurred the horse, but to no purpose ; he would not move. The people came out of their houses and stood laughing. I then bethought myself to lay the reins on the horse's neck. I did so, and he set off at full speed, bearing me out of the town, so that I was presently half-way to Ross. On this I woke, and at once it was clear to my mind that we must sell our furniture, leave this place, and return to Uttoxeter. Those were the resolves suggested by my dream, and when I went down-stairs I found a letter from Imm Trusted of Ross, who wishes me to survey his land, and to take up my quarters at his house whilst engaged in the business.' ".

This seemed to my dear parents an indication of the Divine Will regarding them. My mother adds that they were " both drawn into a great stillness, feeling that nothing more was required from them but a firm reliance on Providence, who would assuredly open a way for them out of their difficulties." The next day being Week-day Meeting at Ross, my father went thither, and took lodgings for his family whilst he should be engaged in his surveying business ; "and," says my mother, "we believed that meanwhile some way would open, under the best direction, for our future movements."

"In the course of three weeks," she continues, "our furniture was sold, our feather-beds, and such things as could be packed in hogsheads and large boxes were sent on to Uttoxeter, and we left Coleford with only £60 in our pockets.

"We stayed three weeks at Ross, the Trusted family, who were Friends, treating us with the greatest kindness.* Whilst we were there, three ministering Friends, Sarah Lumley, Ann Ashby, and Joseph Russell, came on a religious concern to families. In one visit, whilst sitting with us, Sarah Lumley said that 'the cruse of oil should not waste, or the barrel of meal fail, until the Lord sent rain on this barren waste, and that He would bless both basket and store.' One of them also said, in addressing me, that 'the Lord's hand was stretched out to help, and that neither the water nor the fire of this tribulation should overwhelm me.'

"These consolatory passages," continues my mother, "helped to strengthen us both, and enabled us to take sweet counsel together through the solitary path which we had yet to tread."

This fragment by my mother, written some years

---

* A little daughter named Elizabeth had been born just about the time of my birth, and I am glad to record the firm, faithful friendship that exists between my warmly esteemed contemporary and myself.

afterwards, is the sole record we possess of those dark times.  In an interesting little work, however, entitled "Something about Coleford and the Old Chapel," published at Gloucester in 1877, reference is made at page 24 to Coleford being my birthplace, and we learn that I was born in the small suburb called Whiteleeve or Whitecliffe.

"The house," adds the author, "is a mysterious-looking place, with a neglected appearance, as if it had seen better days, which was likely the case.  In one of the windows of an evidently unused room stood for some time a beautiful cast-iron grate, or rather the back of a grate, for a large fireplace circular in shape, bearing date Edward VI., 1553.

"A few years after Mr. Botham's departure another foreigner came upon the scene.  This was Mr. David Mushet.  He had been for some years a celebrity in the scientific world; his writings in the *Philosophical Magazine* were well known, as was also his discovery that the Black Band ironstone in Scotland was not, as hitherto supposed, a wild coal, and despised accordingly, but an ironstone of the greatest value, containing with the ore a proportion of coal, which served in the furnace as fuel.

"It is no exaggeration to say that the Black Band brought many millions of profit to the Scottish iron trade, whose rise and progress, and the prominent rank it has since held in the ironmaking world, date from the era of Mr. Mushet's discovery.

"The Whitecliffe ironworks were not carried on long.  After a time Mr. Mushet had grave reasons for being much dissatisfied with his partners, who had been introduced to him by one of the leading men in London, and he withdrew.  Whitecliffe has been silent ever since."

My parents were again settled at Uttoxeter, and my

father, humble and submissive after his adversity in the Forest of Dean, was speedily to see that God had not forsaken him, but was preparing for him a better lot in the old home than he had sought for himself in the new.

In 1800 a Commission sent out by the Crown to survey the woods and forests decided that "the Chase of Needwood," in the county of Stafford, should be divided, allotted, and enclosed. This forest, dating from time immemorial, and belonging to the Crown, extended many miles. It contained magnificent oaks, limes, and other lordly trees, gigantic hollies and luxuriant underwood, and twenty thousand head of deer. It was divided into five wards, one being Uttoxeter, and had four lodges, held under lease from the Crown, its lieutenants, rangers, axe-bearers, keepers, and woodmote court. To be surveyor in the disafforesting was an important post solicited by my father. Months of anxious suspense had, however, to be endured before the nominations could be known. In June 1801 the Act for the enclosure was passed, one clause containing the appointment of the surveyors. Their names would be published in Stafford on a certain day; but my father felt he could not go thither to ascertain his fate; he should be legally notified if appointed.

On the day when any favourable decision ought to arrive by post, my mother, waiting and watching, saw the postboy ride into the town, then, somewhat later, the letter-carrier enter the street, deliver here and there a letter, and pass their door. She did not speak to her husband of a disappointment, which he was doubtless equally experiencing. But after they had both retired to rest, if not to sleep, they heard in the silence of the little outer world the sound of a horse coming quickly

up the street. It stopped at their door. My father's
name was shouted by Thomas Hart, the banker, and
formerly his political sympathiser in the outbreak of the
French Revolution. He hastened to the window, and
was greeted by the words, " Good news, Mr. Botham. I
am come from Stafford. I have seen the Act. You and
Mr. Wyatt are appointed the surveyors."

It is still a pleasure to me to think of the joy and
gratitude that must have filled those anxious hearts that
memorable night. On the other hand, as a lover of
Nature, I sincerely deplore any instrumentality in destroy-
ing such a vast extent of health-giving solitude and
exuberant beauty in our thickly-populated, trimly-culti-
vated England. On Christmas Day, 1802, Needwood
Chase, a glorious relic of ancient times, older than the
existing institutions of the kingdom, older than English
history, was disafforested. It was followed by a scene
of the most melancholy spoliation. There was a wholesale devastation of the small creatures that had lived for
ages amongst its broadly-growing trees, its thickets and
underwood. Birds flew bewildered from their nests as
the ancient timber fell before the axe ; fires destroyed
the luxuriant growth of plants and shrubs. No wonder
that Dr. Darwin of Lichfield, the Rév. Thomas Gisborne,
and Mr. Francis Noel Mundy, living respectively at the
lodges of Yoxall and Ealand, in the Forest, published
laments over the fall of Needwood, descriptive of the
change from sylvan beauty and grandeur to woeful devastation.

For upwards of nine years the work of dividing, allot-
ting, and enclosing continued. The rights of common,
of pasture, of pannage (feeding swine in the woods), of
fuel, and of making birdlime from the vast growth of

hollies, claimed by peasants, whose forefathers had built their turf cottages on the waste lands ; the rights of more important inhabitants to venison, game, timber, &c., had to be considered by the Commission of the enclosure, and compensated by allotments of land.   On May 9, 1811, the final award was signed, by which the freeholders' portion was subdivided amongst the various persons who had claims thereon.   Practically the two surveyors had to decide the awards.   It was, consequently, a source of deep thankfulness to my father, who had throughout refused gifts from any interested party, that all claimants, from the richest to the poorest, were satisfied with their awards.

From the date of my father's appointment as surveyor in the disafforesting the clouds of care rolled away, more especially as the Messrs. Bishton unexpectedly paid their debt incurred by the losses at Coleford.   With a light and thankful heart he planned with Mr. Wyatt the dissection of the forest.   Some parts, the property of the Crown, were to retain their woodland aspect, but to be opened with ridings ; some were to be laid out in woods and pleasure-grounds surrounding the Forest - lodges ; some to be cut through with roads leading amid extensive farms.   As he laid out the ground he sometimes permitted his children to accompany him, thus enabling us from infancy to become acquainted with the spirit of Nature.   Indeed a great amount of enjoyment came to Anna and me out of the Forest enclosure.   Our knowledge of the world around us became less circumscribed. Our mother, a good walker in those days, would sometimes take us to meet our father at certain points arranged beforehand, perhaps at the house of some Forest farmer, where we could have tea, and return home. pleasantly in the evening.  Our father, always on foot over his land measurements, seemed never tired, and always glad to see us.

I remember particularly one Saturday afternoon, we had gone to the village of Gratwich, about three miles from Uttoxeter.  We were seated at tea with a friendly farmer, his wife, and their little girl about our age, to whom our mother had that afternoon taken a pretty piece of pale blue print for a frock, and were all as cheerful and happy as could be, when in came Thomas Bishop, a clog and pattern maker by trade, but who was constantly in our parents' employ to do all sort of odd jobs.  He had come in hot haste to announce the arrival of two ministering Friends, and as these worthies were always entertained at our parents' house, they were required to return as soon as possible.  It was, I believe, David Sands and his companion from America, and Thomas Bishop was ordered to say that they had written before-hand to apprise my father.

Our little tea-drinking was abruptly terminated, and off we set.  I remember being carried by Thomas Bishop, and must have fallen asleep, for after a consciousness of looking down upon hedges all was oblivion, until I found myself at home; and Anna and I were hurried to bed because of the ministers in the parlour.

Then I recollect a curious little epoch in my life, as we were returning one evening from a Forest ramble with my father.  It was the first evidence to my mind that I could think.  I remember very well the new light, the gladness, the wealth of which I seemed suddenly possessed.  It has curiously connected itself in my mind with passing a pinfold.  That particular spot seemed like the line between rational and irrational existence; and so childish was I in intellectual life, that it seemed to me as if before I passed the pinfold I could only say and think "Bungam"—such was the expression in my mind—but that after passing it I had the full use of all intelligible speech.

Many a long happy summer day had we spent already in the Forest, when, I being then five or six years old, our father took Anna and me with him to be out from morning till evening. Towards noon we were wearied by our long ramble, and were left to recover from our fatigue under the spreading shade of an enormous oak. Around us lay a small opening in a forest glade, covered with short herbage. This was enclosed by thickets of black holly, which in contrast with the light foreground seemed intensely sombre; under these grew the green-wood laurel, with its clusters of poisonous-looking berries, and whole beds of fair white stellaria. In other spots flourished enchanter's night-shade and the rare four-leaved Herb Paris, bearing its berry-like flower at the central angles of its four leaves.

There was an undefined feeling half of pleasure, half of pain, in being left alone in so wild a spot. We heard the crow of the distant pheasant, the coo of the wood-pigeon, and the laugh-like cry of the woodpecker. We watched the hare run past from thicket to thicket. At the same time we remarked a strange unceasing low sound, a perpetual chirr-chirr-chirring somewhere near us.

We asked a stout Forest lad carrying a bundle of fagots, to explain it. He seemed amazed to find two children, like Babes in the Wood, seated hand in hand at the foot of an old oak. Speaking in a low but distinctly articu-lated whisper, he said, "It's my Lord Vernum's blood-hounds. They are out hunting, and yon sounds are the chains they drag after them." So saying, he dashed off like a wild stag. The horror that fell on us was intense. Indeed, had we been left to ourselves and our terror I know not what would have become of us; but our cry of, "Father! father!" speedily brought him to us. "It is the grasshopper, and nothing more," he said, "which has caused this foolish alarm." Listening for a moment, he traced it by its sound among the short dry sunny grass, then held it in his hand before us.

My parents, on returning from the Forest of Dean, had temporarily resided in a small semi-detached house belonging to them, having let the old home on a short lease. By March 1802, however, they must have removed to their usual habitation in Balance Street, with my grandfather for an inmate, as my very earliest recollection is a dim remembrance of the old man delivering, in the kitchen, some piece of intelligence which was received by the assembled household with expressions of joy. I was told later that it must have been his announcing the Peace of Amiens.

My grandfather did not long remain under the same roof, for having, in a moment of great excitement, wounded the little Anna with the large scissors he used to cut out the strong veins of the leaves, which he dried, and feeling it a sad mischance, he was made willing to remove himself and his medicaments. He took up his abode with some good, simple people in a comfortable cottage on the enclosed land, that had formerly been the Heath. At this distance he acquired for us children a certain interest and charm. The walk to his dwelling was pleasant. His sunny sitting-room, with the small stove from which pungent odours issued, the chafing-dishes, metallic tractors, the curious glasses and retorts and ancient tomes excited our imagination ; in after years we perceived that it must have resembled the study of an alchemist.    Here, amongst his drying herbs and occult possessions, he taught the poorest, most neglected boys to read, from a sense of Christian duty, which was generally regarded as a queer crotchet ; for it was before the days of Bell and Lancaster, and when ragged schools were unimagined.

How well do I remember him ! His features were good, but his countenance severe ; over his very grey hair he wore a grey worsted wig, with three stiff rows of curls behind, and was attired in a dark-brown collar- less suit of a very old-fashioned cut, wearing out of doors a cocked hat, also of an old Quaker type, a short great- coat or spencer, and in winter grey-ribbed worsted leggings, drawn to the middle of the thigh.    Although a stickler for old customs, he was one of the very first in the Midland Counties to use an umbrella.    The one that belonged to him was a substantial concern, covered with oil-cloth or oil-silk, with a large ring at the top, by which it was hung up.

Having a reputation in the Society as a minister, he now and then paid visits to other meetings, but never very far from home ; and considering himself connected with Phebe Howitt of Heanor, by the marriage of his stepson John to her aunt, felt it doubly incumbent to repair at times to that Derbyshire village.    With Thomas and Phebe Howitt, the parents of my future husband, we had no personal acquaintance, merely a somewhat disagreeable association from his having obtained from them the plant asarabacca, which had caused my mother violent headaches and was the chief ingredient of his cephalic snuff.

In their society the simple, religious, and therefore the best side of his character was exhibited. He was consequently described to me in after years by my husband as a welcome guest, generally arriving at harvest-time, when he would employ himself in the pleasant field-labour, quoting beautiful and appropriate texts of Scripture as applicable to the scenes around him. This I can well understand, from a little occurrence in my childhood.

Rebecca Summerland, the daughter of my half-uncle John, had married, in 1801, a Friend named Joseph Burgess, of Grooby Lodge, near Leicester. She became the mother of a little boy—William—with whom, when staying at his grandparents', we were permitted to play. On one of these happy occasions, their rarity enhancing the delight, we were enjoying ourselves at aunt Summerland's when our grandfather unexpectedly arrived. Our parents were absent from home—probably at Quarterly Meeting—and he, wishful to look after us, had come to take us a walk. To refuse was not to be thought of. We very reluctantly left little William and started under his escort. But our grandfather was unusually kind and gentle, and to give us a treat, took us to see our father's small tillage farm at the distance of a couple of miles from home.

He talked about the trees and plants in Timber Lane, which, winding up from the town to the top of a hill, was hemmed in by steep mossy banks, luxuriant with wild flowers and ferns, and overarched by the boughs of the oak, hawthorn, and elder, having a clear little stream gurgling along one side. When we came out on the open breezy hill, with the high bushy banks of Needwood Forest extending before us in wooded promontories for many a mile, there were lambs and young calves in the fields, and primroses ; and so as we went on our minds were calmed and interested.    At length we reached the farm of eighteen acres, which we had last seen in autumnal desolation.    Now all was beautifully green and fresh ; the lower portion closed for hay, the upper filled with vigorous young vegetation ; tender blades of wheat springing from the earth, green leaflets of the flax for our mother's spinning just visible ; next, the plot reserved for turnips ; the entire field being enclosed by a broad grassy headland, a perfect border of spring flowers, of which we had soon our hands full.    Our grandfather showed us the tender, delicate flax, and contrasted it with the rougher growth of the turnip and the grass-like blades of wheat, and preached a little sermon about God making every plant and flower spring out of the dry, barren earth.    As we listened the last shadow of discontent vanished.    The walk back was all cheerfulness and sunshine, and we were taken to aunt Summerland's to finish the visit, happier than we had been on our arrival.

This walk gave my sister Anna her first taste for botany.    She probably inherited from our grandfather her passionate love of flowers.    She learnt from his copy of Miller's " Gardener's Dictionary," which became her property after his death, to appreciate the wonderful beauty of the Linnæan system.

It is impossible to give an adequate idea of the stillness and isolation of our lives as children.    Our father's intro-verted character and naturally meditative turn of mind made him avoid social intercourse and restrict his participation in outward events to what was absolutely needful for the exact fulfilment of his professional and religious labours.    Our mother's clear, intelligent mind, her culture and refinement, were chastened and subdued by her new spiritual convictions and by painful social surroundings, which were aggravated by the death of her sympathiser, Ann Shipley. Our nurse, Hannah Finney, was dull and melancholy, seeking to stifle an attachment which she had formed in the Forest of Dean for a handsome carpenter of dubious character and unconvinced of Friends' principles. Each of our reticent caretakers was subjected to severe inward ordeals, and incapable of infusing knowledge and brightness into our young minds. At four years of age little Anna had been unable to talk, and had therefore been sent daily to a cheerful old woman who kept a dame school, and in more lively surroundings had acquired the power of speech.

In fact, after we could both talk, being chiefly left to converse together, our ignorance of the true appellations for many ordinary sentiments and actions compelled us to coin and use words of our own. To sneeze was to us both *akisham*—the sound which one of our parents must have made in sneezing. Roman numerals, which we saw on the title-pages of most books, conveyed no other idea than the word *icklymicklydictines*. Italic printing was *softly* writing. Our parents often spoke together of dividends. This suggested to me some connection with the devil. I was grieved and perplexed to hear our good parents talk without hesitation or sense of impropriety of those wicked *dividends*. Had there been an open communicative spirit in the family, these strange expressions and misapprehensions would have either never arisen or been at once corrected.

Our mother must, however, have taught us early to read, for I cannot remember when we could not do so; but neither she nor our father ever gave or permitted us to receive religious tuition. Firmly adhering to the fundamental principles of George Fox, that Christ, the true inward light, sends to each individual interior inspirations as their guide of Christian faith, and that His Spirit, being free, does not submit to human learning and customs, they aimed to preserve us in unsullied innocence, consigning us to Him in lowly confidence for guidance and instruction. So fearful were they of interfering with His workings, that they did not even teach us the Lord's Prayer; nor do I remember that they ever intimated to us the duty of each morning and evening raising our hearts in praise and petition to God. Yet they gave us to commit to memory Robert Barclay's "Catechism and Confession of Faith," a compilation of texts applied to the doctrines of Friends, and supposed "to be fitted for the wisest and largest as well as the weakest and lowest capacities," but which left us in the state of the perplexed eunuch before Philip instructed him in the Holy Writ.

It was the earnest desire of our father that our attention should be directed to Christ as the one great, all-sufficient sacrifice; yet, nevertheless, so entirely was the fundamental doctrine of the Saviour being the Incarnate God hidden from us, that we grew up to the age when opinions assert themselves to find that our minds had instinctively shaped themselves into the Unitarian belief, out of which we have both been brought by different means. As regards my sister Anna, she has said that she found in reading "Ecce Homo" the exact counterpart of her own youthful views of Jesus, which had grown up in the unassisted soil of her mind. A singular exhibition this of the natural untrained growth of a young ingenious intellect hedged round with the narrowest pale of religious observances, from which all outward expression was excluded, in the belief and in the silent prayerful hope that the Divine Spirit would lead it into all truth.

The Bible, being acknowledged a secondary rule and subordinate to the Spirit, had been neglected in many Friends' families. This led the Yearly Meeting, in the early part of the century, to recommend Friends everywhere to adopt the habit of daily reading the Scriptures; and my father, deputed by the authorities, endeavoured without success to induce the other members of our meeting to comply with the advice. He himself had ever set them the example, and whilst bearing his testimony, that it is the Spirit, not the Scriptures, which is the ground and source of all truth, diligently studied the Bible; at the same time refusing to call it the Word of God, a term he only applied to Christ, the true Gospel.

The right way to understand the Holy Scriptures was to abandon one's own will and wait pliant and obedient on the Divine Schoolmaster. The ground of this belief is given in the following extract :—" As man is composed of body and soul, so also the Holy Scriptures are composed of the letter and the spirit, so that the letter is in a manner the receptacle of the spirit; and as beasts can behold the body of a man and hear his voice, but are incapable of understanding his mind or speech, because they are not endowed with the same spirit as he whom they can thus discern with their eyes; so the wicked can hear the words and see the letter of the Holy Scriptures, but that which is the spirit of the letter, and which pertains to the Divine Mind, they alone understand who are endued with that spirit. The wicked, indeed, can no more perceive it than beasts understand the language of men, of whose expressions they comprehend a few only, and those with difficulty, such as exclamations, chidings, and exhortations and threats. Thus the wicked see in the Holy Scriptures what is related, what is commanded or forbid, but the spirit and, as it were, the marrow of the letter they obtain not."

It was this ardent desire to fathom the deeper teaching of God which made my father value highly and read industriously the life and writings of Madame Guyon, those of Fénélon, S. Francis de Sales, Thomas à Kempis, Michael Molinos, and others, all of a mystical tendency. "Telemachus" was also to him a very instructive book, which he read not as an interesting story, but as a work of deep religious truth; interpreting the aged Mentor, the guide of the young Telemachus, as the Divine Spirit, thus influencing and directing the inexperienced human soul. It was a sort of "Pilgrim's Progress" to his honestly seeking spirit.

The Bible was a book of daily reading and earnest study to our parents; and our father's frequent selection of the Old Testament for family reading is explainable by his constant endeavour to find a spiritual meaning in each verse. The literal Hebraic significance of names was considered most important by him; and he began to transcribe the Book of Isaiah, giving to each proper name this literal significance, as a key to the spiritual meaning of the most unintelligible passages, which thus became clear to him, and full of the deepest teaching.

Each morning a chapter of the Bible was read after breakfast, followed by a pause for interior application and instruction by the Holy Spirit; the purpose of this silence being, however, never explained to us. In the long winter evenings Friends' journals, "The Persecution of Friends," and similar works were read aloud; and when gone through were succeeded by "Foxe's Book of

Martyrs "—a large folio edition with engravings that made our blood curdle ; as to the narrative, we listened, yet wished not to hear, until, proving too terrible reading just before bed-time, it was set aside.

I had also to read to my father during the day, when some mechanical operation left his mind disengaged. Thomas à Kempis was a great favourite with him ; not so with me, as I understood the constant exhortation to take up the cross to refer to using the plain language and plain attire of Friends, and our peculiar garb, many degrees more ungainly than that of most strict Friends, was already a perfect crucifixion to Anna and me. The New Testament never came amiss. On one such occasion I received from my father a stern reprimand for having, when reading the miracle of the loaves and fishes as related by St. Mark, inserted, as he supposed, the adjective " green " in the thirty-ninth verse : " And He commanded them to make them sit down in companies upon the green grass."

He broke in sternly, " Mary, thou must not add or take from Scripture."

" Please, father, it is green grass," I replied.

" Let me see, let me see ! " he exclaimed ; and after looking at the verse, said in a surprised but appeased tone, " I had never noticed it."

We children went to meeting twice on First-day, walking demurely hand-in-hand behind our parents ; and once on Fifth-day with our mother alone, if our father was absent in the Forest or elsewhere surveying. These meetings were far from profitable to me. The nearest approach to good which I remember in these seasons of silent worship was the circumstance that the side-windows were reflected at times, probably owing to the sun's position, in a large window placed high above the gallery, looking down the Meeting-house and opposite to my seat. These windows of light, seen through the larger one, in the sky as it were, represented to me the windows of Heaven.  It was these or similar ones, I imagined, which were open in Heaven when the rain poured down for forty days in the time of Noah.  The sight of these beautiful windows was a privilege, I believed, granted to me when good.  This, I am sorry to confess, was the nearest approach to Heaven which those silent meetings afforded me.  The blotches of damp on the Meeting-house walls presented to me, however, wonderful battles from the Old Testament; the knots in the backs of the old wooden seats merely secular subjects, odd and grotesque heads and faces of human beings and of animals. How grieved would my parents have been at this want of mental discipline!

Our uncle John Summerland, and his wife, lived on the same premises as the Meeting-house, which was divided from their dwelling by a garden; and it was strangely interesting to us children, when paying them a visit, to go alone into our place of worship.  Even now I remember the strange eery effect of lifting the heavy iron handle that raised the ponderous latch and sounded through the empty building with a solemn response.  It was most exciting to us on these occasions to be at liberty to sit even in the gallery, where the preachers, when they came, sat; to go over to the men's side and try how it was in our father's seat or in John Shipley's, and then to go up into the chamber where the "Women's Meetings of Business" were held.

Little William Burgess—the one boy we were permitted to associate with, from fear of contamination—was

our companion in these bold explorations.  He seemed,
however, to be most attracted by the graveyard, a pleasant
little green field into which the side-windows of the Meeting-house looked, and where in the spring-time, a sheep,
with her lamb or lambs, would be turned in to eat the
abundant grass; often breaking the deep silence of some
meeting for worship by their gentle bleatings.  This ever
awoke a peculiar feeling in our childish minds, a sort of
sense of appropriateness from their relationship to the
Saviour, the Good Shepherd, and the Lamb of God.

The visits of ministering Friends, men or women
preachers from a distance, and who, as I have said,
took up their abode at our house, sometimes for two or
three days, always produced a little home-excitement.
A ministering Friend was supposed to be brought into
such close communion with the Divine Source of Light
and Truth, that he or she was permitted to act as the
mouthpiece of the Holy Spirit.  We children, therefore,
never lost a certain awe of ministering Friends, believing
they were aware of the exact state of our souls.  This
was especially the case when their mission was what was
called "paying family visits."  Then they sat alone with
each household, dropping into silence, probably at the
close of the meal, and spoke, it was believed, directly to
the individual souls of those present.

Sometimes a noted preacher came with what was called
" a concern to hold a public meeting ; " and this was to us
children quite thrilling, for our father's factotum, Thomas
Bishop, then delivered circulars from house to house :—
" respectfully inviting the inhabitants of Uttoxeter to
attend a religious meeting of the Society of Friends,
commonly called Quakers, at the club-room of the Red
Lion Inn, that evening, at such an hour."

The excitement was still more increased to us by the Red Lion Inn being in a different part of the town from the Meeting-house; for it was only as a matter of necessity that we children were ever taken through the streets. Our world seemed to enlarge itself simply by going out in an evening, walking through the market-place and the innyard, and through the inn itself, with our eyes wide open and our minds all astir; though meekly following in the wake of our father and mother and the ministering Friend, male or female. Then, too, the sense of importance and suspense when we entered the large club-room, with its chandelier and its side-lights all ablaze, and the raised bench placed for the occasion, having a table in front, on which the minister might lay his hat when he rose to preach or pray—"supplicate," Friends called it— or if a woman, on which she might lay her bonnet, which she took off preparatory to rising to address the meeting. Thomas Bishop was always in requisition on these occasions, showing people to empty seats and preserving order at the door.

Sometimes these meetings, from being very large, the preacher earnest and eloquent, and the audience attentive to the end, notwithstanding the long silence with which they had opened, and even closed, were pronounced very satisfactory by our parents. I cannot but believe that the preparatory silence, the peculiar style of preaching, the long occasional pause in the middle of a sentence, the high rhythmical tone into which the preacher rose as he or she increased in earnestness and fluency, and then the sudden transition by a return to the natural tone of voice, must have struck the unaccustomed listeners as at least very peculiar.

I am not, indeed, aware of any great or good effect ever

being produced by these meetings, held in a room which often served as the stage for far more entertaining, and perhaps even instructive, spectacles to the townspeople. It was used as a theatre by the Stantons, a respectable dramatic company from Newcastle, and it was at the Red Lion that the celebrated Miss Mellon, afterwards Duchess of St. Albans, made her *début*.

When the preacher was of less repute, the gathering would be invited to the Friends' Meeting-house, which our father and Thomas Bishop would then prepare for the occasion, by removing a set of large wooden shutters which separated the upper loft, that usually formed the " Women's Meeting of Business," from the Meeting-room. Thus a large open gallery was formed capable of holding many persons, and which gave a full view of the preacher and the assembly below.   On one such occasion a curious and rather awkward incident took place.   The preacher was a woman-Friend, and concluded her discourse by describing the New Jerusalem, the inhabitants of which should no more say, " I am sick."   With these words, as if impatient to make an end, she sank down into the seat behind her.   On this one of the medical men of the town, who sat in the middle of the meeting, and who evidently had not been paying much attention to the thread of the discourse, sprang up, and leaning forward in the crowd, said in a professional tone, " Is the lady ill? Can I render any assistance? "   A dead silence prevailed —and we must suppose that the truth dawned upon the medical mind, for after repeating the question with the same result, he seated himself, amid the suppressed smiles of all who were not Friends.

Everything was education to us children, even though not in school form; and we learnt much by the pleasant drives to Monthly Meeting at Stafford or Leek, that of Uttoxeter being every third month. I do not think it was a general rule for Friends to take their children with them to these meetings when held at a distance. But as our parents were most anxious to bring us up in the way we ought to go, Anna and I alternately accompanied our parents, sitting between them on a small turn-down seat affixed to the gig for the purpose.

First let us take the road to Stafford. We passed Henry Pedley's, the old weaver's, where our mother went every spring, taking us children with her, to choose the patterns in which he should weave the linen yarn which she had spun in the winter. Beyond the weaver's, the entire road was known to us only by these Monthly Meeting drives. First came the old handsome red-brick hall of Loxley, with its park; then what was called Parson Hilditch's, a pleasant parsonage standing a field's-length from the road; and just beyond, the little red-brick schoolhouse, where Parson Hilditch taught the village boys, who, coming or going, as we passed, made their bow. This was distasteful to my father, as savouring of "hat-homage." If a beggar or other petitioner addressed him bare-headed, he would say politely and kindly, "Put on thy hat;" but if the man, from a sense of duty, humility, or perhaps servility, did not comply, he would become almost angry and say, "Unless thou put on thy hat I shall not talk with thee."

The point of greatest interest, however, on the road to Stafford was the old castle of Chartley, standing close to the highway. It was an ancient, very grey pile of ruins, on the edge of a fine old park, in which were preserved the remains of the original wild breed of British cattle, similar to those at Chillingham. Chartley belongs to the

Earl of Ferrers, and the new house, which had been begun several years before, stood unfinished, owing to a quarrel between the old Lord and his son, Viscount Tamworth. It was a strange, unhappy family, in which murder had at one time brought the head of the house to the gallows. Moreover, in the old castle Mary Queen of Scots had been confined. All this had been told us on the first occasion of our driving to Stafford, and once being told was sufficient. It furnished us with a great deal to think about. Chartley had a romantic history, though at that time we did not know what romance meant. It and its surroundings were all wonderfully weird and hoary. It was the oldest-looking place we had ever seen.

The next point of interest was Weston Hall, a tall-gabled, old Elizabethan mansion, standing a little apart from the road, which was here a long heavy ascent worn rather than cut through the soft sandstone rock. We next looked out for Ingestre, the seat of Lord Talbot, standing far off in the park. We felt in some mysterious way as if the place almost belonged to us. We did not remember when we had not heard of Lord Talbot. My father had a great regard for the family, and knew every inch of their estates. Next came Tixall Hall, with its fine old Gothic gateway.

Of Stafford town itself we knew little, except that it had a castle and was famous for making shoes, which it was currently believed were manufactured for sale rather than for wear. The Meeting-house was a queer old place, older and not so nice, we thought, as that of Uttoxeter; the woodwork of the window-frames and benches was unpainted, and so old that the very grain of the wood stood up in ridges, the softer portions being worn away with time.  The Friends were few and simple, and awoke no interest in us.

Sometimes in these drives we might chance to pass a personage for whom we children cherished the same high regard as our parents, and who seemed in a manner connected with us, from his wearing some of my father's cast-off garments.  It was old Daniel Neale, the worthy Irish beggar.  His figure was short and spare, and considerably bent forward; yet he walked with long strides and a firm step, his tall staff being rather a companion than support.  A cheerful, contented old countenance shone forth between his bushy white locks, his coat was buckled with a broad leathern strap, and over his shoulder he carried a capacious wallet.

He was kindly received and entrusted with messages by the old Catholic families, who, surrounded by Protestant neighbours, at a time when religious differences made a wider separation than they do at present, lived in a dignified seclusion, yet in good-fellowship amongst themselves.  I introduced Daniel Neale in "Wood Leighton;" a work that clearly indicates the effect produced upon my mind by the consistent piety of the Staffordshire Catholics.

The journey to Leek was considerably longer than that to Stafford.  We went out of the town quite at the other end.  We passed the village of Checkley, and never forgot having been shown there, on the first occasion of a drive to Leek, the three tall gaunt-looking stones which met our eye.  They marked the graves of three bishops slain in an ancient battle fought many long ages ago, at a place called The Naked Field, from the circumstance of the three bodies being brought naked from the battlefield three days afterwards and buried there.

At the little town of Cheadle we stayed to bait the horse, and then going forward came to Chettelton, then to Whitly rocks, a wild district of the moorland country to which Leek belonged.

The Friends of Leek had all, with one exception, a cold, bleak, moorland character. They were not a well-favoured race, and were neither good-mannered nor affable. The one exception was Toft Chorley, a gentleman with very little appearance of the Quaker about him. He had a country dwelling on the moorlands, but was always at his town house in Leek. on Monthly Meeting days to receive and entertain Friends.

One spot of surpassing interest to us children was "The Hall" at Uttoxeter. It was a large, irregular brick mansion, standing by the roadside outside the town, and though much dilapidated, must originally have been a place of importance. Here Mr. Thomas Copestake, the great jeweller and lapidary, had dwelt and carried on an important and extensive trade, which in the last century brought much wealth to Uttoxeter. The articles usually made were tiaras, silver buckles, and all kinds of jewellery. Small white pebbles could be abundantly picked up in the neighbourhood, which were purchased by Mr. Copestake, if without fault, at a penny apiece; but after they had been polished and cut, they had the appearance of stones of the first water. He was also entrusted by the Government with orders for "Stars of Honour." It took about three weeks to make one of these decorations, which when finished was worth about £100. Mr. Copestake, when at the height of his prosperity, employed a hundred and forty men, without reckoning apprentices. On the town side of the old hall was a large court, enclosed from the road by an ancient red-brick wall. Round the three inner sides of this court were erected workshops two storeys high, the upper storey having long casemented windows for the greater admission of light, and here in old times Copestake's jewellers and lapidaries had worked.  He had unfortunately damaged his great trade and his reputation by mixing an alloy with gold in the manufacture of gold lace.  Birmingham, Derby, and even London began to compete with imitations and cheap inferior articles, and carried off the demand from Uttoxeter.  In our childhood, therefore, the workshops had fallen into decay, the court was overgrown with grass, and the whole had a strange air of desolation about it.

Now and then, however, the courtyard was turned to account, as on an occasion which remains indelibly stamped on my memory.  Here came an equestrian troop, and no doubt a better place for the exhibition of their feats could hardly have been chosen; the old deserted shops, with their flights of steps outside and their large windows within, afforded tiers of boxes as in a theatre. We, the children of Friends, brought up with Puritanical rigidity, to whom the very mention of a play, a dance, or a horse-rider's exhibition was forbidden, were nevertheless conducted surreptitiously to the show by two young women-Friends who had been permitted to take us a walk.  It was a summer evening, and passing through the weather-beaten door in the old red wall, we came into a crowd and could only get standing-places.  I could not see much, only people laughing.  There was a great deal of shouting and merriment, and a great deal of crushing where we stood.  Nevertheless it was to us little girls very exciting, and it was quite dusk when we got home, where we never spoke of the adventure.

Mr. Copestake's daughter Grace dwelt in the desolate

old mansion, which had the reputation of being haunted. She was a tall, slim, middle-aged lady, attired in the narrow-skirted classical style of those days, which made her look still thinner.  The townspeople, in half-wondering compassion, called her "Poor Miss Grace," from her want of conventionality.  She was in reality a lady in reduced circumstances, who strove to maintain herself, and was certainly one of the earliest of that race of independent, clever women who have given a marked character to the present century.

She introduced "the lace-work," as it was called, into the town, and which, after the lapidary-work ceased, thus became the staple trade of the little town.  Once I accompanied my mother in a call on Miss Grace.  After we had been seated with her in her own room, which was comfortable enough, lofty and wainscoted with dark oak, she led us into a huge barn-like apartment, whose walls, denuded of their original wainscot or tapestry, revealed rude unfinished masonry, than which nothing is more unsightly.  Here the lace frames stood side by side, with girls busily working at them.

Miss Grace, I believe, did not find her establishment sufficiently remunerative to continue it many years.  She retired from it, and the frames became widely scattered through the town.

To my sister Anna and myself Miss Copestake was a perfect heroine.  There must have been some expression in her eyes or tone in her voice that drew us to her and made her lady-like form and face indelible, so that we both have remembered to old age her slim figure attired in black silk, with a large lace shawl held close in her folded hands, her upright carriage and firm step, and her gracious smile.  The force of repulsion or attraction is

most strongly felt when social intercourse is limited, and
none in these days of free interchange of thought and
opinion can understand the singular feeling produced
on our childish minds by persons not "members of our
Society."

In 1804–5 my father was employed by the Corporation
of Leicester for the enclosure of the town fields. He
laid out the race-ground and a new public walk, which
has become a great improvement to the town, from its
fine trees and shrubberies full of flowering undergrowth.
The maps were very handsome, and, to our admiration,
bound with blue ribbon, the colour of the Corporation.
This commission, with surveying in the Forest and for
numerous noblemen and gentlemen, often necessitated
his absence for days and weeks at a time. My mother,
being thus disengaged, would require us to sew or knit
for hours together at her side, whilst she busily plied her
needle or her wheel in the parlour or the garden-porch.
I particularly remember her spinning in the porch, because,
it having a brick floor with a second porch below opening
into the basement storey, the wheel gave a hollow, louder
sound, which caused us to bring our low seats close to
her knee, that we might catch every word of her utter-
ance. Never ceasing our employment—for, to use her
phrase, "we must not nurse our work "—we listened with
breathless attention to exciting tales of her ancestry and
of her unmarried life. She repeated to us "Lavinia"
from Thomson's "Seasons," and other poems she had
learnt from her father. Her mind, too, was stored with
verses which she had met with here and there, both grave
and gay.

Of the former order were the lines written by Charles
the First the night before his execution, and which both

she and we greatly admired, "Auld Robin Gray," "Lord
Rodney's Victory," "Upon yon Belfast mountains I heard
a maid complain," &c.   And amongst her jocular verses,
"Amo, amas, I love a lass," and "The Derby Ram,"
which, oddly enough, had been a favourite of Washington's, and said by him to children for their amusement.
It begins :—

> "As I was going to Derby,
> Upon a market-day,
> I spied the biggest ram, sir,
> That ever was fed upon hay.
> Tow de row de dow,
> Tow de row de da."

During these hours of unrestrained converse she would
become lively, almost merry, even silently laughing.   It
was a revelation of her character quite new to us, and we
were happy under its influence.   There was a term of
endearment peculiar to her, "My precious," and which
had in it a deep tenderness not easily to be forgotten.

Self-withdrawal from her children had become, as it
were, habitual to her, and we were still left an easy prey
to whatever influences might be exerted on us by servants; for by friends or acquaintance there could be
comparatively none.   Indeed the only healthy outlet we
had was the garden and our love for each other.

Hannah Finney, our nurse, unable to conquer her
attachment, had married the worthless carpenter, and
plagued her own heart ever after.   Our parents had
sought long and anxiously for a proper substitute, which
they believed they had ultimately met with in a country-
woman about thirty, who knew her work as if by instinct,
speedily expressed a desire to attend meeting, and by her
irreproachable conduct, sobriety of dress, and staidness of
demeanour, won their entire confidence.   Nanny, as she

was called, equally pleased and, alas ! ensnared us children.
She had a memory stored, I suppose, with every song that
ever was printed on a halfpenny-sheet or sold in a country
fair, which she repeated in a wild recitative, that attracted
us as much as if it had been singing.  She was familiar
with ghosts, hobgoblins, and fairies ; knew much of the
vice, and less of the virtues of both town and country life ;
and finding us insatiable listeners, eagerly retailed to us
her stores of miscellaneous—chiefly evil—knowledge,
under a seal of secrecy, which we never broke.  We
trembled when we heard her utter an oath, but had no
hesitation in learning from her whist—Nanny always
playing dummy and using a tea-tray on her lap as a
card-table.

Nanny's wild, strange communications invested even
our dull surroundings with a life and charm, and whilst
causing us often to put our own or her construction
on the actions of our neighbours, made us realise their
dispositions and sympathise with their needs.

With what shrinking curiosity, for instance, did we
regard the lawyer, Mr. Humphrey Pipe, who was the first
to use an eyeglass in Uttoxeter ; being thereby endowed,
according to Nanny, with a power more malignant than
that of the evil eye !  His wife had deserted him for a
fiddler after studying the " Sorrows of Werther," and her
framed and glazed illustrations of Goethe's romance were
often looked at by us, for they had become the property
of Thomas Bishop.

With what excitement did we note any interchange of
civility between our mother and Mrs. Clowes, the wife of
a clergyman, and who styled herself in consequence the
Rev. Anne Clowes !  After his death she continued to
reside in Uttoxeter.  She was known by everybody, and

was an honoured if not an acceptable guest in the best houses of the neighbourhood; yet she lived without a servant in a narrow alley, and had neither bell nor knocker to her house-door, on which her friends were instructed to rap loudly with a stone. She occupied an upper room, confusedly crowded with goods and chattels of every description picked up at auctions, and piles of earthenware and china, having the casements filled with

THE REV. ANNE CLOWES.

as many pieces of rag, pasteboard, and cobwebs as small panes of glass. She slept in a large salting-trough, with a switch at her side to keep off the rats. This mean and miserable abode she termed, in her grandiloquent language, "The hallowed spot, into which only were introduced the great in mind, in wealth, or in birth;" and on one occasion spoke of "a most delightful visit from two of Lady Waterpark's sons, when 'the feast of reason

and the flow of soul' had been so absorbing that one of
the Mr. Cavendishes, in descending the stairs, had set his
foot in her mutton-pie, which was ready for the baker's
oven."

Each Whitsuntide we saw her marching at the head of
the Oddfellows' Club, with a bouquet of lilacs and peonies
blazing on her breast up to her chin, holding in one hand
a long staff, her usual out-door companion.   She was not
insane, only a very original person, running wild amongst

MRS. CLOWES, ATTENDED BY TWO GENTLEMEN OF THE TOWN, RETURNING FROM AN
EVENING PARTY.

a number of other eccentric worthies, all of whom left
marked impressions on our minds.

In the summer of 1806 we felt brought into very close
contact with the gay world by a visit from aunt Dorothy
Sylvester.   She accompanied our mother from London,
where the latter had attended Yearly Meeting.   As they
arrived late one Seventh-day night, she was first seen
by us children the next morning, fashionably attired for
church, which drew forth the involuntary exclamation

from one of us, "Oh! aunt, shan't thou be afraid of father seeing thee so smart?" We soon perceived that he and our mother, whilst adhering to their rule of life, did not obtrude it on their visitor.

They offered her the best that their house contained, and in her honour gave little entertainments to "worldly people" of their acquaintance. She was driven by my father to all the pleasant places in the neighbourhood; into the Forest, now in its progress of demolition, where at the royal lodges occupied by his acquaintance they were hospitably received. For myself, I only remember being taken on one of these excursions; and this was to Ingestre.

I have already said that my father was constantly employed by Lord Talbot. This was Charles, the second Earl of that name, who, holding serious views and greatly respecting my parent, had long conversations with him about Friends, their principles and peculiarities, and accepted from him Clarkson's "Portraiture of Quakers." My aunt was very handsomely dressed, and I in my best. My father would never allow Anna and me to wear white frocks; but to go to meeting in summer we might have little thick white muslin tippets. In such a cape, precisely like those still worn by some charity-children, a plain little bonnet, a print frock, the pattern so small as to produce merely a grave, sober colouring, with sleeves to the elbow, and opened behind, showing my drab calamanco petticoat; mits covering the arms, and shoes high on the instep like those of boys, though women and girls wore boat-shaped shoes—behold me arriving at Ingestre.

My father seemed quite at home at the Hall. Lord Talbot received him with kindness, and whilst they remained together my aunt and I were conducted by a servant to a magnificent room, where an elegantly attired lady welcomed us.  Next we were led to another handsome apartment, where a splendid dinner was served.  Lord Talbot was then with us, and my father, and all seemed very cheerful.  Afterwards our host sent for his little son, Viscount Ingestre, then five years old, to make my acquaintance.  I was dreadfully shy, and my aunt, doubtless, was very much ashamed of my country breeding. But the little Lord was polite and gentle, and so by degrees I overcame my self-consciousness, and talked comfortably with him at a distance from the others.

We must have been some hours at Ingestre, and returned home delighted, bringing with us an immense mass of greenhouse flowers; amongst which were some splendid geraniums—a plant, I believe, just then introduced—a large bunch of hoja, the Carolina allspice, and the lemon-scented verbena.  I mention these flowers because they were all new to us; and this lemon-scented verbena became so connected in my mind with Ingestre, that I never saw it, even when a woman grown, and when life had produced many richer experiences, without its recalling the memory of my childhood, and that long, long passed away visit.

At length our aunt's stay came to a close, and a farewell party was given, at which a tall thin lady was introduced to our sober family circle as our aunt's travelling companion to London.  How her mincing ways, sentimental drawl, and her gauzy, transparent costume astonished us children!  We approved of our aunt's appearance, her stately form being set off by her rich silk gown and elaborate turban of gold tissue. Nevertheless we were most of all impressed by our mother's calm self-possession, and the quiet grace with which she maintained, in her modest attire, her peculiarities as a Friend.

Let me describe our mother as she was in those days. Not handsome, but of a singularly intelligent countenance, well-cut features, clear grey eyes; the whole expression being that of a character strong and decisive, but not impulsive. She was of middle height; her dress always the same. The soft silk gowns of neutral tints of her wedding outfit were carefully folded away on the shelves of her wardrobe, for her husband disapproved of silk. She wore generally a mixture of silk and wool, called silkbine, of a dark colour, mostly some shade of brown. The dress, being made long, was worn, even in the house, usually drawn up on each side through the pocket-holes; the effect of which was good, and would have been really graceful if the material had been soft and pliable, but the thread of both silk and wool was spun with a close twist, which produced a stiff and harsh fabric. A thin double muslin kerchief covered the bust. Her transparent white muslin cap of the ordinary Quaker make was raised somewhat behind, leaving the back hair visible rolled over a small pad.

In the November of the year 1806 a great event occurred—a baby sister was born, and called Emma. We had hitherto been two sisters; now we were three. Our astonishment and delight over the sweet little blue-eyed creature were unbounded.

In the following May our old grandfather quietly passed away, in his eighty-third year, and was laid to rest in the green graveyard by the silent Meeting-house.

A twelvemonth passed, and fresh surprises awaited us. One summer First-day, at the close of afternoon meeting,

our parents were mysteriously summoned from the
Meeting-house door to visit our father's old half-brother
Joseph, whom, as he had been a confirmed invalid for
many years, we children had never seen.  An hour later
we were fetched from home, and taken for the first time
into a large, gloomy house, along mysterious passages into
a dimly-lighted chamber.  Our parents were sitting there
in solemn silence on either side of an arm-chair, in which
reclined a large-limbed, but fearfully emaciated, pallid
old man.  We were taken up to him.  He spoke to us
in a feeble, husky voice; then, like an aged patriarch,
placed a trembling hand on each of our heads and blessed
us.  We were then quietly led away, our parents remaining with him.

The next morning we were told that our uncle Joseph
had died in the night.  Again, a few mornings later, on
July 9, 1808, we were told that a little brother had been
born to us in the preceding night.  In the midst of our
amazement and yet undeveloped joy arose the question
within us, " Will our parents like it ? " for we had the
impression that they never approved of boys.  The doubt
speedily vanished; their infant son, who was named
Charles, was evidently their peculiar pride and delight.
Under these circumstances, surely there was no family in
the county that was happier than ours.

Anna and I almost lived in the nursery, for we were
devoted to our sweet little sister Emma and our new
treasure, baby Charles.  The nursery, too, was one of the
most cheerful rooms in the house, furnished with every
suitable comfort and convenience.  A light and rather
low window looked over the whole neighbourhood ; there
we sat for hours.  Rhoda, the highly respectable nurse
who had been engaged for Charles, was a new and

interesting character to us.  Her parents dwelt in the market-place, and she told us she had seen the bull-baiting there every year.  It was a horrid, cruel sight, which we should never have thought of witnessing, and our father had tried year after year to put a stop to it.  But Rhoda's description was like a traveller's account of a bull-fight in Spain.  You disapprove, but read the narrative.  Then she had her own books, which she lent us, "The Shepherdess of the Alps" and "The Arabian Nights," over which, as a matter of course, we sat hour after hour reading with unwearying wonder and delight. We, in return as it were for her good offices, brought up into the nursery for her to read the best books we knew of, namely, the "Life of Madame Guyon" and "Telemachus."  The former work was our favourite, from the glimpses it gave us of what our father termed the "dark ages of Popery."  I question whether Rhoda attempted either of them.  Her head was full of private interviews with secret sweethearts.  She wrote her love-letters, and we children must write ours.

I do not think that Anna, who was a year and a half older than I, was bewitched by the sorceries of this dangerous young woman; but I was so far captivated by her talk, that I wrote a letter about love and marriage at her dictation.  When I think of myself, the simple child of nine, brought up, as my parents believed, in perfect innocence, my soul so pure that an angel might inscribe upon it words direct from the Holy Spirit, I feel the most intense compassion for myself.  Poor child!  Nanny had already dimmed the brightness of my young spirit's innocence; now came another tempter, and whilst our parents slept, as it were, sowed the tares and the poison seed in the fruitful soil of my forlorn soul.  "Madame Guyon" lay on a shelf in one of the nursery cupboards, and between the leaves Rhoda laid my unholy letter.

All this had wholly passed out of my mind, when one First-day, after dinner, my father inquired for the "Life of Madame Guyon." It was immediately brought, and he, dear good man! sat down to read it before going to afternoon meeting.

My heart aches to think of the dismay and the astonishment of sorrow that must have filled his soul when he came upon the evil paper in my child's handwriting. He himself had taught me to write, and this was the fruit of that knowledge. What length of time elapsed after this painful discovery, he and my mother sitting together in grieved consternation, I cannot say. Summoned to their presence, I went down without fear or anticipation of evil. I was confounded by the revelation of my enormous ill-doing. Alas! poor father and mother, their sorrow was very great, yet not much was said. It was now time for afternoon meeting, and we must all go.

I suppose I felt something as our first parents did when God called to them in the garden. But, strange to say, I do not think I regarded my offence as the enormity my father and mother did. I was both ashamed and afraid; nevertheless, I had not written those evil, idle words out of my own heart, but at the dictation of another, and with small knowledge of what their meaning implied. A sad silence and solemnity lay on my parents' countenances; they did not, however, inflict any punishment. I was neither degraded nor humbled, only bitterly ashamed.

A Baptist minister of the name of Stephen Chester and his family were my father's tenants in the house adjoining our dwelling. With them lived a most excellent, highly cultivated lady, a Mrs. Parker, or Mary Parker, as she was called in our Friendly fashion; a woman of rare intellect and the highest endowments. She had a day-school of five and twenty or thirty girls, and my parents held her in high esteem.

That very First-day evening, I believe, whilst their minds were still agitated with irritation and sorrow, they requested a visit from her. They laid the whole affair before her. She advised that first and foremost we should be removed from the influence of servants. I think, too, that she must have seconded their own hope that I was but the instrument, and that, like a parrot, I had been made to repeat the offensive words without knowledge of their import. It was her advice to make no great matter of this ugly affair. Let it be forgotten; only fence against any further fall and all further influence of evil. It was the conviction of their own minds.

It was arranged that we should become Mrs. Parker's pupils. My father, still faithful to his idea of separation as a safeguard from evil, stipulated that we should sit apart from the other girls, have no intercourse with them, and that she, the head of all, should have an especial eye upon us.

A happy, pure, and beneficial period now began for us. I was never reminded of my late offence. If my parents and teacher forgot it, so I might have, if the fidelity of my memory, and the knowledge both of good and evil which grew and developed as years advanced, had not kept it alive, and interpreted it like the words "*Mene, mene,*" on the wall. In the meantime the beautiful, lofty, and intelligible moral teaching of our beloved instructress opened my eyes to the loveliness of purity, to the infinite richness of Nature, and so led me up insensibly to the

Creator.    Anna and I no longer mistook evil for good or good for evil; and we soon began to perceive the darkness and ignorance out of which we had come, and to rejoice in the large, bright, glorious world of which we also were denizens.

Our parents, too, were satisfied with our behaviour and progress.    We were exposed to no danger; in going and returning we merely passed from one house to the adjoining.    We sat apart from the other girls, but were friendly with all.    Amongst various injunctions given when we commenced this school-life was the one, that we should always leave on the Saturday morning, before the scholars were examined in the Church Catechism, which concluded the week's lessons.    Nevertheless, either this rule was relaxed, or the hour of instruction must have been altered from our excellent teacher discovering our benighted condition, and feeling it her duty to remedy it.    We never stood up with the class, but by means of listening to it we first learnt by heart the Lord's Prayer and the Ten Commandments.

Happy would it have been for us had Mrs. Parker been engaged from the first as our resident governess, and we committed entirely to her training for the next five or six years; she living with us in the house, taking us walks, and nurturing and cultivating those peculiar talents which afterwards became developed through difficulty, and at the best only imperfectly.    It was a splendid opportunity for our training, spiritually and intellectually, which was disregarded by our parents, who only recognised Mrs. Parker's tuition as a temporary expedient until we could be sent to a Friends' school.

# CHAPTER III.

## GIRLHOOD.

### *1809–1821.*

WE had not been a year under Mrs. Parker's tuition, when the change in our education came. Our governess was anxious to give up her school and leave Uttoxeter; and my parents therefore decided that we should immediately be transferred to the York school. This seminary for girls enjoyed a high reputation in the Society. It was, moreover, conducted by Ann Alexander, through whose involuntary intervention my sister's name had been decided upon.

Ann Alexander, however, informed my parents that she either wished to withdraw or had already withdrawn from the oversight of the school. She recommended most warmly that her little namesake and her younger sister should be sent to a school just commenced at Croydon by two young women-Friends, Sarah Bevan and Anna Woolley, who had been educated for tuition at York school and were in every way well qualified.

We children had never heard of Croydon. Mrs. Parker took the map of England and showed us where it was, above a hundred and fifty miles off; then by what route we should go. "How happy we should be at school," she said, "with companions of our own age; and what a pleasure and satisfaction it would be to be able to improve ourselves more than we could do at home!" We were very sorry that our schooling with Mrs. Parker was over; it had certainly been the happiest, most free and diversified portion of our young existences. Still, she promised to write to us and never to forget us. There was all the excitement of a journey to London before us, and our kind friend and teacher suffered more, I believe, in the prospect of the separation than we did.

How well I remember the gar-ments that were made for us! Our little brown cloth pelisses, cut plain and straight, without plait or fold in them, hooked and eyed down the front so as to avoid buttons, which were regarded by our parents as trimmings, yet fas-tened at the waist with a cord. Little drab beaver bonnets fur-nished us by the Friend hatter of Stafford, James Nixon, who had blocks made purposely for our ultra-plain bonnets. They were

ANNA BOTHAM AT CROYDON.

without a scrap of ribbon or cord, except the strings, which were a necessity, and these were fastened inside. Our frocks were, as usual, of the plainest and most homely fabric and make. Besides our small wardrobes we had few possessions. Anna took with her Mrs. Barbauld's Hymns, as these praises of Creation and Nature were very sweet to her; but when, amidst new scenes, she longed to read those aspirations of a grateful and admiring heart, she sought vainly for the book in the contents of her trunk. It had privately been removed by our teachers.*    I had with me Mrs. Trimmer's "Robins," which was a source of never-failing delight to me.

On the 24th of Tenth Month 1809, I being ten years of age, my sister a year and a half older, we left home for school, under our mother's escort.    Perhaps our parents, in their unworldliness, had forgotten that on the morrow, the 25th of October, all England was to celebrate the fiftieth year of King George the Third's reign.    Be it as it may, we children knew of the approaching festivity, and were thereby reconciled to the pain of leave-taking. We were glad we should be travelling, for in Uttoxeter we should have seen none or little of the rejoicings.    The greatness of our curiosity made us eager to start; and as we drove through the outskirts of our town, by Tutbury and its castle to Ashby-de-la-Zouch, where we had a fresh postchaise, and then on to Grooby Lodge, where we spent the night, we had the delight of watching the busy preparations.    Even our Quaker relatives, the Burgesses, we found in a mild state of excitement in anticipation of the morrow.

Leicester, as we drove through it next morning, was all agog—bells ringing, flags flying, huge bonfires kindling.    The jubilee had set the British population in motion, and the king's highway swarmed with peasants on foot and in waggons, farmers in gigs and spring-carts, gentlefolks on horseback and in carriages.    All were dressed in their best and sporting blue-and-red ribbons.

* In a report of the great Friends' school at Ackworth for 1800 occur these words :—"The London Committee advised the introduction of Barbauld's Hymns and the 'Catechism of Nature ;' but the Country Committee rejected them as unsuitable, and adopted 'The Rational Dame.'" It was this Country Committee that had imparted their views to our Yorkshire teachers.

In this town, bands of music were heading processions of school-children, militia-men and clubs marching to church or chapel; in the next, oxen and sheep were roasting in the streets, and big barrels of ale were tapped or ready to tap. Here, divine service being over, the congregations streamed out to feast. There, a smell of roast beef and mutton pervaded the inn, where we halted; with a hurrying to and fro, a clatter, laughter, singing, and hurrahing that were deafening. On we drove through villages and towns, where the lowest class, including the paupers, were being entertained at long tables in the open air, the families of the squire and clergyman looking on all smiles and good-humour. As the day advanced the madder grew the revel. We felt as if we were out to see the fun. Horses and chaises were not always ready at the towns where we expected relays, and as we waited people in their turn eyed us — the pleasant-looking Quaker mother and her two quaintly dressed little daughters overflowing with ill-suppressed wonder and merriment.

During the evening the sight of drunkenness and sound of quarrelling, although accompanied by strains of the incessant music, somewhat damped our mirth. But it rose again as we entered Dunstable, our night-quarters. The effect was magical. One vast blaze of light, great ' G. R.'s shining forth everywhere, with a dazzled and enchanted sea of spectators. The gentlemen of the neighbourhood had dined at our inn, and a grand ball was about to begin. The obliging landlady led us to an upper gallery, whence we could look down on the arrivals. Our mother, who accompanied us, even permitted us to watch the opening dance. Perhaps she herself enjoyed this glimpse of the gay, moving scene, for she did not reprove me when, overcome by the day's excitement, by the music and flutter, I was seized with an uncontrollable fit of laughter.

The next day we were in London—London! How the very thought transported us with joy and astonishment! But London was not half as brilliant as Dunstable had been—was, in fact, quite gloomy. Extinct crowns, stars, and 'G.R.'s blankly met our gaze, and whilst bearing evidence to the glory that had been, suggested the ashes of a fire that had gone out, or the wrong side of a piece of tapestry.

We dined in London, and in the afternoon proceeded to Croydon. The house which Sarah Bevan and Anna Woolley occupied was at West End, and, I think, No. 2, and opposite to The Rising Sun. It was at the entrance of the town from London; and consequently we were no sooner in Croydon than we were at our journey's end.

The same evening we went with our mother to tea at the house of Frederick Smith. We and two or three grandchildren sat together at a side-table and played with Scripture conversation-cards. Dear mother expressed herself pleased with us afterwards because we had answered so many of the questions. She left us the next morning for London, where she stayed on a short visit to an old friend, the wife of Joseph Gurney Bevan, whose "Life of the Apostle Paul," just then published, I believe she took home with her.

We felt ourselves in a new world at Croydon. I do not remember that we were unhappy or had any longings for home. We were all in all to each other, and had been so through the whole of our lives, and could give to each other the comfort and sympathy we needed. But we very soon felt we were different from those amongst whom we were placed.   Many indeed were the mortifications caused us as the children of rigidly plain Friends out of a remote midland county brought into the midst of London girls, all belonging to the same denomination, it is true, but whose Quakerly attire and life-experience were less precise, were even different from ours.   There were ten or twelve girls when we arrived.   I believe the number was to be limited to sixteen.   We were the youngest, peculiar, provincial, but I do not think in general knowledge we were behind the others.   We seemed to them, however, to have come from the uttermost ends of the earth ; the very word Uttoxeter was to them uncouth, and caused laughter.

Each girl had her fancy-work.   We had none, but were expected by our mother to make in our leisure moments half-a-dozen linen shirts for our father, with all their back-stitching and button-holes complete.   We had never learnt to net, nor had we ever seen before fine strips of coloured paper plaited into delicate patterns, or split straw worked into a pattern on coarse net.   Each girl could do this kind of work.   It was one of our characteristics that we could do whatever we had once seen done.   We could hackle flax or spin a rope.   We could drive a nail, put in a screw or draw it out.   We knew the use of a glue-pot or how to paper a room.   But fancy-work was quite beyond our experience.   We soon, however, furnished ourselves with coloured paper for plaiting, and straw to split and weave into net ; and I shall never forget my admiration of diamonds woven with strips of gold paper on a black ground.   They were my first efforts at artistic work.

We had also the great happiness of being allowed at school our own little garden, which contained a fine holly-tree that belonged exclusively to ourselves. If my sister had a passionate love of flowers, I was equally endowed with a deep appreciation of trees. The Scotch firs in our garden at home, the spruce firs, arbor vitæ, and Weymouth pine in a neighbour's; the group of tall poplars, which I never failed to see when sitting in our silent meeting, had been my dear familiar friends from infancy. It was splendid late autumn weather when we arrived at Croydon, and I do not remember any beginning of winter. It must, therefore, have been a fine season, enabling us to be much out of doors. What a new pleasure we had in finding skeleton ivy and holly-leaves under the alcove-shaped summer-house at the end of the general garden! This delight, however, was soon stopped, as Mary M., who had the character of being the black sheep of the flock, having spoken from the summer-house to some young cadets of Addiscombe College, that part of the garden was closed to one and all of us.

Brought south, and into proximity with the capital, we were met at every point by objects new to our small experience, whose beauty, grandeur, or perfect novelty stirred the very depths of my child-soul. We had both of us an intense love of nature and inborn taste for what was beautiful, poetical, or picturesque. Our souls were imbued with Staffordshire scenery: districts of retired farms, where no change came from age to age; tall old hedges surrounding quiet pastures; silent fields, dark woodlands, ancient parks, shaded by grey gnarled oaks and rugged, gashed old birch-trees; venerable ruins, shrouded by the dusky yew. The calm of this old-world and primitive scenery, together with the peculiar character of sunrise and sunset, and of each alternating season, had profoundly affected our feelings and imaginations. Now a fresh revelation. came to both of us equally, but somewhat differently, so that I had best confine myself to my own recollections.

Much that was attractive in our new surroundings, at the same time, troubled me, filling my heart with indescribable sadness, and awakening within me an unappeasable longing for I knew not what. It was my first perception of the dignity and charm of culture. My impressionable mind had already yielded to the power of Nature ; it was now to feel and accept the control of Art. Yet I was at the time, in my ugly, unusually plain Quaker garb, no better to look at than a little brown chrysalis, in the narrow cell of whose being, however, the first early sunbeam was awakening the germ of a higher existence.

The stately mansions, with all their latest appliances of luxury and ease—their sunshades, their balconies filled with flowers, the graceful creepers wreathing colonnades, heavy-branched cedar-trees, temple-like summer-houses half-concealed in bowery garden solitudes, distant waters, winding walks—belonged to a new, vast, and more beautiful world. No less interesting and impressive were the daily features of human life around us. A hatchment over a lofty doorway, a splendid equipage, with its attendant liveried servants, bowling in or out of heavy, ornamental park-gates, would marvellously allure my imagination. There was a breadth, fulness, perfectedness around us, that strikingly contrasted with the restricted, common, prosaic surroundings of the Friends in Staffordshire.

In our home-life Christmas had been of no account. It was neither a season of religious regard nor yet of festivity. How astonished were we, then, to hear the London girls anticipating a great deal of pleasure and social enjoyment, with much talk of Christmas good-cheer ! We were familiar with plum-pudding and mince-pies, but not with Twelfth cakes, of which much was said, and which were to be brought back with them after the holidays. To our astonishment, the school broke up for Christmas, all the pupils going home except Ann Lury of Bristol and ourselves. She received from her relatives a goodly present of chocolate, Spanish chestnuts, and oranges ; we had no box of seasonable good things.

With the return of schoolgirls two new pupils arrived, who proved, to our surprise, our cousins Mary Ann and Maria Marriage, from Essex. Their mother and grandmother brought them ; and we, sent for to the best parlour, dimly and with difficulty identified the little, dark-complexioned elderly Friend who most kindly invited us to spend the midsummer holidays at her house as the same who some years before had paid an afternoon visit to our father and mother. It was no other than the widow of our uncle, James Botham, and now Rebecca Marriage. On leaving she gave us half-a-crown, which was by no means an unwelcome present. During the new term great misery and discomfort was caused in the school by the teachers, Sarah Bevan and Anna Woolley, listening to the complaints of the London pupils against Mary M., usually called "Mussy," also a Londoner. They allowed an open persecution to be carried on against her, and even rhythmical enumeration of the various Friends' schools from which it was reported that she had been expelled, to be chanted at every corner to catch her ear: "Wandsworth, Plaistow, Tottenham, and Croydon" sounded through the house and garden. This aid and abetting on the part of our governesses was unjust to the girl, injurious to her companions, and a disgrace to themselves.

Anna, in the midst of this social convulsion, found comfort in assisting a fellow-pupil, Rachel Rickman ; and as she suffered from a peculiar kind of blindness, being unable to see at all in the twilight, my sister would at that hour lead her about. She came from Lewes, and was the niece or otherwise near relative of the distinguished Quaker, Thomas Rickman, whose important work, " Attempt to Distinguish the Styles of Architecture in England," greatly tended to a revived knowledge and appreciation of the Gothic.

Rachel Rickman, our cousins the Marriages, Ann Lury, and ourselves kept clear of the hateful squabble of the London girls. Either for Mary M.'s own comfort or at the demand of the belligerents, she had been removed to an upper bedroom ; and the boycotting, to use a very modern term, was at its highest just before the Yearly Meeting. Then came an abrupt termination. Mary M.'s parents arrived, and sat in solemn silence with the assembled school. They spoke words of Christian charity. The kiss of reconciliation went round ; and a book was given to each scholar inscribed with the receiver's name, as a peace-offering from Mary's M.'s father.

The book that came to my share was dull and unattractive ; Anna's still more so, a well-bound volume of Moral Essays. The only one that greatly interested me bore the title of " Richard the Runaway." I borrowed it from the fortunate owner, and found it delightful reading.

In after years Mary M. married. I happened to know some of her husband's relatives, and they described her to me as " a clever, agreeable, though somewhat singular person ; very domestic, with a good deal of spirit, or perhaps some might call it pride."

Although the school management was extremely de-

fective and the tuition imperfect, there was an excellent
custom of making during fine weather long excursions of
almost weekly recurrence. At about eleven the pupils,
attended by one of the mistresses, set out, the train being
ended by a stout serving-woman, who drew after her a
light-tilted waggon containing abundant provisions for
our midday meal. So through Croydon we went to the
open country, to the Addington Hills, or as far as Nor-
wood—all no doubt now covered or scattered over with
houses; up and down pleasant lanes where the clematis,
which we only know as a garden plant, wreathed the
hedges. Now and then we rested on some breezy common
with views opening far and wide. Sometimes we passed
through extensive lavender-fields in which women were
working, or came upon an encampment of gipsies, with
their tents and tethered horses, looking to us more
oriental than any similar encampment in our more
northern lanes.

Surrey breathed to Anna and me beauty and poetry,
London the majesty of history and civilisation. From
the highest point of the Addington Hills we were shown
St. Paul's in the distance. It sent a thrill through us.
Even the visits sanctioned by our teachers to the con-
fectioner's for the purchase of Chelsea buns and Parliament gingerbread enhanced our innocent enjoyment.

Our stay at Croydon was prematurely ended by the
serious illness of our mother. After leaving us she had
caught a severe cold during a dense fog in London, which
brought on an illness that had lasted long ere danger
was apprehended. Then we were sent for. The visit to
our Essex relatives remained unpaid. We returned home
in the care of James Dix of Leek, a Friend whom we had
known from childhood. He was the Representative from

the Cheshire and Staffordshire Quarterly Meeting to the Yearly Meeting in London, and took us back with him after the great gathering had dispersed. Before our arrival at home a favourable change in our dear mother's condition had occurred. We found her weak, propped up in a large easy-chair with pillows, and suffering at times from a violent cough. Still, she was advancing to an assured recovery.

In August of 1810 my sister was sent to a Friends' school held in high repute at Sheffield, but owing to an alarm of fever in the town, was recalled in the depth of the winter. She then remained at home, whilst my mother took me to the same school the following spring. It was conducted by Hannah Killham, the widow of Alexander Killham, the founder of the New Methodist or Killhamite Connection, by her stepdaughter Sarah, and a niece named Ann Corbett of Manchester; all Friends by convincement.

Hannah Killham, an ever-helpful benefactress to the poor, devoted herself to a life of active Christian charity. She treated me as one of the older girls, I being tall for twelve, and often took me with her in her rounds. Once she sent me alone to a woman whose destitute condition so awoke my compassion as to induce me to bestow on her my last sixpence, with the hope uttered, " May the Lord bless it ! " This was followed by self-questionings whether by my speech I had meant in my heart that the Lord should bless the gift to the sufferer or to me—then penniless. Another time, at nightfall, Hannah Killham made me wait in a desolate region of broken-up ground and half-built, ruinous houses while she visited some haunt of squalor. It seems strange that a highly con-scientious woman should leave a young girl alone, even

for a few minutes, in a low, disreputable suburb of a large
town.  But she was on what she felt to be her Master's
errand, and I doubt not had committed me to His keeping; for whilst I was appalled by the darkness and
desolation around me, I saw the great comet of the
autumn of 1811 majestically careering through the
heavens, and received an impression of Divine omnipo-
tence which no school teaching could have given me.

Among my fellow-scholars was Hannah West, from
Uttoxeter.  She was one of a considerable family brought
up as Friends, but not in membership, and who sat in
consequence on the lower benches in the Meeting-house.
We had never at home any intercourse with the Wests.
It is a curious fact that Friends in membership rather
look down upon frequenters who are not.  I was conscious of the sentiment.  However, here now was Hannah
West, a new scholar, shy and unaccustomed to the strict
formality of Friends' principles, and who clung to me
as a sympathetic associate.  My sister and I, who had
always been bosom friends, never sought other youthful
confidantes.  Poor Hannah West, however, came with an
amount of devotion which was new to me.  She was a
warm-hearted girl, and reciprocated my good-will with
passionate devotion.  Her delight was to sit with me in
the twilight and imagine what we should do when we
were women.  Her innocent, highest idea was, that we
should live together, something in the style of the Ladies
of Llangollen, though we had never heard of them; dwell
in a country place, have a beautiful garden, plenty of
money, and be able to travel.

I knew the idea to be absurd; yet, without being dis-
loyal to my sister, I enjoyed her affectionate romance,
and can even recall the sort of intoxication of fancy in

which I indulged her day-dreams. When, however, we both returned home, and I sat with my relatives in the upper part of the meeting, she with hers in the lower, and no interchange of the commonest civility ever occurred, poor Hannah's illusions were dispelled. She ended by marrying a journeyman butcher.

Sheffield never affected me as Croydon had done. The only point of extraneous interest was the fact that the way to meeting led through the Hart's Head and over the doorstep almost of the office of the *Iris* newspaper, making me hope, but in vain, to catch a glimpse of the editor, James Montgomery. He was one of my heroes. Hannah Kilham had advocated with him the cause of the climbing-boys, as the juvenile, much-abused chimney-sweeps were then called; and we had in the school the complete set of his poems. I greatly admired them, particularly "The Wanderer in Switzerland."

It was at Sheffield that I grew painfully conscious of my unsightly attire. The girls had, for fine summer Sundays, white frocks, and sometimes a plain silk spencer. I had nothing but my drab cotton frock and petticoat, a small Friends' bonnet and little shawl. On week-days, when they wore their printed frocks, I could bear it; but First-days were bitter days to me. There was no religion to me in that cross; and I rejoiced that the trying, humiliating day only came once a week, when I had to appear in the school-train, marching down to meeting, the one scarecrow, as it appeared to me, of the little party.

In 1812 I left this school, which was some years later discontinued. When the general peace came the benevolent Alexander of Russia visited England, and admiring the principles and usages of Friends, determined to employ members of the Society in his schemes for improving the internal condition of his Empire. This led to Sarah Kilham accompanying the family of Daniel Wheeler, when, in 1818, he emigrated, by invitation of the Czar, for the purpose of draining and cultivating land on the Neva. Her stepmother, in 1823, went as a missionary to Senegambia in the company of two men-Friends, John Thompson and Richard Smith. They took with them Matemada and Sandance, two natives of Africa who had been redeemed from slavery by Friends and educated in England.

They landed at the then newly founded English settlement of Bathurst, at the mouth of the river Gambia, and after due deliberation formed an establishment not many miles distant at Baceaw, making a treaty with the Alcaide. From the intense heat of the tropical climate, the difficulty of communication by land and water, and other impediments, they had much to bear. Debility and sickness ensued, obliging Hannah Kilham and John Thompson to remove to Sierra Leone. Here matters were not mended, and my former schoolmistress returned home to die.

Richard Smith remained in sole charge of the little missionary establishment, labouring with inconceivable fortitude and patience amongst the people of Baceaw, who seem to have been particularly attached to him. Indeed, when John Thompson and Hannah Kilham, on their departure, requested the Alcaide to take care of their companion, he had replied, "Those who hurt Richard hurt me." After a few months of incessant toil and suffering he sank a victim to the climate, and died July 1824, aged forty. He was a native of Staffordshire, and a convinced Friend, who occasionally attended Uttoxeter meeting; and we girls had little idea of the love of God, thirst for souls, spirit of self-sacrifice, and other Christian virtues which were hidden under his strange and, to us, forbidding aspect.

Before he embarked for Africa he came over to our house to take leave of my parents and sisters. Silence being the rule of his life, he walked into the parlour, sat in stillness with the members of the family for twenty minutes, rose up, shook hands with each, and so departed without uttering a word.

I must here briefly mention a circumstance which produced on Anna and me an effect similar to a first term at college on the mind of an ardent student. It was her visit with our mother to relatives and friends in Wales, an effect which was as vivid and lasting on me as if I had accompanied them. It happened in the late summer of 1813. From Birmingham the journey to Bristol was made in a stage-coach, where, after being closely packed in the inside with our mother's old friend, Evan Rees, two other Quakers, Thomas and Sarah Robinson, bound, like themselves, for Swansea, and a sixth passenger, they arrived, after a long day, at midnight. The intention had been to proceed immediately by packet; but owing to contrary winds, they were detained for three days in Bristol, our mother, Anna, and Evan Rees being entertained the while under the hospitable roof of the Gilpins. Charles Gilpin, afterwards the well-known M.P., was then a little boy just running alone in a white frock. Joseph Ford, an old Friend, who considered it his duty to act as cicerone to all strangers, members of the Society, visiting the ancient city, kindly conducted them to St. Mary's, Redcliff, in memory of poor Chatterton; to the Exchange, Clifton—very unlike the Clifton of to-day; down to St. Vincent's rocks and the banks of the Avon, where they picked up Bristol diamonds, which Anna brought home with her.

At length they went on board, but the wind remaining due west, instead of reaching their destination in twenty-four hours, they were tossed about for three whole days and nights. Notwithstanding the attendant fatigue and discomfort, Anna saw and enjoyed the rising and setting of the sun at sea, the gulls and other marine birds, the moonlit nights, the phosphoric light on the vessel's track —all new and wonderful sights to a girl from the Midland Counties.

At Swansea they parted from their three Quaker· companions, and a life of liberty began for Anna. At our relatives', the Sylvesters, there was no longer any restraint in talk and laughter. Our uncle was jovial, witty, and clever in general conversation. Our aunt, who was always well dressed, was affable, and set every one at ease. Charles, our frank, manly cousin of eighteen, and his young sister Mercy were most cordial.

The first week was spent in receiving calls from our mother's former acquaintance and from those of our aunt, who came out of compliment or curiosity to see the Quakeress. Then followed the return calls. It was a bright, free, gay existence, and my sister enjoyed it. The visit to our mother's intimate friend, Anna Price, then a widow, living no longer at Falmouth, but at Neath Abbey, with her six grown-up sons and daughters, left still more golden memories. There was in the polished circle a freedom of intercourse which was cheer-ful, even mirthful; tempered by the refinement of a high intellectual culture. Quakerism had never worn to Anna so fair an aspect.

Christiana, the second daughter, took the young inexperienced guest into her especial charge, and when walking with her in the beautiful grounds, most tastefully laid out amongst fine monastic ruins by the eldest son, Joseph Tregelles Price (who was, I believe, several years later, the first to introduce steam-navigation between Swansea and Bristol), answered all her timid questions, and even anticipated her desire for knowledge. Edwin Price, who died at the early age of twenty-three, often joined them in these walks, spoke on literature, and re-commended for perusal Rollin's " Manner of Studying and Teaching the Belles Lettres," which was just then en-gaging the attention of himself and his brothers and sisters—all lovers of literature. The young Prices were admirers of Dante, Petrarch, and Spenser, of whose works Anna and I were ignorant. They later fell into our hands, and we devoured them eagerly.

Deborah, the eldest daughter, edited *The Cambrian*, a periodical that dealt with all subjects connected with the ancient history, legends, and poetry of Wales—the subjects, in fact, which later gave such value to Lady Charlotte Guest's " Mabinogion." She was engaged to Elijah Waring, a Friend of great erudition and fine taste, then visiting at Neath Abbey. They became the parents of, amongst other gifted children, Anna Letitia Waring, the authoress of—

> "Father, I know that all my life
> Is portioned out for me,"

and other beautiful and favourite hymns; a patient suf-ferer, content without much serving to "please per-fectly," and though filling what she might call " a little space," having love and respect bestowed upon her in no common measure.

A visit of a week or ten days to our uncle, William Wood, at Cardiff, when our uncle, Roger Lyndon, came over from Merthyr to see his half-sister and niece, gave a bias to Anna's mind which she never lost. She acquired a permanent interest in parentage, inherited qualities and characteristics, and the teachings to be derived therefrom, by listening to our uncle William's genealogical conversations; for he was well versed in the family descent and traditions, spoke much of our ancestors, Woods, Brownriggs, Annesleys, and Esmondes, and gave our mother some of the ill-fated Irish halfpence. His copy of "Lavater's Physiognomic Fragments" introduced her to a new, somewhat cognate. field of study. She imparted the taste to me. We hunted out Lavater's work in the possession of an Uttoxeter acquaintance, and adopting the system, afterwards judged rightly or wrongly of every one's mind and temper by their external form.

Through this visit to Cardiff, Anna and I became first acquainted with the romance of King Arthur. She had been taken to Caerleon, and told there the grand old story of the hero's coronation at that ancient spot, of the knights who were his companions, and the institution of the Round Table. Our uncle, William Wood, seeing the interest which she felt in the legend, gave her a printed account. It must have been brought out by some Archæological Society, for it was a quarto, containing fifty pages or so of large print. Caerleon figured in it largely. We both became perfectly imbued with the glorious historic romance, which never lost its effect on either of us.

Whilst at Cardiff an excursion was made one beautiful September day to the village-like city of Llandaff. Divine service was being performed in the chancel of the ruined cathedral. The cloisters and graveyard were fragrant with the scent of thyme, sweet marjoram, southernwood, and stocks; here and there bloomed monthly roses, the first Anna had ever seen growing in the open air.

The Quaker mother and daughter travelled home by coach through Newport by Tintern, catching a delightful glimpse of the beautiful scenery of the Wye. From Monmouth to Gloucester they had for fellow-passenger a clergyman of the Church of England. He spoke with our mother of the country, the war with Napoleon, and finally of religion. She, full of intelligence and earlier acquainted with much good society and fine scenery, surprised him by her replies. He asked how she knew so much. She answered, in a slightly aggrieved tone, "By conviction and observation." After a pause he said apologetically, "I thought the Society of Friends was too secluded and taciturn a people to interest themselves in worldly matters."

The episode resembled the stage-coach journey of the Widow Placid and her daughter Rachel in "The Antidote to the Miseries of Human Life," a religious novelette of that day.

I must now return to the time when our school-life was supposed to be over and our education perfected. Our father, however, was greatly dissatisfied with our attainments. Our spelling especially was found defective; and though Anna, at Croydon, when failing to spell "soldier" correctly, had the spelling-book thrown in her face by the choleric Anna Woolley, yet it was I who offended most in this way at home. Thomas Goodall, the master of the only boys' school in the town, was engaged to teach us spelling, Latin, the globes, and indeed whatever else he could impart. He was a man of some learning, who in early life, when residing in London, had been brutally attacked in some lonely street or passage by a lawless band of ruffians, the Mohocks. His face still bore the marks of their violence, being scarred with deep wounds, as if made with daggers and knives.

Death having deprived us of this teacher, a young man-Friend of good birth and education was next employed to lead us into the higher branches of mathematics. He made himself, however, so objectionable to us by his personal attentions, that we very soon refused his instructions. Although we never revealed the reason, our father, perhaps surmising it, allowed us to have our own way, and being earnest students, we henceforth became our own educators.

We retained and perfected our rudimentary knowledge by instructing others. Our father fitted up a schoolroom for us in the stable-loft, where twice a week we were allowed to teach poor children. In this room, also, we instructed our dear little sister and brother. I had charge of Emma, and Anna of Charles. Our father, in his beautiful handwriting, set them copies, texts of Scripture, such as he no doubt had found of a consolatory character. On one occasion, however, I set the copies, and well remember the tribulation I experienced in consequence. I always warred in my mind against the enforced gloom of our home, and having for my private reading at that time Young's "Night Thoughts," came upon what seemed to me the very spirit of true religion, a cheerful heart gathering up the joyfulness of surrounding nature; on which the poet says—

"'Tis impious in a good man to be sad."

How I rejoiced in this !—and thinking it a great fact which ought to be trumpeted abroad, wrote it down in my best hand as a copy. It fell under our father's eye, and sorely grieved he was at such a sentiment, and extremely angry with me as its promulgator.

When the summer days were fine and the evenings warm, we carried the school-benches into the garden, and thus did our teaching in the open air, on the grass plat, with borders of flowers and trees round us.

We were very busy girls, and had not through the day an idle moment. Our mother required us to be expert in all household matters, and we ourselves took a pride in the internal management being nicely ordered. Our home possessed a charm, a sense of repose, which we felt, but could not at the time define. It was caused by our father's correct, purified taste, that had led him to select oak for the furniture, quiet colours and small patterns for the low rooms. The houses of our neighbours displayed painted wood, flaming colours, and large designs on the floors and walls.

I feel a sort of tender pity for Anna and myself when I remember how we were always seeking and struggling after the beautiful, and after artistic production, though we knew nothing of art. I am thankful that we made no alm-baskets or hideous abortions of the kind. What we did was from the innate yearnings of our own souls for perfection in form and colour; and our accomplished work, though crude and poor, was the genuine outcome of our own individuality. Before speaking of some of these efforts I must mention a style of ornamentation which influenced our minds as the A. B. C. book of classic form and beauty. I refer to the paste or plaster decorations of mantelpieces. A man named William

Taylor, who had a bow-windowed shop at the corner of our street, had been a maker of them when in demand. As the taste for them decreased the supply exposed in the window grew dusty, yet their beauty remained unchanged to us. They were round or oval medallions to be let into wooden mantelpieces, which were mostly painted white; there were also border ornamentations, the design often floating nymphs bound together by chaplets of flowers festooned from point to point with lovely medallions and trophies. These elegant designs were perfectly classic, exactly in the style of Flaxman and Wedgwood.

Kindred to these chimney-piece decorations was the Wedgwood ware. The black Wedgwood inkstands and teapots, with their basket-ware surfaces, were in almost every house. The delicate blue vases and jugs, with their graceful classical figures, were less common. These we greatly admired, and borrowing one now and then from some friendly acquaintance, made in a very humble way a *replica* of the figures. To do this we took the thickest and finest writing-paper we could obtain, and laid it in boiling water, so that it became a pulp. Pressing the water out of it, we applied the soft paste-like paper carefully over the design, and leaving it to dry, we obtained a clean, fair copy of the admired group or figure; often extremely perfect, and which, being cut round or oval, made a sort of medallion. Of these we formed a considerable collection, which caused us great pleasure.

Again, we very successfully etched landscapes, flowers, and figures on pieces of glass. Although we could make no use of them, they might very well have furnished panes for a casement. We also made transparencies simply by different thicknesses of cap-paper. The best that I remember was after an engraving of Tintern Abbey. The effect of light and shade was excellent; the long perspective was accurately given; there were the broken arches, the black thickness of ivy, with the loose trails hanging here and there in the light. It was about the size of a moderate pane of glass, and survived many of our other works of art. Our attempt at imitating the inlaying of ivory and ebony with black paint on white wood remained mediocre.

To refer to a far more important subject. In the summer of 1815 came the news of the battle of Waterloo, and with it terminated the long war with France, a time of conflict that had cast slant shadows over our childhood.

The great adversary of England was not spoken of as Buonaparte but Napoleon, and many religious persons, our father probably amongst the rest, thought that he was the Apollyon, the man of sin, whose coming foretold the speedy approach of the Last Judgment. Our father restricted himself to reading one weekly newspaper, and did not communicate the contents to us children, and yet from our infancy upwards we were aware of the terrible war which became year by year more awful and menacing. News of bloody battles, ending in glorious victories, set the church bells ringing, and the tidings penetrated our house. Fast-days were proclaimed every now and then, but never being observed by our parents, remained unintelligible to us, and became associated in my mind with our neighbour, Stephen Chester, the Baptist minister, and the people who attended his meeting-house, as we termed his chapel.

The chamber formerly occupied by our grandfather, but now empty, adjoined our playroom. The window looked into the street, and from it we eagerly watched the town lads playing at soldiers, and even young recruits being exercised before our house. The very air was full of soldiery, military excitement, and terror. An excellent woman once nursed our mother in an illness, whose husband was an English prisoner in France, and now and then she received a letter from him, smuggled out of the country, and arriving long after date. She dwelt in Uttoxeter, and the advent of such a letter quite entranced us.

Our parents took little drives in the pleasant summer evenings, mostly one of us children going with them. They talked together of the war, of fearful battles, the increasing price of food, the distress of the poor, the increase of the army, of the jails being filled with young men-Friends who were resolutely determined not to serve in the army. The hatred and bitterness against the French that rose up in our young hearts I cannot describe. We were frightened out of our wits at the prospect of an invasion ; but I remember consoling myself with the thought, when driving through Lord Vernon's park at Sudbury, that at all events those frog-eating French would marvel at such magnificent trees, because they could have nothing like them in their miserable France.

When sixteen this lifelong incubus ceased ; we were freed from a terrible anxiety, yet very naturally still talked and thought of the awful human conflict. I have before me a letter of the period, addressed to me by my faithful correspondent, Mrs. Parker, in which, speaking of the current literature, she says : "I shall first mention Walter Scott's popular poem on the battle of Waterloo, which, I believe, falls far short of the public expectation,

as I am sure it did of mine.   It has been smartly said by
some that Mr. Scott himself fell at Waterloo.   But I am
chiefly interested by a small volume entitled 'A Visit to
Flanders by a Scotch Gentleman,' which, besides an
account of Antwerp and Brussels, contains the relation
of a visit to the field of Waterloo soon after the battle,
which is affecting in the most awful degree—to think of
two hundred thousand men collected for the express
business of slaughter.   The field, it seems, at a little
distance appeared as if covered with crows, so thickly
strewed lay the caps and hats of the dead.   From the
then appearance of the soil, it had been literally flooded
with blood.   The tremendous roar of cannon lasted from
morning till night, and was heard in Brussels, the distance
of nine miles, like one continued peal of thunder for
eight hours.   Whole ranks lay dead, with horses innu-
merable, and the roads were filled with the wounded,
creeping and dropping as they moved, while others were
trampled to death by the horses and baggage waggons.
At Brussels and Antwerp several large buildings were
made to serve as hospitals, and here some anecdotes are
related of a shocking nature, particularly that the wounded
French lay mimicking the convulsive contortions of their
comrades dying in adjoining beds.   The author mentions
an officer's lady who had just heard that her husband's
head was shot off.   They saw the poor creature running
wildly about the market-place, while her little boy followed her crying and screaming also.   'He is not dead,'
cried she.   'My husband's head is not cut off—he is
coming.'   Contemplating these horrid features of human
crime and misery, the pious mind is excited to fresh
ardour in the support of those public institutions which
have for their object the disseminating the glorious gospel

of peace.  In this order the Bible Society appears divinely illustrious."

This closing remark of Mrs. Parker's introduces us to a new and prominent feature in the religious world.  I think it must have been in 1815 that our Uttoxeter Bible Society became a branch of the British and Foreign Bible Society, which had been established in 1804.  To constitute it as such, the Rev. J. Owen and the Rev. C. Steinkopff, two of the secretaries and founders, came to Uttoxeter and dined at our house with Mr. Cooper, the clergyman of Hanbury, and an Independent minister of Tutbury, who had compiled an "Epitome of the History of the Christian Church."  The Friend, William Masters, who accompanied the two latter guests repeated some lines that had passed between the Dissenter and the Churchman on the road, when seeing a windmill and a church.

The Independent :—

> "Yon turning mill and towering steeple
> Proclaim proud priest and fickle people."

To which the Episcopalian had replied :—

> "Yon busy mill and lofty steeple
> Provide with grace and food the people."

This was after some ready and witty remarks between the two ministers at table concerning immersion and sprinkling.

A public Bible meeting was held in the Red Lion, with Lord Waterpark in the chair; and Anna and I were greatly puzzled what attitude to assume when prayer was offered and the doxology sung.  Large circulars were distributed through the town, headed either with the royal arms or a portrait of George the Third, and below

was printed His Majesty's desire that every child in his
kingdom should read the Bible.

Our father was a most zealous and steady supporter of
the Bible Society.  This and other benevolent institutions
brought him in contact with pious and excellent individuals of various religious denominations, amongst whom
he ever behaved as a most strict and consistent Friend.
He never spoke of a chapel any more than of a church—
a word which he had a scruple in using excepting in its
highest spiritual sense.  He never, however, like some
ancient Quaker worthies, called it "the steeple-house"
or "daw-house," but would say the "parish meeting-
house," or in a half-depreciative tone, "the church so
called."

The Methodists just about this time established themselves in the town, and had built a large and what was
then thought a handsome chapel.  Celebrated and eloquent
ministers preached occasionally from its pulpit; and the
Methodists altogether made an impression in the town,
more especially as they began to count every now and
then some important conversion among the townsfolk.

They had first appeared in the neighbourhood in
our grandfather's days, and this through a respectable
family of the name of Sadler, dwelling at the old Hall in
the near-lying village of Doveridge.  These Sadlers were
most earnest in the new faith; and a son named Michael
Thomas, not then twenty, a youth of great eloquence
and talent, preached sermons, and was stoned for it.
Sir Richard Cavendish and the clergyman of Doveridge
countenanced their farm-servants and some rough fellows
who pelted both the boy-preacher and his listeners.
Michael Thomas Sadler wrote a stinging pamphlet that
was widely circulated.  It shamed his persecutors, and

almost, I think, wrung an apology from them. The ardent young man went to Leeds, which he represented later in Parliament. On one of his visits to Doveridge he came to Uttoxeter and called on my father, who greatly respected him. His gentlemanly bearing, handsome dress, intelligent face, and pleasant voice we thought most unlike the usual Uttoxeter type.

John Wesley was not equal, in our parents' opinion, to George Fox; yet his followers formed a worthy Christian body, and were less offensive than the State Church, from their demanding neither tithes nor rates.

A new mortification and trouble had in the meanwhile come into our lives, with the wearing of caps and muslin neckerchiefs. The fashionable young Friends' cap had a large crown, which stood apart in an airy balloon-shape above the little head, with its turned-up hair, which was seen within it, like a bird in a cage. This was a grievous offence in our father's eyes; our caps were accordingly small and close-fitting to the crown, which gave them to our undisciplined minds the character of a nightcap. Dresses in those days were cut low on the bust, and the muslin kerchief we were expected to wear, not being shaped to the form, required much pinning and folding. Anna having pretty, sloping shoulders, could wear her kerchief much more easily than I mine, which tore with the pinning, and looked angular in spite of all my pains.

In the autumn of 1815 or 1816 our parents went for a tour in North Wales. We greatly enjoyed their absence. The weather was stormy, and I remember our taking off our caps and running in the garden with our hair flying, and a sense of delicious freedom came to us as the wild wind lifted our hair. The few leaves that were left on the apple-trees were sere and flew about with every blast, and a few frost-touched apples still hung on the boughs.

Susanna Frith, a young Friend, who was considerably older than ourselves, and possessed independent means, much general knowledge, and refined manners, was now residing with our widowed aunt Summerland, also her near relative. She sympathised with us in our insatiable love of reading. She came constantly to see us during our parents' absence, and read to us some manuscript poetry of a pastoral character; as it described the declining autumn, we were much pleased with it. Two lines remain with me :—

> " In this sick season at the close of day,
> On Lydia's lap pale Colinetta lay."

We had a feminine love of dress, to which we gave vent in a very innocent manner. We could not make pretty, fashionable gowns for ourselves, as we should have liked; for we had only one style cut from a permanent paper pattern. Our friend, Miss Martha Astle, however, although poor, might wear a dress in the height of fashion, and being no needlewoman herself, whilst sewing was to us second nature, we made two summer gowns for her in the privacy of our own chamber. We could not wear muslin collars, but we indulged ourselves by drawing pretty patterns and embroidering them for Martha. Once she went to the subscription ball, and what interest we took in her attire !—a white muslin and green satin bodice, which we thought elegance itself.

Oh! those balls given at the White Hart, the chief inn of the town; what a trial they were to me! I confess to a jealous feeling of repining that we likewise, beautifully dressed, could not be conveyed in the one

post-chaise of the town, which I heard rapidly careering
from house to house, bearing the ladies to the ball, and
have thus our share in the general enjoyment.  The wife
of Squire Hodgson lent her private sedan-chair to her
intimate female friends; but to that honour I did not
aspire.

We took Martha Astle with us on our botanical
rambles, for we pursued the study of botany with the
most ardent undeviating industry.  She had no taste for
it, but liked our company.

We had been on terms of civility with the Astles from
our infancy.  Martha was about our own age, and dwelt
with her mother, Jane Astle, as we called her, in lodgings.  There was also the husband, Captain Astle, who
lived alone with the son Edmund in another part of the
town.  "Daniel Astle," in Friends' parlance, was one of the
oddities of the locality; yet he was a very clever man, had
been an acquaintance of Dr. Samuel Johnson, and was
the artist of the sketch of the great lexicographer and
himself inserted in Boswell's "Life of Johnson," edited by
Hazlitt.  Captain Astle, although trained for the Church,
had entered the army and served in America, but was
said by my parents and every one else in Uttoxeter to
have run away at Bunker's Hill and hidden in a pig-sty.
The very street-boys would shout at him, "Bunker's
Hill, Bunker's Hill; run, the cannon-balls are coming."
This made him very irate.  He had on his return to England entered the Church, and though generally called
Captain Astle, was the incumbent of Bromshall.  He
never could read the lesson from the Old Testament if it
referred to the pathetic history of Joseph and his brethren,
the clerk performing that duty in his stead.

Mrs. Astle was a thorough gentlewoman.  She prided

herself on coming of the great and ancient family of the
Kerrs of Northumberland.  Her sister was the wife of
Sir Richard Glynn, the London banker.  She always sat
by the fireplace, having on a table by her side a big
book and her fan.  She never did any needlework.  Our
mother used to think her a "feckless" person, but was
very kind and neighbourly to her.  Sometimes, as children, we were sent with a little present of game or fruit,
and our "mother's respects and inquiry after her health."
Then she would often puzzle us by replying, "Indifferent,
thank you," for we did not know whether to say we were
glad or sorry.

Although our parents had usually next to no acquaintance with the vicar, yet an exception was made in the
case of the Rev. Jonathan Stubbs, from his joining our
father in the attempt to suppress bull-baiting, one of the
most popular amusements of the wakes.  He was a good
and learned man, who met with his death about 1811 in
consequence of being thrown out of his gig.  The grief
of his parishioners was great, that of our parents no less
sincere.  My mother felt drawn, in tender sympathy, to
call on his afflicted widow, and took me with her.  When
we were ushered into the room where Mrs. Stubbs and
her only child, little Jonathan, sat sorrowfully side by
side, and I found myself for the first time in the company
of a widow in weeds, it was to me a most solemn occasion.
What my mother said I know not, but she and the widow
wept together, and were ever after friends.  And when
our eager, persistent system of self-education had begun,
when we borrowed books wherever we could, and spent
many hours every day and late into the night reading,
Anna and I found Mrs. Stubbs of the greatest assistance.
She lived near us, and retained her husband's library of

the classics, the best English and foreign divines, and standard works on history and topography. They were all beautifully arranged, "ready," as she said, "for Jonathan, who was to be educated to walk in his father's footsteps. In the meantime the books were at our service, with one proviso, every volume taken out must be restored to its place."

I can never sufficiently return thanks for the unrestricted range of that scholar's library, which not only provided us with the best books to read, but made us aware of the beauty of choice editions—Tonson's "Faerie Queen" and other important works, handsomely bound in quarto and embellished with fine plates, at which we were never tired of gazing, some of the landscapes remaining in my memory still. Nor have I ever forgotten Piranesi's magnificent engravings of Rome, brought from that city by the Evanses of Derby, and lent by them to their friend, Mrs. Stubbs.

Our father having been induced again to speculate, had done so, fortunately for us, in partnership with Mr. Bell, the banker, with whose two charming daughters, considerably older than ourselves, we were permitted to be intimate. We loved Mary Bell for her brightness and amiability, and we admired Dorothy more particularly for the delicate beauty of her features. Intercourse with these superior and intelligent young women and their parents was doubly an advantage and a comfort to us, from our peculiarities as Friends never making any difference with them, whilst they treated our craving for knowledge, our love of flowers and all that was beautiful, as a matter of course. They resided in a fine old house, where the Duke of Cumberland had been lodged and entertained on his way to Culloden. The bed he had slept in remained in the tapestried chamber he had occupied. From the shelves of the handsome well-furnished library Mary lent us the first novel we ever read, "Agatha; or, The Nun," written by her cousin, Miss Rolleston. Possessing the current literature of the day, the Misses Bell supplied us with Scott's metrical romances and Byron's poems.

It was from their maternal uncle, Mr. Humphrey Pipe, if I mistake not, that we borrowed Dugdale's "Monasticon" and Camden's "Britannia." These heavy volumes could not be hidden away, like many borrowed books, in our pockets, and thus being seen by our mother, afforded her the same intense pleasure as ourselves, she spending many hours, I believe, in conning their pages and in studying the grand illustrations of the "Monasticon."

Our associate, Susanna Frith, lent us "Elizabeth Smith's Life and Letters," with a few similar works. She was a distant relative of the Howitts of Heanor, and told us much of the sons, especially of William, who possessed remarkable talent and great learning.

In the winter of 1815–16 our cousin, Martha Shipley, was married to our cousin, John Ellis, of Beaumont Leys, near Leicester. They likewise were related, but not so closely as to make the union objectionable to our Society. Before the wedding an unusual event occurred, inasmuch as Anna and I spent a couple of days with the bride-elect. During the visit, launching forth into our favourite topic, poetry, she in response took us into her bedroom, and producing out of a drawer from between her shawls a small volume, read to us the "Hermit of Warkworth." Fascinated by the delightful ballad, we likewise procured it, but not without difficulty, and what appeared to us a great outlay.

The Ellises, like the Shipleys, had never been on very intimate terms with our family, from the elder members having imbibed the old prejudice against our mother as proud. A better understanding was now brought about. In the early autumn of 1817 Anna and I paid a delightful visit to our warm-hearted cousin, Rebecca Burgess, at Grooby Lodge.

Going on First day to meeting in Leicester, we thus saw and were seen by the family at Beaumont Leys. They invited us to their house, and the visit extended for weeks. Cousin Martha had died the preceding January in giving birth to a little son. The widower's mother, a quiet, consistent Friend, kept his house. His sister, Anne, a very agreeable young woman, devoted herself to the motherless baby, Edward Shipley Ellis, who, like his father, became in after years so prominently connected with railways.

Cousin John Ellis and his intimate companion, a handsome young man from the north, named Daniel Harrison, who was to him as a brother, were, to our agreeable surprise, truly intellectual. We became in consequence extremely communicative, and many times since have I hoped that we girls did not make ourselves absurd by our display of knowledge. We were deep in history at the time, and soon perceived that in many branches of the vast subject we were better read than they. Our cousin John delighted in the acquisition of every kind of knowledge. Daniel Harrison was especially fond of eloquence. He carried in his pocket a little book, "The Constellation," out of which he enjoyed reading aloud fine passages. He was somewhat troubled with religious doubts, warred desperately against the eternity of punishment, and induced us to study Scarlett's "Translation of the New Testament," in which "age-lasting" is put for "everlasting." It was a work that met with our father's disapproval.

Amongst the many subjects on which Anna and I expressed ourselves very fully at Beaumont Leys was our low estimation of the endowments and culture of ordinary young men-Friends, amongst whom, we had, be it said, would-be suitors. Anne Ellis declared us mistaken, and mentioned some shining lights. "There was," she said, "the young Irishman, Thomas Knott, whose speech at a Bible-meeting at Southampton had been printed and greatly admired. There was David Drape; but neither of them equalled William Howitt. She had made his acquaintance at an excursion of young Friends to Kenilworth, after Warwick Quarterly Meeting. He was more than a scholar—a born genius, and most agreeable."

Her brother and his friend made merry at her eulogy of William Howitt. We had, however, received a similar testimony from Susanna Frith, and took her part.

The news of the death of the Princess Charlotte at Claremont on November 6 wrung the heart of all England. It was like a thunder-clap at Beaumont Leys, where the young wife had met with the same death ten months earlier. Our cousin John, who for the last few weeks had astonished every one by his cheerfulness, bowed under the public sorrow as if it had been his private grief. A gloom fell over the household. Cousin Anne, Daniel Harrison, Anna, and I heard the funeral sermon delivered on the occasion by the celebrated preacher and writer, the Rev. Robert Hall, then pastor of the Baptist congregation at Leicester. It was the first time I had attended other public worship than that of Friends.

Again it was autumn, twelve months after our Leicester visits, when William Howitt came to Uttoxeter to see his cousin, Susanna Frith. We were delighted to accept her invitation to meet him.

He addressed us with great cordiality, and spoke in gratifying terms of his desire to make our acquaintance, having learnt much of our tastes and pursuits from his cousin.

Botany was the first intellectual topic on which Anna and I ventured to open the treasures of our knowledge to our new acquaintance. It was in a walk which he took with his cousin and us that same afternoon. Crossing pleasant pastures, where we had gathered in the spring the meadow fritillary, a peculiar and beautiful flower, which this accomplished botanist told us he himself had never found, we went by the banks of the sweet, placid Dove to the old mill, where all around was peaceful and picturesque. It is nearly sixty-seven years since that walk, which comes back to me with such fresh, fragrant memories as I write. Thanks be to the blessed Lord, the great Botanist, for the simple, natural tastes which He had given me! It was the first link in the golden chain of His providence which united my life with that of one of the best and purest of men.

Before the close of the year I became the affianced bride of William Howitt. He was six-and-twenty, and I nineteen. My father, although he never allowed his emotions, or even his affections, to evince themselves, to our surprise, almost laughed when the important matter was settled, hiding his pleasure by the remark, "It was all in the usual order! The young women of Uttoxeter Meeting were always sought in marriage, those of Leek but seldom."

The tastes of my future husband and my own were strongly similar, so also our mental culture ; but he was in every direction so far in advance of me as to become my teacher and guide.  Knowledge in the broadest sense was the aim of our intellectual efforts ; poetry and nature were the paths that led to it.  Of ballad poetry I was already enamoured.  William made us acquainted with the realistic life-pictures of Crabbe ; the bits of nature, life, and poetry in the vignettes of Bewick ; with the earliest works of Wordsworth, Coleridge, and Shelley ; the first marvellous prose productions of the author of "Waverley," *The Edinburgh Review*, and other works of power and influence.  I say us, because Anna was, as it were, the very double of myself, and shared in every advantage that came to me.

We had always enjoyed walking, but girls alone cannot tramp the country as boys and men can.  With William as a most delightful and efficient companion, we could enjoy to the full the Arcadian scenery that surrounded us.  We took him to our favourite Alton Towers, that wonderful region of beauty and romance, which was growing up year after year under the Earl of Shrewsbury's taste and religious ardour ; to the secluded ruins of Croxden Abbey ; to the airy heights of the Weaver Hills ; to the ancient lordly oaks and birches of Bagot Woods ; to the still more hoary fragment of nature's antiquity, Chartley Moss ; to Tutbury and Sudbury.

It was a happy time, yet accompanied by some little clouds and rufflings of the smooth current of daily life, which must always be the case when strong characters are brought into juxtaposition.

Opposition to my father was never thought of by his

family, which consisted entirely of submissive women, with the exception of his young son, who, strange as it may seem, had his will in all things, and would, seated on the hearth-rug, laugh and talk all sorts of boyish nonsense unreproved.

William's family, on the contrary, consisted of but one female, the mother; whilst the father and his six sons, who were not of a rigid type of Friends, talked freely, laughed loudly, and maintained their own opinions, each differing more or less from the rest. His character was fortunately amiable, unselfish, but full of strong individuality, originality, and dislike to all coercion. This caused him to examine and discuss every subject with a freedom of thought and expression that surprised Anna and me.

I recall one First-day evening in the early days of our courtship—one of those long silent First-day evenings when we sat with our books round the table ; my mother looking weary, as if she wanted her knitting, an occupation which beguiled many dull hours on a week-day. My father was seated apart in his arm-chair, with a candle on the mantelpiece shedding its light on the pages that he was perusing in " John Woolman " or " Madame Guyon."

It was in such a scene that I was shocked and startled by William suddenly bursting out with, " Mary, what is thy opinion of the Godhead of Christ ? "

I knew not what to say. I had, in fact, never thought of it. My mother looked up with a kind of quiet astonishment. My father closed his book, and remarked with solemn gravity of tone, " We have nothing to do with such subjects, William."

Had the latter attempted to argue the point, it would have been felt a profanation—a touching of holy things with unclean hands.  Religious discussion was never heard in our family, where the aim, as I have said, was to preserve the soul in passivity for the divine inward revelation, which was not to be subjected to the natural reason of man.

On the 16th of Fourth Month, 1821, we were married, I wearing my first silk gown—a very pretty dove-colour —with bonnet of the same material, and a soft white silk shawl.  Shawls were greatly in vogue, especially amongst Friends, and my attire was thought very appropriate and becoming.  For a wedding-tour my husband took me to every spot of beauty or old tradition in his native county —romantic, picturesque Derbyshire.

# CHAPTER IV.

*MY HUSBAND'S NARRATIVE.*

*1792–1821.*

I WILL now impart to the reader some characteristic traits and incidents which my husband wrote down of his family and his youth, as they form a fitting prelude to the history of our married life.  He tells us :—

The Hewets dwelt in the reign of Henry the Eighth on their estate of Killamarsh, which was situated three miles from Eckington and ten from Chesterfield.  Of the two sons, William, the eldest, went up to London, and became an opulent mercer.  He dwelt at his shop on London Bridge. In 1547 the nursemaid of his only child, Anne, was playing with the infant at an open window, when she accidentally dropped her from her arms into the Thames, flowing sixty feet below.  The prentice-lad, Edward Osborne, leaped instantly into the river and brought the child safe to land.  She grew up, and was given, with large estates purchased by her father, then Sir William Hewet, in marriage to her preserver.  ˙Osborne was knighted in 1582, when Lord Mayor, and became, with his wife Anne Hewet, the progenitors of the ducal house of Leeds.  Sir William Hewet, likewise Lord Mayor of London, whose name still survives in his munificent charities, shines forth the one bright example of prudence, industry, and benevolence ; for the descendants of his brother were, from generation to generation, a rude, jolly, carousing lot.

The property of Killamarsh passed to the Osbornes; but the junior branch of Hewet, from whom I am descended, obtained through marriage Wansley Hall, Nottinghamshire, and other estates. Whilst dwelling at Wansley, the family changed the name from Hewet to Howitt.

My great-great-grandfather, Thomas Howitt, married, in 1680, Catharine Charlton, only child and presumptive heiress of Thomas Charlton of Chilwell, Esq. Chilwell is a village a few miles from Nottingham, on the Derby road, and the Charltons had possessed property there for generations. Thomas Howitt, then of Eastwood, Wansley Hall being already sold, so disgusted his father-in-law by his drunken, rollicking life, that Mr. Charlton told his daughter, if she would consent to leave her husband he would settle the estate upon her and her children. The daughter refused to part from her husband, worthless as he was; and the old squire, cutting her off with a shilling, adopted Mr. Nicholas Charlton, a barrister, whose name he had seen in a trial case, and left him his property. The prodigal, thus suddenly ousted, did not seem to resent the intrusion of the stranger in his place, for my father used to relate that the disinherited man frequented the house of the new proprietor at Chilwell.

The Charltons still flourish at Chilwell. The present squire, Thomas Charlton, married a daughter of the late Mr. Walter, proprietor of the *Times*. I well remember not only his father, William Charlton, a captain in the Nottinghamshire militia and county magistrate, but his grandfather, a colonel in the same regiment. This Colonel Charlton came frequently to our house; my father being the manager of a colliery at Heanor, the joint property of Colonel Charlton and of Edward Miller Mundy, Esq., of Shipley Hall, about a mile from Heanor; the moiety of

Mr. Mundy being leased to Colonel Charlton.  He was a well-bred county gentleman, easy and unaffected in his manners, and, according to my conceptions as a mere boy, extremely well informed.  He would get me to read the newspaper to him, correcting my pronunciation of proper names, which I uttered as they were spelled; Strachan, for instance, which I did not give, as customary, *Strawn*, but as if spelled Stratchan.  He also strongly recommended me to read the works of Pope, whose poetry, he asserted, was by far the most perfect in the English language.  To my father, "Tom," as he always familiarly called him, he was uniformly kind and even generous, and always anxious "to make some reparation for the injury inflicted," he said, "on you by *your* ancestor, not mine."

The Howitts had continued by their jollifications to dissipate their property, and the broad lands had fallen away piecemeal.  Younger sons had been rectors of East-wood.  They were hunting, feasting parsons, persecutors of Quakers and other religious vermin.  In its turn East-wood was sold, and the Howitts, reduced by the extrava-gance of their roystering forefathers, possessed hardly more than the roof over their heads.

A spirit of thrift, economy, and sobriety came into the race with my father, Thomas Howitt; and it was a maxim with him, that "a man who gives his children habits of truth, industry, and frugality provides for them better than by giving them a stock of money."  In 1783, when twenty years of age, he was received into the Society of Friends at Codnor Breach Meeting, in the county of Derby.  Three years later he married, at the same Meeting-house, Phebe Tantum, only daughter of Francis and Elizabeth Tantum of The Fall, Heanor.

The family bearing the singular name of Tantum, the Latin for "only," is the *only* family that I ever heard of possessing that cognomen. The first we know of is Francis, born in 1515, and dwelling in Loscoe, a neighbouring village to Heanor. The Tantums were amongst the first to embrace Quakerism, and that probably directly from George Fox, who came preaching thereabouts in the days of the Commonwealth. They resided for upwards of two hundred years at The Fall, cultivating their own land. It had considerably diminished in course of time, and when my grandfather had it, was reduced to a mile in length.

At the period to which my memory runs back, my grandfather Tantum must have been near the close of his life. I was only in my third year when he died; yet I have a vivid recollection of him as a man of middle stature, but of substantial build, dressed in a dark Quaker suit and broad hat, and with gentle, kindly manners.

From my mother's account of his character, he was decidedly of an intellectual turn and poetical taste; and I have no doubt that my brother Richard's literary idiosyncrasy as well as my own were derived from him. He occasionally wrote verses, but they were rather satirical squibs on the follies of some of his neighbours than any more ambitious attempts. His love of the best English writers was intense, and furnished him with the greatest enjoyment of his life. Addison's "Spectator" was an immense favourite with him, and I still possess his copy. He was very fond of Shakespeare; of all writers, however, Milton was his admiration.

The circumstances attending his decease were very peculiar. He had often said, in his profound love of nature, that if he might choose the manner of his death, it should be to pass quietly away seated on some flowery bank in the pure moonlight of a balmy May night. It was the ideal of peace in the bosom of nature that his imagination suggested as the sweetest close to a life in which the deepest sympathies of his soul had been in perpetual conflict with the asperities of his fate. His wife, Elizabeth Redfern, was a fiery, domineering dame, who had very little feeling for herself or others. One of his greatest solaces, therefore, was to steal away in an evening from a home made desolate by an unequal yoke and enjoy the society of John Dunn and his wife; old and dear friends in the next village of Loscoe, and, like himself, belonging to an ancient Quaker stock.

On the night of May 10, 1795, John Dunn and his wife, who had early retired to rest, were surprised at ten o'clock to hear the well-known knock of Francis Tantum solemnly sound thrice at short intervals on the front-door. John Dunn called anxiously to his friend from the window. There was no reply. Hurrying on his clothes, the old man hastened downstairs. He opened the front-door; there was no one. Filled with a strange and foreboding alarm, he closed it, put the key in his pocket, and set off for The Fall; and when about half-way, he saw his friend seated on a flowery bank, evidently in calm contemplation of the beauty of that still, odorous May moonlight night. He approached him, saying, "Dear Francis, what is amiss?" Receiving no answer, he went close up to him, and saw the gleam of his eyes gazing on the moon, as it were in a trance. But he was dead; and the desire of his poetic soul was accomplished.

In that same year, 1795, my father bought a house, with about thirty acres of land, in the village of Heanor. His colliery affairs had prospered in his hands, for he had a quiet, leisurely sort of industry about him, liking better to be employed than idle ; and he had, moreover, received my mother's small dower of £300, which enabled him to complete the purchase.   I and my three older brothers

HOME OF WILLIAM HOWITT AT HEANOR.

(Tantum, my parents' first child, died in his fourth year) were born in the same parish, at Heanor Wood, the house of our paternal grandparents ; my three younger brothers at the new home.

This village of Heanor, the scene of my childhood, boyhood, and youth, is photographed, with every house, field, wood, common, footpath, and dell, with the most absolute and familiar distinctness on my memory.   It is in reality dreadfully metamorphosed by the increase of population and the dismal devastation of smoky collieries. My memory only commences at the house my father purchased. It was a rambling old place. The portion of it looking up the sloping village street was much more recent than the half overlooking the garden and country. The view on the garden side was very airy and pleasant. It included the ample vale of the Erewash, with Eastwood, formerly the abode of our family, and its church lying opposite on the hillside at two miles distance.

The garden was large and old, and below it was a big orchard; they were both well stocked with a great variety of all kinds of the most excellent fruit-trees; so excellent, indeed, that I have had grafts from them repeatedly to introduce into other counties. Whoever planted that orchard knew admirably what was the very best in English fruit-growth. At Heanor Fall—so called from the fall or steep descent from the village—there was, on the contrary, the remains of a very old orchard, in which the trees were of a most primitive and almost wild kind; top apples about as hard as wooden tops and choke pears, the juice of which had the property of drawing your throat together as by a vice.

About The Fall, which was an old grange, there were always dogs and guns; for shooting and coursing appeared from time immemorial to have been pursued with much gusto by the Tantums. My mother's only surviving brother, Richard, was in my boyhood the great sportsman.

I well remember my paternal grandfather, William Howitt, with white hair and having all the appearance of a man of family. Like his ancestors, however, he had lived freely, enjoyed his bottle, and was suffering the consequences in the torments of gout.  I used to see him at Heanor Wood, generally sitting on what was called a squab, a wooden couch, which has given place to the more luxurious sofa, propping his head on a stout cane and swaying to and fro; a habit I suppose he had acquired in the paroxysms of gout.  He was mostly, however, very cheerful, and was greatly amused by the cock-and-bull stories I used to tell him of my adventures in coming across the fields from my father's house at Heanor.

He had married, in 1750, Mary Bestwick, a collier's daughter; a homely woman of good, shrewd common-sense.  I remember her by a curious piece of grand-motherly kindness.  In the winter after attending school at Heanor Wood, I used to run up to my grandmother, who had always ready for me a large hot roasted potato, which I carried in my hands, to keep them warm on my way home.

My grandfather died on November 6, 1799, when I was nearly seven years of age.  I remember my father coming in greatly distressed.  He had just witnessed his decease.  He sat down on announcing the event to my mother and gave way to a paroxysm of tears. I was much affected by the scene; and certainly moved by some influence beyond my childish mind, I went quietly away into a distant room, got a chair, and reached up to a bookcase containing a large Family Bible.  I took it down and carried it, as a considerable load for me, into the room where my father was sitting sunk in his grief.  The book seemed to open almost of itself, and I began to read the first words that caught my eye.  They were in the 14th chapter of St. John: "Let not your heart be troubled: ye believe in God, believe also in Me. In My Father's house are many mansions: if it were not so, I would have told you.  I go to prepare a place for you."  I was carrying the book away, when my father stopped me, took and opened it, and read the words in evident astonishment.  He then said, "I was not aware there were such words."  He dried his tears and seemed wonderfully comforted.

The school to which I have already referred was kept by William Woodcock, originally a baker of Leicester, who had married my father's only surviving sister Mary. He was a short, rather stout man, of a somewhat prosy and confident manner; and as the villagers were wonderfully addicted to calling people by nicknames, so he was generally known as Billy Woodcock, Billy Bingo, or Billy Button.  He had not been fortunate in his baking business, and had come to this village and set up there in the united professions of baker and schoolmaster.

All we village lads were his scholars, or rather his wife's, for so long as she lived I have no recollection of his ever taking part in our lessons, except, perhaps, setting our copies.  He always appeared on the best terms with himself, whistled and hummed tunes cheerfully, and produced most excellent toffy, gingerbread, and buns, irresistible magnets to whatever pence we had in our pockets.  After his wife's death he gave up his bakehouse and confectionery, retired to a smaller house, and used to cook his solitary dinner of a mutton-chop or beefsteak in a Dutch-oven before the school fire, making all our laddish mouths water by the most savoury odour which it diffused.  To my notion poor Woodcock had a perfect master-hand for seasoning his steak with salt and pepper.  He had it punctually ready at twelve o'clock, and sent us all pell-mell out of the school, to eat our cold dinner under some sunny wall or old tree; and it seemed to my boyish fancy that such a luxuriously fragrant, artistically cooked dinner must be the great consolation of his isolated life. Poor old Woodcock! he had lived in towns; had taken interest in national and other events; was therefore fond of his newspaper from Nottingham or Derby, which he got duly on every Saturday evening by the carrier, and thus enlightened the neighbours, and especially the smutty coal-dust circle of the Jolly Colliers, on the world's doings. It was always a proud thing for him that my brothers and myself had been attendants of his school; and when, in his old age, he heard I had even published a book, he said exultingly, "Yes; I laid the foundation of all that!"

My mother was one of the most truly pious and affectionate women that ever lived. The apathy of my father and her sensitive and energetic nature were in striking contrast. Wherever there was distress her immediate desire was to relieve it. At home the love of her children was ever lively, ever on the watch for their welfare and comfort. Amongst the poor she was a general mother. In all their troubles and sicknesses, night or day, she was the first person who came into their thoughts and for whom they sent. From her mother she had derived a knowledge of many simple remedies, which she was always ready to apply when she saw they would serve, or she sent off immediately for the doctor. In their spiritual troubles she was equally their comforter and counsellor. Very little ghostly comfort was to be derived from the clergyman, and till the Methodists got a strong footing in the parish, she was the only person to whom the villagers could have recourse on their beds of sickness or death. But no friend could they have on such occasions who could more sincerely strengthen and encourage them. She had the most fervent love of the Saviour, the most profound faith in Him and in His promise that whosoever came to Him He would in no wise cast out. She would read to them from the Gospel the most beautiful instances of Christ's all-embracing regard for His people. The lost, the erring, the long-time denier and rejecter of Him, she showed them, were still welcome to Him. His pardon had no narrow limits, His love no scantiness; these were infinite, like all the Divine attributes; and the inimitable parable of the Prodigal Son showed that God was ever ready not only to forgive the most abundant sin, but to run to meet and welcome back the sinner, when he came home truly penitent. Great was the solace of her constant declaration that Christ said that He came not to call the righteous but sinners to repentance.

The blessing she was in the long-benighted parish it is not easy to conceive. People of all sorts sent for her as freely, and without any idea of apology, as they would send for any minister or doctor whose duty it was to attend them. In the most winterly nights she would be called up to people taken ill, and often she had to go for a mile or more through the dark solitary fields, crossing the single plank of the brook, or wading deep through the miry lanes often in frost and snow, often in deluging and pelting rain, or roaring and whistling winds. Nothing could prevent her going. She would put on a thick cloak and hood and strong shoes, and with her maid-servant, Sally Wilton, equally muffled up and carrying a lantern, away they went.

But though my mother was firmly convinced that Jesus Christ was the certain and unchangeable Saviour of sinners, she was the last to attempt to salve over unhealed wounds.  She was plain and uncompromising in her denunciations of the hardened impenitent.  Many a combat she had with the wicked ones of the parish, and spoke thunder and lightning to them, which often made them tremble.

Boyhood in the country!  Paradise of opening existence!  Up to the age of ten this life was all my own, and I revelled in it.  My mind and faculties were so far expanded as to be conscious of all the charms of rural life, and I took in its pleasure and attractions in unlimited draughts.  These and succeeding years in the same scenes stamped on me for ever the indelible love of Nature and all her objects, and an intolerance of long abode in towns.  Those early days and habits modelled the whole of my existence, and exerted an indomitable influence on my fortunes.  With that charming country all around me, I was as Adam in Eden before the Fall.  All within that horizon had an attraction for me.  I knew of no other world, and therefore cared for nothing beyond.

I was allowed to range about very much at my own will, in a manner at which I am now astonished.  I wandered far and wide, through fields, woods, and by streams, without any care or fear.  I have no recollection of any of my brothers being my companions in these rambles; some of the village boys often attended me, bearing the familiar names of Chicky Pig, Tom Spink, Ned Newton, and so forth.  They were always under my command, and each daring feat was left to me, such as climbing the loftiest trees, scaling high walls and the precipitous sides of stone-quarries after birds' nests.  My grey pony, Peter Scroggins, and my white terrier, Pry, made a large figure in my life.  Peter I rode far and wide, and Pry was always my attendant.  A day I have not forgotten, was when I was sent on Peter to the Friends' families for some miles round, to invite them to the burial of my paternal grandmother.  This was called " Biddin to the berrin."  At all the country funerals then people got their black crape hatband and pair of gloves, but the Friends not wearing mourning, we gave a pair of drab gloves ; at the funeral the guests were treated to wine and cake made for the purpose, called " berrin cake," and when the funeral left the house each person received the customary gloves and a square piece of " berrin cake " wrapped in white paper and sealed, but not by Friends, with black wax.

When I was sent to school at Ackworth, near Pontefract, in Yorkshire, my eldest brother, Thomas, had finished his four years' course there, and my next brother, Emanuel, was there then.

This Ackworth school is a fine, large stone building, standing on rising ground, and presenting a 'handsome appearance, the centre having a pediment and an ascent of broad steps.  At each end of the main building is attached a colonnade, which connects it with wings of the same character.  An ample space lies within the embrace of the buildings, extending a good way below them, and terminated by a sunk fence, which gives free view over equally ample gardens below.  The playground, or green, as it is called, is divided by a broad pavement of flagstones, and on the boys' side of the pavement it is gravelled, on the girls' side is grass.  Though the boys and girls occupy the opposite sides of the main building, and have their schools in the opposite wings, during play-hours brothers, sisters, and cousins were allowed to walk together on the central pavement.  It was generally understood the bonds of relationship were pretty widely extended on this common walk. The boys had gardens below their wing, and a playground also behind, surrounded by a wide colonnade, where they could resort in wet weather, and where on a bench were ranged the boxes containing their books and play-things. There was also a little field behind the main building, to which

ACKWORTH SCHOOL

the boys, and I suppose the girls, were occasionally admitted for variety, but on different days. Thus, though the children were not allowed to go out of bounds, except once a month, for a long country walk, or for a half-day's play on the common, they had abundance of room for exercise and amusement. Parties of boys, too, were draughted off to work in the gardens in summer, gathering peas, weeding, and the like. Others were selected to work on the farm. These were boys who were from the country, and knew something of agricultural labour.   I was often one of these detachments, the farmer, Samuel Goodwin, having been at my father's, and knowing my liking for such employments.   In fact, the days thus spent out in the fields were to me the most delightful of holidays.

The establishment had been originally a foundling hospital, but not having answered, it had been bought by Friends as a school for a plain English education for all members of the Society.   In fact, we got there a very excellent English education.   We were well grounded in English orthography and grammar; for our superintendent, Dr. Binns, had published a spelling-book, and Lindley Murray, a member of the Society, a grammar.   There was also a succession of reading-books, compiled by Lindley Murray, through which we went; but that was about all.   At that time provision for teaching geography, history, or natural history was very defective, or rather was non-existent.   There was no attempt to supplement arithmetic with mathematics or algebra.   Neither Latin nor French was taught.   This was a great loss to the children, and occasioned an awful waste of time.   Long before I left I had learnt all that was there taught, and used to spend a great portion of my school-hours in reading any books that I could borrow ; and these were all such as had undergone a strict examination by the superintendent or committee of the masters ; and it may be supposed what was the Quaker rigidity of this censorship when, long years afterwards, when I had published the "Book of the Seasons," this being sent to one of the boys by his parents, it was taken away by the superintendent on the plea that it was "a worshipping of Nature."

I managed, however, to scramble together a considerable number of books one way or another, chiefly from borrowing; for though there was a school library, it consisted of the very driest of Quaker journals, and other books equally so.  Amongst those that I got from this library, and the only ones that I remember with interest, were Durham's "Physico-Theology," Zimmermann's "Solitude," "Elegant Extracts from English Literature," and Mavor's "Collection of Voyages and Travels."  This last was a source of infinite delight, and has often caused me to wonder that no one amongst the endless schemes of publication has ever thought of bringing out a cheap, new, and portable edition of voyages and travels on the same plan.

Of the details of the life at this school, I have given a full and true account in my "Boy's Country Book," that book, indeed, being a real transcript of my youthful life.  Of many of the most striking characters who then lived at Heanor and its neighbourhood, and impressed themselves on my imagination by their originality, independent humour, and oddities, I have also written in various places; in "The Rural Life in England;" in "Tait's Magazine;" in articles entitled "Nooks of the World," in "Jerrold's Magazine;" in the tales called "The Hall and the Hamlet;" in the "Heads of the People," reprinted in "The Year-Book of the Country," &c., all drawn from the life; also in my novels, "Madam Dorrington of the Dene" and "Woodburn Grange."

Some time after I had been at Ackworth, scarlet-fever broke out in the school, and the children had to be quickly sent away.  As I recollect, I was at home about half a year.  When I returned it was alone, my elder brother having completed his fourteenth year.  Once more, in 1804, my father appeared to call me home in order to gratify his mother, who, now on her deathbed, was anxious to take leave of all her grandchildren.  This was granted as a great favour, it not being the custom for children to leave on such occasions.  Altogether, therefore, I was about three years and a quarter at Ackworth.  In that period I acquired an intense love of reading, which always remained with me, and wrote poetry, such as it was ; some stanzas on Spring being afterwards sent by my Tamworth master to the "Monthly Magazine," the same journal in which Lord Byron's first production appeared.  This juvenile effort of mine was given with my name and as written at the age of thirteen.  Somebody afterwards showed it me, to my great surprise.

The original of this poem is still extant, written in a round boy's hand, in now faded ink, on yellow paper; and I interrupt my husband's recital to introduce the verses.  They are as follows :—

### SPRING.

Lo ! sturdy Winter quits his sullen sway,
And Spring returning gives the vernal day.
Loosed from the freezing influence of the north,
The leafless trees their tender buds put forth.
The fields o'erspread with verdant green appear,
The beauteous raiment of the new-born year.
The vegetable tribes at Spring's command
By slow degrees their tender leaves expand,
Till all the country round at once is seen,
In one bright robe of universal green.
Yet still uncertain Winter lingers round
And spreads his gelid pinions o'er the ground.
Seized by the nipping frost the evening-dew
Spreads a bright shining substance to the view,
Whit'ning the landscape, far as eye can strain,
The expanded forest and the silent plain.
But when bright Phœbus lifts his beauteous head
The transitory vap'ry scene is fled.

> At length the orchards by advancing year
> And hedges white in blossom full appear.
> Lured by the vernal sway return again
> The timid birds that fled at Winter's reign.
> Now beauteous May bedecks the field with flowers,
> Where Nature's songsters sing in fragrant bowers.
> Cool in the balmy air the zephyrs stray
> And waft sweet odours round them as they play.
> The feathered race begin their annual toil,
> And range the country for the downy spoil.
> With busy care they ply their little bills,
> And gather moss upon the neighbouring hills,
> To form their nest with industry and care
> With wondrous art and in precision rare.
> How changed the scene where late the wintry storms
> Distress'd the world in many direful forms !
> The woods around in shining verdure bend,
> The groves enlivened by the feathered throng
> That chant unseen the umbrageous boughs among.
> Warm'd is the air by Horus' genial rays,
> Where sun-bred nations sport their transient days.
> In verdure thick the plains are clad around,
> While health and beauty, joy and love, abound.
> O ! may the country be my loved retreat,
> To study Nature and its Master great !

By W. HOWITT, aged thirteen years.

*Addressed to* " PHEBE HOWITT, HEANOR."

Since my Ackworth schooldays the plan of education has been much extended and improved, Latin, French, and, I think, German being now taught, with more attention to history, geography, and natural history.

On returning from Ackworth I remained a short time at home, resuming all my rural amusements and employments with undiminished zest. I extended my miscellaneous knowledge by the perusal of the translations of Homer, Virgil, and Horace, and of Fénélon's " Telemachus," of the " Spectator " and " Guardian," " Pilgrim's Progress," " Hudibras," an edition with woodcuts, which I found most amusing. I had, moreover, learnt the inhumanity of robbing birds'-nests, though I never lost the admiration of their beauty, and even now am fond of peeping into one and luxuriating on the loveliness of their construction and of their eggs. I was soon after, however, despatched to a Friends' private seminary at Tamworth.

The only principle on which I could ever discover that we were sent for another year of education to this school was, that it was conducted by a Friend of the same district or Quarterly Meeting as my parents, and one of a family with which they were acquainted, and to which they wished well. The master, Joseph Hudson, was a very young man, scarcely older than some of his pupils. The school had been conducted by his uncle, who, dying without children, left it him. What were his previous qualifications for such a charge I know not. In his school were youths who would be called to engage in business of considerable extent, but I do not recollect any teaching likely to prepare them efficiently for such occupations. One thing, however, was taught, and which I most absurdly omitted to avail myself of, and that was French. Monsieur Bruno Hamel, a French *emigré*, who kept a shop of sundries not far from the school, including a good assortment of walking-sticks, canes, and fishing-tackle, was the teacher, and was naturally anxious that I should join his class. But my father had put it to my option, and, like a young simpleton, I declined! I thought to myself, " I am an English country lad. I am not likely to go to France. I have no inclination to do so. Why should I learn the language?" My resolve was one that I have severely rued ever since. It has been my lot to wander about a great deal in the world, and everywhere I have felt the want of a ready expression in French. Youth is the only time when this can be acquired, and though afterwards I learned to read the language with perfect ease, I have never spoken it to any extent. That twelve months, during which I might have grounded myself thoroughly in the principles of the language and had the opportunity of conversing with the worthy and sociable old Bruno Hamel, I occupied in devouring miscellaneous books, and simply confirming that bent towards literature which might have been more lucratively diverted towards trade or one of the learned professions, say of medicine or law.

For the rest, that twelve months at Tamworth remain in my memory as a most pleasant time. Our master, Joseph Hudson, if he was neither anxious nor qualified to carry on our education to any great height, was extremely desirous that we should enjoy ourselves, and have abundance of healthy action. Again the "Boy's Country Book" gives a perfect picture of our doings there—our long walks in the bowery lanes of the country round to distant villages and past old halls; our delicious bathings in the Anker and the Tame; our nut-gatherings; our visits with some of our schoolfellows, the Fowlers, to Alder Mills, cotton-mills and pleasant villas inhabited by the Fowler brothers, about a mile from the town; Gemgate and Briggate, and the old toffy-woman's shop opposite to the school, and my fishing from the bridge at the bottom of Briggate for perch amongst the broad leaves of the water-lilies. These are all living, delicious pictures, as it were, of a long-gone and other life; with wanderings on the slopes of the old castle, all set round with escutcheons of the Ferrers, Lords of Tamworth, from the simple horse-shoe, the sign of the original profession of the family, *ferrieri* or smiths. But oh! that insane neglect of

French; it lies like a black spot amid all the boyish pleasures of that epoch.

As my year drew to a close, our master had concluded to remove his school from Tamworth to Castle Donnington, a pleasant and healthy village, much nearer his native town of Nottingham. He was desirous that I should stay during the midsummer holidays and assist him to flit. I had often been his assistant in a workshop in an attic, where he used to work late in an evening when he was making apparatus for chemical experiments; for we had had a chemical lecturer at Tamworth, whose lectures one or two other boys and I had attended, and had become strongly bitten by the chemical mania, giving in my case a turn to my future.

Our master now prepared to convey his goods and chattels by canal; he, one or two other boys, and myself were to go along in the boat with them. It was a piece of adventure which appeared very alluring. I had romantic visions of our sailing slowly along through an unknown country and villages, cooking for ourselves in the cabin and sleeping on board. It was a piece of interesting new life I was not destined to experience. I had been reading incessantly through long days and deep into the night, and my eyes now felt the consequence. They became much inflamed and studded with little white specks that were called pearls, but had to me the sensation of sand. I was quite unfitted for the projected voyage by canal, and had to return home, then and there terminating my school education.

Between leaving Tamworth when about fifteen, and going out 'prentice at seventeen, I returned to rural occupations at home. From my eldest brother Thomas, who was the principal manager on the farm, I had contracted a taste for shooting and angling. In the winter days we used to wade through the deep snows of the fields, with one gun betwixt us, after redwing or Norway thrushes, fieldfares, and now and then a hare or a partridge, which then were neither so numerous nor so rigidly watched over as now.

In our winter evenings we used to amuse ourselves with "fox-and-goose," draughts and dominoes. Cards were interdicted, and by Friends looked upon as devil's books. We also spent much time round the kitchen fire, where many a country tale was telling, in making beehives of straw, sewing the rounds of the straw together with split blackberry briars. We made mole-traps also, and wove nets for bird- and fish-catching. Books also we got; the "Spectator," in which Roger de Coverley, Will Wimble, and the wanton widow doing penance by riding backwards on a black ram, were never-tiring favourites. "Robinson Crusoe" and "Pilgrim's Progress" had many a reading, feasting our eyes on all their personages represented in the quaint woodcuts; so, too, Philip Quarles' "Emblems." The "Eccentric Mirror," in several volumes, illustrated, in which all the odd characters of various countries figured, was an immense favourite.

But of all the books that ever fell into our hands, none had so bewitching an effect as Winterbottom's "History of the United States." It was a book that fired us up to a spirit of emigration, that, had we been as free to act as we were willing, would have carried us over to America, and turned us all into Republicans of the thoroughest grit. We were clamorous that our father should sell his property, take us over, and buy a "wide, wide world" of his own—Howitt County at least. In fact, had he taken our boyish advice, it would have been the wisest thing he ever did.

Our day pursuits were as full of interest to me as our evening ones. I remember getting up of a winter moonlight morning at about four o'clock, and going off to examine my mole-traps set in distant fields, take out the moles caught, and reset the traps. Such zest has the young mind in what it engages in. My days used to be joyfully spent in driving the plough, helping to hack up frozen turnips for the sheep and cattle, helping to cut hay and fill racks and cribs with hay and straw for horses and cows. Early in spring, about March, I used to be up betimes in the still, bitter frosty mornings to look after the ewes and their lambs.

As the spring advanced, my employments were weeding corn, driving plough, and helping to hoe crops. I used to delight in listening to the stories of the labourers, who were long employed on the farm, and seemed almost to make part of the family; and remembering those times, I can well understand what a vast amount of pleasure is enjoyed amid youth and health in country ife, in scenes and amongst people of whom the world is ignorant.

Then came, in their season, mowing, mushroom-gathering in the pastures, nutting in the woods, collecting acorns for the swine by bucketsful as they pattered down on a windy day from the trees; threshing, taking in corn-stacks, and killing rats and mice, collecting hen, duck, geese, and guinea-fowl eggs. Then came jolly Christmas, with its gathering together of old and young; blind-man's-buff, hunt-the-slipper, forfeits, mince-pie eating, and fishing for the ring in the great posset-pot. Life may have its more intellectual pleasures, but it has none so full, so intense, so perfect, as young existence, whilst health, vigour, and enthusiasm are in their united glory, and time, death, and deception have not yet written over our heads, "*Sic transit gloria mundi!*"

Fond of rural occupations, I never had the idea of becoming really a farmer. In fact, I had no particular inclination for any profession. How few boys have! My father began now to say I must learn a trade. He had imbibed the notion of Rousseau, that every lad, whatever his position, should be set to learn a mechanical trade, so that, if everything else failed, he could always get his bread by the labour of his hands. An absurd idea, because it must take up a certain number of years just at the time that a boy should be learning the profession to which, after all, he would have to devote himself; and because such proper professions, in nine cases out of ten, would be found amply sufficient to keep a man from absolute starvation. In fact, the case is so plain, that the sophisms of Rousseau have long fallen in this matter before common-sense. Yet how many men at that time suffered from them! I had once occasion to call on Mr. Davenport at Wotton Hall, Staffordshire, where Rousseau had found a home when in England, and on mentioning the name of Rousseau, Mr. Davenport said, "That is to me of all names the most odious, for I had the misfortune to be brought up on his principles by my father, who was a convert to his opinions."

I do not believe that my father ever read a line of Rousseau's, but he had adopted his opinions from hearing them discussed and applauded probably in the Liberal newspapers, but more probably by Colonel Charlton. Be it as it might, my father was bent on carrying out

Rousseau's theory amongst his six sons. It was thought that the profession of an architect or builder would suit me. Heaven knows on what data or ideas of my particular fitness for such a profession this conclusion was arrived at. I had not the slightest fancy for such an occupation; I had not the slightest fitness for it. Calculation, so necessary for an architect, was my aversion. In fact, I had never seriously employed a thought on the future. All that I knew was, that I was very fond of the country and of books. Well, to be an architect, according to my father's notions, I must first be a carpenter. I might just as well have been a bricklayer or a smith; they are also mechanical trades, without which houses cannot be built; and I have no doubt that it was a mere chance that I did not commence life by wielding a trowel or a sledgehammer. Rousseau would have approved any of the three.

My father was acquainted with a Friend at Mansfield, one Richard Hallam, who carried on the mixed business of builder, carpenter, and cabinetmaker. He had a great respect for him as a man who had come into the Society by convincement, according to the Quaker phrase; and it was arranged that I should go thither for four years, *i.e.*, till I was twenty-one. I made no resistance. I had not the slightest intention of following any such business, and I went to this *pro tempore* employment regardless of the awful waste of time that it was.

Mansfield was a quiet old town, which formerly lay in the heart of Sherwood Forest, the great haunt of Robin Hood and his merry men, and the extensive remains of the Forest still came up near it. It was a place that, by its agreeable memories and the spots and traditions connected with it, pleased my poetical imagination and rural tastes. I went, therefore, mechanically through my daily duties, and spent my leisure hours in early mornings, long summer evenings, and on Sundays in rambling about and making myself acquainted with the local amenities of the neighbourhood and their historic memories. The Forest, a vast waste of heather, undulating with hill and dale, scattered with spreading oaks, and enlivened with clear trout-streams rippling away over bright sands—the whole region was sandy—amongst freshest grass and flowers; the larks carolling overhead and the linnets of different kinds twittering and singing in the gorse and broom; with here and there a wood such as Harlowe Wood, and a clear lake or dam as that of Inkersole, abounding with wild-fowl, made it an enchanted region to me, where I nursed my poetic feelings and left behind me the real world as completely as Robin Hood and Little John, Will Scarlet and Friar Tuck, had done there long before. Was there not Fountain Dale, where Friar Tuck and Robin Hood had their lusty encounter? Were there not ruins of a hermitage still by the Rainworth Water? Was not Newstead Abbey, with the dawning fame of Byron already upon it, not more than five miles distant, in the very heart of the Forest; and Annesley and Mary Chaworth just beyond?

On the road from Mansfield to Sutton-in-Ashfield, which was three miles distant, about half-way was an old water-mill, celebrated as the scene of the ballad of the King and the Miller of Mansfield. The actual mill of the ballad had long disappeared, but this was also a very old mill standing exactly on the same site, at the head of a great dam, and which brought back to the mind the King riding up from the chase in Sherwood, where he had lost his attendants, and the many adventures with John, dubbed by the King Sir John, and with dame Cockle.

On another side of the town, at about a mile or a mile and a half's distance, was the village of Mansfield Woodhouse, its name sufficiently indicating that it had ages ago been simply a house in the woods of Sherwood Forest. The name of this place was familiar to me from George Fox, always one of my greatest heroes, having preached to the people from the churchyard, and having been thrown by the mob, instigated by the parson, over the church-wall on to the road, and severely injured. There was an old hall, once the property of the Digbys, with grand old gardens, having old-fashioned alleys, quince and medlar trees, and sundials, all things exciting my admiration. There was also not far distant from the village, in the fields, the remains of a Roman villa. There were the foundations of walls, and remains of tessellated pavements in highly coloured patterns, retaining their original colour perfectly. No care, however, had been taken by the proprietor of the field or the archæologists of the neighbourhood to protect the remains, and the people who had visited it had very much destroyed the pavement by taking away some of the cubes.

I had frequently to carry out bills to country-houses, an errand that I very much liked, for it gratified my fondness for rambling through the country and the villages, and amongst the old English halls, then inhabited, long before the days of railroads, by rude squires that rarely reached London, but spent their lives in hunting and shooting. I was sent one summer's day to Kirkby and Linby. These were primitive farming villages buried in trees, and as old-world and obscure as possible.

Returning from these sleepy hollows of old Nottinghamshire agricultural villages, where the quiet, the thick foliage, and the slumber of ages seemed to brood, my way lay past Newstead. It would be difficult to describe my sensations as the view of the abbey opened upon me. First, I came upon the lake below, lying in the wide valley, where the old lord, as he was called, the poet's grand-uncle, had piled up artificial rocks, and in which had been found the brazen eagle thrown into it by the monks as they fled at the locking-up of their establishment in Henry VIII.'s time, and now forming the reading-desk of Southwell Minster, not many miles distant. There stood forth the western front of the old abbey, with its large window of Early English style, and the queer old fountain, with its quaint figures of animals on the green in front ; and to the left another lake, an old water-mill, and sham fortifications. All was silent, no soul anywhere was visible, and I seemed to have suddenly walked into a scene of the Middle Ages, and should not have been surprised to see monks issue from the dark, venerable pile, or to hear the hunter's horn sounding amid the ferny slopes, and to see the deer trooping beneath the low and great old spreading oaks of the park.

Lord Byron had published his original volume of poems and the scathing onslaught on his Scotch critics. He had made some hasty and insufficient reparations of his ancestral abode, had held those licentious revels there with his young college companions and women of " uneasy virtue " that he himself describes, and was gone abroad to bring us back the rich and most beautiful of all his productions, " Childe Harold." All this I knew. I had drunk in with youthful avidity, not only his poems but his stinging satire, which appeared to me the grandest piece of poetical justice ever inflicted on the critics, not excepting the " Dunciad " itself. The mad fame of the old lord was the familiar property of all the country round, my native village lying only nine miles off. The report, for instance, that he had erected a statue to the devil in one of the alleys of the garden, and his cutting down his woods, and even young plantations, to damage the estate as much as possible, in wrath at the spendthrift conduct of his heir, Captain Byron, the poet's father, I had heard over and over again by our own fireside. My father, indeed, had picked two young poplar-trees, mere wands, out of a cart-load of such trees cut down or torn up on the Newstead property by the old lord in his devastating fury, and which were passing our house in a baker's cart. These two trees he planted at the head of a fish-pond in the field below the house, where they now stand, trees of a great height and bulk.

Then my father, in rebuilding his house at Heanor, employed a builder from Mansfield who had been working for the poet at Newstead, and strange were the stories that he and his workmen had to tell of the riotous doings there ; of the young women dressed in men's clothes, of the dog's tomb, and the revelling out of the cup formed from a monk's skull.

My imagination was full of all these things, and I was extremely anxious to get a peep into the place. I did not know whether I could gain admittance, but I hastened up some steps in front and rang a bell by pulling a chain that hung by a small door. All continued silent ; I then seized a queer old knocker and gave a lusty pounding. Within, the sound was re-echoed with a strange hollow dreariness, indicating emptiness and solitude. At length a little wicket opened in the door, and an ancient visage presented itself, took a survey of me, and asked my business. I replied I was a great admirer of the poet, and, casually passing, would much like to see the house and garden. This was old Murray, the sole occupant of the abbey in the lord's absence. He asked how many persons there were; and on my replying only myself, he gave a sort of unsatisfactory "Humph!" and I thought my chance was gone. But the sight of a half-crown, which I showed at the wicket, turned the scale. He opened the door, saying he was just cooking his dinner, but I might go into the garden, and when he had finished his dinner he would come to me. Nothing could have suited me better. I told him not to hurry; I could amuse myself in examining the gardens as long as he pleased. He opened a side-door, and descending some steps, I was alone in a perfect wilderness.

I was just behind the western façade of the abbey church. The church was gone, but the front was left, like a tall screen, with its great window, its pinnacles, buttresses, and carvings. Before me, in what once was the nave, but now a plot of bushes and tall grass, stood conspicuously the dog's tomb. I read the noted epitaph, which I had already seen in print, and then turning, saw a tall wall on which were the remains of figures in fresco, which I remembered a curious old cobbler, Bobby Powell, in Mansfield, had described as "red shanks and limners," meaning, I suppose, full-length figures in antique costumes and bright colours. Before me lay the old gardens, which I entered: there was a large pond, long, straight walks all overgrown with weeds, and the shrubs and bushes of both flower and kitchen gardens, roses, lilies, gooseberries, and currant-bushes all smothered by a wild growth of Nature's sowing. The place appeared left entirely to itself.  There was no trace of human hand or foot anywhere.  I strolled on in wonder at such desolation, where art once had made a pleasant scene of terrace, grove, and lawn, with all the beauty of flowers and fountains.  Towards the end of the gardens I passed under alleys moss-grown and overshadowed, made, in fact, dim and gloomy with trees, and there I discovered what the simple country people had called "the old lord's devils." They were merely leaden statues of fauns, satyrs, and other rural creatures of mythology.

I had scarcely made my round when old Murray appeared, and took me through the house.  What struck me most sensibly was the ruin that was fast hurrying through the building again.  Byron had replenished the house in a somewhat showy style, without first repairing the roof, and the rains had poured in over gilded cornices, great mirrors, and rich silken curtains.  In the kitchen were painted upon the wall over the ample fireplace words that, according to Byron's own account and that of others, had been very little regarded : " WASTE NOT, WANT NOT." In the drawing-room stood in a cabinet the celebrated skull cup, and over the fireplace the full-length portrait of Byron in a sailor's dress by Phillips, engraved in Moore's Life of him, in the act of starting on his voyage, and when he may be supposed to say, in the words of his own verses,

> " My boat is on the shore,
> And my bark is on the sea."

In his study, though the books were gone, there remained two tall graceful stands of wood, on which were placed very perfect and finely polished skulls, and betwixt these hung on the wall a crucifix, as though he had been a Catholic.

Some time after this I was sent with others to carry out extensive repairs at the house of Colonel Need at Mansfield-Woodhouse. It was the old hall of the Digbys, that he had purchased, and wished to transform into a modern dwelling. One day I was nailing a plinth along the base of a gallery hung with tapestry; the scenes displayed were mythological. The colonel, accompanied by Mr. Wilkinson, the architect, stopped just by me, discussing the precise subject of a part of the arras. They did not agree, and, in fact, were both quite wrong in their ideas of the scene and personages represented. With a sudden impulse I rose up and said, "Excuse me, gentlemen, for my apparent presumption, but the subject is so-and-so." "Egad," said the architect, "but that is it." With an air of surprise on both countenances of the gentlemen, they asked me how I came to possess such knowledge. I told them that I hoped I had picked up a good deal more knowledge than of Greek mythology at the schools I had been at, and from my own reading. This only increased their surprise. They asked me who I was, and why I was in so mechanical a situation. I told them I was doing penance for the absurd theories of Rousseau, which had infected my father's head, like those of many others. "And who is your father?" said Colonel Need. I told him. "Ha!" he replied; "ha-a-a!" drawing out his "ha" to a great length. "I know him well; I have met him at Colonel Charlton's. How odd!" "So," said Wilkinson, "and for that he made you a carpenter?" "Yes," I returned, with a significant smile; "as a first step to your own profession, architecture." "Bless me! how odd!" said he; and the two gentlemen, bidding me a cordial good-morning, walked on.

From that day, whilst the repairs went on, the architect had always a pleasant smile and greeting for me; and when he wanted anything done with particular nicety in the rooms, would call me to do it.

When my twenty-first birthday arrived I had gained a good deal of skill in a profession acquired only to be abandoned. I received my indentures from my worthy master; accompanied by commendations and good wishes, took my way homeward over Sherwood Forest, and as I went, tore up the indentures and scattered them on the winds.

I had now a new profession to select and acquire, but I felt no urgent haste, and my father felt none. I suppose he thought he had discharged his duty towards me, and was content that for a while I should work on the farm. Four of us six brothers were at home: two were at school. Whole days from early morning I used to spend in angling. Izaak Walton was become one of my fanatically favourite authors, and thus angling and sauntering along the banks of streams amid the grass and flowers of spring and summer made my elysium, as they made his.

During the seven years betwixt my return from Mansfield and my marriage my whole time was not spent in rural labours and amusements. I was constantly studying and continuing my education. I devoted much time to the acquistion of French and Italian. Of course, as I had no instructor, my pronunciation must have been unique; but my object was chiefly to read the best works in these languages, and so far I succeeded very well. I read many French authors, and procured from Derby a pocket-set of the Italian classics, including Dante, Tasso, Boccaccio, Petrarch, and Guarini's "Pastor Fido."

I was at the same time an indefatigable student and experimenter in chemistry, botany, and the dispensation of medicine. I also learnt Latin of an Independent minister at Ilkeston, the Rev. Joshua Shaw, who had been a fellow-student of Dr. Pye Smith, Dr. Bennett, and other leading Independent ministers. He was a great advocate of the Bible Society, and had established a local branch. The annual meetings were generally held in Eastwood church as a central situation. The gentlemen and clergy entered fully into the plan; and there appeared no jealousy betwixt Church and Dissent in the matter.

The first Bible-meeting that I attended was in Eastwood church. I was greatly astonished at what appeared to me the eloquence of Dr. Bennett, then of Rotherham. I thought how useful it would be to acquire this ease and freedom in public speaking, if one were ever called on to defend oneself on any occasion. I therefore consented to take a resolution and make a short speech. The first rising, however, before a few hundred people, without any preparation by means of a debating society, was something startling and strange. It was a new sensation, and when I had staggered through a speech of some ten minutes, I was most glad to find myself once more in my seat without an actual breakdown. The circulation of the Bible was a thing that I thoroughly accorded in as a self-evident duty in a Christian nation. I began now regularly to attend and speak at Bible-meetings and committees, the benefit of which as training for public speaking I felt at an after period.

which still remained me of very most pleasant ... based ... enjoyment rides by Annesley and over ... lanes ... On one of these occasions ... some ... about a mile from Newstead. I saw a young gentleman approaching, leading his horse. Looking attentively at him, I observed that he limped on one ... and it instantly occurred to me—Lord Byron! As he came up I took a close survey of him, and saw that it was really he. I could recognise him not only by this limp, but by the portrait I had seen at the abbey. He was coming from the direction of Annesley, and had probably been indulging some sad remembrances by a visit round by the residence of Mary Chaworth. He had now published the first cantos of "Childe Harold," and was in the zenith of his fame.

"During this period the "Sketches of Geoffrey Crayon," by Washington Irving, had appeared. These produced the liveliest impression of pleasure on me. Here we had the scenery and people of England delineated by a foreigner in a manner that threw over them a new and poetic light. He had seen everything in England, especially its rural scenery and life, through the poetic atmosphere of a reverential affection for the land of his ancestors. All was Arcadian beauty and dreamy legend, as of Rip van Winkle and the loves of village life. I was very much inoculated with the spirit of this book, and making a pedestrian tour through the Peak of Derbyshire, I felt that my model of style and sentiment was in the pages of "Geoffrey Crayon." This tour I printed in a quarto literary paper, called *The Kaleidoscope*, published by John Smith, one of the editors of the *Liverpool Mercury*, under the title of "A Pedestrian Pilgrimage through the Peak," by Wilfrid Wender. I

... us are similar. If I were to rank it now I should be considered as the little wonders made our great own differences innocent and the like.

In the summer of 18— I paid a visit to a relative, Susanna Birch, at Uttoxeter, and there first saw Mary Bodham, destined to become my true friend, constant companion and wife.

Whilst Susanna and I were talking of old family affairs, in came a very county and bright young lady-friend, to whom I was introduced. She was Susan Bodham. I was greatly pleased with her grace and intelligence. Very soon came in another sister, whose lively and clever appearance charmed me. I had heard much of the Bodham family, though the only member I had ever known was their old friend John Bodham, these young ladies' grandfather. I accompanied them home to call on their parents, who received me most cordially.

My visit to Uttoxeter proved an actual piece of idyllic life. We had a series of tea-parties or walks in the very pleasant country round, and excursions to distant places of beauty and interest; and the result was that I felt persuaded that in Mary Bodham I had found the true future companion of my life. Soon after my return home I proposed, and was accepted.

During the next two years frequent were my visits to the quiet old town of Uttoxeter. Many charming rides and rambles we had. My bride-elect and her sister were extremely fond of botany, which gave an unvarying interest to our walks. They were enthusiastic lovers of poetry, especially of the ancient English and Scotch ballads, and were, besides, extremely well read in English literature in general. They, as well as myself, wrote poetry.   In a word, we were extremely congenial in our tastes and pursuits.

Early in 1821 a chemist of Derby, who had opened a concern at Hanley, in the Staffordshire Potteries, wished to dispose of this business.   As a commencement, though with no view of permanent settlement there, I purchased it; and on April 16, 1821, I married Mary Botham in the little Meeting-house of Uttoxeter, and we went to reside at Hanley.

W. H.

# CHAPTER V.


*FIRST YEARS OF MARRIED LIFE.*

*1821–1824.*

I WAS not elated by the change in my circumstances
when I accompanied my husband to our home at Hanley,
in the Staffordshire Potteries; nor, I think, was he.
William, however, simply regarded the business he had
taken as a temporary concern, with which he should part
so soon as he could assure himself of a good position
elsewhere. It was speedily discovered by some of the
more active spirits of the place, that he was not a mere
tradesman, but a man of talent, bold independence of
thought, and great originality; and they flocked around
him, eager to engage him as a champion both in public
and private.

I am astonished, when I remember the strict observance
of our religious duty which prevailed at my home, that
my father made no objection to my going to reside at a
place in which there were no Friends, and where the
nearest meeting was at Leek. I likewise ought to have
felt it a melancholy change, and should have done so if
the religion in which I had been educated had taken
vital hold of my soul. As it was, I do not remember,
during the seven months that we dwelt at Hanley, that
either William or I went on the Sunday to any place
of worship. Our life and education as Friends had
not, it seems to me, in recalling years of spiritual dead-

ness, even excited any curiosity about other forms of faith.

The Staffordshire Potteries were strongholds of Dissent. Of course, the Church of England was there, but though probably some of the richer master-potters might be members, the great body of the people were Dissenters of every variety of opinion. Large chapels abounded; and to the Potteries came the wildest experimenters in religion; amongst others, Thomas Mulock. We had been told much of this extraordinary man, who had been private secretary to George Canning; and, as an exception, we went to hear him. Lord Byron mentions him in a letter to Moore, December 9, 1820, as "Muley Moloch, the lecturer," who had endeavoured to convert him to some new kind of Christianity.

The place of worship was a large, bare, whitewashed upper room in a china-factory. Seated on benches made of planks, supported on piles of bricks, were about fifty persons; there were several ladies of wealth present; the remainder of the congregation consisted of potters in their working clothes, their wives and children. The room was lighted by means of rude chandeliers, consisting each of two laths nailed crosswise, suspended from the ceiling by a piece of string, and having three nails driven in near each end of the laths, to form sockets for the candles.

A round three-legged deal table served as pulpit and reading-desk, placed in the middle of the great room. At it stood Thomas Mulock, a young, handsome, well-bred man. He was clad in a blue dress-coat with gilt buttons, a buff kerseymere waistcoat, then the fashion, and white trousers. His linen was beautifully fine and clean; his hands adorned with rings, and delicately formed.

In his harangue he plainly intimated to us, that since the days of the apostles, the true faith had been revealed to no one but Thomas Mulock. All preachers, all missionaries, were engaged in an occupation they knew nothing about. The only honest man he had heard preach was the clergyman of Stoke, who candidly confessed that he "knew not God."

When he had ended, a very tall working potter, in his long white apron, knelt down and prayed that our hearts might be changed, and returned heartfelt thanks to the Almighty for having sent amongst us such a "burning and shining light." Yet no sooner had he resumed his seat than the preacher rose and severely reproved him.

He declared the potter's prayer an astonishing instance of the blindness of the human understanding. He had been for a long period teaching and explaining the real nature of the Christian religion; now he heard a prayer put up that our hearts might be changed. Had he not told them a hundred times that our old hearts could never be taken away? A new heart might be given us; but the old Adam's heart would still remain within us, and be perpetually trying to corrupt the new heart.

The poor potter looked down in humiliation at this reproof; and the ladies wept.

Mr. Mulock grew to be greatly admired in the neighbourhood; he married a rich wife, and had a handsome chapel built for him at Stoke. It was later purchased by the Society of Friends, and became their Meeting-house.

There was, at the period of our sojourn at Hanley, a small body of Unitarians, who were endeavouring to introduce their opinions to the great mass of chapel-goers.

My husband, whose mind had a tendency to Unitarianism, was eagerly sought after by them, particularly as he was discovered to be an able disputant. He had no little pleasure in advocating their cause against the vast majority of Nonconformists, who, he thought, showed a spirit of intolerance towards them. In this way he was not without an agreeable excitement in a life otherwise uncongenial.

William likewise had the enjoyment of authorship, furnishing to *The Kaleidoscope*, and still under the pseudonym of Wilfrid Wender, some papers on Uttoxeter, which he called Deckerton. Thus I find myself writing to my sister Anna, from Hanley, "9 Mo., 30th, 1821, 1st Day evening :—

"Dost thou recollect some months ago, in the *Nottingham Review*, some lines by Keats on Autumn? And canst thou procure a copy of them for Goodman Wender, who is just now vastly occupied in running up and down the country in the neighbourhood of Deckerton, visiting old halls, hunting, hawking, fowling, and fishing, talking to every old man and woman he meets, peeping into churches and ancient houses ; amassing together all the antique usages of our ancestors, and introducing the reader to the acquaintance of certain worshipful old gentry, partly who have been seen by our eyes, and partly who have been created by his brain, and upon whom eyes of Christians have never alighted? He is very good-tempered in his wanderings, and never halts or grows weary."

On "5th Day, 12 Mo., 13th, 1821," I write to the same correspondent :—

"We are preparing for a decampment. I am sitting in a perfect chaos of books, papers, valuables, and rubbish. I suppose we shall be ready to depart from here on

Second-day; so you may, if you please, send the gig for us; and I shall thank thee to see that I have a cap made up to wear at home."

My husband had accepted an advantageous offer of disposing of his business to a gentleman of good means, who was engaged to a young lady of Hanley, and wished to settle there; and I believe William gained considerably in a monetary view by the bargain. After a short delightful visit at Uttoxeter we proceeded to Heanor, where my parents-in-law had invited us to reside with them, until we could suitably establish ourselves in Nottingham.

I was very kindly received by my husband's relatives, who, I speedily noticed, were not only hospitable, but clannish. Thus any member of any branch of the family, be it ever so remote, was welcome. The house was roomy, if not large, and three or four additional persons sitting down to table made no difference.

The father, Thomas Howitt, was a large, important-looking man, with a personality not easily forgotten. He sat for hours at his old high desk, or near it, sometimes busy writing, and sometimes poring over old manuscripts, copies of old wills, and deeds connected with county families. He took immense interest in pedigrees, and was considered an authority upon them, even by lawyers. He knew the most remarkable instances of longevity in the county of Derby, and could relate endless anecdotes. Amongst others of Friends, one such occurs to me:— "As Michael Fletcher of Romsey was walking with a young woman-Friend from London, on the Terrace at Windsor, King George and Queen Charlotte drew near and freely entered into conversation with them. His Majesty asked Michael whether

many of his Society resided in that neighbourhood,
adding 'they were a people he greatly respected.' Then
turning to the young woman, he inquired if she were one
of the Society, and being answered in the affirmative, the
King inquired, 'Is there not too much gauze here?'

THOMAS HOWITT OF HEANOR (WILLIAM HOWITT'S FATHER).

She acknowledged that she had deviated from the rule,
and was sorry for it. Upon which George the Third
said, 'And I am sorry for it too, for when persons once
begin to deviate, they do not know where to stop.'"

Phebe Howitt, religious, warmly affectionate, and from
her childhood exercising the greatest self-sacrifice, was
also gifted with a singular talent for the study and prac-

tice of medicine.   Thus the constant treatment of the sick and the preparation of vegetable medicines carried on most efficiently at Heanor made me quickly perceive what a fascination the place and its mistress must have had for my old grandfather Botham.

My husband, inheriting the same taste from his mother, ought to have been educated for a physician.  Now, however, deploring for himself the time lost in his training, he had determined that the future of his youngest brother Godfrey should be provided for.   He had become his tutor, and after educating him in all the preparatory branches, had induced the parents to send Godfrey as a medical student to Edinburgh.

In the spring of 1822 we resolved to visit Scotland, whose scenery, history, traditions, and literature had become part of ourselves; and as Godfrey had just very successfully completed his studies at Edinburgh, pay him a well-merited compliment by joining him in that city, and accompanying him home.

Supplied, therefore, with absolute necessaries in a light valise, and attired in clothes that defied all changes of weather, we started from Heanor one April morning at five o'clock, seated on saddle and pillion, which proved a most easy and sociable mode of transit, and rode through ill-kept lanes, overhung with thick trees, and across open commons to Derby.  The next day it snowed as we travelled on the top of a coach from Derby to Liverpool.   On April 11 we set sail from Liverpool, and had our first experience of a steam-packet and the sea.

On the 12th we were put ashore by a ferry-boat at Dumbarton, and set foot on Scottish ground with an emotion of pleasure.  Our ferrymen dissenting in their opinions about the best inn, we entered the first we saw, which presented a respectable appearance. A very bonny, barefooted, sandy-haired girl met us at the door, and accosted me with, "Come in, lassie; ye'll be wanting a room, I'm a-thinking." She showed us one, but we perceived our mistake before we reached it; the house had every symptom of filth and poverty; the room had never been visited by the painter; there were naked walls, naked wood, a dirty-looking deal table, and a bench; and in the adjoining one, of which we got a glimpse, were a man, woman, and a parcel of dirty children, eating crowdy. We purchased a little whisky, and then decamped with an appalling apprehension of Scottish fare. From these fears "The King's Arms" relieved us, and notwithstanding sufficient evidence that it was not an English inn, we felt ourselves at home, were well accommodated and handsomely attended.

The next day, Sunday, we spent in exploring the neighbourhood. The famous castle, now a garrison, a lofty cliff, whence we had our first view of Ben Lomond and its beautiful loch; the remains of Dumbarton college, and the ruins of Douglas tower were the principal scenes we visited.

On Monday, April 14, we started on foot for Loch Lomond, up the beautiful Vale of Leven; saw on our way the monument erected to Smollett's memory, and the scenery of his "Roderick Random," by which name this native poet is chiefly called here. In the afternoon we sat down on a sunny bank at a short distance from Loch Lomond, and were joined by an old merchant, who travelled from Renton to the different villages on the loch-side, supplying them with the staff of life, cakes and gingerbread. He carried on the top of his basket of good things what he deemed the greatest necessity and luxury of all, a well-worn Testament, out of which it was his wont to read a few passages, and expound and dialogue upon them with the good dames and hoary shepherds to whom he administered his temporals; and from the specimen he gave us, we thought he had a very extraordinary gift of discernment that way. He strongly recommended us to lodge at Rowardennan, where there was "a very fine, clever, discreet woman, who bought bread of him."

We took tea at Luss. With the exception of the inn and one or two other houses, it consisted of a cluster of genuine Highland huts amidst a group of trees, then covered with a profusion of blossom. Our walk after tea led us along the margin of the lake. The sound of the many torrents became more perceptible as the silence of evening came on. The lake slept still and beautiful in the last rays of the sun; and the mountains around, as the twilight stole over them, assumed successively a variety of the softest hues, purple, deep blue, grey, then wrapped themselves in awful obscurity. By the time we arrived at the ferry of Rowardennan it was deep twilight; and the ferryman, snugly seated at his whisky, desired us "to wait a wee." Not being inclined to wait, we applied to another proprietor of a boat, who ordered a boy to take us across. The lad had his cows to milk, and he therefore desired us "to wait a wee." It was only by force of menaces that we got him off at length, and then, either to revenge himself or alarm us, or both, he led us down through a rough hollow, across a deep-ploughed meadow into a wood, where it was too gloomy to discern anything many yards; here he stopped and whistled, but seeing we discovered nothing but a desire to get over, he at length led us to his boat, and out we pushed into the lake. If ever we were in a scene of gloomy grandeur, it was then, paddling at nine o'clock across the water with scarcely enough light to discern our course, but enough to perceive the savage cliffs that rose around, and which seemed to cast down from the sky a deep stillness upon us.

The inn at Rowardennan we found after some stumbling about in the dark, every window and door being closed; and on entering, discovered a goodly family, father, mother, and a troop of children, seated round a blazing wood-fire. Our appearance seemed to excite that sort of surprise and anxiety which unprepared-for guests occasion. A candle was lighted, and we were requested to walk upstairs; but having full assurance that we were then by the only fire in the house, there we determined to seat ourselves. Our landlord had much the air and attire of a gamekeeper, and our land-lady was a comely matron of superior stature. She begged to know if we would wait for a "fool" to be cooked. Declining this offer, we managed to make a supper of their oat-cake, their whole stock of eggs, three in number, procured a glass of whisky toddy, none of the best, and added a supplement out of our own budget.

Our landlord's conversation made us some amends. He had been up Ben Lomond as guide to Sir Walter Scott; like everybody else, he had read his works; and it was in this very house that young Rob Roy celebrated his marriage with his fair captive, and stayed a few days before he proceeded to his own dwelling. The kitchen where we sat was a scene fit for the pencil. Around the ample fireplace hung several pairs of tartan hose, wet with traversing the spongy moors. On the floor, among sticks, dust, half-roasted and half-crushed potatoes, crowded the whole tribe of dirty half-naked children and several large shepherd-dogs. Overhead were guns and a variety of household implements. About one-fourth of the room was occupied by a press-bed with sliding panels, which from its aspect appeared to be the nest of the chief part of the family.

In our bedroom the sheets were so thoroughly saturated with peat-smoke that we did not lose the odour of it for days. In the morning we heard our host and hostess engaged in a warm debate. He dropped a word now and then in a subdued tone, but our "fine, clever, and discreet woman" was loud and impetuous; and from a few of her shrill accents that reached us, we gussed that a lack of viands for our breakfast had raised her fiery indignation. At length mine host fled into the wilderness, and after a long delay our breakfast appeared —good tea, raw sugar, boiled eggs, mutton-ham, and dirty salt. Such was our sojourn at Rowardennan, the Duke of Montrose's inn. Alas that our old merchant had not arrived here before us with his wheaten loaves! This was the only place in Scotland of which we had reason to complain; and the poverty of the people was evidently the cause.

A little before ten o'clock we set out to climb Ben Lomond, at the foot of which we had slept. The ascent is reckoned about six miles, and we found it a laborious task of four hours. We waded deep in heather, crossed rocky and impetuous torrents, laboured up acclivities only to see unsuspected hollows which must be descended; but the most impeding obstacles were the black and trembling bogs, which intercepted our course every few yards, and which required a good deal of boldness, contrivance, and circumspection to pass. As we advanced, however, and paused at intervals to rest, the most extensive and grand prospects opened before us, whilst we became more and more impressed with the profound silence which reigned over the immense barren and lofty solitude in which we were. Not a sound seemed to live there but the twitter of a small bird always found in heather, the casual call of the raven, the less frequent and more plaintive cry of the plover, or the bleat of the solitary sheep wandering on a far-off slope, or coming to look down gravely with its grey face from some eminence above.

About a mile from the top the ascent became suddenly more steep, the summit rising up like a cone, whilst the apex, torn out, presented a black and terrible perpendicular hollow of two thousand feet deep. This tremendous hollow, open to the north side of the mountain, in naked and rugged gloom, revealed its ghastly and dizzy depth at our feet, to which the snows of many winters sleeping in it gave an air of greater desolation. Labouring with increasing ardour, we at length stood upon the summit. What a prospect! At the south-west foot of the mountain lay Loch Lomond in full view, an expanse of water twenty-eight miles in length, scattered with as many beautiful islands; the Clyde, Dumbarton, and the southern part of Scotland; Argyleshire, with its lochs, woods, and mountains; the coast of Ireland—but it would be useless to enumerate the distant places visible from it. Yet we were not so much amazed at the vastness of this extensive survey as at the tempestuous sea of mountains which the Highlands exhibited.   They lifted their bare and abrupt peaks into the sky; some brown in the nearer view, some splintered and desolate, some shrouded in snow, some black beneath the frown of a passing cloud, and some blue in the softened distance.

When we had surveyed this magnificent scene about ·half-an-hour, the clouds began to gather, and at length closing upon us, involved us every moment in deeper gloom.   The wind began to whistle with the hollowness of an approaching storm.   It became suddenly extremely cold, and the snow fell as thick and heavily as in the depth of winter.   We were upon the very edge of the tremendous chasm, which could hardly be distinguished from the solid mountain, except by the snow in its bosom.   The darkness became so great that we could not discover each other at more than an arm's-length.  We were therefore obliged to hold each other's hand, and in this manner we endeavoured to retrace our steps till we could get below the cloud.   Fearful of stepping into the chasm, we held so much in the opposite direction that we speedily bewildered ourselves amidst a chaos of rocks, which forbade all further progress and almost any return.   At length we regained our old station, and, by a more successful effort, the path by which we had come up.   Then descending below the region of cloud, we found we had again diverged, but continued our way, and in the space of two hours, sometimes stopped by precipices, sometimes by torrents, and sometimes fearful of being engulfed in the tottering bogs, and all the time sinking deep in the wet spongy moss, the rain pouring down plentifully, we escaped in safety to a farm-house at the foot.

Women, children, and clamorous dogs had long noticed

us descending, and were assembled at the door gazing in astonishment at our temerity; but as we approached they all withdrew into the house, and when we reached the door everything was so still there might have been no soul in it; we found, however, a family of no less than thirteen persons. It was a genuine Highland hut, built of rough stones and thatched with bracken. Two goats, the first we had seen, came and presented their bearded visages at the door. Having sat, chatted, and rested ourselves with the solitary family, we crossed the river by some stepping-stones, and pursued our way down the sublimely desolate Glen Dhu.

Our road led us to the borders of beautiful Loch Ard, and we found ourselves in the scenery of some of the most interesting incidents in the Waverley Novel of "Rob Roy." We passed under the rocks where poor Bailie Nicol Jarvie was suspended from a tree by the skirts of his riding-coat. The authorship of the tale had not at this epoch been definitely determined; yet with whatever person we conversed about "Rob Roy" we were told that the Rev. Dr. Grahame of Aberfoil had furnished Sir Walter Scott with many materials worked up in that story. A similar testimony is borne by the author himself in a note to the novel. Dr. Grahame afterwards said to us, "It is in vain to look for any other man in whom all the qualifications for such authorship meet. Whilst Sir Walter might be supposed to be studying the scenery of 'Rob Roy,' I accompanied him twice to most of the places in this part mentioned in it. When we were sitting by this cascade, Sir Walter, his daughter, and myself, I noticed the effect it had upon him. Apparently aware of my observance, he requested his daughter to sing, in order to divert my attention. Whilst she sang he sat with his eyes fixed on the surrounding scenery. I thought it would not be long before I saw this spot placed in a prominent situation, and the appearance of the tale of 'Rob Roy' realised my suspicions. Helen Macgregor gives her ever-memorable breakfast to Bailie Jarvie and Frank Osbaldistone in this beautiful and romantic scene."

At the clachan of Aberfoil we found, as the author of "Rob Roy" had promised, instead of the old hut immortalised by the contest of the worthy Bailie, in which he valiantly set fire to Garschattachin's new plaid with a red-hot ploughshare, a neat little inn. In the morning we called on Dr. Grahame, the venerable minister, the author of "Sketches of the Picturesque Scenery of Perthshire," and one of the inquirers into the authenticity of the poems of Ossian. We were received at the door by the aged minister, wrapped in his plaid, treated with great kindness, and on taking leave of his amiable family, he, together with a young lady visitor and a youth, his pupil, accompanied us to the beautiful cascade already mentioned, and put us into the way for the Trosachs.

We traversed a wild heath and a winding road of the roughest description. In front of the celebrated defile, a patch of cultivated land and two good houses contrasted pleasantly with the wildness of the scene. Loch Achray stretched along the eastern side of the valley.

As we approached, a dark storm shrouded the mountain chaos before us, sending before it a solemn sound of wind and waters, which warned us to escape to the nearest house for shelter. The storm proved as tremendous and enduring as it had promised. The lady of the house, Mrs. MacFarlane, received us with a good deal of dignity, followed by much kindness and hospitality. As we were

obliged to remain with the family some hours, we spent
them very pleasantly, in eating an excellent dinner and
in conversing on subjects of local interest.   They told
us that John Wilson, the author of the "City of the
Plague," &c., the leaping, wrestling Professor of Moral
Philosophy, of Edinburgh, and his lady had been there,
equipped much as ourselves, and, moreover, carrying
on their backs two loads of portable soup and other
provisions; he about a quarter of a hundredweight,
she about a stone.   They were on a pedestrian tour in
the Highlands and Western Isles.   Our narrators described Mrs. Wilson as a very lady-like woman, in high
spirits, appearing to perform her journey with great
ease, and he to be a very singular fellow.

The storm over, we found there was literally a gulf
fixed between us and our progress.   An Alpine bridge
over a rapid stream was, with the exception of a single
pole, carried away by the waters.   A barelegged High-
lander was called to carry us over, and Mrs. MacFarlane
and a gentleman walked with us to the place.   The
stream was indeed deep, rapid, and fearfully clear, and
the pole slippery with the wet, yet appearing to us
passable, with care; by the assistance of our umbrella,
and by holding each other's hand, we got over.   When
we turned round, we saw Mrs. MacFarlane holding up
her hands in terror and astonishment.

We read "The Lady of the Lake" on the banks of
Loch Katrine, and were surprised that it did not express
more.   We read it afterwards, and were then surprised
to find it express so much.

From Callander we walked through the small town of
Doune and the park of Blair-Drummond to Stirling.
This was to me one of the most interesting places we

had visited, from the historic associations connected with it. *The Lady of the Lake* steamer conveyed us down the Links of Forth to Edinburgh. We reached it on Saturday night, April 19, and found Godfrey well, and very snugly established in his bachelor quarters, which were six storeys high.

Liverpool, where we had spent a day sight-seeing before embarking for Scotland, had, by its bustle and magnificence, amazed us. We had, in our simplicity, compared it to ancient Rome and Athens. Yet, after seeing Edinburgh, our enthusiasm was cooled. We dwelt opposite the College, and admired the richness and beauty of its Grecian architecture; and noted the same character in other public buildings, feeling, however, there might be a little too much monotony of design. We walked the princely streets of the New Town, and breathed the invigorating breezes which sweep from the ocean through them, feeling an exultation of heart at the power and prosperity of man. No words could convey our delight and enjoyment of the magnificent prospects visible in all directions.

But what pleased me most were the relics of Mary Queen of Scots preserved in Holyrood; above all, her workbox, covered by embroidery on white satin, representing Jacob's dream, the work of her own hands. It was impossible to look at the angels ascending and descending upon the ladder without involuntarily forgetting the mighty space which had intervened since she had deftly traced out those figures, and without admiring the simple taste and piety demonstrated in the choice of the subject.

We had the curiosity to attend service at the Gaelic Chapel, originally erected for the accommodation of the

National Guard, consisting of Highlanders, and which, since its abolition, had been continued for that of the servants and work-people of the city, who were principally mountaineers. There were a few liveries in the congregation, which had otherwise a most plebeian and workaday appearance, and was composed chiefly of old people. Large nightcaps and snuffy noses were seated all the way up to the pulpit-door. A little, round, fat minister of the Gospel preached in Gaelic to them. He also addressed to us a short portion in English, during which the Gaels took the opportunity of clearing their throats, coughing, spitting, scraping with their feet, and making a most outrageous uproar.

The Friends we found a very small and orthodox set, uncontaminated by the fopperies of fashion. They received us with much kindness. We learnt they made but few disciples in Scotland. Once an old woman did by chance get into the Friends' Meeting at Edinburgh at First-day worship, and after sitting two hours in all the fidgety torment natural to those who have not been accustomed to "the subjection of the activity of the natural will," on coming out, said to the person next her, "An unco' place this, where there's neither prayer nor praise!"

On the 30th of April we set off on a ramble into the county of Fife. We directed our course towards the eastern extremity of Lochleven. It was evening when we got sight of it. A long roll of thick white mist was stretched across it like a curtain, leaving the nearest part of the lake perfectly clear, and over it appeared the summits of various hills.

The next morning we sailed to the castle, so interesting as the scene of Queen Mary's imprisonment and flight.  We entered the boat near the site of old Blink-hoolie's house, where the light was displayed as the signal for the escape.  It was a lovely morning, and the crystal waters of the lake were beautifully still.  The castle, now a ruin, is situated on a small island about three-quarters of a mile from the nearest point of land. The only inmates we found to be a host of cormorants, daws, and loch-whistles, and the only appurtenances a few scattered and battered old trees, and on the ledges and crevices abundance of wall-flower.  We saw all the places to which Scott, in his " Abbot," has so delightfully given almost a new identity.  The keys of the castle, which on the night of Mary's escape young Douglas threw into the lake, had been found, the summer before our visit, on the shore by the brother of the boy who assisted in rowing us across.

We had a fine walk from Auchtermuchty to Cupar, and impatient to reach St. Andrews, we left the flourishing little capital of Fife after tea and walked on to that place in the moonlight.  The ancient and ruinous city of St. Andrews had a most wild and impressive aspect as we entered it at ten o'clock.  Passing through the old western gate and advancing up the long, ill-paved street, the deep silence of the night, the dilapidated Gothic palaces and convents, the lofty skeleton towers of the ruined cathedral at the eastern extremity, partly discerned in the dim moonlight, the roar of the ocean close under the town, were enough to touch the least imaginative with a sense of awe and solemn, melancholy pleasure. In the morning we beheld time-worn and demolished buildings and quiet, grass-grown streets, in which pro-fessors in large black gowns and a few boy-students in long red ones were walking about.

We returned to Edinburgh by the delightful shores of Largo, Dysart, and Kirkcaldy, and bade farewell with regret to the queen of cities on May 4. Accompanied by Godfrey Howitt, we proceeded by coach to Lanark.

We were deeply interested in Robert Owen's enthusiastic dreams of the perfectibility of human nature, and hoped to make the acquaintance of the philosophic philanthropist, but in this we were disappointed. We were prepared, by his proclamations of the excellence of his theory and practice, and by the reiterated praise of visitors to his model factories and dwelling-houses at New Lanark, to find the utmost practical perfection, and in this too we were disappointed.

On the Sunday morning we went down to New Lanark, and found the younger children in the schoolroom, with three or four masters. One of the latter ascended a pulpit, with which the room was furnished, and read a chapter of the Bible; another, succeeding him, uttered a prayer. During this service the children were perfectly heedless of everything but playing tricks and talking to each other. We never saw a more insubordinate little crew. Remarking this afterwards to the teacher who had delivered the prayer, we inquired if they never proceeded to some species of coercion to effect order. He replied, "No, never; it is contrary to Mr. Owen's system."

We had, the evening before, been attended about the grounds by a boy, whose uncommon acuteness and intelligent remarks on all subjects of our inquiries had excited our admiration. We had asked him, amongst other things, whether the masters ever flogged the scholars. He replied, with a look round to see that the coast was clear, "Joost sometimes!" We were more disposed to believe the boy than the master.

As we returned towards Lanark, a considerable number of work-people were going up to kirk.  To one of these, a shrewd old man, we addressed ourselves, by observing, "What a pleasant situation they had, and how happy they must be."  He replied, "Why, very well, very well."  We observed that their establishment had been much talked of in very distant places.  "Aye," said he; " the farther off the more talked about, I dare say."  "But you have a quiet, orderly little village here, and must be very comfortable," added we.  To which he rejoined, "Why, if a man drinks or thieves, he must be marching; but there are other things besides these, enough to prevent the place being too pleasant."  "Well, but we suppose you find things so comfortable as to induce you to stay here."  "Aye," answered he; " it's a long way to travel to the next factory, and then there's a chance of not getting work."  "But you get good wages?"  "Small, small."  "However, if your wages be small, such is the excellence of Mr. Owen's system, that you find them sufficient; and then you have your children brought up in a manner that must render them happy and virtuous for life."  "Well, a deal has been said about it," replied the old man.  "Mr. Owen has a many fine notions, but" (in a low tone, and coming close to us) "though it is treason here I must say it, 'tis but patching up poor human nature, that, if it be stopped in one place, will break out in another."  "A prophet is not without honour, save in his own country."  Such were the things and feelings of which we got a glimpse at the very fountain-head of this system of social regeneration.

From Lanark we went down Tweeddale to Peebles. Nor did we fail to visit the Abbey of Melrose, and as much as possible after the direction of Scott, "in the pale moonlight." We slept at the inn at Melrose; and the next morning, seated at breakfast, we heard a carriage drive up to the door. Then in rushed a waiter, exclaiming, "If you want to see Sir Walter Scott, it's he!" We hastened to the window, and beheld the greatest genius in the North. He was seated quietly reading a newspaper while the horses were changed. He and a friend were taking a drive to Kelso, and although they had only come three miles, had put their horses into a foam.

With eyes not satisfied with seeing, nor ears with hearing, we set out on our way to Selkirk by Abbotsford. We walked into the gardens, then gay with brilliant borderings of blue gentian, passed the house, saw Lady and Miss Scott through the plantations, gathered plenty of flowers and leaves as relics, and bade a silent and contented adieu. We pursued our course through Selkirk and Ettrick Forest to Hawick. The next day we walked down Teviotdale, and on the following along the Border by many a moss-trooper's tower to Gretna Green.

Here the whole population was alive and astir, believing us gentlefolks in disguise, who had been just married. We might be supposed such, as William, Godfrey, and I all wore tartan cloaks. We were told at the inn that the number of marriages were on the increase, and that David Long accomplished them by reading over the English marriage-service at various prices, from a glass of whisky to one hundred pounds. From his habit of loitering at the blacksmith's shop, the notion had spread that it was the smith who performed the ceremony. David Long's only trade, however, was that of Gretna parson.  It was an established custom for him and the post-boys at Carlisle to share profits; a plan so effectual, that whenever a couple reached Carlisle, they might consider themselves secure.  The happy pair were driven along towards Gretna by a guide, who seemed to have his spurs rowelled with lightning, and horses that would run down the sun.  But, alas for the pursuer! not a soul would stir.  The horses were all engaged, or they were lame, and the post-boys were lame and blind too; and if they did actually convey their impatient cargoes out of Carlisle, there might be half the kingdom married before they would arrive at Gretna.

We took our leave of Gretna and Scotland together after a most delightful ramble, and with this sapient remark, that as Dr. Johnson travelled through a good part of Scotland and could not find a single tree, we had walked five hundred miles, ridden and sailed a considerable distance besides, and yet did not see a single guide-post till we arrived at Gretna.  What objection the Scotch had to these useful things we knew not; but a traveller, we felt, had far more reason to be provoked with the want of them than of trees; as we found, to our frequent misfortune, when several roads diverged from one point on a lonely heath, where perhaps there was not a house within some miles, and not a soul passing once in a day.

An enlarged narrative of this pedestrian journey, with descriptive original verses, was furnished by us in 1824 to the *Mercury*, a Staffordshire paper, and entitled, " A Scottish Ramble in the Spring of 1822, by Wilfrid and Wilfrida Wender."

I find the remainder of our tour noted in a letter

to my sister Anna, dated Heanor, 5th Mo., 15th, 1822 :—

"After leaving Gretna we slept at Ireby, the commencement of the beautiful scenery of the English lakes. Except the views from Ben Lomond, the scenery of the Trosachs and Loch Katrine, we have seen nothing finer than Keswick vale and lake. Tell mother, one of the most delightful spots in Keswick vale is Ormathwaite Hall ; a fine old house, situated under Skiddaw, overlooking the most enchanting and paradisiacal landscapes, with a sweet view, both of Bassenthwaite and Derwentwater. Dr. Brownrigg was still highly spoken of, and my aunt Wilkinson was known there. An old man, who lives in a cottage by the Hall, and says he has lived under the family for threescore years, knew me to be of the Brownriggs immediately. He recognised the family likeness before I told him my relationship. The yew-trees, which accompany this, we got out of the grounds, as we thought mother would like a memorial of the old place.

"We climbed Helvellyn on First-day morning ; walked down by Grasmere and Rydal. The sun shone out over the mountains, and danced in living light over the little lakes. The gaily-dressed villagers were sitting at their doors or walking about, and seeming at least to enjoy every delight that man can know. Wordsword's cottage on Rydal Mount is truly an abode that should satisfy a poet's heart. Miss Wordsworth we saw, a tall, rather proud-looking lassie, but the old bard was invisible.

"We looked back with sorrow upon the mountains we were leaving, and reached Kendal about nine o'clock. We left that town the next evening at six by coach, and passing through Lancaster and Manchester, reached Mansfield yesterday."

THE SAME TO THE SAME.

"*Heanor, 7th Mo., 7th (after returning from a visit of five weeks to Uttoxeter).*—My short journey was concluded at five o'clock on the afternoon that I left you. I found William waiting for me (at Derby), and Daniel (Harrison) was arrived; so we drank tea with him, and he walked about six miles on the way with us, promising to spend the Sunday at Heanor, where he arrived at nine yesterday morning. We all walked to meeting at Codnor Breach, and back, and spent a very pleasant day. In the evening he and William discussed the old subject of foreknowledge and predestination, which so often furnished a topic at Beaumont Leys. I rejoiced to hear these two, whom we have so often wished to see together. The more I know of Daniel, the more my old predilections in his favour are confirmed. He is a charming youth, and the prospect of frequently seeing him gives me much pleasure."

A busy and, in some respects, agreeable life now began for us at Nottingham. I write from that town to my sister Anna, in August 1822:—

"I like the situation of our new abode. It is open and lively. Just below, but quite in sight, is the new Methodist chapel, a handsome building of its kind, and whence the sound of psalm-singing issues, as when, in the days of the Covenanters, the solemn chanting of multitudes was heard in the stillness of evening. Our house —alas for it! What shall I say? small, good—I am fearful it is a well. We quarrelled with Hanley over and

over again because our borders were limited, but could
we have seen this, our new habitation, we had chuckled
in pride and exultation over the despised Hanley.

"Of our manuscript volume of poems I must say something.  There is a printer in this place with whom we
have become a little acquainted, whom we thought of
as our printer, having, of course, the work published in
London.  But the learned insist upon its being both
printed and published there.  On this we are at present
undecided.  It seems strange to me, and I cannot reconcile myself to the thought of seeing my own name staring
me in the face in every bookseller's window, or being
pointed at and peeped after as a maker of verses.  But
enough!  The season of trial is not yet, and before then
I will assume as much indifference as possible."

My husband and I had arranged a joint collection of
poems in manuscript, which some judges of poetry had
urged us to print.  Earlier literary attempts had always
been made in partnership with my dear sister Anna.  As
girls, Milton, and Pope in his translation of Homer,
had possessed our fancy.  The sonorous, heroic measure
became our gauge of the mechanism of poetry.  We
commenced a grand epic, laid in the early days of
British history.  It was called "Quindrida," from the
heroine, the daughter of an archdruid, herself a priestess
beautiful and good, and loving her country with a pure
devotion.  Then came the Roman legions, and all was
warfare; in the style of Homer, rendered by our favourite
Pope.  We did not write it together, but each produced
separate parts and united them.  It was never finished
in writing, but the whole plan of the epic was clearly
defined by us.  It perished, no doubt, like many other

of our great beginnings. As a prose work, for instance, which was to consist of a number of short tales, supposed to be written by some young authors, unknown to fame, and laid together till completed in a parcel, the whole to be opened on some great family occasion, under the title, "The Packet Unpacked." The style, however, appeared to us too poor and meagre for preservation. Thus it perished, with much more, in one of those holocausts which very properly occur in the experience of most young ambitious authors; the day having come when scales fall from their eyes and the gold of their youthful enthusiasm shows itself as dross. Grand heroic poems and prose were given up, and our after efforts were confined to short poems. Occasionally Susanna Frith, who took such a kindly interest in our intellectual efforts, encouraged us to read them to her; with this exception, we had no auditor or critic. Yet I remember in those young days, when our *sanctum sanctorum* was the little school-room, sending privately, with Anna's co-operation, two poems to a pocket-book signed "Mary of Uttoxeter." It was first in 1827, many years later, that we accidentally learnt they had duly appeared.

Here again are some passages, taken from my letters to my sister :—

"*Oct.* 1822.—Thou heard, I suppose, that the Duke of Sussex visited this town. I, among the rest, went to get a peep at a royal prince. He entered the town amongst thousands of the rabble; it being the low party that assembled to welcome the Radical Duke, with their miserable flags, all tattered and torn, as they were left at the last election. He sat in an open carriage, bareheaded, bowing to the people and smiling very graciously; a good, jolly, merry-looking man—one to laugh with. He came from Newstead. Major Wildman accompanied him in the carriage. After staying about an hour in the Exchange rooms, receiving the freedom of the town, and making a speech of which hardly a word was heard, the great man and his attendants returned to Newstead.

"Our volume of poems will to-morrow journey up to London, to issue from the press of T. Davidson, Whitefriars; for we are not so orthodox as to employ the Friendly firm of Darton & Harvey."

"10*th Month, First-day evening.*—The church clocks are striking, and this reminds me of the hour at home. I can fancy you and Emma preparing for a visit to old Molly's (at the Almshouse). I see you this wintry evening, wrapped up in cloaks and shawls, setting off in joyful anticipation of the pleasure which this next hour and a half will bring. It may be that you mention me, never thinking that I at this moment am picturing to myself the little round white table and the few books upon it, the high chairs with their cushions, the little carpet spread for the ladies' feet, and the poor old (Almshouse) women seated round in all those attitudes in which age and pain have fixed them; while the garrulous Molly, with her semi-Quaker bonnet, her stick propped by her side, and her foot extended and turned on one side, is either discussing the merits of the sermon, or reading 'a godly hymn out of poor Mr. Stubbs's hymn-book.' All this is present to my mind; and, right or wrong, I like to indulge in it, because I have so often seen it and made one of the little company.

"Thy fishing-song has brought the tears into my eyes, and I have read with an emotion of soul—

> 'Eaton's woods are in their pride,
> Dove's green banks are fresh and fair,'

until I wondered not at the languishing attachment of the absent Swiss to his country. We have seen those Uttoxeter scenes at every season, and be we ever so distant, they will still be present. Indeed, I could foolishly believe I should know a leaf which had grown in some places, though I might be puzzled to tell how it differed from any other."

"11*th Mo.*, 15, 1822.—This is Sunday evening, and quiet and alone, and happy as loving, contented hearts can make us, we are now sitting, like Darby and Joan, by our own fireside, which is to us what the vine and the fig-tree were to the old patriarchs, and where we may sit and none make us afraid.

"We have not yet been officially visited, though we understand that it has been certified to Friends that our walking has hitherto been orderly. We have not much intercourse with our brethren. Of the young Friends I know nothing, as I have scarcely exchanged with them more than a cool and courteous 'How do *thee* do?'"

"1*st Mo.*, 29, 1823.—I have been reading John Wilson's beautiful 'City of the Plague,' and the first volume of Joanna Baillie's 'Plays on the Passions.' I have heard much of this celebrated lady's works. Walter Scott has called her his highly gifted friend, and indeed she is a woman of most extraordinary powers. The last I have read is 'De Montford;' it depicts hatred. I am proud that a woman writes thus; it is nobly done.

"*2nd Mo.*, 8, 1823.—Oh! the treasury of old poesy we have found. What a feast of antique words, with their supernumeraries! It really does my heart good to find in some beautiful old story that stray stanza or those few unconnected lines which, from the days of our earliest childhood, we have remembered and treasured from Nanny's curious hoard of medley verses. Then, too, there is mother's everlasting treasury of old songs, such as were in vogue when she was young, and such as my grandmother taught her. They come in now and then so charmingly, that Emma and I almost fancy we must tire William with our constant recognitions. This work is Percy's 'Reliques of English Poetry.'"

"*4th Mo.*, 6, 1823.—Our poor book in London will, I verily believe, never see the good light of the sun. I turned over two lists of this month's publications with an awe, quite expecting to see my own self presuming to stand in the row of divines, philosophers, fools, and poets; but there was no occasion for alarm; neither William nor I was in such company."

A few days later "The Forest Minstrel, and other Poems," printed by Davidson, but published by Baldwin, Cradock, & Joy, Paternoster Row, must have appeared. The verses were descriptive of country sounds and scenes, and had arisen, as stated in the Preface, "not for the sake of writing, but for the indulgence of our own overflowing feelings." They were presented to those who, like ourselves, were devoted disciples of natural beauty and of simplicity.

The copy before me bears the inscription, "Richard Howitt. Nottingham, May 1823." This younger brother of my husband was my contemporary, and at the time of which I am writing, our fellow-inmate. He possessed a most poetical, sensitive mind, was caustic, humorous, a quiet punster, deeply versed in Nature, and sympathising in all noble movements and vital human interests. Although thoroughly awake in congenial society, he would lose himself in some poetical dream when uninterested in his companions. This reminds me that once a very ordinary individual walked with Richard from Nottingham to Heanor, and asked him suddenly, "What bird that was?" No reply was vouchsafed for the distance of several miles, then without uttering another word, the wished-for information was given. He was well versed in literature, and was fond of old-fashioned poetry, but it must be choicely good.

In the summer of 1823 my husband and I removed to the market-place, Richard remaining in the small house we had been occupying in Parliament Street, and taking oversight of the chemist and druggist business there, which finally became his own. Our new residence was opposite the Long Row, just facing the lower corner of the Exchange. It was part of a fine old mansion built by a French architect for his own abode, and its history is recorded in the annals of Nottingham. In its best days it must have had a good deal of internal decoration. It had lofty doors, much carving over the great mantelpieces, handsome ceilings, and several wainscoted rooms. I greatly liked the house, and felt much at home in it.

In the late autumn of 1823 my sister Anna became the happy wife of Daniel Harrison. I was at the wedding, and, according to the custom of those days, both her bridesmaid and I accompanied her to her new home at Everton, a suburb of Liverpool. At the beginning of November I returned to Uttoxeter, where I found all my dear family in their usual good health; and then journeyed on to Nottingham, to find my husband and our faithful dog both glad to see me. Nevertheless, a few weeks later, my father, after a very short illness, quietly expired on December 19, 1823.

I again met Anna at the funeral, and she afterwards returned with me to Nottingham, where, on January 15, 1824, my beloved daughter, Anna Mary, was born. A long and dangerous illness followed. My husband and Anna watched and waited by my bed of sickness; and whilst I lay utterly unconscious, offered in their agonised hearts a prayer that was mercifully granted. They saw me awake, rescued from death.

# CHAPTER VI.

*IN NOTTINGHAM.*

*1824–1830.*

THE next twelve years of our life, which were spent in Nottingham, proved an extremely busy and, to us, eventful period. Literary labour industriously went on, and at the same time mental improvement, for never did we cease in the pursuit of knowledge. The remarkably well-supplied public library of Bromley House furnished us with constant fresh stores of literature; and if by any chance a rare or, to us, useful book was not there, William did not hesitate to purchase it. Some memorable occurrences likewise left their impress on our characters.

Resuming now the chronological thread of events, I write to my sister Anna, from Nottingham.

"*7th Mo.*, 18, 1824.—Poor Byron! I was grieved exceedingly at the tidings of his death; but when his remains arrived here, it seemed to make it almost a family sorrow. I wept then, for my heart was full of grief to think that fine eccentric genius, that handsome man, the brave asserter of the rights of the Greeks, and the first poet of our time, he whose name will be mentioned with reverence and whose glory will be uneclipsed when our children shall have passed to dust, to think that he lay a corpse in an inn in this very town. Oh! Anna, I could not refrain from tears.

"Byron's faithful, generous, undeviating friend, Hobhouse, who had been his companion in his youth and in
his travels, who had advised him as a Christian and a
man of honour, yet even when that proud spirit refused
his advice, and was suffering from having spurned and
neglected it, stood by him to the last, his friend through
good and evil,—he only, excepting Byron's servants and
the undertakers, came down to see the last rites paid.
Hobhouse's countenance was pale, and strongly marked
by mental suffering.

"But to particulars. On Fifth-day afternoon the hearse
and mourning coaches came into Nottingham. In the
evening the coffin lay in state. The crowd was immense.
We went among the rest. I shall never forget it. The
room was hung with black, with the escutcheons of the
Byron family on the walls; it was lighted by six immense
wax-candles placed round the coffin in the middle of the
room. The coffin was covered with crimson velvet, richly
ornamented with brass nails; on the top was a plate
engraved with the arms and titles of Lord Byron. At
the head of the coffin was placed a small chest containing
an urn, which enclosed the heart and brains. Four pages
stood two on each side. Visitors were admitted by
twelves, and were to walk round only; but we laid our
hands on the coffin. It was a moment of enthusiastic
feeling to me. It seemed to me impossible that that
wonderful man lay actually within that coffin. It was
more like a dream than a reality.

"Nottingham, which connects everything with politics,
could not help making even the passing respect to our
poet's memory a political question. He was a Whig; he
hated priests, and was a lover of liberty; he was the author
of 'Don Juan' and 'Cain.' So the Tory party, which is

the same as saying the gentry, would not notice even his
coffin.   The parsons had their feud, and therefore not a
bell tolled either when he came or went.   He was a lover
of liberty, which the Radical Corporation here thought
made him their brother ; therefore all the rabble rout
from every lane and alley, and garret and cellar, came
forth to curse and swear, and shout and push, in his
honour.   All religious people forswore him, on account
of his licentiousness and blasphemy ; they forgot his
' Childe Harold,' his ' Bride of Abydos,' the ' Corsair,'
and ' Lara.'

" 'The next morning all the friends and admirers of
Byron were invited to meet in the market-place, to form
a procession to accompany him out of town.   Thou must
have read in the papers the funeral train that came from
London.   In addition to this were five gentlemen's carriages, and perhaps thirty riders on horseback, besides
Lord Rancliffe's tenantry, who made about thirty more,
and headed the procession, and were by far the most
respectable ; for never, surely, did such a shabby company
ride in the train of mountebanks or players.   There was
not one gentleman who would honour our immortal bard
by riding two miles in his funeral train.   The equestrians,
instead of following two and two, as the paper says they did,
most remarkably illustrated riding all sixes and sevens.

" William, Charles, Thomas Knott, and that odd Smith
(thou rememberest him) went to Hucknall to see the
interment.   It, like the rest, was the most disgrace-
ful scene of confusion that can well be imagined, for
from the absence of all persons of influence, or almost
of respectability, the rude crowd of country clowns and
Nottingham Goths paid no regard to the occasion, and
no respect or decency was to be seen.   William says it

was almost enough to make Byron rise from the dead to
see the scene of indecorum, and the poor, miserable place
in which he lies, though it is the family burial vault.

"That mad-headed, impetuous Smith was, like the rest,
enraged at the want of respect which was the most
marked trait of the interment. Although he had that
day walked in the heat of a broiling sun fourteen miles,
he sat up and wrote a poem on the subject, which I send
as a curiosity. He composed and copied it by three
o'clock in the morning, went and called up Sutton, very
much to his displeasure, had it sent to press by six
o'clock, and by nine had the verses ready for publication.
Byron's servants took four-and-twenty copies, and seemed
much delighted with it.

"Is it not strange that such an unusual silence is
maintained by the poets on the subject of his death?
It reminds me of the Eastern custom of breaking all
instruments of music in any overwhelming grief, or on
the occasion of the death of some favourite. It seems a
theme too painful for any but a master-touch, and he is
gone that could do best justice to such a subject."

On 10th Mo., 28, 1824, I write, however, to my sister:—
"Thou hast heard, I suppose, of 'Lord Byron's
Conversations,' by Captain Medwin. By the extracts
given in the different papers, as kittiwakes to the appe-
tite of the public, I am more offended and disgusted with
Lord Byron's sentiments than I ever thought to be. We
have his bust on the chimney-piece, and so angry am I
that I should like to demolish it, were it not ornamental.

"Speaking of Byron reminds me of an anecdote I
heard related the other evening. Some of Byron's friends
were in Italy, Trelawny, Leigh Hunt, and Westmacott

among the number.  One evening, in high spirits, warmed with romantic sentiment, they wandered along the banks of the Arno to the valley *delle Donne*, mentioned in the 'Decameron.'  Sitting down, they imagined that the spirits of Dante and Boccaccio might unseen be hovering around them, when, in the midst of the conversation, Leigh Hunt begged them to be silent, and desired Westmacott not to stir, for upon his hat had settled the largest and most beautiful butterfly he ever saw.  All admired it amazingly, but the greatest wonder was, that it was perfectly black.  Then, resuming the conversation, one suggested the idea, that as the Greeks symbolised the soul by the butterfly, some one of their friends in that country might then be dead, and his soul have made them a passing parting visit in the shape appropriate to Greece. The idea struck all.  They noted down the day and hour, and soon after the news reached them that on the same date, April 19, 1824, Byron had died at Missolonghi, in Western Greece.  Now, there is a good ghost-story of the nineteenth century, worthy of all acceptation.

"So Daniel has bought the 'Improvisatrice.'  Did thou know that L. E. L. was a ward of Jerdan's, the editor of the *Literary Gazette?* whence his abundant and extravagant puffs of her.  She is, I understand, rather short, but interesting-looking, a most thoughtless girl in company, doing strangely extravagant things; for instance, making a wreath of flowers, then rushing with it into a grave and numerous party, and placing it on her patron's head.  Bernard Barton sent her one of his last volumes, and in reply, after some remarks on the poetry it contained, she sent him, in high glee, a full account of a ball she had just attended, particularising all the dresses, forgetting she was writing to a sober Quaker.  However, she

is but a girl of twenty, a genius, and therefore she must
be excused.

"We have had, since I last wrote, the company of
Joseph John Gurney for three days in Nottingham.  We
were a great deal with him, and I was very glad to understand he professed himself much pleased with us, but it
was nothing to the pleasure his society diffused.  We
had a sort of carnival then, not only on his account, but
to honour Jeremiah Wiffen, the translator of Tasso, who
was in Nottingham for ten days.  Joseph John Gurney
has a most comely person, gentlemanly manners and
deportment, is an agreeable companion, and, above all, is
a good man.  He told William he did not quite approve
of the almost *unqualified* praises bestowed on Byron in
the 'Poet's Thoughts;' * at the same time, he remarked,
after reading in his deep, sweet voice some of the stanzas,
that he must confess 'it was a beautiful, very beautiful'
thing,' and then almost complimented William on his
poetic talent.  I abominate flattery, but commendation
from persons on whose candour and judgment I can rely
has charms, and such praise, whether given to William or
myself, is always welcome.  This was much from a *Quaker
minister*, was it not?  Bless the good man, and prosper
his goings, is my farewell to Joseph John Gurney.

"Give my dear love to Charles, and say I hope he is
well and happy.  He knows not the anxiety and fond
wishes I have for him."

Although we were aware of my brother Charles's
passion for the sea and shipping, and even dreaded its

* "A Poet's Thoughts at the Interment of Lord Byron, by William Howitt,
one of the authors of the 'Forest Minstrel,' &c.  London : Baldwin, Cradock,
and Joy, 1824."  It was later inserted in "The Desolation of Eyam, and
other Poems."

consequences, yet we had cast our fears away, when he consented to being articled in October 1824—the date of my last letter—to Mr. Rowland Roscow, a merchant of Liverpool.

After the death of my father, ten months previously, the first question with his widow, daughters, and sons-in-law had been, What was Charles to do? And the handsome, manly, generous-hearted boy, although but fifteen, having no occupation at home, was as anxious to fix on a profession as any of us. My father had thought of the law for him. There seemed some uncertainty, however, whether as a Friend he could conscientiously fulfil all the duties and enjoy all the privileges of an attorney. Richard Phillips was a lawyer, it was true, but he had a partner not belonging to our Society, to attend to business done in the law-courts; and were Charles, as in his case, reduced to mere conveyancing, he would find little employment in Uttoxeter. We all, therefore, unanimously approved of his practically studying commerce at Liverpool. We knew the enjoyment he would find in the society of Anna and her husband, with whom he could spend his leisure hours, and he was to board with an elderly Quaker couple, Joseph and Mary Nicholson.

Alas! how little attention do parents and guardians pay to the innate tastes and abilities of the young! Had Charles, who displayed great skill with his lathe, been placed with a shipbuilder, instead of with a merchant, his sad fate and our misery might have been averted.

The pride and hope of his family, and the admiration of all beholders, Charles had hitherto led a most guarded and secluded life. His mind had been carefully trained in moral and religious principles by his indulgent but anxious father, and his attractive exterior and manners subjected to the peculiarities of Friends. Now placed in a more exposed situation in a large seaport, the natural bias speedily asserted itself. His dress, language, conversation, the tone of his voice, assumed so completely the character of a sailor, that a stranger would have supposed him born and bred at sea.

How carefully and accurately he had studied the building of a ship is proved by a three-masted schooner, about a foot in height, of exquisite workmanship, pronounced by connoisseurs to be perfect in all its parts, which he constructed in his spare hours, and, calling it the *Anna Mary*, sent as a present to his first little niece, my daughter. A young man, not a Friend, was Charles's fellow-boarder at Joseph Nicholson's. He had been in the army, was at the bombardment of Copenhagen and in the battle of Waterloo, and had thrilling tales to relate of his travels and exploits. Some seafaring youths at the same time made Charles's acquaintance, and learning that he was the only son of a widow, by artful persuasions led him, in the simplicity of his heart, to suppose that he would relieve his mother of a monetary burden if, following his inclination and providing for himself, he went to sea; and although giving great satisfaction to Mr. Roscow, in August 1825 he suddenly disappeared.

He left his lodgings one First-day morning, attired in his best suit, which awoke no suspicion in the minds of Joseph and Mary Nicholson, until the next day came and he had not returned. Moreover, the sailor's jacket and trousers, which he wore sometimes, when employed about the shipping, and his worsted stockings were missing. A letter, addressed to his sister Anna, and brought to land by a pilot, informed his distracted relatives, that, "but for his mother, he should earlier have carried out his resolution to go to sea. He hoped, however, that, as she would henceforth be burdened with no expenses on his account, she would allow herself greater comforts. He expected to be out for three months, and would write again from Quebec, where he should be in about four weeks."

We learnt by inquiry later, that he had engaged himself with Captain Bell, part owner of the trade-ship the *Lady Gordon;* that his indentures were procured, but owing to the hurry in which the vessel went to sea, were left unsigned ; that Bell had been detained by a broken leg, and his place supplied by a Captain Clementson, who had received Charles, with the other apprentices and sailors of the *Lady Gordon,* as those who were to work her to Quebec.

Nothing more was to be ascertained, and though the thought was bitter of the idolised son and brother having thus severed himself from his relatives, we believed he had acted from good but mistaken motives, and would ultimately do well wherever placed. In the second week of November the shipping intelligence mentioned the *Lady Gordon* as lying off Quebec. She would then be homeward bound, and no letter from Charles having arrived, we concluded we should not receive direct tidings until he himself was in port ; and my mother hastened to Liverpool to meet him.

A few days, however, before the *Lady Gordon* sailed up the Mersey, a letter came to her from Charles, written in Quebec, October 26, with an account of his having hurt his leg in climbing the rigging. He was obliged to quit his work and go to his hammock, where for four days he remained without notice, the captain supposing he was sulking ; but when it was discovered that he was

really ill, he was supplied from the cabin-table. When
the ship reached Quebec he was so much reduced, and
the wound had become so bad, that he was taken, he
said, to a "Nunnery hospital," where he was receiving
every attention. The *Lady Gordon* was to leave for
England in three weeks, and he would write by her.

On December 18, 1825, the *Lady Gordon* came into
port, and brought no letter from our beloved Charles, but
one from Dr. Holmes, the chief surgeon of the Hôtel
Dieu Hospital, addressed to our mother, stating that
our poor brother had undergone an operation, his leg
being amputated a little above the knee; but his constitution was so reduced he sank under it. Dr. Holmes
had been with him when he passed away, and his last
words were of his mother.

Charles had asked his physician if there were any
Friends in Quebec, and he had replied he knew of none,
but that he himself was very much of one, having been
educated at a Friends' school in England, and that he still
corresponded with some Friends. From that moment Dr.
Holmes felt a still greater interest in the noble, patiently
enduring youth, and they became mutually much attached
to each other. The gentle nuns, overflowing with love
and pity, soothed and tended the sufferer in his sisters'
stead. The priest was also very kind in regularly visiting him; Charles, however, preferred the company of
Dr. Holmes, who read to him in his own Bible, for which
he had sent to the ship.

The statements of the crew of the *Lady Gordon*,
and especially of the ship's carpenter, told a terrible
tale. Soon after leaving Liverpool the vessel encountered head-winds and heavy seas; the sails were split
by the hurricane, and as soon as new ones were put

up they were rent in twain. The ship had been out a month when Charles met with the accident, and he lay for three weeks, often delirious, before port was reached and medical aid obtained. The captain, however, had him removed from his hammock to a berth, and the sailors, rough, hearty Cumberland men, showed him every kindness; he being especially waited on by the carpenter and a little lad.

Anna had later a visit from a Quaker sea-captain, named William Boadle. He had been in a provision-shop in Quebec, when a French physician entered, and after observing his attire and mode of speech, told him that a youth, a stranger from England, and one of his Society, who was lying ill at the Hôtel Dieu Hospital, had requested him, if he saw any Friend, to ask him to call on him. Captain Boadle went immediately. He sat some time with Charles, who confided to him the whole sad story, from the moment of his forming the desperate resolution of going to sea to the occasion of his being in the hospital. He lamented most deeply the error into which he had fallen, but spoke of the comfort he derived from the Scriptures, expressed the most yearning affection for his beloved, distant relatives, and the most unbounded gratitude to his devoted caretakers. He thought the doctors and nuns did more for him than for any other patient.

And we, in England, his sorely bereaved relatives, whilst believing that Divine love had found our treasure and borne him to the haven of peace, where the wicked cease from troubling and the temptation to sin is at an end, nevertheless felt for long weeks and months that we must still wake from a terrible dream to find our bright, buoyant Charles in our midst. Then came a formal attestation of our loss in a document signed by the Earl of Dalhousie, Governor of Canada, certifying that " Charles Botham, a mariner, aged seventeen years, died on the 3rd of November, and was buried on the 4th of November 1825, in the burial-ground of the parish church of the Protestant parish of Quebec." We could cherish illusions no longer; the pitiful story was all too true.

In February 1826 a little son was given us, who, by mutual desire, received the name of Charles Botham.

Shortly after—2nd Mo., 21st, 1826—I wrote as follows to my sister :—

"Would thou believe that William Howitt, Quaker and orthodox Christian, and good, loyal subject of the King's most excellent Majesty, is become dear and very excellent friend to no other than William Hone, of political parody notoriety? But so it is. Do you see his 'Every-day Book'? A right, pleasant book it is too. We have taken it for about a year, and now my good man has flung a whole purse into his treasury, and got a bow down to the very ground for it.

"I hope you do not experience, as too many do now, the effects of these most melancholy times. It is, indeed, enough to make the most thoughtless considerate. On all hands are we surrounded by misery. Rich and poor all participate. The poor are starving, and the rich and respectable classes are reduced to distress as bad to them as actual want."

At the end of the same year—12th Mo., 13th—comes the following :—

"I am rather engaged just now preparing our manuscript volume for the inspection of Baldwin & Co. They request to see it, and I have no doubt Campbell's favourable opinion—for he notices in the *New Monthly*

*Magazine*, in a very handsome and encouraging way, my poem on Tyre—will operate considerably in our favour. Everything in the literary world is done by favour and connections. It is perfectly a miracle to me how our former volume, when we were unknown and without one influential person to interest himself or say a good word for it, got favourably noticed. In many instances a book is reviewed which has never been read or even seen externally. I lately was the means of getting a favourable notice of a little book, and was told by the reviewer that he had written it merely in compliance with my request, but in total ignorance of the contents. Criticism sank in my estimation twenty fathoms."

" *Nottingham, 2nd Mo., 19th,* 1827.—I had a letter from Bernard Barton yesterday. He says poor Mrs. Hemans is in great sorrow for the death of her mother, to whom she seems to have been fondly attached. They had hardly ever been separated, all her children having been born under their grandmother's roof. Do not think me vain, dear Anna, when I add something more about Mrs. Hemans. I had a letter from Zillah Watts; in which she says Mrs. Hemans particularly inquires after me, and expressed herself an admirer of my little productions. I hope the time may come when I may be one among the high-souled and truly noble, and may look back to these days, as one does to a dim and cheerless morning that ended in a bright and glorious evening."

" *4th Mo., 22nd,* 1827.—We are, whether we will or not, very dependent upon circumstances, and such trifles as those attendant on universal cleanings are enough to derange the order of one's mind for a month. I do not

wonder at very deep and philosophic old gentlemen pro-
hibiting the entrance of a broom and duster into their
studies, as rigidly as a Mussulman does the entrance of a
woman into the temple of Mecca; for such internal con-
vulsions have we experienced, such disturbing of clouds
of dust, such breaking of sundry arms and legs of certain
figures and casts, that we began in no small degree to
resemble some venerable ruin of an antique temple; and
so great has been our demolition in this species of house
adornments, that our worthy friend, John Chambers, who
thinks us little better than pagans or *papishes*, might
satisfy his conscience that we were visited with such a
signal destruction as came upon Bel and the Dragon
and the god Dagon. I am glad, however, to say the
Quarterly Meeting is over, with its attendant troubles.
Woman's work, however, is never done—stitch, stitch,
stitch. I am, however, completely come from under the
bondage of very neat sewing; no more counting of
threads and three hundred and sixty-five stitches to the
inch for me; and I hope thou, dear Anna, hast embraced
the same doctrine.

"I hunger and thirst after acquaintance who are highly
gifted in mind or profound in acquired knowledge, and
for this reason should prefer decidedly a large town or a
capital, where, in general, talent congregates. Nevertheless, there is many a fine mind, brilliant imagination, and
much sound judgment to be met with even in obscure
places. Think of Wordsworth fostering in quiet seclusion one of the loftiest and purest imaginations of the
present time. Many, indeed most, and to their great
loss, consider him as only fit for a child, writing of his
'Little Celandine,' his 'Leech-gatherer,' pedlars and
potters. But the fault is in themselves, not in the poet,

who, like a true alchemist, turns all things to gold.  He
is the philosopher of nature and poetry.

" Speaking of men of superior minds in obscurity, reminds me of an old man in this place, William Haslam,
the very prototype of Wordsworth's Matthew.  He occasionally calls on us, and his piety, refined and elevated
sentiments, and his very correct judgment, joined to a
most enthusiastic taste for the higher order of poetry,
render him a most agreeable companion.  Such persons
are rare, but occasionally meeting with those possessed
of higher intellect makes me pine for more society of
the kind.  Our humble old friend always strikes out
some new idea, and furnishes food for thought, sometimes for days afterwards."

William's and my joint-work, entitled " The Desolation of Eyam, and other Poems," duly appeared in 1827,
and I write to Anna from Nottingham, 6th Mo., 24th :—

" Nobody that has not published can tell the almost
painful excitement the expectation of first opinions
occasions.  Really for some days I was quite nervous.
William boasted of possessing his mind in wise passivity,
and truly his imperturbable patience was quite an annoy-
ance ; I therefore got Rogers's beautiful poem ' Italy ' to
read, and so diverted my thoughts.  William had, a few
days ago, a letter from Wordsworth.  It was merely to say
that, the evening before, he had returned from a journey,
when he found the volume, which he is pleased to call
' elegant,' and that he immediately wrote, though he had
time only to turn over the pages, in doing which ' he was
glad to find several poems which had afforded him no
small gratification before then.' "

"*7th Mo.*, 18*th*, 1827.—Hast thou, dearest Anna, by any chance, seen the notice of our book in the *Eclectic Review?* The writer considers us anti-Quakerish, licentious in style, evidencing the same in sentiment, devoted body and soul to poetry and Lord Byron; and, moreover, William is *atheistical.*

"William has received a charming letter from David M. Moir ("Delta" of *Blackwood*), and he says as much for the book as Conder of the *Eclectic* says against it.

"I have just now received a letter from Mrs. Hemans. It is a great encouragement. She says, to use her own words, 'if she has the pleasure of seeing us at Rhyllon, she can prove to us how long she has admired and derived pleasure from our writings by many manuscripts of them.' She selects as some of her favourites the very things the *Eclectic* abuses. She congratulates me, I can fancy, with a mournful reference to herself, in possessing in a husband a kindred spirit and a friend; and still more, she invites me, if agreeable to myself, to continue the correspondence."

"*8th Mo.*, 7*th*, 1827.—Dearest Anna, please let me know how you are, and particularly thy dear little Mary. She seems fixed in my soul, and gladly would I wait on her night and day. I cannot think of her and thee without tears; for dear as you always are, how inexpressibly dear in sorrow do you become! When I look at my own children, strong and happy, playing about me, I almost feel miserable; for I can imagine thy little patient sufferer lying on the sofa, a source of painful solicitude to thee by night and day."

"*8th Mo.*, 12*th*.—I rejoice that the danger is now removed.

A child never twines itself so much in one's affections as when, in suffering, it shows a meekness and uncomplaining patience. You could die for it; you are almost sorry, as Leigh Hunt says, that you have so much to praise. The affection of parents is a wonderful and a mighty thing, coming with the little helpless stranger, and becoming more strong and imperishable as the object which excites it may require its guidance or protection. How could the love and oversight of the Almighty be presented to our hearts more touchingly than in the love of a parent? He has represented Himself to us in that character, and has Himself implanted in the heart that holy principle which we all feel and venerate, and upon which He founds the resemblance. Therefore I would regard Him with love rather than fear, and rest assured that as a father seeks the well-being of his children, and punishes but to amend them, so does our great Father act; only with more mercy, with more justice, and without caprice or passion. I am sometimes bewildered and almost overpowered with the astonishing idea of the state for which this must be a preparation. *What are we to be?* almost stupefies me. We know, dear Anna, that we are here; we know not whence we came; we have hopes and desires for the future, and the wonderful organisation of the whole structure of Nature to convince us that we are under the superintendence of some mighty and mysterious power. But of the secrets and marvels of the future existence we are ignorant; yet are we supported with a secret assurance that the object of our existence is for our ultimate happiness, when or where we can only conjecture. I have some idea of a gradual ascent in the scale of existence, and I do not think it irrational, though perhaps a little unscriptural. Whatever our destiny may be, I hope, with all sentimentalists, that the affections may be more than flowers meant only to adorn our earthly pilgrimage; and that those we love and cherish in this life may be allowed to share with us, and we with them, the more refined and more holy ties of a spiritual existence. There is no one beside our own family, William and my dear children, to whom my soul seems bound with an undying love, and I cannot imagine, according to my own feeling, a perfect Paradise without them.

"Art thou not grieved to hear of poor Canning's death? I have not mourned for the dead, for long, so sincerely as I have mourned for him. I made up my mind on Fifth-day not to mention his name, that I might not hear he was dead, for I had a conviction that must be the case. William was from home. I thought I would not go to bed with that sorrow on my spirit, so shut myself up for the evening, when the demon of perversity sent a man under the window crying the suffering and death of the lamented statesman; and I do not know, in truth, when a more melancholy mood beset me."

"*Nottingham, 2nd Mo., 17th,* 1828.—We have had a thoroughly winterly week. Fifth-day was a day of snow, like the snows of our childhood: knee-deep in many places. But what is snow in the town, dirty and drab as it falls? I thought of the purity and stillness and fairy-land-like beauty of our garden, when the firs hung like plumes of nodding feathers, and the pyracantha was covered, save its bunches of red berries, at which the birds fluttered and pecked all day long.

"How glad I should be to live in a house surrounded by a woody garden! At all seasons a garden has its beauties; and the memories connected with ours at

Uttoxeter, in our happy companionship there, are such as hallow that spot, and make every garden dear for its sake. The love of rural pleasures and occupations is not deadened in me after seven years abiding in the narrow precincts of a town-house."


" 3rd Mo., 10th, 1828.—Is not this pleasant weather? I took a solitary walk to-day, which I enjoyed very much, the atmosphere was so delightfully balmy and bright, revealing the clear, blue distance, till every object on the horizon, to the distance of between twenty and thirty miles, was brought forward quite in strong relief. In front lay our fine green meadows stretching away down to the Trent, that looked like a river of polished steel more than silver ; and between it and the horizon were the dark woods of Clifton and Thrumpton, showing even at that distance a hue of life which they never assume till this season. But perhaps the greatest beauty in the landscape was one peculiar to our meadows—our inimitable crocus-beds. It is impossible for any who do not see them to conceive their extraordinary beauty, shining out clear and bright in many places to the extent of twenty acres, one entire bed of lilac flowers. Not a faint tint of colouring, but as bright as the young green grass, with which they so charmingly contrast. The fields of Enna never could be more beautiful than our meadows. A bed of asphodels or roses could not look half so delightful as these, because, growing close to the ground, they entirely cover it. There is another charm attached to these flowers besides their beauty, and it is the pleasure they afford to children. You see them flocking down, as if to a fair, all day long, rich and poor carrying their little baskets full, and their hands and pinafores full, gathering their thousands, and leaving tens of thousands behind them, for every day brings up a fresh supply."

"*4th Mo.*, *13th*, 1828.—How strangely and suddenly are my prospects changed, and my heart covered, as it were, with a thick cloud! I hardly know, my dear Anna, how to write; my thoughts seem tossed. I have much to say on one subject, and yet I almost fear encountering it. Alas! how much sorrow have I known since I last wrote! I have seen our dear little Charles cut off in a moment, in the midst of his childish beauty and winning ways, and, above all, with his heart overflowing with the most remarkable affection.

"While in health, he was possessed of exceedingly strong passions and an impatient temper, though, to use a familiar expression, 'cut down' in a moment by a word or look of reproof. Two days before the sad event which took him from our care, he became, to our surprise, totally changed. Never was martyr more patient or meekly submissive. My heart runs over with anguish when I recall his obedience in taking the most nauseous medicines almost hourly. Their effect was extremely trying, producing a nervous irritability beyond belief; yet he tried, at our desire, to compose himself, shutting his dear eyes and attempting to sleep, poor little fellow! as if with a desire to soothe us. He was parched with a burning thirst, and for twelve hours, while sleeping and waking, incessantly murmured, 'Water, papa!' Dear, ay dearer than the blessed sunshine, as he has been in his health and joyfulness, never was he so dear as in those days of suffering. William was to him the soul of comfort, and the last word he articulated was 'Papa!' Oh Anna! I

hope thou may be spared the pangs of waking from a
dream of confidence and proud hope, from delight in the
present and joyful anticipation of the future, to a reality
of suffering and death.   It is indeed as much as human
nature can support.

"Thou can hardly imagine how the dear boy has
impressed a memory on almost everything, and months
must pass before we are restored to a quiet state of
acquiescence with our loss.  We miss his merry shouts
and bursts of laughter, his vehement joy, which contrasted so much with his sister's quietness, his arch
and mischievous little tricks, that kept us in a continual
state of activity.  Then his joy when he heard William's
step, which he knew at any audible distance, and his
actual scream of delight when papa promised him a
walk.  I wish thou had heard his voice, so loud, rich,
and deep, always reminding me of the silver tone of a
bell.  Could thou but have heard him, in his merry health,
singing to himself while he twirled round a bit of string
or stick for a hand-organ, or played the little organ thou
sent him, thou would have thought, as I often did, it
was a voice which surpassed all music.  It was a lovely
sight to watch him and Anna Mary together, forming
such a contrast.  Dear, dear children, they have been
my jewels, proudly worn and prized.  Poor Anna Mary
will miss him too.  He was her man Friday, when for
day after day she has acted Robinson Crusoe.  It was
wonderful to me to think how, at two years of age,
he could comprehend the character; he marched about
with a hearth-brush on his shoulder, pretending to shoot
different things for game, sat down by Anna Mary and
did as she bid him, like Friday himself.  Then he has
walked with two sticks, pretending to be an old lame

man. His merry antics have amused me as much almost as they have him. Our house seems silent and forlorn, and there is a void in my heart, which no other child can ever fill.

"'Though, dear Anna, I have spoken yet only of sorrowful memories, I must not ungratefully forget the mercy which has been mingled with judgment. Never before—and my heart is full in writing it—never did I know the value of many a blessed promise in Scripture. From the pleasant books, in which, in the sunshine of my security, I took such delight, I have turned with distaste, and found in the beautiful and assuring words of Christ comfort and hope; and dear Anna, without affection, I can truly say, were the power to recall the dear boy given us, we would not do it. The blow has been a severe one; but there are some things that call for thankfulness in it, and assure me that there was a sparing and a merciful hand under all, so that I hope it may tend to our good, and not lightly be forgotten.

"Dear mother has also been a comfort to us. It seemed almost in the ordering of Providence that her visit was deferred to the time when her presence was most needed, and just in time to see her only remaining boy before he was taken from our eyes for ever."

" *Uttoxeter, 7th Mo., 20th, 1828 (after a visit to Liverpool).*—How hast thou lived in my remembrance since we parted! I think of thee and thy two dear children till my heart is sad; and sad and sorrowful seemed my journey here, from having left thee behind, and from the sense of the many days which must assuredly pass before we meet again.

"I found William here, as he proposed, and quite well, as were both mother and Emma. The day after my return we went to Lichfield to see Chantrey's monument of the two children, the daughters of the Rev. W. Robinson, in the cathedral. We were exceedingly pleased with this stately and beautiful edifice, which of itself would have repaid the journey; but with the celebrated monument we were indeed delighted. I must confess for a few moments I was disappointed, I believe owing to the face of the youngest child having less of ideal beauty than we look for in such works. Very soon, however, its truth to Nature, the confiding and simple innocence of its attitude and expression, effaced the first impression, and the whole became to me almost painfully beautiful. The design is most chaste and appropriate; the two sleeping children, the younger lovingly reposing in the embrace of the elder; and retaining in her hand a few snowdrops, seem to speak most mournfully, yet beautifully, of the unconscious innocence of childhood, even in its sports lying down to die.

"What a triumph of art it is when the cold marble can speak so powerfully! It is the only thing of the kind at all worth looking at in the cathedral; for though Johnson, Garrick, Anna Seward, Addison, and Lady Mary Wortley Montagu all have monuments, they are commonplace productions, which excite no pleasure or satisfaction."


"*Nottingham*, 11*th Mo.*, 6*th*, 1828.—I think, upon the whole, the 'Winter Wreath' is as good a book as most of the annuals, for they are a chaffy, frivolous, and unsatisfactory species of publication, and are only valuable

as works of art.  How little, how very, very little, good
writing there is in the whole mass of them!  But that
they serve to keep a young author alive in the mind of
the public, and often draw upon him the favourable
notice of reviewers, and bring in a little cash, I would
forswear the whole community of them.  The chapter
on 'Woods' (in the 'Winter Wreath') forms a small
part of William's forthcoming volume, which is now
getting into a tolerable state of forwardness, and will,
in truth, be one of the greatest treasures a lover of the
country, and of its healthy and pure pleasures, ever
received from the press.

"I received two days ago a very nice, kind letter from
Maria Jane Jewsbury.  Thou knowest the interest I
have long felt in this really clever and amiable girl.
She also sent me her last volume, 'Letters to the Young,'
a work very different from her former ones, but of a most
worthy and excellent character.  I do not pretend to
any experience in religion myself, but I do admire the
sense and acknowledgment of religion in others, where
it is unaccompanied by cant or pretence.  Thus is it in
this little volume."

"12th Mo., 6th, 1828.—Thou hast no idea how very
interesting William's work, now entitled 'The Book of
the Seasons,' is become.  It is nearly ready for printing.  It contains original articles on every month, with
every characteristic of the season; a garden department,
which will fill thy heart brim-full of all garden delights,
greenness and boweryness, and dews and flowers; with a
calendar of all garden flowers as they come out.  Mountain scenery and lake scenery, and meadows and woods,
hamlets, farms, and halls, storm and sunshine—all are

in this delicious book, grouped into the most harmonious whole. Besides, there are calendars of English botany, entomology, and of the migration of birds, with their habits and haunts."

"*1st Mo.*, *25th*, 1829.—How cold it is, dear Anna! Excuse me talking of the weather, but in faith I must to-night; I am shivering, though close to the fire. Cold is like love; 'he'll venture in where he dare'n well be seen,' and where a midge cannot enter, he'll find out the way. But to think of the poor; my heart is troubled indeed when I consider them, poor children and poor *old* people. I think of the aged, with their chilled blood, which is always cold; of their stiff limbs, which cannot use quicker motion; and their scanty clothing of many carefully kept but thin garments, till I am really distressed. Our poor old uncle, James Botham! I have even remembered him; yet he was a comfortable man, with his greatcoat and worsted gloves and short gaiters. Cannot thou see him, dear Anna, with his hurried steps, in the very impotence of age endeavouring to hasten along; yet a child of four could soon have distanced him! Well I have remembered our poor old uncle thus, till my eyes have been full of tears. So it is, the longer we live the more we look to those who have been, with a chiding of spirit, as if we had disregarded them while living. Our dear, dear father, many sad remembrances crowd in my heart some-times, when I think of him."

"*Nottingham, April* 18th, 1829.—I will give thee an account of what we have done since thou left us. After breakfast I determined that Anna Mary and I should take a long walk. What a glorious morning it was, full

of spring sights and sounds and feelings!  But, my dear
Anna, the thought that thy pleasant visit was over, and
that thou wast beyond recall, pressed heavily upon me,
and in spite of sunshine and spring gladness, my heart
was sad.  Poor Anna Mary mourned more than thou
can imagine.  I was determined not to let her pretend;
therefore I said nothing to her of my feelings; but she,
in the afternoon, sat down by the fire and talked of little
Mary till her heart was full, and she burst into tears and
cried bitterly.  Poor child! I loved her all the better for
it, and promised that she and Mary should often meet
again and grow up as loving friends.  Give our dear love
to Mary, and tell her from her cousin that 'we went to
her wood, and that Anna Mary found very beautiful larch
tassels, like little knots of crimson silk, that the gorse
was yellow over with flowers, and the larks and all kind
of birds were singing, as if they were all so very glad that
spring was come.'

"Charles Pemberton, the performer of 'Old Butterboat,'
is just arrived, and has promised to spend to-day and
to-morrow with us.  We shall have, I hope, plenty of
tragedy and comedy."


"*April 26th*, 1829.—I wish, dearest Anna, thou couldst
have enjoyed the amazing talent of Pemberton, as I
did last week.  Truly it is wonderful.  Such power of
passion as I could hardly have imagined; he really is
tremendous.  We Friends, who are brought up from our
earliest infancy under such calm rule, and are so much
taught to subdue all emotions, cannot form any conception of the force and sublimity of human passion.
Not bursts of fury—those *we do* sometimes witness—but
of the stronger and more lofty passions: grief, love,

indignation, remorse. These were some of the traits he gave us, in the characters and feelings of Macbeth, Virginius, and Shylock. Feeling the truth and sublimity of these representations, I still more admire the human heart and soul, which, like a deep ocean, though often calm and clear as a mirror, can be wrought up to such awful storm and reveal such rich and unfathomable depths. Depend upon it, dear Anna, there is a very great deal to be learned from such acting.

"If the second part of Sir Richard Phillips's tour, 'Derby and Nottingham,' falls in thy way, turn to it and see what he says of 'Messrs. Howitt, husband and wife.' It is a very imperfect account of Nottingham; strangely defective and full of misstatements; nevertheless I am not offended at his mention of us, which, for its urbanity and politeness, quite surprises me."

I interrupt the epistolary narrative to add a few particulars about poor Charles Pemberton. He was a man of good family but of erratic genius, both an actor and lecturer, and his life a perfect romance of adventure and misfortune. He had been a good deal in America, where he passed through every variety of experience, and had brought back with him a nature fresh as that of a child. When in London, he dwelt principally in the circle of the religious lecturer and (later) Member of Parliament, W. J. Fox, and his friends, the Misses Flower. Of these ladies, the younger sister became Mrs. Adams. She was the authoress of a sacred drama, "Vivia Perpetua," and other religious poetry, but is chiefly known by her exquisite hymn, "Nearer my God to Thee." Her sister was a splendid musician, whose performances on the organ caused the chapel of W. J.

Fox to be visited on Sundays by crowds, who were not exactly followers of that gentleman's religious teaching. Pemberton had married in his early manhood a handsome actress, who was the misery of his life. They had been parted some years, when he happened once to be staying with us in Nottingham, at the time of the great autumn Goose Fair. He was always a partisan of the people and their sports, and took a lively interest in the booths and travelling circuses. At the door of one such exhibition Pemberton recognised a showy woman, painted and bedizened in feathers and tinsel, as his wife. Fortunately my husband was with him, as he seemed momentarily out of his mind ; he uttered some terrible exclamation of despair, and forgetting everything but his grief, rushed out of the crowd. After this occurrence, we saw him no more for many months. I do not remember, indeed, that we ever saw him again in Nottingham. He came to see us at Esher when in broken health, and on the eve of his departure for Egypt, whither he was going by medical advice. If he did not die in Egypt, he must have done so shortly after his return.

I write to my sister from Nottingham, June 14, 1829 :—

" My heart glowed when thou spoke in thy welcome letter of thy strong sentiment towards flowers. I remember thy early love for them, when not a violet or wild strawberry could thou pass on the banks ; there is no propensity more genuine in thy soul than thy delight in flowers.

" Thank thee for thy thought about William's book. It has come back from Longmans' as it went ; they decline it. We have been for the last three days more busy than thou can imagine with it. When it came back, we resolved to remodel its appearance, to put out all that we had an internal half-sort of a feeling would be better omitted, to introduce several new articles, and to copy again all blotted or illegible sheets. We worked hard all Sunday and Monday, sitting up till past midnight, and writing till our fingers ached and our eyes were as dim as an owl's in the sunshine, to try to complete it by this evening. But this day's hard work has convinced us that it is impossible, so for respite I have taken up this sheet, and then I shall be 'at it again.' We make it much more *personable*, and I hope really more worthy. I must confess that after Longmans' letter came, I sat for about three hours in a cloud; but looking over the rejected manuscript, I was convinced it was a worthy book; confidence returned, and in that confidence I am as strong as granite."

"10th *Mo.*, 18th, 1829.—Speaking of beautiful poetry, there is a piece of Miss Bowles's in the *Souvenir* that is to me perfect; its tenderness and pathos haunted me for days. It is the dying mother to her infant. Miss Bowles is certainly a most charming woman. Have I ever told thee what kind, cordial, sisterly letters I have had from her? In her last she speaks a great deal about herself. She has, she says, long ceased to be young, and has known many tossings and tribulations, and so I can believe. Her heart has known sorrow, and therefore she sympathises with it so kindly."

"*Nottingham, Nov.* 8, 1829.—I would make no secret to thee of any of our literary ventures if thou wert near, but much that is easily said seems formidable to write. As thou art generously interested for us, I will, however, tell

thee that the tide runs favourably for us just now.    Every
periodical speaks our praise ;  and  such  overwhelming
commendation has been heaped upon a certain 'Old
Man's Story' in the *Amulet*, which I, in very idleness,
wrote one summer evening, that I have blushed for
myself, and with Lady Morgan and the little old woman,
have said, 'Sure this is none of I.'"

"*Nottingham,* 12th *Mo.,* 13th, 1829.—Thou art quite
right about Mrs. Hemans's poetry, and thou art not by
any means peculiar.   But it is no stately undertone of
*German* in it that offends thee.   She wants true simplicity.    Her  heart  is  right,  but  her  taste  is  rather
vitiated.    It is just like her dress ; it has too much glare
and contrast of colour to be in pure taste.   I *felt* this
when I saw her.

"Now, dear Anna, what wilt thou say when I tell thee
William  and  I  set  out  for  London  the  day  after  to-
morrow ?   My heart beats at this moment to think of it.
I half dread it.   I shall twenty times wish for our quiet
fireside, where day by day we read and talk by ourselves,
and nobody looks in upon us.   I keep reasoning with
myself that the people we shall see in London are but
men and women, and perhaps, after all, no better than
ourselves.   If  we  could,  dear Anna,  but  divest  our
minds of *self*, as our dear father used to say we should do,
it would be better and more comfortable for us.   Yet it is
one of the faults peculiar to us Bothams, that, with all the
desire there was to make us regardless of *self*, we never
had confidence and proper self-respect instilled into us; and
the want of this will give us a depressing feeling, though
I hope it is less frequently seen by others than felt by
ourselves.   This is the only thing that casts a cloud on

our proposed journey.    In every other respect it is delightful, almost intoxicating.    I recall to myself the old
fame of London, its sublime position in the world, its
immensity, its interesting society, till I feel an impatient
enthusiasm, which makes quite a child of me again.
Think only, dear Anna, to hear the very hum of that
immense place, to see from afar its dense cloud of smoke!
These things, little and ordinary as they would be to
many, would, I know, under particular circumstances, fill
my eyes with tears and bring my heart into my throat till
I could not say a word.    But then to stand on Tower
Hill, in Westminster Abbey, upon some old famous
bridge, to see the marbles in the British Museum, the
pictures in some of the fine galleries, or even to have
before one's eyes some old grey wall in Eastcheap or the
Jewry, about which Shakespeare or some other old worthy
has made mention, will be to me a realisation of many a
vision and speculation.    We do not intend to stay more
than a week, and thou may believe we shall have enough
to do.    We are to be with Alaric and Zillah Watts, and
have to make special calls on the S. C. Halls, Dr. Bowring, the Pringles, and be introduced to their ramifica-
tions of acquaintances; Allan Cunningham, L. E. L.,
Martin the painter, and Thomas Roscoe we are sure to
see, and how many more I cannot tell."

"MY DEAR ANNA,—Actually and truly I write from
London, and in great haste, just to prove to thee that
thou art not forgotten.    I cannot pretend to tell thee
one-tenth of the sights we have seen or one-twentieth
part of the kindness of our friends.    Alaric Watts is
one of the most gentlemanly and obliging persons I ever
saw, with a nice, well-bred wife and a dear little boy.

"I am also exceedingly pleased with Thomas Pringle; he is a good man. We have met L. E. L.; she is a pretty, merry, fidgety little damsel. Mrs. Hofland is a very ordinary-looking, very countrified old lady, but very kind and motherly. We have not yet seen Barry Cornwall, Allan Cunningham, and Geoffrey Crayon; Dr. Bowring has, however, promised to invite the latter to meet us to-morrow evening. T. K. Hervey is visiting at the Watts's at this time. He is a very singular-looking young man, but very agreeable."

# CHAPTER VII.



*IN NOTTINGHAM—(continued).*

*1830–1836.*

THIS was the period when the annuals—those "butter-
flies of literature," as L. E. L., herself a butterfly, called
them to me—found favour with the public.  Alaric
Watts was the editor of the *Literary Souvenir*, one of
the very best of this class of productions.  Both he and
his wife had become our beloved and valued friends.
Zillah Watts, the sister of two remarkable men, Jeremiah and Benjamin Wiffen, was highly gifted, and born,
like myself, in the Society of Friends.  We were the
same age, and greatly attached to each other.  The
chief bond between us at this time was literature, and
the style of our correspondence may be seen in letters
given in the "Life of Alaric Watts," by his son and my
son-in-law, Alaric Alfred Watts, which was published
in 1884.

In our visit to London at Christmas 1829, my husband
and I first made the personal acquaintance of Mr. and
Mrs. S. C. Hall.  He was then editing the *Amulet*, and
his wife had accepted the editorship of the *Juvenile
Forget-Me-Not*.  This acquaintance grew into a lifelong friendship.  Allan Cunningham edited *The Anni-
versary*, and Thomas Pringle the *Friendship's Offering*,
whilst our friend William Chorley, at Liverpool, was
editing the *Winter's Wreath*.

It was on a visit paid to my sister Anna that I first came in contact with the interesting Chorley family. I met Henry Fothergill Chorley, the youngest brother, in the drawing-room of his aunt, Rebecca Chorley, and was soon afterwards introduced to his accomplished mother, Jane Chorley, and his sister, Mary Anne. The father must have been dead some years, and the Quakeress, Jane Chorley, her three sons and one daughter, dwelt with her brother, Dr. Rutter. William, the eldest, especially devoted himself to literature. John, the second, was brimful of elegant scholarship and music. Henry, then twenty, and equally musical, was of a delicate constitution, and suffered from shyness. He was very affectionate and generous-hearted, and became to me as a brother. He was himself devoted to authorship, and assured me that "no good work could ever be accomplished without time, reflection, and prayer." In 1833 he settled in London, became a regular writer on the staff of the *Athenæum*, and three years later he issued his "Memorials of Mrs. Hemans."

This amiable and accomplished poetess, a native of Liverpool, and my senior by five years, had been brought up in the seclusion of North Wales, and without being regularly educated, had acquired the knowledge of several languages, and stored her memory with everything worth possessing in the whole range of poetry. She resided at Rhyllon, near St. Asaph, having a kind, protecting friend in the Bishop, until the marriage of her sister, in 1828, broke up the household. She then removed to Liverpool for the education of her five little sons, arriving there in the autumn of 1828. She settled in the village of Wavertree, and writing to me in the following December, speaks of "many things pressing on her heart, amongst these, the want of hills, the waveless horizon, wearying her eye, accustomed to the sweeping outline of mountain scenery. It was a dull, uninventive nature around her."

On my next visit to Liverpool I found Mrs. Hemans the object of tender solicitude to the Chorleys, who were her chief friends. She was persecuted by sightseers, especially by the homage of importunate young ladies, so that she trembled to see a muff enter her little parlour, lest it should conceal an album "within its treasure caves and cells," saying she considered it "unjustifi- able in people always to come armed with their pocket-pistols."

It was summer-time when we met; and once, as we were sitting together, little Charles Hemans ran into the room holding a dark Bengal rose, and exclaiming, in gleeful admiration, " Oh mamma, the red rose of glory ! " Upwards of forty years later I gave him, in Rome, a bunch of the same roses, and attached to them, in writing, his juvenile appellation.

I must not omit one great and lasting benefit which we derived from our intercourse with Mrs. Hemans and the three brothers Chorley. They were all enthusiasts for the German language and literature, and inspired us with the same taste. William Chorley especially aided and encouraged us, directing our studies and supplying us with books from his large collection of standard German works.

Returning now to my correspondence with my sister Anna, I find the following, under the date April 27, 1830 :—

"I look out into the market-place and up to the blue sky, and anticipate with almost childish impatience the happy day when, after three months' caging, I may again breathe the free air in the green fields. The baby is doing delightfully, a really pretty, bonny little fellow, and the best child, surely, that ever came into the world. I know you want to hear what he is to be called. Truly this naming of either book or baby is a hard matter. The giving unto Tristram Shandy a name was not an affair of greater consideration than it seems likely to be in our case. Anna Mary has spelled over every name in her spelling-book, from Aaron down to Zedekiah, and cannot satisfy herself. It really was amusing to hear her. 'A-b-e-l—Abel—Abel Howitt; oh! no, that won't do at all. A-g-n-e-s—Agnes; but that's a girl's name,' and so on; and for lack of a better, she and I call him Harry. The whole house was in horror at this, when she announced belowstairs that mamma said he *should* be called Harry. Nurse thought, 'To be sure, Harry was *more genteeler* than Henry, but, for her part, she thought Stephen or Jonathan would be much prettier.' Our faithful Ann came up to remonstrate on such a choice, and really so much did I enjoy the consternation, that it seemed a pity to undeceive them. The name, however, is to be Alfred William, he being called by the first.

"Dear Anna, if thou carest to see me in a London party, how I looked, and how I behaved, thou wilt find it in the first volume of 'Romance and Reality,' page 149. There are several other literary people, Miss Jewsbury as Miss Amesbury, Kennedy, Allan Cunningham, Crofton Croker, the S. C. Halls, &c.; some of whom thou wilt recognise by their works. I am not very accurately described; nevertheless, I suppose it was

Miss Landon's impression, and for the kind compliment I am obliged to her."

"*Nottingham, June* 14, 1830.—Why, dear Anna, if thou feels the disadvantage and absurdity of Friends' peculiarities, dost thou not abandon them? William has done so, and really I am glad. He is a good Christian, and the change has made no difference in him, except for the better, as regards looks. I am amazed now how I could advocate the ungraceful cut of a Friend's coat; and if we could do the same, we should find ourselves religiously no worse, whatever Friends might think. I never wish to be representative to any meeting, or to hold the office of clerk or sub-clerk. All other privileges of the Society we should enjoy the same. But I am *nervous* on the subject. I should not like to wear a straw bonnet without ribbons; it looks so Methodistical; and with ribbons, I again say, I should be nervous. Besides, notwithstanding all his own changes, William likes a Friend's bonnet. In all other particulars of dress, mine is just in make the same as everybody else's. Anna Mary I shall never bring up in the payment of the tithe of mint and cummin; and ·I fancy Friends are somewhat scandalised at the unorthodox appearance of the little maiden. As to language, I could easily adopt that of our countrymen, but think with a Friend's bonnet it does not accord; and I like consistency. I quite look for the interference of some of our exact brothers or sisters on account of my writings, at least if they read the annuals next year, for I have a set of the most un-Friendly ballads in them. What does Daniel say about these things? I hope he does not grow rigid as he grows older.

"I trust thou hast plenty of nice little shelves and odd nooks for good casts and knick-knacks. I love to see these things in a house, where they are well selected and used with discretion. Let us accustom our children to elegant objects, as far as our means permit. I think one might manage so that every common jug and basin in the house were well moulded, with such curves as would not have offended the eye of an Athenian. There is much in the *forms* of things. I wish I had my time to live over again, for with my present knowledge, even in the buying of a brown pot, I could do better. Thou wilt perhaps smile at this as folly, yet so fully am I impressed with its importance, that I point out to Anna Mary what appears to me good and what faulty. Morally and intellectually we must be better for studying perfection, and it consists a great deal in outward forms. Even a child can soon perceive how in houses some things are chosen for their grotesqueness or picturesqueness, which is distinct from beauty. I do not know why I have written thus, for thou feels these things just as much as I do."

"*Nottingham, Dec.* 26, 1830.—It is impossible to tell thee how I long for some mighty spirit to arise to give a new impulse to mind. I am tired of Sir Walter Scott and his imitators, and I am sickened of Mrs. Hemans's luscious poetry, and all her tribe of copyists. The libraries set in array one school against the other, and hurry out their trashy volumes before the ink of the manuscript is fairly dry. It is an abomination to my soul; not one in twenty could I read. Thus it is, a thousand books are published, and nine hundred and ninety are unreadable. Dost thou remember the days when Byron's poems came out first, now one, and then one, at sufficient intervals to allow of digesting them? And dost thou remember our first reading of 'Lalla Rookh?' It was on a washing-day. We read and clapped our clear-starching, read and clapped, read and clapped and read again, and all the time our souls were not on this earth. Ay, dear Anna, it was either being young or being unsurfeited which gave such glory to poetry in those days. And yet I do question whether, if 'Lalla Rookh' were now first published, I could enjoy it as I did then. But of this I cannot judge; the idea of the poem is spoiled to me, by others being like it. I long for an era, the outbreaking of some strong spirit who would open another seal. The very giants that rose in intellect at the beginning of the century, Southey, Coleridge, and Wordsworth, have become dwarfed. Many causes have conspired to make literature what it now is, a swarming but insignificant breed; one being the wretched, degraded state of criticism; another is the annuals; and, in fact, all periodical writing, which requires a certain amount of material, verse or prose, in a given time."

"*Nottingham, April* 3, 1831.—I know, my kindest sister, thy warm interest about us and our literary progress, and therefore I am glad to think thou wilt be pleased to see the triumphant course of the 'Book of the Seasons.' I dare say thou hast seen the notice in the *Athenæum* some weeks ago. This month there are excellent reviews of it in the *New Monthly,* the *Eclectic,* the *Westminster Review,* and *Blackwood's* in the "Noctes." Our literary friends have been most kind, Delta, Bowring, the Halls, and above all, our indefatigable friend, Alaric Watts. Josiah Conder, too, has made the *amende honorable* for his former offences against William by his gracious criticism."

I cannot resist imparting to the reader the notice in the "Noctes Ambrosianæ," as it also contains pleasant allusions to some of our relatives and associates. It is taken from the works of Professor Wilson, edited by his son-in-law, Professor Ferrier, Vol. III. :—

APRIL 1831.

QUAKER POETS.—THE HOWITTS.

*North.* Your head, my dear James, is now touching Howitt's "Book of the Seasons." Prig and pocket it. 'Tis a jewel.

*(The Shepherd seizes it from the shelf, and acts as per order.)*

*Shepherd.* Is Nottingham far intil England, sir? For I would really like to pay the Hooitts a visit this simmer. Thae Quakers are, what ane micht scarcely opine frae first principles, a maist poetical Christian seck. There was Scott o' Amwell, who wrote some simplish things in a preservin' speerit o' earnestness;—there is Wilkinson, yonner, wha wons on a beautifu' banked river, no far aff Peerith (is't the Eamont, think ye?), the owther o' no a few pomes delichtfu' in their domesticity—auld bachelor though he be—nae warld-sick hermit, but an enlichtened labourer o' love, baith in the kitchen and flower garden o' natur;—lang by letter has me and Bernard Barton been acquent, and verily he is ane o' the mildest and modestest o' the Muses' sons, nor wanting a thouchtfu' genie, that aften gies birth to verses that treasure themselves in folks' hearts;—the best scholar among a' the Quakers is Friend Wiffen, a capital translator, Sir Walter tells me, o' poets wi' foreign tongues, sic as Tawso, and wi' an original ore;—and feenally, the Hooitts, the three Hooitts—na, there may be mair o' them for aught I ken, but I'se answer for William and Mary, Husband and Wife, and oh! but they're weel met; and eke for Richard (can he be their brither?); and wha's this was tellin' me about anither brither o' Wullie's, a Dr. Godfrey Hooitt, ane o' the best botanists in a' England, and a desperate beetle-hunter?

*North.* Entomologist, James. A man of science.

*Shepherd.* The twa married Hooitts I love just excessively, sir. What they write canna fail o' bein' poetry, even the most middlin' o't, for it's aye wi' them the ebullition o' their ain feeling, and their nin fancy, and whenever that's the case, a bonny word or twa will drap itsel' intil ilka stanzy, and a sweet stanzy or twa intil ilka pome, and sae they touch, and sae they sune win a body's heart; and frae readin' their byuckies ane wushes to ken theirsels, and indeed do ken theirsels, for their personal characters are revealed in their volumms, and methinks I see Wully and Mary——

*North.* Strolling quietly at eve and morn by the silver Trent.

*Shepherd.* No sae silver, sir, surely, as the Tweed?

*North.* One of the sincerest streams in all England, James.

*Shepherd.* Sincere as an English sowl that caresna wha looks intil't, and flows bauldly alang whether reflectin' cluds or sunshine.

*North.* Richard, too, has a true poetical feeling, and no small poetical power. His unpretending volume of verses well deserves a place in a library along with those of his enlightened relatives—for he loves nature truly as they do, and nature has returned his affection.

*Shepherd.* But what's this " Byuck o' the Seasons?"

*North.* In it the Howitts have wished to present us with all their poetic and picturesque features—a Calendar of Nature, comprehensive and complete in itself—which on being taken up by the lover of nature at the opening of each month, should lay before him in prospect all the objects and appearances which the month would present, in the garden, in the field, and the waters—yet confining itself solely to those objects. Such, in their own words, is said to be their aim.

*Shepherd.* And nae insignificant ane either, sir. Hae they hit it?

*North.* They have. The scenery they describe is the scenery they have seen.

*Shepherd.* That circling Nottingham.

*North.* Just so, James. Their pictures are all English.

*Shepherd.* They show their sense in stickin' to their native land—for unless the heart has brooded, and the e'e brooded too, on a' the aspecks o' the outer warld till the edge o' ilka familiar leaf recalls the name o' the flower, shrub, or tree frae which it has been blawn by the wund, or drapped in the cawm, the poet's han'll waver, and his picture be but a haze. In a' our warks, baith great an' sma', let us be national; an' thus the true speerit o' ae kintra'll be breathed intil anither, an' the haill warld encompassed an' pervaded wi' poetry and love.

*North.* As a proof, James, of their devotedness to merry England——

*Shepherd.* Not a whit less merry that it contains a gude mony Quakers.

*North.* Our Friends have described the years, without once alluding —as far as I have observed—to the existence of Thomson.

*Shepherd.* Na—that is queer an' comical aneuch;—nor can I just a'thegither appruve o' that forgetfulness, ignorance, or omission.

*North.* It shows their sincerity. They quote, indeed, scarcely any poetry but Wordsworth's—for in it, above all other, their quiet, and contemplative, and meditative spirits seem to repose in delight.

*Shepherd.* I canna understaun' why it should be sae; but wi' the exception o' yoursel', sir, I never kent man or woman wha loved and admired Wordsworth up to the pitch, or near till't, o' idolatrous worship, wha seemed to care a doit for ony ither poet, leevin' or dead. He's a sectawrian, you see, sir, in the religion o' natur'.

*North.* Her High-Priest.

*Shepherd.* Weel, weel, sir; e'en be't sae. But is that ony reason why a' ither priests should be despised or disregarded, when tryin' in a religious speerit to expound or illustrate the same byuck—the byuck o' natur', which God has given us, wi' the haly leaves lyin' open, sae that he wha rins may read, though it's only them that walks slowly, or sits down aneath the shadow o' a rock or a tree, that can understaun' sufficient to privilege them to breathe forth their knowledge an' their feelings in poetry, which is aye as a prayer or a thanksgiving?

*North.* The "Book of the Seasons" is a delightful book, and I recommend it to all lovers of nature!


On May 3rd I say in a letter to my sister Anna :—

"My little Anna Mary is gone again to Uttoxeter; and Emma was also to have gone at that time but for unexpected guests, who have been with us a week to-day; no others than Mrs. Wordsworth and her daughter. This day week, as we were dressing in the morning, Mr. Wordsworth was announced. Of course, we were very glad to see him. He was on his way home from London, and Mrs. Wordsworth, who was with him, was taken ill on the road, and had arrived in great agony in Nottingham, the night before.

He came, poor man! in much perplexity, to ask our advice. We recommended that Godfrey should see her, and insisted on her removal to our house, which was accomplished with some difficulty the same afternoon. Here she has accordingly been since. She is now nearly recovered, and I suppose will leave us the day after to-

morrow.  Wordsworth greatly pleased me.  He is worthy
of being the author of the 'Excursion,' of 'Ruth,' and
those sweet poems so full of human sympathy.  He is a
kind man, full of strong feeling and sound judgment.
We very much enjoyed the little of his society that we
had, for he stayed but one night with us.  My greatest
delight was, that he seemed so much pleased with
William's conversation.  They seemed quite in their
element, pouring out their eloquent sentiments on the
future prospects of society, and on all subjects connected
with poetry and the interests of man.

"Not less are we pleased with Mrs. Wordsworth and
her lovely daughter, Dora.  They are the most grateful
people ; everything we do for them is right, and the very
best it can be.

"I am glad to tell thee that they are quite delighted
with Emma.  'Here the dear creature comes!'  Mrs.
Wordsworth constantly says, when she hears her foot
on the stairs; and I do not wonder at it, for a kinder,
gentler, more affectionate nurse than she is cannot be,
perpetually doing, silently and unknown, some pleasant
and acceptable service."

The year 1831 was not only memorable to us by
this visit from the Wordsworths, but from the riots in
Nottingham.  A few years earlier the lowest class in the
town, elated with prosperity, had become a perfect nuisance to society by braving all order and defying all authority, and had taught us that, if once inflamed by rage,
these roughs would make Nottingham a dangerous place.

After the accession of William IV., in June 1830, we
looked forward with fearful apprehension, till, in November, the Grey Administration was formed, and then we

again began to hope. Those were certainly melancholy times. The poor were suffering dreadfully. Labourers in the southern counties toiled like slaves for sixpence a day, and with every spark of independence smothered, from the necessity of receiving parish relief. No wonder, then, at the spirit of insurrection among these poor peasants. Nay, sensible men, well-wishers to their country and the cause of humanity, began to consider the incendiary spirit as one likely to produce good, that nothing short of it would turn the attention of the rich and influential to the miserable condition of these hewers of wood and drawers of water.

The people of Nottingham depended very much for a market on France and the Netherlands, and after the disturbances on the Continent the trade in Nottingham suffered dreadfully. Poor people worked incessantly sixteen and seventeen hours a day, and could then only earn from sixpence to eightpence. No wonder, therefore, at attempted revolution ; more especially as the toilers heard of the country's money being lavished by millions. I, who never in my life had been a politician, and whose prejudices from childhood had been in opposition to democracy, now most cordially allied myself in spirit with the party who cried out for radical reform.

On October 7, 1831, the Reform Bill was rejected by the Lords ; and three days later Nottingham Castle was burnt in the political excitement.

My husband, in some unpublished notes, thus describes the scene :—

"From the top of our house, which was flat and leaded, we had a full view of the burning of Nottingham Castle, the property of the Duke of Newcastle. Well do I remember the time. First in the dusk of the evening, the vast market-place of six acres filled with one dense throng of people, their black heads looking like a sea of ink, for the whole living mass was swaying and heaving in the commotion of fury seeking a vent.  Suddenly there was a cry of 'To the castle! to the castle!' to which a fierce roar of applause was the ominous echo, and at once this heaving, raging ocean of agitated life became an impetuous, headlong torrent, struggling away towards Friar Lane, leading directly to the castle.

"Anon arose a din of deafening yells and hurrahs from the wide castle-court.  The mob had scaled the walls.  They surrounded the vast building as a stormy tide surges tumultuously round an ocean rock.  Anon and a red light gleamed through the different rooms in view, followed by the hoarse roar of the monster crowd without.  The flames rapidly spread, filled the whole place with a deep fiery glow, mingled with clouds of smoke that burst from the windows and streamed up roofwards, tipped with tongues of flame, hungry for the destruction of the whole fabric.  Through all this, even when fire seemed raging through the whole building, there were seen figures as of black demons dancing, as it were, in the very midst of the flames in the upper rooms, whilst cries as dread and demoniac were yelled forth from below.  In fact, numbers of these incendiaries, made drunk with their success, were still dancing in the rooms, in delight over their revel of destruction.  When all access by the staircase was cut off, and only when driven by the aggressive flames, did they issue from the windows and descend by the projection of the stonework, which, luckily for them, was of that style in which every stone stands prominent, leaving a sunken band between it and its fellow.

"Soon the riotous, voracious flames burst through the roof, sending down torrents of melted lead, and to heaven legions of glittering sparks and smoke as from a volcano. The scene was magnificent, though saddened by regret for the destruction of a building which, though not antiquely picturesque like its predecessors, was invested with many historical memories, and by its size, symmetry, and its position on the bold and lofty rock, formed a fine feature in the landscape. It was a steadily rainy night, yet the wet seemed to possess no power over the raging mass of fire. Frequently parts of the roof or beams within fell with a louder thunder, and sent up fresh volumes of smoke, dust, and coruscating sparks. The rioters had torn down the wainscotings of cedar, piled them up in the different rooms and fired them, and the whole air was consequently filled with a peculiar aroma from the old cedar thus burning. In the morning the great fabric stood a skeleton of hollow doorways and windows, blackened walls, and heaps of still smouldering and smoking materials within."

Returning to my letters to my sister Anna, I write from Nottingham, February 4, 1832 :—

"It is a common thing for thee to be without thy husband for weeks together, so it occasions no extraordinary want in thy mind; but to me, who am like a spoiled child, an absence of ten days makes me feel as if I had lost my right hand or my eye, or as if some dark cloud hung over the house, making everybody in it stupid and uninteresting, and I the stupidest of all. William's errand to London is to dispose of his old-world legends, which he calls 'Pantika.'

"No one knows how dear, how inexpressibly dear to

me are those I love.  My heart does not covet many friends; I care not to be personally admired, though I have some ambition to be distinguished in my day.  But this is a feeling distinct from that of love.  Let me be known to the world, but let me be loved by those who are dear to me, and let me live among those who love me, is the craving of my soul.  Though my husband and children are like daylight to my eyes, thou knowest not, my dearest, oldest, and kindest friend, what thou art to me, and what thou hast been in those unalloyed days of our maidenly happiness; and the memory of it will go down to the grave with me.  I am not, dear Anna, much changed since a girl; what were my ruling passions then are so now, and what were my pursuits are so still, except gardening, which circumstances have denied.

"I am reading Cobbett's work on gardening, and it makes me long for a plot to sow endive and cauliflower in.  I am not yet come to his remarks on flower-gardening, but I expect that it will be more disquieting than the cabbage and salad dispensation.  What a clever writer he is!  Whatever his faults may be as a politician, he has true genius, and that he shows by the extraordinary interest he gives to common subjects."


"*June* 15, 1832.—We like our summer quarters at Wilford wonderfully.  We are most comfortably situated with some most kind and civil people, who for cottagers are very well to do.  He is a basketmaker, and keeps a few cows.  We have butter and milk from them—plenty of warm, new milk for the children.  We have quite a state bedroom, neatly papered with three different sorts of green paper, as clean as if done yesterday, white dimity curtains to the two little casement windows, Faith, Hope, and Charity, and the Four Seasons, on the walls. We have had to muster some of our pieces of carpeting for the brick floor of the sitting-room, which, with a good supply of flowers and our own books, makes a very respectable appearance. The family consists of the man and his wife; he a sturdy old English peasant, she a woman who has lived in her youth in good service, but is now lame of the 'rheumatics;' a daughter tolerably pretty, a sort of village belle; a son rather given to company, to whom we hear not seldom grave advice given, but a very good sort of person notwithstanding; a little nurse-child, hight Lorenzo; a pet lamb, a cat and a kitten, and a large family of hens and chickens."

"*Nottingham, Oct.* 16, 1832.—Were you not grieved at the death of Sir Walter Scott? Never did there live a man who has so largely contributed to the happiness of his race. He seems to me to have been at this particular time an especial benefactor, because sorrow and care are, as it were, let loose in the world, and man needs recreation; like the poor Paisley weaver who said the greatest pleasure he enjoyed in these bad times was reading Sir Walter Scott's tales."

"*Dec.* 19, 1832.—I suppose you have been very much interested about the elections. We have, to a certain degree. Here it was so sure from the beginning, that though the contest was carried on to the last minute of polling, no one felt at all anxious. The only thing in the election that at all interested me was the immense groan that hailed and attended the Tory candidate on his final withdrawal from the poll. It was such a groan as I could not have imagined, and such a thing as one cannot forget; sent forth from three thousand throats. All outbursts of human passion are to me intensely interesting. I almost go wild with an enthusiastic shout, and a demonstration of public sorrow is to me overwhelming.

"William is very busy writing a history of priestcraft. It will be a work of wonderful interest, and one well suited to the general feeling and to the topics which occupy the public mind. Such a thing, in short, as ought to be written. I am glad William does it, because, while he shows the tyrannical spirit of priesthood in all ages and nations, he will treat moderately, comparatively speaking, the subject of priesthood in the present day; that is, he will war with the principle, and not with the men. I have no doubt it will be generally read and much approved by the Liberals; the *Conservatives*, as they call themselves, will call him a Radical leveller and overturner of religion, whereas he will be only overturning the *abuses* of religion.

"Tell dear mother, please, that we are much obliged to her for John Wilbur's Letters. How wonderfully all Friends write alike! This is the exact style of Friends of what may be termed the middle ages of the Society. I do not like it. It has not the quaintness of the early Friends. It is the manner of Friends' preaching, and that, to my thought, wants reforming, like many other things. The matter is often better than the manner, and the sense than the form of words it is put in."

"*Nottingham, Feb.* 1833.—William is just bringing his 'History of Priestcraft' to a conclusion. When my book ('Seven Temptations') will be published I know not, for the times are sadly against poetry. A part of it is now in London, and has been seen by some

of our literary friends, who give it such extraordinary
praise as almost terrifies me.  I fancy myself it is the
best thing I ever did, but I do not know whether it
deserves the quantity of praise they give.  However,
it is singular that the terms of commendation have been
nearly the same from all quarters, though the parties
had no intercourse with each other, and had not the
same portions of the work to read.  But enough of
egotism.

"Write soon and tell us about you all, and about
Emma's preparation and prospects of marriage.  Heaven
bless her and make all turn out for her happiness."


"*April* 22, 1833.—One's heart grows sore with looking upon the present prospects of English society.  Any
change, it seems to me, provided it affected the aristocracy and the immensely rich as well as the middle
and lower classes, must be an improvement.  One grows
almost reckless about political changes, so utterly hope-
less are human affairs becoming.  Were it not for the
tie children are of necessity, and the obligation they
impose upon us to have a fixed home, I could like to
turn gipsy or lead the life of a wild Indian, and have
no home or hardly any country, except such as chance
and circumstance gave us.  At least, such a life I should
very much like to try.  I dare say, dear Anna, thou wilt
think I have lost my senses or am grown very wicked
to have such strange notions.  I am not going to do
any wild thing, nor am I doubtful of Providence.  But
what thoughtful person can look round on the strange
disorganisation of society without regarding that life
as the best and most rational which reduces one's wants
to the smallest number, and makes us less dependent

upon others, than the present state of things necessarily obliges us to be?

"Our approaching journey to London is partly one of business; nevertheless, we cannot anticipate a visit there, particularly at this season of the year, without having many delightful visions of much to be seen and done. I wish it were possible to persuade you to take just this once a trip to Babylon. Only think what we might do! Why, we would go down to Croydon for a day, and we would live our schoolgirl rambles over again; go down those lanes which I fancy I know so well, but in which, I suppose in reality, I should soon lose my way; and we would see those green hills where were actual shepherds, and where on the white stony tops we sat down and ate our dinners.

"I hope, dear Anna, thou wilt let me have a full account of the wedding, a real womanly account, with beginning, middle, and end, for from Emma I could not get so good a one, she being actor."

"*Nottingham, June* 15, 1833.—With this you will receive a copy of the 'History of Priestcraft.' I do not anticipate its entirely meeting with your approbation, though I must be free to say I think George Fox, William Penn, and Robert Barclay would have hailed it as a book of good-fellowship; but, some way, Friends have adopted a more timid policy in these days, and are more inclined to concede to the powers that be than stand boldly opposed to them. Perhaps you have heard that this book of William's was denounced in the Yearly Meeting by Luke Howard as a libellous work, and one which he cautioned Friends not to read. This in reality would do the book good, the very caution inflaming curiosity and attracting attention to it. Though perhaps you may think some portions written in too vehement a spirit, I am sure there is a great deal that will delight you; you will feel that the general tone is manly and right, and that it contains much beautiful writing.

"I thank thee, dear Anna, for thy most pleasant letter with the welcome news of the wedding. All seems to have been as it should be—quiet, holy, and full of kindly affection. I am glad to think that our dear mother has seen Emma not only happily married as far as prospects go, but so much to her mind and sufficiently near for her to feel the separation less.

"The account of your journey interested me extremely. I can believe thou wouldst long to have a quiet little pastoral home in one of those valleys thou so beautifully describest. Thou would feel that even as far as thy children were concerned, it would be better for them to have the free range of the wide hills and valleys, with the ever-changing but ever-beautiful sky above them, than for them to live among the narrow bounds, noise, and confusion of a town, and exposed, more or less of necessity, to its pollutions, its vices, and its misery. I am sure I have often felt this, and wished there could be some blessed way of freeing our children from such scenes. I suppose, however, it cannot be; one of the penalties of our human nature is to suffer, and another to look on and mourn and aid; and children cannot be exempted from them. But, dear Anna, it always is a joy to my heart to find that the relish and the glad enjoyment of these pure pleasures still remain and that we have a feeling of the beauties of Nature, and the ennobling and deeply religious sentiment which mountains and the solitudes of Nature always must excite, when the soul is not spoiled by too much intercourse with the world; and I could so well understand what thou saidst of thy feelings in such scenes that I longed to be with thee, and there take sweet counsel together.

"I suppose thou wilt, dear Anna, expect some account of our London visit; but really I have very little to tell thee. I attended one sitting at Yearly Meeting, but one more unedifying I never did attend. There was so much petty weighing of small matters, and so much interruption from two or three-worded ministers, who popped up here and there continually, that, to my mind, it was anything but profitable. I was, however, very much struck with the beauty of the uniformity and singularly pure-looking apparel of so many hundreds of women, who really resembled a large flock of doves more than anything else.

"I can imagine you will be inclined to censure me for not making a point as of duty in attending the Yearly Meeting. But let me beg you to remember one thing—mother can understand it, I am sure—what a serious obstacle is the distance of places one from another in London. We were three miles and a half from meeting, with persons not Friends, who, therefore, had no arrangements made for attending meeting; and to walk backwards and forwards that distance, with no Friend's house to rest at, was what I could not do, and to take a coach was what we could not afford; therefore we were obliged to reconcile ourselves to stop away, and did the more easily from the specimen I had; and especially because there was nobody there we cared to see.

"With the neighbourhood of London, especially with the more celebrated places of Hampstead, Highgate, and Richmond, we were extremely pleased. They, indeed, deserve their fame.  The banks of the Thames are less beautiful for pastoral effects than the banks of the Trent, and this is owing to the tide, which leaves a muddy shore for part of the day.  But when you come to Richmond, where such trees as you see in pictures or fancy in poetry grow in their bountiful luxuriance to the river's banks, it is all you can desire for rich river scenery ; and the view from Richmond Hill is certainly one of the most glorious of the kind that can be conceived, such an excess of fertile beauty as no pencil can represent, and you wonder at the audacity of any painter pretending to do it.  Ask dear mother if she remembers it, and if it be not as I describe.

" For a quiet, little, less-pretending place of great beauty we like Highgate, and should not be disinclined to take up our abode there.  A modest cottage in a garden buried among trees would be the height of my ambition. How happy should I be to make thee and thine welcome in such a spot at Highgate !

" I hope thy dear children are all well.  What a great deal Anna Mary could tell her cousins if they were but near !  She has been a happy and privileged child, and I think is much better for her journey."


" *Dec.* 9, 1833.—No ! I did not expect you would like the baby's name, but you must call him Middleton.  It is quite curious to hear remarks on the said name. ' Well, what is he called ? ' one person asks.  ' Claude Middleton.'  ' Ha ! Claude *is* a pretty name, but I don't quite like Middleton.'  Then another says, ' Claude !  Dear me, it is a new name !  I don't think I quite like it !'  I remark, however, that there are two who like Claude to one that likes Middleton.  Poor old nurse is quite perplexed about the name. She calls him Claus, and Lord, and supposes it to be French. It was given out at Monthly Meeting as Claudy.

"You are very kind to take so much interest in the 'History of Priestcraft.' It is doing wonderfully well. A new edition, with three additional chapters and great improvements, will, William hopes, be out by the opening of Parliament."

"*January* 1834.—I wish I could send you some specimens of Anna Mary's drawings. She is now illustrating my 'Seven Temptations.' She designs heads to illustrate the different characters. William has them with him in London, and has astonished several artists with them. Dear child! it is a fine talent, and, I doubt not, given for a good purpose.

"William has been in London for the last week. If you see the London papers, you will have noticed his name mentioned for good or evil according to the politics of the paper. Joseph Gilbert and he were delegates from this place to the great meeting in London. He has attended several other meetings, and been so warmly received that in one instance he was obliged to come down from the platform before he could put an end to the people's marks of approbation."

Until the publication of the "History of Priestcraft" my husband had lived in great privacy in Nottingham, where the Radical portion of the population now claimed him as their champion. This led to his being deputed, in January 1834, with the Rev. Joseph Gilbert—the husband of Ann Taylor, joint-authoress with her sister Jane of the charming "Original Poems for Infant

Minds"—and a third Advanced Liberal, Mr. Hugh Hunter, to present to Government a petition from Nottingham for the disestablishment of the Church.*  They had in consequence an interview with Earl Grey, and presented their memorial praying for the separation of Church and State.  His Lordship, after reading the petition, told the deputation that he was sorry to find the expression of such sweeping measures, which would embarrass the Ministers, alarm both Houses of Parliament, and startle the country.  He wished they had confined themselves to the removal of those disabilities connected with marriage, burial, registration, and such matters, for on these heads there existed, both in himself and his colleagues, every disposition to relieve them.  He further added, that if personal disabilities were removed, he could not conceive what actual grievance would press upon Dissenters.  Did they want entirely to do away with all establishment of religion ?

The delegate, who, as a Friend, had been brought up to reject all dependence on "a man-made Ministry" and the outward ceremonies of religion, and who believed that compulsory payments for the propagation and support of Christianity were not sanctioned by its Divine Founder, replied from his conscience, "That was precisely what they desired."  On this Earl Grey declared de-

---

* We are told in the "Autobiography and other Memorials of Mrs. Gilbert," edited by her son, Josiah Gilbert, 1874, vol. ii. p. 129, that "the first public meeting in the kingdom to consider the abolition of a Church Establishment was held in Nottingham in 1834, and Mr. Gilbert moved the first resolution, in which he endeavoured to set the tone of the meeting, and to imbue it with his own religious spirit.  A deputation to Earl Grey was decided upon, a leading member of which was Mr. William Howitt.  The blunt straightforwardness, racy English, and ready tact in his interview with the Premier tell with quite dramatic effect, even in the dull pages of the 'Annual Register.'"

cidedly that he should give his strenuous opposition to every attempt to remove the Establishment. He belonged to the Church, and he would stand by it to the best of his ability. He considered it the sacred duty of every Government to maintain an establishment of religion.

"People are not so easily frightened at changes now-a-days," replied William Howitt, adding that "to establish one sect in preference to another was to establish a party and not a religion."

My husband held the opinion that if a State religion be deemed advisable for each nation, it should for the Irish, owing to the belief of the majority, be Catholic; and he felt a deep concern at the coercion sometimes practised on them to enforce an alien creed. In this he had a warm sympathiser in my mother, who, from an early experience in Wales, had learnt a wise method of treating the Irish. She had heard, when a child, a gentleman say to her father at Cyfarthfa, "Mr. Wood, the Welsh are a sensitive people. They still consider themselves a conquered nation. You may lead them by a fine thread, but I defy any man to draw or drag them with a cart-rope." Her father had acted upon the hint, and no people were, in consequence, more esteemed by all classes than he and his wife. At one time the Uttoxeter vestry made it a rule that Irish labourers passing through the town should not be relieved at the vagrant office. Mr. Bladon, a highly respected draper, went, therefore, in haste to my father to fix on some mode of relief, and they jointly undertook to provide a small fund, could any one be found to act as relieving officer. My mother immediately offered her services, and, aided by her husband, assisted in the course of time four hundred Irish.

Famine was then prevalent in their country, and she

took care to inquire of each applicant how much he or his friends had received of the money sent from England. She always obtained the same answer; the funds were entrusted to the Protestant clergy, who refused to dispense them to those who did not attend their ministry. My mother, warning the labourers to speak the truth, as she should commit the statements to paper and make inquiry, carefully noted the name and address of each clergyman mentioned. Joseph Burtt, a Friend connected with Ireland, after assuring her that she had been terribly imposed upon, took the written statements for the purpose of obtaining their contradiction or confirmation. He brought them back the next time he visited Uttoxeter, with a written remark affixed to each, such as— "This is true," "This is correct," "Sad but true." Nor did she ever forget how the Irish labourers, calling after my father's death, on hearing the tidings, knelt down and, with tears, prayed for his soul.

My husband combined with his intense appreciation and love of nature, and his affection for all that was good and true, a fiery detestation of every form of human injustice or oppression; and this made him a violent partisan in real and sometimes in imaginary wrongs. His hatred of what he felt to be priestcraft had been engendered from infancy by the ignorance, brutality, and petty tyranny exercised by the incumbents in his native village, and whose conduct and ministrations were in most glaring contrast with those of his mother, the servant and consoler of the parish.

In Nottingham he found a warm ally in Mr. Benjamin Boothby, a powerful and remarkable man, of strong intellect and strong prepossessions, anti-Church to the core, philanthropic, and an active agent in the improvement of the borough.   Mrs. Boothby, a most excellent wife and mother, was much occupied with her family, so that whilst our husbands met frequently to discuss their views and arrange plans of action, we had the pleasure of seeing each other only occasionally.

My husband had published his "History of Priestcraft" with Effingham Wilson, and I shortly afterwards made my appearance from that house in a very humble guise, a small square volume, with poor woodcuts, entitled "Sketches of Natural History;" in a very unattractive form, I thought, in comparison with Mrs. Austin's "The Story Without an End," which Wilson had just before published.   My husband used to amuse our children with off-hand explanations of Bewick's vignettes.   It is impossible to describe the fascination of those evening hours, when the father, with the children clustered round him or on his knee, told the imaginary story of the wonderful picture, only a couple of inches, perhaps, in dimension : the two old cronies talking together leaning on their spades—the blind fiddlers—the village lads riding astride on the gravestones—the pigs in the garden, and so on. It was a never-ending series of village life, related in a rich comic vein, or with true pathos and tenderness.   My little poetical sketches had reference to Bewick's woodcuts of birds and animals, and were written down because the children liked them.   They still live, and other children read them, under one of the various titles with which Messrs. Nelson are too fond of disguising old friends.

To my sister Anna I write, February 28, 1834 :—
"Have you chanced to see a good notice of 'Seven Temptations' in the last week's *Athenæum*, the only

review which has yet appeared, excepting the *Literary Gazette*, which was designed, in the technical phrase, to 'damn the book'? The cry is, 'Poetry don't sell;' and perhaps it does not as much as it did. If, however, my volume is unsuccessful, I suppose I shall adopt the cry rather than allow that mine is not either good or original. The new edition of the 'History of Priest-craft' will be out in a very few days. It contains four entirely new chapters, and is much improved."

" *Wilford, Aug.* 4, 1834.—We have again taken up our abode in our accustomed little old cottage, and now that the season has been unusually dry, find the place more agreeable than ever. Wilford is a pleasant village, within a mile of Clifton Grove, by the river-side, which river, in going to Nottingham, we cross by a ferry, far pleasanter and more picturesque than the best of bridges. Alfred is a sunburnt, active lad; but what a dialect he has picked up—'Oh! papa, oi've had such a *nois roide!*' However, that will be got rid of, and the stock of health and strength, I trust, will remain and give him a good start for the winter. Anna Mary rides capitally on her pony—a perfect beauty. It is amusing to me, and rather flattering, to hear people's remarks as I come after, all divided in admiration between horse and rider. Now for Claude, and I shall have gone through the family. He has very little hair, and what he has is so white, that his head looks like an ivory ball; nevertheless, he has a sweet face, a merry smile, and funny little ways, that make one love him very dearly.

'Our own children in our eyes are dearer than the sun.'

"This line of Wordsworth's reminds me of the death

of Coleridge.  It is not an untimely death.  He has been like a shock of corn full ripe ; nevertheless, I mourn his departure.  It is like the breaking up of that old brotherhood of great poets, who have made poetry honourable, and been like stars in literature.  Wordsworth one naturally looks for next.  Their latter days ·have been clouded by looking forward to expected evil.  The aspect of things is naturally gloomy enough, both to Southey and Wordsworth.  I wish they could take a hopeful view of the changes that are progressing, for one likes not that such fine spirits should be darkened in their closing years, for they have brightened many hearts, and, strangely enough, helped, though they cannot see it, to bring about the revolutions that are now coming upon society."

"*Nottingham, Jan.* 11, 1835.—You will be glad to hear that a third edition of the 'Book of the Seasons' is preparing for the press, and that the whole edition of my 'Sketches of Natural History' is about sold, so that I shall presently have a fresh one.  William is going on with his 'Rural Life of England ;' that will be a work to thy mind.  His 'Pantika, Legends of the Ancient World,' is just finishing printing.  You, I expect, will not like them ; this I say to anticipate your judgment. Still, if you like Milton's 'Paradise Lost,' you cannot disapprove of these.

"Thou would be sorry to hear of poor Abby Whitlark's illness.  She is no better.  It makes my heart ache to see her wasted to a skeleton and aged in countenance, but with large, beautiful eyes still full of youthfulness, and to hear her deep, hollow voice, which sounds like tones from a sepulchre ; to see that she is surely on her deathbed, and to hear the merry voices and hearty laugh

of those five little creatures below.  If ever there was
an affectionate - hearted, grateful being, it is she.  I
cannot tell thee how much she feels any kindness or
even ordinary attentions.  When I see her, and feel at
how little expense of time I can make a fellow-creature
thankful even to tears, I feel as if one owed human
nature more than one is willing to give it.  A kindly
smile, and even a passing glance of sympathy, would do
much to make the burden of suffering lighter.  Human
nature, with all its weaknesses and sorrows, is a holy
thing, and our common brotherhood a sacred tie and full
of many deep obligations of love, pity, and sympathy.
The man who does most good to his kind approaches
nearest the Divinity, and ought to be reckoned the
greatest and noblest of men.  When people estimate
worth by this standard, the world will have made a vast
step towards a better order of things."

"*Feb.* 10.—Thou wilt see the announcement of William's
next work, ' The Rural Life of England.'  It is full of
English scenery and feeling, and of everything that
makes a country life delightful, with a fine spirit of
human sympathy running through it.  I am busy, too,
in writing ' A Year in the Country ; or, The Chronicle
of Wood Leighton '—a great effort for me, being nothing
less than three prose volumes.  I began it about New
Year's Day, and have finished one volume.  It is an
engagement with Mr. Bentley.  Wood Leighton is
Uttoxeter, and I have imagined a legacy of property
there, coming to us from an old bachelor relative.  The
place is all new to us.  We go to take possession, find
there an old housekeeper—our own Nanny.  Finally, we
are so pleased, we determine to remain a year.  Then

follow descriptions of the country and all kinds of character and story.  Tell me what thou thinks of it."

"*March* 1835.—I was glad to hear that good opinion of the 'Seven Temptations.'  It is encouraging to know, when one's desire has been to serve the cause of virtue, as was mine in writing those dramas, that one has not been beside oneself.  I could say something on the subject of 'The Old Man,' and thus far allow me.  If old age were free from moral weaknesses, it would be wicked in any writer to represent it otherwise ; but why should not its besetting frailties—a repining, querulous spirit—be spoken of ?  There are elderly people, dear Anna, who have felt in that drama a strong lesson.

"Thou cannot conceive, dear love, how old times have come upon me while I have been creating events for my book of 'Wood Leighton.'  I tread again our old haunts. I have had something to do to disguise the names.  Of Daniel Neale I have a good deal ; and I think a pleasant paper might be written on the old women in the alms-houses, with their excellent names."

"*Nottingham, 9th Mo., 20th,* 1835.—William is about to write a series of papers on Friends, their domestic manners, opinions, and the state of the Society at large, for *Tait's Edinburgh Magazine,* at Mr. Tait's request, and which I think will be extremely interesting and useful.  They will give a more correct view of the Society in every respect than has ever been given before.  Do you see this magazine ?  It is a very good one, and contains articles every month on some topic of general and important interest, political or otherwise, which would, I am sure, interest Daniel.  Some of the very best articles William ever wrote are there, full of right-mindedness and true Christian benevolence.

"Dear mother will be curious to know what is done about our leaving Nottingham. Nothing at present, I am sorry to say."

"*November* 5, 1835.—You would receive a *Nottingham Review* this last week. It was sent for you to read 'The Death-cry of a Perishing Church,' an article which has made the town all alive this week. It seems as if the Archdeacon and William were never to cease their controversy. Samuel Fox is so delighted with the article, that he has had it printed on a large sheet of paper, and circulated gratis the whole town over."

"*December* 29, 1835.—Oh! dear Anna, how glad I should be to be able to peep in upon you, and see all those three young ones, who are strangers to me! Anna Mary has described dear little Alfred, with his beautiful eyes, so large and soft, with an expression like that of a lama, full of love and intelligence. I know the kind of eyes, such as thine were.

"Dear Anna, if anything particular occurs in your meeting respecting these questions of dissent amongst Friends, tell us, wilt thou? I do not mean that anything thou says is to be made use of in William's papers, but for our own information, for we like to know the truth. For my own part, I should be deeply sorry to involve myself in any party feeling, and am thankful to be out of the way of squabbles and dissensions, and to be able to live in a quiet state of Christian charity with all about us; still, I should like to know whether any persons in whom I am interested in Liverpool join the Beaconites."

On December 31, 1835, my husband, against his will, was elected by the Council an alderman of the borough of Nottingham, and was regarded by the Radical party as their chief representative. His political sentiments at this period are well reflected in his correspondence with our valued friend, Miss Bowles.

On April 25, 1835, addressing her at her place of abode, Buckland, Lymington, in the New Forest, he says :—

"I sincerely sympathise with you on the havoc made in your beautiful woody lanes. When Lord Denman gets into office, I shall use all my Radical influence to get a rat-catcher's place in your Forest. Then you and Mary and I will set our heads together, and write such things about it as shall make every oak-tree sacred. Not an axe shall be lifted upon a tree, except for the legitimate purpose of shipbuilding. When reform gets a little vent, depend upon it, it will not be so rampant as it is now. It is pent up, and therefore ready to break everything down that it can. It is chafed, and therefore puts itself in an attitude of destructiveness. When the mind and *gentlemanness* of the country see that reform must go on, they will gradually fall into its ranks, and infuse a little more taste, a little better blood, into the cause.

"The Whigs have a sort of mushroom liberality. They are liberal that they may be thought so, not for the love of it ; and the Radicals are more politicians than people of taste. These things will change for the better, I hope. Of one thing I am sure : the Whigs and Radicals have a great deal to learn with regard to the honour and the strength derived in respecting kin and party. For myself, I am as aristocratic about *old oaks* as you can be."

On February 9, 1836, he writes to the same correspondent :—

"We are anxious to know whether you have been progressing gloriously into the land of poetry or of that noble prose which you know so well how to write, what you have been speculating on, doing, or suffering.  In that sweet retirement of yours, what but thoughts and feelings for your own and general delight ought to spring up ?  If such a little paradise were mine, I would forget politics and be poetical and happy spite of Churches, Constitutions, Houses of Lords, Humes, or O'Connells. But it is my fate to be dragged into public botheration, and I shall never be free from it till I am free of Nottingham.  I am anxious to complete my 'Rural Life of England,' but am daily driven away from it by the nuisance of a Town Council that I sincerely wish at Van Diemen's Land.  I wish we lived near you.  I think our individual Radicalism and Toryism would then amalgamate into something very rational, very generous, and very beneficent.  I often think of your dear place and country, and the time I strolled about with you and sat with you on stiles in that fine autumn weather by woodland walk or hurrying stream with great affection. I should have valued that journey if it had left me only that pleasant memory, but it has left many ; and I sometimes talk to Mary of places and things that I encountered that fill her with poetry, some of which is already in print."

On March 6, 1836, I write to my sister :—

"Well do I remember, dearest Anna, how thou began to study botany by thyself from the Introduction to Miller's ' Gardeners' Dictionary,' before I was wrought up to the proper pitch to begin with thee.  I remember many things besides—the beautiful flowers thou drew, and all thy pure elegant tastes so like thyself. I was very different to thee, dearest. Thou wast more meditative; thou loved Nature better than society: I society better than Nature. I remember it well as a child.

"If we cannot visit you, do thou visit us. What walks we would have, and how thou wouldst enjoy this country! for it is pleasant, though less Arcadian than our own Staffordshire scenery. Thou shouldst sit and talk about all old feelings and old pleasures, not only within four brick walls, but on dry sunny banks, in fields, and among woods and by watersides. Dearest Anna, to think of it only makes me quite impatient, and in thought I have thee with me at every one of my favourite places: at dear Annesley, the most melancholy of all old houses; at Thrumpton, with its grand English hall, its fair and flourishing village, and its views like the most beautiful of Turner's landscapes. Then, to go no farther off, to have thee in our meadows, at Wilford and Clifton, and even in our park, that would be a delight. I know that, however much in appearance we may be changed, thou wouldst find our tastes and manner of life as simple, and, what is far more than either, our religious opinions and feeling entirely accordant with thine.

"I want to make thee, and more particularly dear mother, see, as I have done long, that I am not out of my line of duty in devoting myself so much to literary occupation. Just lately things were sadly against us. Dear William could not sleep at night. The days were dark and gloomy. Altogether I was quite at my wits' end. I turned over in my mind what I could do next, for, till William's 'Rural Life' was finished, we had nothing available. Then I bethought myself of all those little verses and prose tales that for years I had written for the juvenile annuals. It seemed probable to me I might turn them to account. In about a week I had nearly all the poetry copied; and then who should come to Nottingham but John Darton. He fell into the idea immediately, took what I had copied up to London with him, and I am to have a hundred and fifty guineas for them. I must call this a signal interference of Providence for us. Is it not a cause of thankfulness, dearest sister, and have I not reason to feel that in thus writing I am fulfilling my duty?

"I do not know whether you would see a *Nottingham Review* I sent two weeks ago to mother, containing an abstract of William's speech at the Irish meeting. The effect of that speech was really wonderful. I was not well, and could not go out, or I should have attended the meeting, and seen the effect myself. I am told that the audience was quite carried away—now all enthusiasm, again perfectly breathless, now all in tears. The greatest and richest men wept like children; one old man covered his head with his handkerchief to weep in private. Yet when William entered the hall he had no idea of saying more than about half-a-dozen sentences. He said it seemed to him like inspiration, and he wondered at himself; and even when he sat down in the thunder of applause, he himself wept, and returned thanks to the Almighty that he had been so enabled to advocate a great cause."

"*March* 22.—This day I was looking over the advertisements in a newspaper, and saw the Bible advertised which thou said you were taking in; the very sight of it filled my heart anew with affection, and I determined to work

hard and finish a pinafore I had in hand, and so secure
an hour in the evening to finish my letter. Now, therefore, I am writing, the children being in bed, and William
gone to meet a committee anent a grand O'Connell
dinner, which we are to have on Easter Monday in Nottingham; a very great concern it is to be, and one in
which I take vast interest. I will send you an account
of it by newspaper.

"I do not know whether I ever told thee that I have
a district which I visit for the Nottingham Provident
Society. I used even to question whether such visita-
tions were proper for females. My opinion, however,
altered with consideration, and I volunteered my services. Now, I must confess I never had more entire
satisfaction with anything I ever did than with this.
I cannot tell thee the almost love—I suppose it is
*charity*—I feel for my poor people, nor the benefit I
have been able to do to some of them. I say this not
in boasting, but in thankfulness, because I never could
have imagined, with the little we have to spare, our
being able to serve so essentially any poor families. I
have actually shed tears both of sorrow and joy with
these poor people. Then there is another view in
which this work interests me, but in a far inferior degree, and that is in the variety of character which we
find among the poor. In a common way, one looks on
them as on a flock of sheep. All seem alike. All
have many children, little leisure, poor clothes, and are
all more or less dirty. But one does not sit with them
many five or ten minutes once a week without soon
detecting very marked and curious varieties, and hearing many most touching and interesting bits of family
history, of trouble or sorrow, or equally interesting

display of human nature, which has often made me think better of my race for their sakes."

It was William Howitt's speech in the Town Hall on the Irish question, in which he eloquently referred to O'Connell, that led to a spontaneous determination by the audience of inviting the "Liberator" down to a public dinner. He came, being met in the suburbs by a committee of gentlemen in carriages, and conveyed through the town amid the acclamations of immense crowds. This visit brought us into personal and very friendly contact with Mr. and Mrs. O'Connell.

My husband at this time, when most anxious to complete his "Rural Life of England," was daily debarred from literature by the duties imposed on him in the Town Council. We therefore deemed it prudent for him to withdraw from the arena of public debate to a more secluded place of residence, where, unconcerned in municipal affairs and national measures, he could, in the study of Nature and the pursuit of general literature, laudably satisfy his intellect and his affections.

On August 30, 1836, I write from the village of Wilford to Miss Bowles :—

"This letter must be one of explanation; and first of all you must know that we have left Nottingham as a place of residence, but are now returned to it for a few days after a three months' tour in the north of England and Scotland. On our return we found your volume, for which accept our sincerest thanks. We have not yet read it steadily, for we have been back only a very few days, and we had our dear children to gather again about us, to talk and listen and idle with them ; therefore this letter of mine is but to inform you that your volume is

received, and will have an early perusal; then you shall
hear again from us, and at that time I hope to be able
to tell you of our whereabouts, which is to be somewhere in the neighbourhood of London, and to which, as
you will believe, we are impatient to be hastening, for as
yet our habitation is unselected, and we have a pleasant
vision of being settled down in our new home before
winter.

"We heard of your volume in several places during
our rambles—in Liverpool, at Rydal Mount, and especially
at Edinburgh. It was a great pleasure to find you spoken
of everywhere, not merely as the author of a new volume,
but as a fireside favourite. You would have rebelled, I
suppose, had you heard, as we did, Professor Wilson,
in his most unqualified manner, prefer you to Mrs.
Hemans.

"I should extremely like to give you some idea of our
most delightful journey, but that I hardly know how to
begin. A great deal of it you will find embodied in
'The Rural Life of England;' to gain information for
which work the journey was especially taken, at least
in the north of England. We saw a great deal of *the
people*, especially in the Yorkshire dales and in Northumberland, and much to interest and please us. Above
all, we received much kindness from persons whom we
met as strangers. Our journey in Scotland was entirely
of curiosity, not of business, and accordingly we moved
along much more rapidly, and dwelt much more on
generals than particulars. Some time or other we may,
perhaps, have the great pleasure of talking over with
you our visit to Staffa and Iona, our sail up the Cale-
donian Canal; our Sunday at Kilmorack, during the
administration of the Sacrament to the Gaelic congrega-

tion; certainly one of the most striking ceremonials—
the time, place, and people being taken into consideration—that we ever witnessed.

"What a fine incident is that of yours which you call
'The Mechanic!' I could tell you much that we have
seen in the lives of the poor that you could tell as
touchingly. Human hearts are holy things."

In connection with the pleasant tour above alluded
to, I would add, that at Blackburn we visited my beloved
sister Emma and her husband, Harrison Alderson, cousin
to Daniel Harrison. We then paid a most interesting
visit to Stonyhurst College. We drove, likewise, tandem
with a young Friend, who was anxious to show us all
the wonders of the wild Yorkshire scenery round Ingle-
borough, by Weathercote Cave, Hurtle-pot, and Gingle-
pot. We wandered amongst the simple, primitive dales-
people. After a delightful stay of several days at
Rydal Mount with the Wordsworths, we proceeded to
Newcastle-on-Tyne, on a pilgrimage to the haunts of
Thomas Bewick. His two daughters, maiden ladies,
became, from the date of this visit, particular friends
of ours.

We went to the ruins of Lindisfarne Abbey, in Holy
Island; to Warkworth, remembering the delight which
Anna and I had in our first knowledge of "The Hermit
of Warkworth," whilst my husband had rejoiced over the
same beautiful ballad as a schoolboy at Ackworth. To
many another romantic or historic spot we wandered,
which my husband afterwards graphically described in
his "Visits to Remarkable Places."

We had a delightful stay in Edinburgh. Immediately
after our arrival, a public dinner was given to Campbell,

the poet, at which the committee requested my husband's attendance, and that he would take a share in the proceedings of the evening, by proposing as a toast, "Wordsworth, Southey, and Moore." To this he consented.

This banquet was our first introduction to Professor Wilson ("Christopher North") and his family. I sat in the gallery with Mrs. Wilson and her daughters, one of whom was engaged to Professor Ferrier, who likewise took part in the speeches below. We could not but remark the wonderful difference, not only in the outer man, but in the whole character of mind and manner, between Professor Wilson and Campbell—the one so hearty, outspoken, and joyous, the other so petty and trivial.

The Wilsons were extremely kind to us during our stay in Edinburgh, as indeed were each of the several classes of literary society which gave such a distinguishing character to that intellectual centre. There was the Blackwood clique, to which, of course, the Wilsons belonged. Then the set who composed Mr. Tait's stronghold for his magazine. By Mr. Tait we were invited to a tripe supper, and introduced to Mrs. Johnstone and the rest of his local contributors. I found it very agreeable and amazingly entertaining in its way. There was the group connected with *Chambers's Journal;* and, happily for us, Robert Chambers, that most genial, intelligent, and interesting companion, made himself our *cicerone* in Edinburgh, showing us every place of interest, and presenting us to every person of character or note, not omitting Mrs. Maclehose, the Clarinda of Burns. She was then a very old woman, and, pleased by our call and our admiration of the poet, wished us to drink out of a couple of glasses given to her by Burns.  This, however, her servant would not allow ; she locked them up in the cupboard whence they had been produced for exhibition, put the key in her pocket, and brought in their stead three ordinary wine-glasses.

There was a fourth little group in this wonderful old city that showed us much kindness, the Friends' family of William Miller, the Nature-loving artist and admirable engraver.  I have a most pleasant remembrance of break-fasting with these excellent Friends : the abundantly supplied table, the pure white linen, the kind, courteous, quiet manners, with the reading of the Scriptures and the solemn pause of silence that ended it.  There was a young poet of great promise in Edinburgh, by name Robert Nicoll.  We took the liberty of introducing him to the Millers.  He accompanied us on this occasion, and was very much impressed by the peculiar character of breakfast in a Friends' family.

From Edinburgh we went to the Western Isles, taking the steamer at Glasgow.  Our experiences at Staffa, Iona, later at Kilmorack and the field of Culloden, are all duly narrated by my husband in his "Visits to Remarkable Places."

We must have walked some hundreds of miles on this tour, than which I can imagine nothing more delightful. I am thankful that now, at the age of eighty-six, I can still retain such an unbroken sense of the Divine goodness to His two unworthy children ; who did not, I fear, though they enjoyed the good which He so liberally bestowed, remember that it all came from His gracious hand, and thus did not thank Him as He deserved.

# CHAPTER VIII.

## AT ESHER.

### *1836–1840.*

WE took possession at Michaelmas 1836, almost without self-exertion, of a charming home at Esher, in Surrey, procured by the instrumentality of our kind and efficient friends, Mr. and Mrs. Alaric Watts. They had removed from London to Ember Lodge, Thames Ditton, and at the distance of three miles had seen a house which they rightly conjectured would suit us.

West End Cottage—for such it was called—was an old-fashioned, roomy dwelling, lying at the foot of the ridge, on which extends the pleasant, mile-long village of Esher. It had a young, well-stocked orchard, a most productive garden, convenient paddock, and a fine meadow by the river Mole ; with the right of fishing and boating to the extent of seven miles. The furniture was to be disposed of with the lease ; and it being but scanty, we supplemented it with purchases made at Hampton Court, and in 1837 at the sale of Talleyrand's furniture in London ; for the old and noted ambassador had returned to France and retired from public life.

We were speedily settled in our charming home ; and I had the delight of sharing the children's joy over cow, pig, poultry, pony and chaise ; and my husband's satisfaction in his study lined with books, and in the attractive features of the neighbourhood.

VOL. I. R

On December 3, 1836, I write to my sister :—"Thou wilt be glad to know, dearest Anna, that our prospects are brighter than ever they have been, and our income will be better than it was in our most flourishing days at Nottingham. In consequence of an article that William wrote on Dymond's 'Christian Morality,' Joseph Hume, the Member for Middlesex, wrote to him, and has opened a most promising connection for him with a new Radical newspaper, *The Constitutional.* O'Connell seems determined to make him the editor of the *Dublin Review;* * and even when he just lost his wife, wrote him, on November 27, a most kind letter—and a letter which has materially promoted his interest with the party. I cannot but see the hand of Providence in our leaving Nottingham. All has turned out admirably. We have, indeed, much to make us thankful. A new life seems opened before us ; and I sleep as I never have slept since I was young."

"*Feb.* 9, 1837.—It is very long since I wrote to thee. It is quite astonishing, and yet when I consider the vast quantity of needlework I have had to do, it is not so very astonishing after all. When we first came here, establishing us and helping to do the upholstery work quite filled up my time. Then when that was done, and I began to look at our several wardrobes, the mending and making had accumulated to such a degree, that I was . like a hardworking seamstress, sewing from morning till night, and never reading a word of any book. I never led so unintellectual a life. I have not yet even a mantua-

---

* O'Connell deemed William Howitt admirably adapted to deal with political and literary topics ; but there was, as he affirmed, a most serious obstacle to his becoming the editor of the *Dublin Review,* for it was " emphatically and polemically Catholic."

maker, for Esher is but a village, and I have no great notion of village gown-making.

"And so dear Mary and Margaret Ann are gone to Ackworth. Thou wilt, I am sure, be much interested with the general style of the school. I was when I visited it with William. The very concourse of children brought with it the feeling to my heart of how much domestic affection was bound up in each little individual. How dear it was to some hearth and hearts, though perhaps widely separated from them! was a reflection that filled my eyes with tears. Looking on the school in this way it was a most pleasing sight, to say nothing of the general cleanliness, wholesomeness, order, and cheerfulness of the whole establishment. But then of its details I can say nothing. The long, unbroken school term, without a holiday, seemed to me melancholy, and I should fear the pupils' notions becoming sectarian and contracted. As to thy dear children being so long exiled from home, I hope thou wilt do as thou said, go over and see them at other times than the General Meeting. Give my best love to them. I do most earnestly hope they may be happy.

"Nothing has given me a more unpleasant confirmation of my opinion of Friends' contracted and sectarian feeling than our experience in this neighbourhood, including the town of Kingston. Some Friends came from that meeting to announce to us the receipt of our certificate, with the utmost solemnity and shut-up-ness. They never said they were glad to have an addition to their meeting, that they hoped our residence had proved so far agreeable, or that it might do so, or even that we might have our health. They had no congratulations, no good wishes. Perhaps they felt none. But if so, it was not according to my notions of Christian charity, that wishes good to all men. They warned us against literature and politics, and when William inadvertently used the word Radical, the man-Friend asked *if he thought that word a desirable one for a Friend to use.* Everything, with these Kingston Friends, was warning and prohibition. They would not read books. They would not go into society. They would not look at a newspaper, nay, even would not admit a newspaper into their houses. Now, is not this a miserable state to be in? Yet these are among the approved and most orthodox members.

"This county of Surrey is really a most beautiful one, and at the same time very unlike a Midland county. There the generality of the land is farms, one farm after another, with their homely houses over a whole district, and a gentleman's seat coming in now and then as a grand variety. A common, too, in such counties is quite a novelty, and so is a village green. Here, on the contrary, all is one gentleman's seat after another, with beautiful cottages and mansions in the midst of woods and grounds; and the intervals seem to be made up of vast commons covered with moss—such moss!—finest heather, and about us, with what is now become native to the soil, the Scotch fir. It grows in woods open to the roadside, and in which we can ramble with as much freedom as if they were our own.

"Then, besides this, all the meaner buildings are so quaint and picturesque. They have such a Saxon character about them, one can fancy them such as stood there in the days of Alfred. Many of them wood, with every variety of roof. It must also be a glorious land for a botanist or entomologist.

"William has already begun to rejoice in the voices of such a great variety of birds, even in our own garden. How thy dear children, with their strong household affections, would have been delighted with the robins and the linnets that the severe weather made our pensioners for crumbs! I do not remember at Uttoxeter the birds coming very near to be fed. Here, as we sat at breakfast, we saw them congregating from all round, as if they saw through the glass that the meal was begun. Then one bold old robin, the king of the beggars, sat on the window-sill, peeped in, and if not immediately attended to, tapped on the glass, and would even make a most angry scuffling, being most clamorous in his demands."

"*Esher, May* 30, 1837.—I do not think there ever was a time when I had so strong a love for my own kith and kin, or such a yearning desire to see them. Some of the Friends here are ten times more formal and dress ten times more absurdly than in the North or the Midland Counties. For instance, I have seen men-Friends all in drab, with horn buttons and little pudding-crowned hats; and women there are who will not have a gather or plait in any garment, and who wear cloth bonnets.

"We have been up to London to attend one or two sittings of Yearly Meeting. But as it was Seventh-day and we not very knowing in such matters, we found the regular sittings were not held—at least of the women-Friends. I therefore spent the time with Christiana Price at the White Hart, opposite the meeting, which house, I dare say, dear mother will recollect as a great resort of Friends. I was very much entertained by the passing in and out of the dowager-like old lady-Friends, who came sweeping in, with their long, dark serge gowns and large crape shawls ; the assiduous attendance of their quiet, well-fed servants ; and, above all, with the original style of conversation of Christiana Price.  She is a very pleasant woman, and retains a most kind and delightful recollection of thy visit to Swansea.  We talked it all over.  She related many anecdotes, to which I had to respond, 'Oh yes; and I can tell thee something more.'  Very amusing indeed it was to see the strong and faithful impression all that thou had told me had made on my mind.  Christiana said it was like an echo of her youth coming back.  I saw her brother Joseph also, and was very much entertained by his apparent astonishment at my dress.

"Among the stately old ladies was Elizabeth Fox, of Falmouth ; I think a really handsome woman.  She was very inquisitive after dear mother.  She said she knew her well in their young days, and loved her dearly, and had stayed some time with her before any of us were born.

"Saturday night we spent with some friends of ours near Tottenham.  In going there we passed a long array of the wealthy Friends' houses.  Tottenham is a sort of court-end, and all looked so bright, rich, and well-to-do.  There were such traces of wheels in and out, and such a quietly dawdling in and out of stout, handsomely-dressed Friends.  There lives William Ball, who married the rich Ann Dale, and whom we had seen at the Wordsworths', for he is building a mansion at Rydal.

"On First-day morning we went to meeting, and to Devonshire House, rather thoughtlessly, for Newington would have been the right meeting to attend to see the grandees of the Society.  But I was glad we went as we did.  The sight of Friends in meeting is beautiful.  The women-Friends in such multitudes, all so pure, so gentle, so sweet-looking.  Nothing is more striking than the perfect quietness with which they sit, hundreds of them, side by side, like images in marble, all in the same style, with their heads a little inclined on one side, and the head always looking small in proportion to the body, and the effect of that is good.

"Sarah Grubb's sermon, however, was the strangest I ever heard, full of denunciation, and in a spirit of animosity and division.  There she stood, a good-looking woman, in garments sufficiently flowing to give effect to her figure and gestures, raising her arm and pouring forth a really eloquent, but to my mind un-Christian, sermon, and, like some ancient sibyl, repeating in a high, shrill key her denunciations, which were meant to be prophetic.  'It is coming! It is coming! It is coming!' she said, speaking of judgment on the Seceders, and so continually, that it really produced an effect on the meeting.  It was such a sermon as Christ could not have preached.  The Seceders may be wrong, but they have, many of them, erred in the desire to do right; and with a feeling of this kind they ought to be spoken of, especially in public, with consideration.

"Our garden is now so lovely that I feel as if we had no business to have all its beauty to ourselves.  The lilacs are out; so is the broom, white and yellow, and the guelder-rose, that tree for which we had so great a desire at Uttoxeter.  Our garden would of itself furnish us with employment; and it seems to me that it would be such a pure and heavenly life, especially if we at the same time wrote books that did the world good.

"Now I must give thee an anecdote to prove how much

I think of thee. There is a large guelder-rose in the middle of one long border, and under that tree nothing grows. The boughs almost reach the ground, but not quite, so that the dry bare soil under it looks unsightly. We had often said, 'What must we set here?' and we talked of violets and primroses. However, one night I dreamed I walked with thee in the garden—how I wish I could! and I asked thy opinion; and thou said, just as was natural, 'If I were you I would plant lilies of the valley.' It was the very thing that was wanted, for of all flowers this situation would suit them best. As we had not a single lily of the valley in the garden, William brought some from Nottingham, and they are now flourishing and looking green and pleasant. Surely thou hast been in spirit in our garden, seen that dry ground, and thought of the lilies."

"*Esher, July* 28, 1837.—Dearest Anna, we have had a great disappointment, and a great source of uneasiness and anxiety, from what promised when we first came here to be a satisfactory engagement. I mean William's employment on *The Constitutional.* He was engaged to write for it at Mr. Hume's instance. He did more, in fact, for it than any other person about the office. He worked and wrote like any slave. In the end, after a series of the most harassing and vexatious conduct on the part of the newspaper company, he was swindled out of every farthing. Oh! it was a most mortifying and humiliating thing to see men professing liberal and honest principles act so badly. As thou may suppose, this was a great blow; and the very money we had calculated upon for our summer expenses was not forthcoming.

"A month ago, when in the very depth of discourage-ment and low spirits, I set about a little volume for Darton, to be called 'Birds and Flowers,' and have pretty nearly finished it. William in the meantime has finished his 'Rural Life,' and sold the first edition to Longmans."

My husband, in some private memoranda, says regard-ing his connection with *The Constitutional:*—

"It was an attempt to establish a daily Liberal paper which should especially support the political, economical, and financial reforms advocated by Joseph Hume. The misfortune was, that it was commenced without sufficient capital.

"Joseph Hume requested me to write one or two articles weekly. Busy as I was with my own more agree-able labours, I did not feel justified in absolutely refusing to lend a helping hand to a good cause. The papers used to be sent down to me in the morning, and I had to read them and have my article ready by ten o'clock in the evening, when the post left for town. *The Constitu-tional* did not seem to make its way. I heard more and more of many difficulties. Sad news was soon given me by the editor. There were no funds. The proprietors were going on in desperation, without being able to pay a single contributor. He told me that they had a corres-pondent in Portugal, who had been sent out to report on the disturbances there, who was totally destitute of funds, and was writing the most imploring entreaties for remit-tances. He said Laman Blanchard, who had a wife and five children dependent on his pen, was writing daily articles, and for months had not been paid.

"One day Major Carmichael Smith, the active manager, told me that he had sent for his son-in-law, Mr. Thackeray, from Paris, where I understood he was correspondent for a London daily paper, I think the *Morning Post*, to come and take the editorship of the paper. Just as I was going out of the office, which was in Fleet Street, I met on the stairs a tall, thin young man in a long dark-blue cloak, and with a nose that seemed some time to have had a blow that had flattened its bridge. I turned back and had some conversation with him, anxious to know how he, Thackeray, proposed to carry on a daily paper without any funds and already deeply in debt. He did not seem to know any more than I did. I thought to myself that his father-in-law had not done him much service in taking him from a profitable post for the vain business of endeavouring to buoy up a desperate speculation. How much longer *The Constitutional* struggled on I know not. That was the first time I ever heard of or ever saw William Makepeace Thackeray. I withdrew from the paper."

"My dear Brother"—I write to Richard Howitt from Esher, June 18, 1837—"thou hints of low spirits that *will* haunt thee, and a solitary feeling that *will* sadden thy heart in spite of the crowds that are about thee. God help us! we all have the same; and at this present moment, with anxieties about many things, I feel as heavy-hearted as if there was no hope left in the world. Depend upon it, then, dear Richard, we can, and do, sympathise with thee, and I think of thee many a time till my heart aches with affectionate interest.

"But what just at this particular moment determined me to write was this. I came up here into my own quiet room resolved to get on with a poem I have in hand, but really the very power of poetry seemed gone, the very springs were dry. I took up thy volume of poems to freshen myself; for there are particular books that do me a great deal of good.  My table is strewn over with them— the Bible, Keats, Shelley, Tennyson, Wordsworth, Barry Cornwall, and thyself.  I just run over their names as my eye glances on them.

"Thou canst not conceive the delight I have had in reading this little volume this morning, nor how it seemed to clear away the clouds that lay on my spirit.  I feel as if I should find 'the way open,' as Friends say, to write again, and as if my soul would find pleasure in it.

"Richard, thou once set off and walked into Yorkshire. I know we thought it quite an extraordinary thing, but is it to remain the one extraordinary journey of many years?  Is there no possibility of thy mounting the coach and coming in another direction?  We see many things in our neighbourhood that would fill thy soul with poetry.  The kind of woodland that one feels the spirit of in Keats, leafy and *lush*, full of primroses below and nightingales above; full of cottages and gentlemen's houses, with their flower-gardens sloping into green fields, bordering on commons too—and such commons as sweetly picturesque as the Forest of Ardennes.  I am sure the scenery of Keats's poetry was gathered up in such as this.

"A thousand pities that we, any of us, should have the enjoyment of such scenery spoiled to us by devouring cares and anxieties.  Yet it is plain enough to my understanding, that if thou would but leave Nottingham for a fortnight and come here, we too would have a holiday of the heart, and turn out day after day to a thorough enjoyment of the good things that surround us.

"Only think of those beautiful poems thou wrote to Anna Mary when a child.  If thou could love her then, how much more is she worthy to be loved now! She has grown up fulfilling all the promises of her childhood, and is such an one as thou wouldst hold pleasant communion with. Mr. Pemberton described her as 'a bit of religion dropped down from heaven to earth'—very quaint, I grant, but very expressive.

"I am afraid of urging thy coming lest I should seem troublesome, but it is a thing I earnestly covet."

Again turning to my husband's memoranda, he remarks :—

"We took long drives in our pony-chaise over the heathy commons and through the woods. On one occasion, being in the oak-woods on Bookham Common, which have, or had, an undergrowth of holly, and in spring abound with nightingales, and are richly carpeted with violets and primroses, we heard the hounds coming up behind us. Peg, our pony, was generally rather dull, and was at least twenty years old, having belonged to the Earl of Tyrconnel, who, after selling Claremont in 1802, had continued to reside in the neighbourhood. I had my two boys with me, and I thought we might see the hounds sweep by without molestation. But I was mistaken. No sooner did old Peg hear the hounds and the tally-ho of the huntsmen than she pricked up her ears, began to snort and caper, and as the hounds and huntsmen came up, defied all my efforts to keep her in. Away she went like a three-year-old, and all that I could do was to keep clear of a smash against one of the old gnarled trees. Over stock and stone she flew, over heath and hollow, and was in at the death. Glad was I indeed that we escaped so well, but the effect on her old blood was wonderful. All the way home she went at a jovial trot, saying, as plain as action could, ' Bravo! once again I have had a taste of the jolly old times!' I found, indeed, that in Lord Tyrconnel's days one of his grooms had regularly ridden her to the hunt.

"In an evening drive on July 27, 1837, with a young friend staying with us, as we passed by the little rural hamlet of Stoke d'Abernon, I was struck with two singular female figures at a little distance before us. They were both young, the one about the middle size, the other rather taller. The latter was dressed in a dark cotton bedgown, dark petticoat, grey stockings, and shoes. On her head was tied a yellow silk handkerchief, and in her hand she held a long, stout hazel wand, recently cut from the hedge. The other had on also a short bedgown, but of a pink colour, striped and figured with white, a dark petticoat, and ankle-boots. On her head she wore an old straw bonnet. As we drew near they came running up to us, and, one on each side of the pony-chaise, began begging most importunately:—'Will you give us sixpence? Do give us sixpence. Do, dear gentleman, give us sixpence. Dear lady, do tell the gentleman to give us sixpence!'

"It was only necessary to cast a slight glance at the faces of these beggars, and to hear one tone of their voices, to know that it was a frolic, that they were *ladies* of education and family thus dressed up. They had hair and eyes jet black as any gipsies, but were handsomer than any gipsies I ever saw. Irresistible as such beggars might appear, I resolved to refuse them, in order to see how they would keep up the attempt, and how they would take a refusal. I therefore said, laughing, 'Oh! I have no sixpences for beggars like you: you certainly are very charming beggars; you have chosen a very rustic costume;

you act your part very well indeed, and I hope you will enjoy your frolic.'

"All this time I kept driving on at a good pace, but the resolute damsels still ran on importuning for sixpence. One dropped behind—the taller still ran on with her stick in her hand, in a voice of much softness and sweetness still begging for sixpence, as they 'were poor strangers, who had got nothing all day!' As she ran, this sort of badinage passed :—'Where do you come from ?' 'Oh! we have come all the way from Epsom to meet our young man here, and he has deceived us.' 'Well, I hope no young man will deceive you more cruelly.' 'I should like something, for I am very tired; and what is sixpence to you? You have a very good horse in your chaise; I have no doubt you are a gentleman of independent fortune—*do* give us sixpence!' 'No; I wish I were half as rich as you are.' Here the Queen of Love and Beauty stopped, and turned round with an air of very beautiful disdain. As she went back to join her companion, we were again struck with the grace of her form and the buoyancy of her carriage.

"As we returned, we met these gipsies coming up a hollow woody lane near Bookham Common, and behold! they and a military-looking young man with light moustachios were walking familiarly on together. It was evident that they had found 'their young man.' The moment our actresses saw us, they motioned their escort to move off to the other side of the way and to walk on, and again renewed their importuning as we passed.

"As we proceeded, I stopped and asked of all the country-people I met, Who was that gentleman? and who the ladies dressed as beggars? The miller thought the gentleman was from Bookham Lodge, the seat of Captain

Blackwood. 'But the women, sir, they are Dutchwomen,' meaning German broom-sellers. The groom at the Parsonage gate 'didn't know the gentleman in the moustachios; but the women, bless you! they were no *ladies*.' 'Why?' 'Oh! they came ringing at the bell like new 'uns; six or seven times they called us out—they would take no nay.'*

"Driving one day near Hook, on the Brighton road, some four or five miles from Esher, we met Charles Dickens, who had, in 1836, become a favourite with the public through his 'Sketches by Boz.' He was walking with Harrison Ainsworth. I have no doubt they were both on the look-out for facts, images, or characters to weave into their constantly appearing fictions; and in Dickens's next production, 'Master Humphrey's Clock,' I was amused to see that our stout and wilful pony, Peg, had not escaped his observation, but had been set to do service in Mr. Garland's chaise. By the bye, all down the Portsmouth road about Esher you see traces of his quiet notice of everything; in poor Smike's journey with Nicholas Nickleby; in the names of Weller, the Marquis of Granby, and the like; as in later years you could trace his names in the Hampstead Road, as Sol's Arms, in his long walks from Tavistock House round by Highgate and over Hampstead Heath back again."


Writing to my sister from Esher, October 10, 1837, I ask :—

"Have you read William's paper on the 'Domestic

---

* The incident is given in the "Rural Life in England," under the heading, "Gipsies of Fashion" (p. 191). They were, in fact, two of Richard Brinsley Sheridan's gifted granddaughters : the Hon. Mrs. Blackwood (later Lady Dufferin), and her taller and younger sister, the Duchess of Somerset.

Manners of Friends' in this month's number of *Tait?* I am rather doubtful as to what may be the general impression of the Society respecting it; but I am sure it is one of the very truest pictures of Friends that ever was drawn. They are a most singular people, and they, living almost exclusively amongst themselves, are not at all aware how peculiar their lives and customs are. We live a good deal out of the line of demarcation, and we see and feel these peculiarities in their full force. We can see dispassionately what is excellent and what is faulty in their system. And this too is true, though many of the more rigid Friends would hardly give us credit for it, that there are no members of the Society more sincerely attached to what is admirable in it than we are. This paper is to be followed by another, 'Friends at the Yearly Meeting.' It is written and in Mr. Tait's hands, but he is so consumed by politics that there is no calculation when it will appear. It is a very graphic and interesting paper, and everything that it describes we ourselves saw, but perhaps it is as well not to say as much."

Great changes have taken place in the Society of Friends since an article appeared in *Tait's Edinburgh Magazine* for October 1834 entitled, "George Fox and his First Disciples; or, The Society of Friends as it was and as it is," by William Howitt, and which was reprinted as a pamphlet in Philadelphia in 1837. The article gave great offence to the elder portion of the Society, but was accepted with such avidity by the younger as showed that it was quite prepared for the reforms that have since gradually taken place in the course of the last fifty years. Singularity of dress and speech no longer remain standards of orthodoxy.

The strictest Friend would not now take umbrage when William Howitt says :—" The use of peculiar names for the days and months proceeds from a laudable desire carried to excess—a desire to keep clear of names once belonging to idolatry—into which there is now little danger of falling. The adoption of *thou* to a single person, *you* only to more than one, is a violation of modern grammar without in these days an adequate use. The first Friends made no change in their dress, if we except Fox's suit of leather, which no one imitates. William Penn was dressed as became a gentleman of the time. Christianity is not a religion of caps and coats of a certain cut, but of high, ennobling sentiments, and of the practice of everything which tends to bind man to man and prepare the heart for heaven."

"The outward testimonies" were, however, great essentials to zealous Friends in the first part of this century. Thus a letter was gravely circulated among the members of a certain meeting, written by Isaac Wright in Second Month, 1839, in which he says :—

" Very soon after sitting down in your meeting a tender cry was raised in my mind, ' Oh that the Lambs of the Flock would but enter into the Fold by the door, that they would take Christ, the Light, for their leader ! . . . Oh that these Babes, in their Christian course, might be willing to bring all superfluous things to the pure witness for truth in the conscience, *i.e.*, the Light ! ' and methought one effect would be that the Muffs, the Tippets, the Boas, &c., would not appear so commonly among us ; and may I not kindly suggest whether, for example's sake, the Veil might not often be dispensed with ?"

In October 1837 my little volume of poems, called

VOL. I.                                                       S

"Birds and Flowers," appeared.  In sending a copy to Miss Bowles from Esher, October 23, 1837, I say :—

"In a short time you shall receive two much more worthy tomes, the long-talked-of 'Rural Life of England,' the proof-sheets of which Mr. Howitt is now receiving daily.

"I quite despair of making you at all conceive of the entirely rural, nay, perfectly wild region in which we live.  The land is full of fine places, it is true, but they lie only here and there in the midst of woods.

"Poverty, in its squalid sense, as we knew it in the manufacturing districts, we have never seen here.  The people are ignorant and improvident, but the cottagers are seldom without a pig, and they all have a garden, and right of common, upon which they raise large flocks of geese, keep a cow, and often a pony.  The men appear always employed, and whatever they have to sell, as fruit, geese, mushrooms, and such things, they ask a great price for.

"Much of the open land about us is sufficiently hilly to give great diversity and character to it, particularly as it is covered with heath, fern, and gorse.  We have often stood in the midst of these solitary wilds and looked round us for miles on extents of brown common and wood, and wondered how it was possible that we could be only about two hours' drive from London.

"The sole feature the country wants is running water. There are none of those pleasant little, pebbly, clear, and living streams that we have found elsewhere in scenery of a similar character.  Another want there is also, and that is the village church, with its goodly spire or tower of old grey stone.  The churches are few and most grotesque, low wooden erections, more like dovecots than parish churches. They are, in fact, exactly like those one sees on old Dutch tiles; but even these, in the midst of woods, often produce a very picturesque effect.

"Dr. Southey's description of Brixton and its neighbourhood as it was when he wrote 'Joan of Arc' there, might be taken, in many respects, for the neighbourhood of Esher; but then we possess what Brixton never did, and that is rich old memories, for the whole district is full of them. 'The tower of Asher, my Lord of Winchester,' as Shakespeare says, whither Wolsey fled in his trouble, is a short quarter of a mile from us to the left; at the same distance from us, to the right, Claremont, with its fine woods. Hampton Court is but a walk, and there are the cartoons of Raphael, to say nothing of the historic old palace and its stately gardens. Richmond, Oatlands, Windsor, Runnymeade, Chertsey, the retreat of Cowley, and St. Anne's Hill, the abode of Charles James Fox, are but short drives. Then we have a grand old Roman Camp, called Cæsar's, just by us, in a hilly region of wood and fern, commanding one of the most splendid views I ever saw. Do not, my dear Miss Bowles, despise our residence as a cockney box in a cockney neighbourhood; such a place would have been little enticing to us. William must have space to range over, and here he finds it, and freedom equal to the freedom of your ancient forest."

William Howitt to his Brother Richard.

"*Esher, Nov.* 5, 1837.—We often wish thou had a little cottage somewhere here. What glorious rounds we would then have amongst old book-shops in London, and through the woods and up to the top of the hills about here!

"I must just tell thee a good anecdote of literary fame. One day, as I had Alfred and Claude in the pony-chaise with me, at the entrance of Chertsey I asked two old women who were sitting under a hedge which was Cowley's house, for it has an inscription on it. 'Cowley? Cowley?' they said. 'What is he?'—'What is he?' I replied. 'He *was* a poet; but he has been dead almost two hundred years.'—'A poet? a poet?' they said. 'What's a poet?' The children were fit to burst with amusement, and for days after they were chiming over and laughing again at it. 'A poet? a poet? What's a poet?' Behold the extent of poetic fame, and of the wisdom of our Surrey Arcadia!"

The same to the same.

"*Esher, Feb.* 25, 1838.—I am very glad to say that 'Rural Life' is doing very well, and Longmans are very anxious for another book from the same author. I am working hard at 'Colonisation and Christianity,' and mean it to be out in May. If thou canst give me any hints, or furnish me with a good motto or two, I shall be glad. I take a rapid review of the behaviour of the *Christian* nations of Europe to all the natives of the countries they have seized in all quarters of the world. After May I shall begin the 'Visits to Remarkable Places,' which I hope to make an interesting volume.

"Do you know that the wife of our surgeon here, Mrs. Neville, is an old friend of John Keats? I believe I might say an old flame. Many of his verses were addressed to her; and a very lovely young woman she was, I doubt not. She sent us the other day three sketches of him to look at—one of them in youth and health; one lying in his berth reading while passing through the Bay of Biscay on his way to Italy; and one as he lay with his head on the pillow just before death. They were done by Mr. Severn, the young artist who went to Italy with him, and are very interesting."

On March 3, 1838, I write to my sister Anna:—
"Thou wilt want to know about the baby. He is unlike any of the other children. He has clear, sharp eyes, and looks very intelligent; and by Yearly Meeting-time will, I expect, be a very nice child, fit to present to anybody. We were sorely puzzled for a name; he is, however, called Herbert Charlton."

"Colonisation and Christianity" is an able and good book, that has now long been out of print. Its publication led to the formation of the British India Society, which issued in a separate form the part of the work relating to India. My husband, amongst other important facts, pointed out that, were the native tanks kept in repair, and the grand native system of irrigation only properly sustained, the awful famines in India would not occur. John Bright, made acquainted with the abuses of our Indian system, took up the question in the Chamber of Commerce in Manchester, and then in Parliament, which dissolved the East India Company and introduced measures of reform. He and Professor Fawcett both powerfully protested at these reforms in India being inadequate, and especially against the neglect of the obvious means to prevent famine.

William Howitt writes to his brother Richard, November 21, 1838, and when he was again hard at work; this time on the "Visits to Remarkable Places:"—

"I have been to Penshurst, and to Stratford and all the haunts of Shakespeare.   I was passing a school on my way to Shottery to see Ann Hathaway's cottage, when I asked the schoolmaster whether he should raise another Shakespeare amongst his lads.  'Sir,' said he, 'I have a Shakespeare in the school, a descendant of Shakespeare's sister. See if you can find him out.'   He set his lads in a row, and glancing down it, I said, 'That is a Shakespeare,' and I was right; so you may suppose there was some likeness.   The lad's name is William Shakespeare Smith. I was at Justice Shallow's too, and saw his portrait, his monument and effigy in the church, and his descendants, who are very nice people indeed.   But I must not tell you too many good things at once."

MARY HOWITT TO MISS BOWLES.

"*Jan.* 3, 1839.—A very happy New Year it must needs be to you, and you must allow William and myself to congratulate you most cordially on the era which it is to accomplish in your life.   Now, I wonder whether you thought we should be surprised.   I can tell you no.   Mrs. Bain called one day and told me to guess who was going to be married.   As she glanced to the books on the table, I asked, 'Is the lady literary?'—'Yes.'   Well, as it was not likely to be Joanna Baillie, I said, 'Miss Bowles.' —'Oh! you are a conjurer,' replied my friend—'but the gentleman?'   Admiral Bain, my friend's husband, intending to give me a hint, said, 'I have been at his house.'   That, however, was no clue; still, I did not hesitate, and said, 'Dr. Southey.'

"Now, will not this convince you what a natural, joyful thing it seemed to be?   I had the pleasure of making William guess, when he came in from his walk; and then we paid a delicious mental visit to your cottage, and gave you our entire heart-sympathy. May the Almighty bless you, and crown your life with such happiness as you so well deserve.

"I am quite cheered to know that you did not disapprove of 'Colonisation and Christianity.' William felt the least in the world sorry afterwards that a copy had gone to you. Not that he feared you could disapprove of its general spirit, but that there might be reasons why such a volume should not be quite to your taste. I thought it was horrible and dismal reading for a lone lady. Dear Miss Bowles, this again reminds me of your future. You will have more cheery company than the cat and the canary-bird, and the portraits of the dead ancestors. I shall never pity you of a winter's evening now, let you be reading ever so melancholy a book.

"On the very day your last letter came I was going to write to you to request the permission to inscribe my little volume of 'Hymns and Fireside Verses' to you. William is going to send you a book, which you can present to some young boyish cousin, if you please. It is 'The Boy's Country-Book,' being the real life of a country boy. The engraver, Mr. Williams, has embellished it, I think, very beautifully. The hero, Will Middleton, is drawn by him from our eldest boy, Alfred, and the little brother from our second son, Claude. Alfred's likeness is very good. Claude's is a failure, except where he and his brother stand with the gardener.

"You have been so very good as often to inquire after our daughter. She is a dear, lovable girl, with a fine poetical spirit. In the little volume, which I hope shortly to send you, you will find some of her designs for the principal poem.  I think you will like them.  They represent the spirit of Christianity under the guise of a child, in different scenes and circumstances of human life.  There is also in her papa's book an embellishment, a tail-piece to Chapter XVI. from a drawing of hers—the runaway boys shelling peas at the cottage-door.

"I must not forget to tell you what you ought to have known long ago respecting the Rose of May.  I will not vouch for its flowering in the one-and-thirty days of our May.  It must have been the May of the old style.  I very much question, also, whether it would at all equal your expectations, for the situation in which it grew, and its poetical name, gave it a charm and grace to my fancy, and hence the poem.  I found last year, after the terrible frost had killed the most of our beautiful and thirty-years-old evergreens, that a large, straggling rose-bush was brought to light.  It bore flowers in the very beginning of June.  It had even pink buds in May, and I immediately recognised it as not unlike our Rose of May, excepting that it was double; but as its form was very irregular and defective, its beauty was lost from this cause.  The true Rose of May is single, and has a cinnamon-like perfume.  When we sent to William's mother for the cutting, she said it was also called the Whitsun Rose, or, as the country-folks say, 'the Wissun Rose.'

"You would be shocked, as we were, to hear of poor L. E. L.'s death.  We feared, when she went with her husband to Africa, that her days might be looked upon as numbered, but we never thought they were so few. It is indeed a melancholy fate, and reminds us of poor Miss Jewsbury.  It was dreadful to think of her dying attended only by such a strange being as her husband,

Mr. Fletcher. Her relations have not received one syllable from him to this day.

"Poor Miss Jewsbury! It was she who gave us most of the carols which are quoted and alluded to in 'The Rural Life.' She knew how I doted on carols and ballads, and, half in joke and half in earnest, she collected at Manchester and its neighbourhood all the halfpenny carols and songs that she could, and had them bound for me."

I make mention, in the above letter, of Admiral Bain. This excellent and enlightened man, deploring the crass ignorance of the labouring class in Esher, succeeded, with much difficulty and opposition on the part of the gentry, in setting on foot a village school at his own cost. The affluent feared making their servants and labourers intellectual by teaching them to read and write. On our arrival at Esher, the only school-building in the neighbourhood * was in the distant and obscure hamlet of Oxshott, due to the beneficence of the Royal Family. It bore the inscription, "The Royal Kent School, founded in 1820;" but it was no longer used. The windows were broken, and the whole premises in a state of dilapidation. The farmers were glad that so it should be, as the peasants, if educated, would no longer be beasts of burden. In Esher the benevolent Admiral would not be thwarted, and the poor children began, about the year 1836, to receive a useful English education.

. Lady Noel Byron, the poet's widow, was actively engaged in promoting national education. She favoured my husband's religious and political views; and in 1836,

* A dame-school had been commenced by the Princess Charlotte in one of the lodges of Claremont Park, but was discontinued after her death.

admiring his "Address to the Society of Friends," an article which had appeared in the April number of *Tait's Magazine* for that year, had been desirous for its publication in a tract form for general circulation. She was living at Fordhook, near Ealing, when we resided at Esher, and made our acquaintance through our mutual friend, Mrs. Joanna Baillie. Here I may add that we first owed our pleasant personal intercourse with this admirable and excellent poetess to her approval of my volume of dramas, entitled, "The Seven Temptations," which she valued "as a work of great moral value, vivid imagination, and which ought, she felt, to be instructive to youth."

Lady Noel Byron introduced us to her son-in-law and daughter, the Earl and Countess of Lovelace, who, like herself, were extremely interested in the formation of industrial schools. She had organised a school in 1834 in Ealing Grove, under the charge of Mr. E. T. Craig, in which boys were successfully educated for agricultural pursuits; and when we became acquainted with her, was anxious to meet with a suitable schoolmaster to form and manage for her a similar institution at Kirkby-Mallory, in Leicestershire. Such an individual was procured for her by my husband.

During our life at Nottingham, William had discovered and encouraged the intellectual ability of a poor man named Ephraim Brown. He put into his hands works that were calculated to soften down a natural ruggedness of character and to cultivate his mind, which was of no mean order. Brown evinced genuine gratitude to his benefactor, and a most anxious desire to help others of the labouring class to think, reason, and reflect. Village education was confined to reading, writing, and arithmetic, without any attempt at the culture of the understanding, the intellectual powers of the child being totally neglected. His great ambition, therefore, became to help to draw public attention to the subject of popular education, so that, suitable measures being enacted, he might still live to see his beloved native land enjoying, like her favoured sister, Scotland, a wise, flourishing, and enlightened rural population. He embraced most thankfully Lady Byron's offer, learnt the system in her model school at Ealing, and then commenced a fellow-establishment at Kirkby.

I well remember, when staying at Lord Lovelace's seat, East Horsley Park, during a long drive through a southern most remote portion of Surrey, how here and there a solitary peasant in white slop stared at the ladies dashing by in carriage and four; and how Mrs. Hippersley Tuckfield, another guest of Lord Lovelace's, explained to his two sisters, the Hon. Misses King, and myself, as we bowled along, the system of education which she was carrying out on her estates near Bristol. She had the most needful instruction imparted to poor children by voluntary or paid teachers in cottages. She was opposed to the erection of expensive school-premises and great gatherings together of children, believing that the formation of their moral and religious characters could only be individually effected in small centres of tuition. She maintained that by her method the entire juvenile population could in a very few weeks be put to school almost without effort or sensible cost.

In Lord Lovelace's schools we saw, during our first visit, a hundred and thirty bright, happy, busy children; the boys acquiring the most common handicraft trades, and the girls learning dairy, laundry, and other household work.

To this period belongs a " First Book for Reading " that

I wrote, and which was published, I believe, at the cost of sixpence.

Returning now to my correspondence with my sister Anna, I thus address her, February 1, 1839:—

"Alfred and Claude are my pupils. We try to be as regular at lessons as possible, but it is difficult to avoid interruptions.

"William sent thee and thine a couple of 'The Boy's Country-Book.' It is a general favourite, and has already sold so well that a second edition is preparing. I hope there will be no objection to thy children having the book at Ackworth. It would be delightful reading to them; and as it describes William's life there, would have a double zest.

"And now, dearest sister, it is impossible that anything so kindly meant as thy remonstrances could offend us. But I really cannot tell to what it alludes. I have never contributed to any periodical for these three years at least, except *Chambers's Journal;* and to that five articles, 'The Decayed Gentlewoman,' 'The Friend's Family,' 'Letting a House,' 'The Minds of Children,' and 'The Demon of Perversity.' To none of these can thy remarks apply. 'The Friend's Family' is the only one that describes Friends, and I had no desire in it of 'ministering to a depraved public taste.' I myself should feel great interest in a faithful sketch of a Moravian family.

"Then, as to William's contributions to periodicals, it can only be to *Tait's Magazine,* for he has not written in any other for years. His articles on Friends there contain not one word which is not true, and had any object but that of pandering to bad passions. Their aim has been to make known to the public what is really noble and peculiarly Christian in the profession and practice of the Society; and he has done so more than any other writer that has written on the subject. I grant that he has spoken freely of many of their *outward* peculiarities; and that he has done with design, because he saw clearly these it was that were sapping the foundation of the Society's simplicity and usefulness, and that they had come to be regarded by the Society itself as the essentials of the faith, or at least of its practice. He firmly believed this, and he did, in my opinion, quite right to speak of them as they deserved.

"I think thou art wrong in saying they have injured his reputation in the literary world, for we have continual evidence with how much interest they are read—and that not by gossiping, idle readers—and how much they have tended to the better features of Quakerism being understood. Owing to these very papers William has been employed to write the article, 'Quaker,' for the new edition of the 'Encyclopædia Britannica;' that is anything but a proof of his good name having suffered. On the contrary, we looked upon it as one of the most flattering and gratifying testimonials to his fair reputation; for none but acknowledged and first-rate writers have ever been employed on that work. That part of the 'Encyclopædia' is just about being published, and the article, therefore, will soon be before the public. William has gone carefully through upwards of a hundred Friends' books, old and new, in order to make it perfect. The former article was very unfavourable to Friends, and especially to the character of George Fox.

"My dearest sister, if thou knew how earnestly desirous we are, how it is the frequent cause of our humble supplications, that, in our day and generation, we may be

enabled to do good by making virtue lovely, and teaching
how simple and glorious is Christianity, thou would not
suspect us of any such false designs as thou speaks of.
With such desires it is impossible that we can ever
willingly or knowingly have perverted our talents.  Perhaps the young lady at Chester may allude to a paper in
the December number of *Tait*, on the state of society in
the neighbourhood of London, drawn from our own experience here.  If so, she knows nothing of what she
speaks, for it is one of the most valuable papers William
ever wrote, and will do great good.  Gentlemen have
called on him from villages all round London to express
their satisfaction with it, and to bear testimony to its
wonderful truth."

"*Esher, July* 14, 1839.—I believe that Dr. Godfrey
Howitt, with his wife and children, his brothers-in-law,
John and Robert Bakewell, and brother Richard will
emigrate to Port Phillip next month.  I am thankful
that we have no emigrating mania upon us.  Our children may please themselves, but we will abide by old
England."

"*Aug.* 9, 1839.—I am sure thou wilt be glad to hear
that thou hast another little *niece*.  The baby was born
this day week, on a fine sunny afternoon, when we had
company in the house.  We talk of calling her Margaret.
I like the name greatly, and I fancy we shall decide
upon it."

"*Sept.* 23, 1839.—My beloved sister, I congratulate thee
on the happy event, and I rejoice from my heart that it
is a girl.  My new daughter flourishes excellently, and I

hope the dear little contemporaries will live and be comforts to us all, and that they will learn to love one another.

"You want to know something about our emigrants. They all came down to see us, and William and Anna Mary spent a little time with them in town, remaining with them to the day before they sailed. It was to have been a Friday, but owing to a sailor's superstition, they did not set sail until the Saturday. Unfortunately the wind changed and became contrary before they got into the Downs; and there they lay tossing and tacking about for ten days. The same adverse winds continued in the Channel; and on the night of last Saturday week, in the midst of a severe storm, another ship struck against them, and they almost suffered shipwreck. Their vessel is the *Lord Goderich*. The other, the *Sophia*, bound from London to Sydney, and also carrying Australian emigrants, suffered dreadfully, and was towed back to London by an Irish steamer. The *Lord Goderich* put into Portsmouth to refit, and there they still are. William went down to see them, and Richard returned with him here last night, and is this morning gone down to Nottingham and Heanor.

Now, I dare say a great many people will think all these disasters are a sign that this emigration is not favoured by Heaven. I see nothing of the kind in it, but rather the direct interference of Providence. They had not been many days at sea before they discovered three terrible things: that their ship was wanting ballast; that they had not hands enough on board to work her; and, what seems to me the worst of all, that she was insufficiently victualled, and that an actual famine must be the result if the voyage was continued,

for the ship was to call nowhere on her course.  Their
being compelled thus into harbour again may therefore
be looked upon as the salvation of the ship.  It is believed that she is insured for more than her value, and
that the proprietors care not if she goes to the bottom ;
and she might have done so had it not been for this
providential opposition of the elements.  The passengers
are all resolved to compel a proper refitting and supply
of all necessaries, and not to leave port without every
requisite appointment.  It is quite singular to hear the
reasons the sailors give for the misfortunes of the voyage.
There was a little black kitten on board.  An ill-
tempered passenger in a petulant mood threw it over-
board.  The sailors were indignant, and, as in the case
of the Ancient Mariner shooting the albatross, they pro-
phesied coming judgments.  The adverse winds accordingly rose.  The dead kitten was declared and believed
to dodge the ship for many days ; and Richard says that,
could the sailors have come at the offending passenger,
he believes he would have suffered at their hands.  Do
you not admire the spirit of humanity even in this
superstition ? "

On October 2nd the *Lord Goderich*, still in a state of
much confusion, and indeed not sufficiently repaired,
put out to sea.  The night was stormy, and suddenly a
brig came down upon the vessel midships.  Some of the
passengers gave up all hope ; but the brig righted herself and dropped astern.  It was a hairbreadth escape.
A terrible storm followed, but by October 7 the ill-
fated ship was safely out of the Channel.  The voyage
then became pleasant and prosperous.  Richard wrote
to us while they were becalmed in the tropics, eight

degrees from the line.  On December 28, 1839, I thus reply :—

"I have many things to thank you for; first of all for that beautiful sonnet.  Dearest brother Richard, you know not how this touched me ; and then came a poem which you gave to Ephraim Brown, the most soul-moving that you ever wrote, beginning, 'Alas ! upon a reed I leant.'  The verses are penetrated through and through with feeling, and the agony of a wounded spirit, and sink into my heart like my own experience.  May God bless and prosper you, and send you your heart's wish ten times over.

"You cannot tell the rejoicing that your letter brought to our fireside.  There was but one drawback, which was, that a month had passed since it was written,  Oh ! Richard, I could not help feeling thankful that I was not in your ship, and thankful also was I that you would come back to the dear old Continent, with all its old memories and ruins and associations.  Nay, even I do believe that its very abuses, its old expensive monarchies, and its neck-bowing, priestly establishments would seem respectable and venerable in such a situation.  Heaven knows, but you will perhaps return a very good Tory; such things have been.  How glad shall we be to see you back again !  We picture you living near us, and we like the picture extremely.

"It gladdens our hearts to hear poor Ephraim Brown speak of you.  You had a little band of fast friends at Nottingham, and that ' corner house ' must have been like holy ground to them.  William has written a review of ' Festus ' for the *Eclectic*—a very just and proper one, which will gratify young Philip Bailey."

To my sister Anna I write on my birthday, March 12, 1840 :—

"Time fleets away so fast, and though we flatter ourselves that we do some little good, looking back from one year to another, the evidence of it is very small and unsatisfactory. Oh, how sincerely do I desire to employ my few talents to a good purpose! I make compacts with myself to do some great and good thing ; but, alas! I remember the same feeling when we used to 'do our afternoon lessons' in the best parlour, with that small mahogany desk before us, and we kept our journals and commonplace books, and read 'Watts on the Mind' and 'Locke on the Human Understanding.' I had the same aspirations then, and was full of hope ; now they are dimmed by there being no fruition to satisfy me."

My husband revisited the north of England this Spring for his work on "Remarkable Places," and, in so doing, paid a visit to our relatives in Liverpool. On May 13, 1840, I say, in a letter to Anna :—

"William quite interests me by what he hints of a certain conversation he has had with thee on the state of the Society of Friends. It is deplorable, and marks decline every way. I wish there were a fine, right-minded, active, and liberal body of Christians that one could join fellowship with. There is something very good and very comfortable in a religious community, if it were but established on Christian, not on sectarian principles. I can imagine something so holy and affectionate in true religious fellowship and brotherhood. I doubt if we must not wait for its enjoyment till we get to the Better Land.

"We try to make our children Christians without reference to any sect or party whatever, and except in the fundamental doctrines of old Quakerism, such as abhorrence of war and principles of universal religious and political liberty, Anna Mary is no more a Friend than the Archbishop of Canterbury. The boys will grow up the same. Alfred is full of thought, has an interesting mind, and holds, young as he is, very decided opinions. Even Claude, though a wild lad as ever lived, thinks for himself, and now and then gives his opinion most oddly. The other day he held an argument with a gentleman, whom we do not know, on the Opium Question—taking the side of the Chinese, of course. He told us when he came home, for he was much excited, and what arguments he had used.

"The two little ones will, I think, be brought up in excellent order. My young Friend in the nursery, Eliza, is a real jewel. It is quite affecting to me to see her nice methods, and to visit her and the children at the nursery-breakfast, Charlton sitting quietly in his small chair to hear a chapter of the Testament read. She is a good young woman, and the children love her. My only fear is her health. She was an invalid for years, and still looks delicate, but does not complain. I love her, and nothing touches me more than a humble, conscientious fulfilment of simple duties."

We had at this time made arrangements to reside for some years abroad, being attracted by the alleged advantages attending education in Germany. At the beginning of June 1840 we were in London, at 20 Ely Place, whence I write to my sister on the fifth of that month, telling her we were so far on our way. I add :—

"We dined on Sunday with the women-Friends who are delegates from America to the Anti-Slavery Convention, and with that noble American abolitionist, William Lloyd Garrison. The English Friends, whose women go up and down preaching, and who have their meetings of discipline, have, nevertheless, refused to receive these women-delegates from America. I wish thou could see and hear Lucretia Mott. She is a glorious, noble-minded woman, and a plain Friend too. The English Friends will not receive her because she is a Hicksite. They also say they think women thus sent by an entire nation are out of their sphere.

"We go on board our vessel to-morrow, the *Batavia*, for Rotterdam, *en route* for Heidelberg."

# CHAPTER IX.

## *IN GERMANY.*

### *1840–1843.*

WE made a prosperous and merry journey from London to Bonn, in the delighful companionship of Clara Novello, now Countess Gigliucci. We then sailed up the Rhine, which we found worthy of its fame, as far as to Mannheim, and thence drove by carriage to Heidelberg.

We were directed in that city to a widow lady, who could speak English, and were able, immediately on arriving, to rent the first-floor in her abode. We had scarcely done so, when Lord Lyndhurst's brother-in-law came to engage it for him. It was, in fact, a favourite dwelling. There Jean Paul Richter had been wont to enjoy an evening revel. The Emperor Alexander of Russia, when proceeding on his march to France in the rear of Buonaparte, had taken up his quarters in it to his great satisfaction, and left above its door a brass plate with an inscription, calling on every Russian hereafter to respect and spare the house. It faced the river Neckar, having at its back overhanging woods and terraced walks, with a secluded footpath ascending to the famous castle of Heidelberg, which, once the home of the unfortunate Princess Elizabeth Stuart, and destroyed in turns by lightning, fire, war, and finally by its own princes, still proudly stands on its vantage-ground. The castle-gardens, open to the public, were just above us;

and thence we surveyed the vast plain of the Palatinate stretching away beyond the Neckar valley, with the distant Vosges mountains shutting out France.

Mrs. Jameson had furnished us with an introduction to Rath and Frau Räthin Schlosser. They were a noble-hearted and highly-accomplished couple, who gathered around them the noted and cultivated of all nations at their country-house, Stift Neuburg. It had once been a convent; was situated two miles from the city, on the opposite bank of the Neckar, and filled with choice works of art. Mrs. Jameson had also given us a letter to young Wolfgang von Goethe, the grandson of the famous poet, whom, most painfully shy and averse to society, we nevertheless met a fortnight after our arrival, at a ball given at Stift Neuburg, in honour of his relative, Rath Schlosser's birthday.

Wolfgang von Goethe, plain in person, yet bearing a remarkable likeness to the portraits of his grandfather, proved, on nearer acquaintance, a very intellectual and interesting young man of a most retiring and sensitive nature; but although he was kind enough to say that he felt with us unusually happy and at his ease, we saw but little of him. He shunned the company of his fellow-students in the University, preferring to lead the life of a modern hermit; and, shutting himself in his room, perused religious works of Rath Schlosser's selection.

Fascinated by the novelty of the situation, we were far less fastidious, and willingly mixed with some of the large moving population of the dear old University town. We found the students—who, with abundant masses of flaxen or black hair under very small caps, were addicted to smoking, beer-drinking, and fencing,

OUR FIRST HOME AT HEIDELBERG.

which they dignified by the name of duelling—on the whole, gentlemanly, agreeable, and unassuming.

The colony of our country people was small in those days. It contained, however, for some months after our arrival, the novelist, Mr. G. P. R. James, and his wife. He was an amusing companion, brimful of anecdotes. Captain Medwin, noted for his "Conversations with Byron" and his friendship with Shelley, was a resident; he was a man of culture and intelligence, aristocratic in his tastes, and finding my husband unprovided with an English newspaper, politely sent him regularly the *Court Journal*.

For the sake of our children we sought German acquaintance, we read German, we followed German customs. The life seemed to us simpler, the habits easier and less expensive, than in England. There was not the same feverish thirst after wealth as with us; there was more calm appreciation of Nature, of music, of social enjoyment. In all the first delight of glorious weather and unexplored scenes, we let our new acquaintances introduce us to quiet valleys, with their fast-flowing streams, rich grass, gorgeous flowers, and incessant chirp of the grasshopper; to deep woods full of bilberries, whence we obtained wide views over forest and plain. We let them conduct us to many sweet spots—Neckarsteinach, the Wolfsbrunnen, the Stiftmill, where, in the spring, grew the little turquoise blue squill; and to other quaint old mills and half-timbered homesteads with ancient walls and orchards, where peasant girls, with clear eyes and picturesque dresses, were washing and drying the linen on the delicious green hillsides. After days of happiness unclouded as the sky above us, we returned home, when the sunset cast an amber and lilac glow over hills and woods, to tea, music and merriment.

Anna Mary, then seventeen, spent a very joyous winter. It seemed to her the happiest of her life. Her young German friends found waltzing as needful to them as food or air. Thus there were many impromptu dances and much delightful singing.

OLD MILL NEAR HEIDELBERG.

Our practical knowledge of the Christmas-tree was gained in this first winter in Heidelberg. Universal as the custom now is, I believe the earliest knowledge which the English public had of it was through Coleridge in his " Biographia Literaria." It had, at the time I am writing of—1840—been introduced into Manchester by some of the German merchants established there. Our Queen and Prince Albert likewise celebrated the festival, with its beautiful old German customs. Thus the fashion spread, until now even our asylums, schools, and work-houses have, through friends and benefactors, each its Christmas-tree.

We kept the festivity in true German fashion, all the arrangements being made, at our expense, by some willing, indefatigable natives of Heidelberg. The whole affair surpassed anything that we, with our Quaker education, could have imagined.

After months of mystery, we were at last, on Christmas Eve, ushered ceremoniously into our own drawing-room. At one end stood the tall tree, glittering with numberless wax-tapers, with dainty cakes, bon-bons, and gilt walnuts and apples, and ornamented with a small image of the Christ-child. Tables covered with white cloths, each lighted by a row of tapers cleverly fastened into green moss, were placed round the room, one for each member of the family, and containing the beautifully arranged presents. These were gifts from us all to each other, but procured and disposed of by our friendly agents with the most tantalising secrecy. The joy of the children was intense; at first sub-dued by surprise, then bursting forth into a clamour of delight.

Our young folks and their friends danced in the New Year. At twelve o'clock punch was handed round on a tray, with a pile of neatly folded notes addressed indivi-dually to the assembled company; and each person pre-sent thus received New Year's wishes in the form of a pretty and appropriate poem. It was gracefully done, and so German.

The frost had set in with unusual severity early in December; in a few days the Neckar was frozen over, and so too was the Rhine. With the first snow, sledges of every description appeared, from the handsomely painted and ornamented vehicle of the Grand-Duke of Baden to the old wicker basket on a few poles rudely knocked together of the peasant. Wheel-barrows were turned into sledge-barrows. Tubs, baskets, and bundles were all conveyed on sledges. Our elder boys had each his little sledge, and with it a vast deal of amusement.

Our indefatigable German friends, the caterers for our entertainment, induced us to give a sledging party; and at last, after a great many preliminaries and much organisation, it came off. The seven handsomest sledges in the city, drawn by its best horses, were put in requisition; and I, with my gentleman attendant, heading the train, having four horses, and being preceded by seven outriders dressed in blue jackets, long black boots, and loudly cracking their whips, we dashed through the town. The whole of the inhabitants seemed in the streets to see the gay procession.

We drove to Neckargemünd, a village about six miles up the Neckar valley. There, in the warm saloon of a very comfortable inn, we partook of excellent coffee, and amused ourselves, from the oldest to the youngest, with games, such as were played in England some two hundred years ago—"Jacob, where art thou?" "The Black Man;" "Blind-Man's Buff"—called the "Blind Cow"—and so forth.

In the evening we returned home, very merry, by torchlight. It was beautiful at a turn of the road to see the procession of sledges rushing along, the whole scene illuminated by the ruddy blaze of the torches or cast into shadow by the dense smoke. The hills were visible covered with snow; so too the frozen river, and the suddenly illuminated road stretching before us. Our party was pronounced by judges the most perfect of the season, but oh! at what a cost!

Then came the gaiety of Carnival. There were masked balls; and at Mannheim a most splendid procession, representing the marriage of the Emperor Frederick the Second with a Princess Isabella of England. The whole was the most gorgeous spectacle we had ever seen. Each detail was in keeping. The men and women looked as if they had stepped out of old pictures, the costumes were perfect, and the horses, in their beauty and correct equipment, almost equalled their riders.

The first symptom of spring was the sudden breaking up of the ice. On the very night on which the boatmen had prognosticated the going of the ice, we were actually awoke at midnight by the swift galloping past of a horse and the loud cry of a man, "The ice goes! the ice goes!" My husband, describing the picturesque scene that followed, says:—

"Now there came a wild and awful sound of contending elements through the darkness; sounds of grinding, crushing, cracking, of rushing, roaring waters, and the sweep of winds bringing from up the valley the heavy, dull explosions of ice-masses. Along the banks flared hundreds of torches. The cries of human voices, those of men, women, and children, came on all sides. Guns were firing rapidly near the city. One could perceive through the darkness white and spectral masses moving on the waters, and then the rending away of fresh sheets of ice, as those rushed against them. Below, from the bridge, where the gigantic pieces were continually striking against the piers, came dull and incessant thunders as of a distant battle.

"I hastily threw on my clothes and ran towards the

city.   People were hastening in dishabille, and often with their cloaks or their gown-skirts thrown over their heads, to the river-side.   All was life, wakefulness, and animation ; the fear being that the houses might be endangered by the sudden breaking loose of the ice and the rapid rising of the waters by the thaw.   Accompanied by a good-natured student in a long dressing-gown and a red cap, I watched the scene from the bridge, where, though the ice was two feet thick, it was moving off in as orderly a style as could be expected ; and though wild-looking throngs, made conspicuous by the glare of the torches, watched the chafing ice-blocks and the vexed waters, there was no apprehension."

On April 2, 1841, I write to my sister Anna :—

" William is just now on the eve of his departure for England, for a stay, I expect, of about three months—the longest separation it will be which we have had since we were married, and it makes me low-spirited.   He has completed his last three months' work ; that is, ' The Student Life of Germany,' which a young German friend of ours, himself a student, has this winter written for him, and which William has translated from the original MS.   It is a clever, curious, and interesting work, but I am not quite sure whether you, and especially our other dear relatives, will not see great cause to find fault with some things in it.   For instance, the drinking-songs ; but unless this very characteristic feature of student life had been given, the book would have been incomplete.

" We have passed a most pleasant winter, and have received our friends every Monday evening.   The farewell reception was on Monday, and though we were all very cheerful, we felt sorry that it should be the last. Some students intend to accompany William to Mannheim, to see him on board the steamboat and wish him health and a happy journey. I like these warm-hearted German customs.

"The spring here is like weather come down from heaven. All appearance of winter has long been gone. The hillsides are getting green ; the almond-trees are all in flower, many trees in early leaf. We take long walks into the hills and woods. The nightingale, we are told, has already been heard, and the blackbirds, thrushes, and woodlarks sing all day long. I greatly regret that William must leave Germany this sweet spring season, for to one like him, whose eyes and ears are so open to all natural objects, and who always took such delight even in an English spring, where every object was familiar, this coming on of the season in beautiful scenery, with all its new characteristics, would have been a source of daily delight. Anna Mary and I would keep a journal of the advance of the season, but then we should never be able to walk as far as he would, and thus penetrate into the very heart of old woods and go down into the far-off valleys of the hills. What old-world places are they !

" I wish just for one day we could transport thee and Daniel into some one of those valleys, where little boys lead goats by a string, and women stand bare-legged and bare-headed washing linen at running waters. All the valley is shut in by round-backed hills covered with beech-woods, the ground scattered over with huge mossy stones, that look as old as the hills themselves. Such a region of profound seclusion and quiet, that it seems to the mind like a picture, a dream, or the realisation of some old-fashioned tale or poem. Yes, I am sorry William has to leave these places under their spring influences; but then, if he did not go to England, he could not finish his second series of 'Remarkable Places,' nor could 'The Student Life' be correctly and safely published.  So business, like the devil, drives.

"Did I ever tell thee that among our student friends is the grandson of Goethe?  He is a most peculiar young man, of a most poetic temperament, but timid and bashful to a painful extent.  He never will join our parties, but comes to us alone.  We like him much, in spite of his peculiarities, and mean to do our best to make him a little more in love with his fellow-beings, and tolerant of their society."

After the return of my husband from England, we both, accompanied by our eldest daughter, made a tour in Germany.  We set out in pouring rain, at the beginning of August, for Carlsruhe.  It so happened that one of our student friends, having passed his examination, was the same day going to take possession of a government post which he had received in Bruchsal, between Heidelberg and Carlsruhe.  In student phraseology, he was leaving the *Burschen* heaven and entering the land of the Philistines.  Of course his friends accompanied him.  As we drove down the main street of Heidelberg, we saw before us the three carriages of the procession.  At the first stopping-place our friend and his best friend came to our carriage-door, and mutual salutations passed.  We congratulated him on his office, he us on our journey.  Again we all drove off, we seeming to swell the train in his honour.  At his destination, a stupid, melancholy-looking place, with an old, neglected palace, vast barracks, big town hall, and a poor, dirty population, we took leave of the new State official.  The tears were in his eyes as he shook hands with us again and again, declaring that such a happy winter as the last could never return to him.

Carlsruhe seemed to us a town of sleep or death, so dull, heavy, and uninteresting was its aspect. Yet many a poor student has come there for his examination with a fearful heart, and has even sometimes turned back when the city gates were before him. Thus thinking of our student friends, we looked on the building in which the examinations took place with intense interest.

From Carlsruhe we went to Baden-Baden, beautifully situated in the midst of the Black Forest, which, with its immense pine-woods, covers the hills for miles round. The watering-place consisted of fine buildings, with the most delightful, well-kept walks. Its bane was its frequenters, English and French nobles, with other pleasure-seekers, time-killers, and gamblers. Tieck, the poet, who was very fond of Baden-Baden in its earlier days, had said, so soon as the waiters at the inns began to speak French instead of good, honest German, he would leave, and so he had done. On all hands nothing but French or English sounded in our ears, and the waiters were most persistent in using those languages. We could quite sympathise with Tieck.

We visited the splendid " Conversation House," where company assembled every night to stroll about, listen to fine music, and to gamble. We, like hundreds of others, stood at the *rouge et noir* and the *roulette* tables to watch the play go on. It was melancholy to see men and women, young and old, rich and poor, entering into the game, laying down their gold and silver, and mostly having it swept away into the great gambling-bank, which, like a pit, seemed ready to swallow up all that came. Many an anxious and many a hard, merciless countenance did we watch. One person, however, in spite of the disgust and sorrow which filled our hearts, really amused us. It was a fat, French lady, who came as a matter of course, sat down, untied her bonnet, unpinned her shawl, changed her gloves, took out her vinaigrette and scent-bottle, which she placed, with her fan, beside her in the most methodical manner; took out her large purse, placed it with the card and pin with which she pricked the progress of the different games; and looking round her with a very well-satisfied air, settled herself down for the night. Each evening she did the same, and each evening she was the only object which amused us.

From Baden we went to Wildbad, another fashionable bathing-place, situated in Würtemberg, where no public gambling was allowed; and, therefore, much quieter and more respectable. All round it lie the hills of the Black Forest. The people are chiefly employed in felling trees, in sawmills, burning charcoal, and making articles of wood, especially the noted Black Forest clocks. The great rafts used on the Rhine and Danube are also supplied from this neighbourhood. Never until I was in the vast and ancient Black Forest did I know the full beauty of the silver fir. It grows there, tall and straight, and without branches to near the top. It would, I dare say, grow to the height of two hundred feet; but when the trees have attained an elevation of about a hundred feet they are cut down, being the size most manageable for rafts. They are indeed magnificent, with a bole as straight as a marble column, scarcely tapering till near the top, and of a silvery whiteness.

Through this elevated, wild, and solitary region we

travelled on to Stuttgart, a comparatively modern capital, the King of Würtemberg being one of Napoleon's monarchs. There we spent a very pleasant Sunday, the hotel-keeper driving his English guests, some eight or ten in number, as a little diversion, to the favourite resort, Cannstatt.

The same evening we called, in Stuttgart, on Gustav Schwab, the poet. He did not possess any great originality, but was of a poetic temperament, which found beautiful expression in verse, and some of his poems William had translated for "The Student Life." We found him a man of fifty, very old-fashioned, with a homely wife, dwelling in a simply-furnished house. The rooms were supplied with great wooden presses, full of homespun linen, hard couches covered with blue-and-white check, and with books, engravings, and casts of the famous writers of Germany. The poet himself, in homespun, resembling a farmer from the plough, was evidently pleased by our attention. He regarded us as benevolent strangers, who bade him be of good cheer, and go on in the straight but unfashionable path of poesy. At least, so we interpreted his broad smile and his bows down to the ground, repeated over and over again, cordial, yet so embarrassed, and to us so embarrassing.

Nor can I forget our visit to the studio of the great, renowned, and pious sculptor, Dannecker, a native of Würtemberg. Amongst other glorious works, he produced a grand conception of Christ. The marble statue was purchased by the Empress Maria Feodorowna of Russia, but he had given the colossal clay model to the Hospital Church of Stuttgart. We could not look at the representation of our Lord without tears of love and devotion, for there seemed to breathe perceptibly

from it a spirit of holiness. We did not wonder at the
Princess of Thurn and Taxis having a marble replica for
her husband's tomb. Whilst Dannecker was employed
upon the model in his studio, a little child suddenly
entered, full of fun; but the moment it saw this divine
statue it exclaimed, in a soft, low voice, "The Saviour!"
and folding its hands, fell on its knees before it. I can
well believe this, for so touching, so inspiring a countenance I never saw. The sculptor was, at the time of our
visit, eighty-three. We asked, "Could we not see him?"
and accordingly we were shown an old man with long
white hair, resting on a raised seat in his garden—that
was Dannecker! Whilst we were looking at him with
a feeling of reverence, the attendant went and told his
wife, I suppose, of our enthusiasm. We were then
invited to walk into the garden and shake hands with
him. We did so, of course, and greatly pleased he
seemed. He took us round his garden and showed us
his flowers and his trees, evidently thinking, dear old
man! that they would give us just as much pleasure as
his immortal works had done. He died before the close
of the year.

From Stuttgart we went to the university town of
Tübingen, a place so ancient that we felt the students
must imbibe exclusively old divinity, abstruse sciences,
and black art. Here we paid a visit to the renowned
German poet and native of Tübingen, Johann Ludwig
Uhland. It seemed as if he had lived all his days in
the glorious world of his own fancies, untroubled and
unvisited by anything so material as three English
travellers, and appeared in consequence both unhappy
and uncomfortable until his wife came. She arrived
from the garden with her knitting-basket on her arm

and a book in her hand, which she had been reading there—it was Milton's "Paradise Lost" in English. She took such an incursion naturally and easily, and made us kindly welcome.

One day, as we were travelling along—this is put in by way of episode—we stopped at Waldenbuch, a most wretched village, that our horses might have some food. We needed nothing for ourselves, and preferred sitting in the carriage. The landlord, having found that we were not to be tempted to alight by any offer of meat or drink, suggested we should go and see an old castle on the hill. He himself would be our guide. It seemed ungracious to refuse, and we alighted. It was the former hunting-lodge of Duke Carl Eugen of Würtemberg. Dannecker had been born in this village, and served as stable-boy at the castle. After our guide had shown us the vaulted stables, he said we must see the dungeon. It was not underground, but merely a vaulted hall. We read the word "Apothecary" on the great iron-studded door; and when it was opened, we entered a vast, cold, dimly-lighted hall, full of drugs, and smelling of them.

A little, pale, thin, anxious-looking man in spectacles, who on our appearance started as if he had seen a ghost, gave a melancholy smile and laid down the book he was reading. It was "Don Quixote" in Spanish. We expressed our surprise, and then we found he could speak English too. He told us he had even paid a visit to London, but had remained merely eight days, it was so immensely great a place. He led us into the next room. It was a beautifully clean little shop, and behind the desk was his bed.

There was something about this poor apothecary which

touched us greatly: how much more so when our host
told us that he was a very learned man, who since his
wife's death, some years before, held intercourse with no
one, spent his time in reading and in preparing medicines
for the poor, and walked out in the evening! I thought
so much of the sad and solitary man, reading his foreign
books in the prison chambers of the old decaying castle,
that I formed with him quite a mental friendship.

After leaving Tübingen, we devoted a day to the
beautiful scenery of the Swabian Alps, especially attracted
thither by Hauff's fascinating romance entitled "Lichten-
stein." The castle of that name had been a ruin perched
on a lofty crag, until the appearance of the popular
historical tale; then great interest being awakened in it,
Count William of Würtemberg, the King's cousin, re-
built it, and at the period of our visit, was having it
richly decorated with frescoes and painted glass, after
designs by noted artists, and appropriately furnished in
antique style. It seemed to us like a glorious castle in
a fairy-tale.

I pass much more rapidly on paper through Ulm and
Augsburg than we did in reality, and so reach Munich.
With this bright and enterprising seat of art we were
delighted. We visited galleries and studios, and were
particularly impressed with "The Destruction of Jerusalem," by Kaulbach, and our visit to this great painter's
studio. It was in a picturesque building, standing amid
deep grass, full of wild-flowers, bushes, and poplars, in
the St. Anna suburb. This visit was especially memorable from its effect on the mind and imagination of our
daughter, of whose inborn talent for art mention has
already been made.

From Munich we journeyed to Linz. Here we embarked on the Danube for Vienna. The steamer had not been able to get up to Linz from the lowness of the water. It lay at the distance of twenty English miles farther down, and we must be conveyed thither in a common Danube boat. It was very wet weather, and there was neither a cover from the rain nor seats for the hundred passengers of all ranks requiring conveyance. As we went on board, however, benches and an awning were being hurriedly arranged. On the plank down which the passengers had to descend into the boat stood up, some couple of inches, a stout nail. It caught the skirts of every lady that went down, tore several, and over it some gentlemen stumbled. At length our turn came; my gown caught; my husband disengaged it, and calling to a man with a hammer, had the nail knocked down. An American immediately afterwards addressed us in the boat, saying, " Sir, excuse my freedom, but I know you are an Englishman by the simple fact of your having immediately ordered the driving down of that nail." To do so, he had noticed, never occurred to the German gentlemen; some seemed apathetic, others nonchalant; they would stumble, curse it, and go on.

We spent a fortnight in Vienna, the capital not merely of Austria, but of German gaiety; thousands and tens of thousands were seated in the gardens, netting, knitting, listening to the musical bands, drinking coffee and sugar-water, and eating ices. There was the Folk's Theatre, with its comic representations; the Opera; there were concerts, and fireworks all in full action. Imperial gardens and parks were open, and the public walked in them, and through the very courts and gateways of palaces, as if they were their own. We were already aware of the freedom thus enjoyed by the people, from our experience

in Baden and elsewhere. We had noticed the Grand-
Duke come into a country inn, call for his glass of ale,
drink it, pay for it, and go unceremoniously away. The
Emperor of Austria and the King of Prussia might also
be seen walking about amongst their subjects. Arch-
dukes and princes sat in public places with their friends,
unassumingly drinking coffee. These royal and ducal
personages were treated with quiet respect, and whilst
everywhere popular, were exempted from all crushing
and being stared at.

We grew quite tired of sight-seeing, and looked forward to our two days' and nights' continuous travelling
in an *Eilwagen* over the whole extent of Bohemia as a
season of respite and relief. We started on September 7
for Prague, journeying on without stopping, except to
eat and change horses. Oh, how different was the heavy,
lumbering *Eilwagen* in appearance from a smart English
mail-coach! In England the horses were harnessed into
the least possible space. In Germany, on the contrary,
the leaders were about three yards distant from the
wheelers; so that Hood, in his clever book, "Up the
Rhine," had good reason for making the leaders turn
round to look if the *Eilwagen* were coming. On we
slowly went through a most dreary part of Germany, the
old kingdom of Bohemia, desolate wood and unbroken
plain, varied only by the melancholy, forlorn villages.

Scarcely had we been a couple of hours in our *Eilwagen*, a curious, long-bodied coach, with several seats
placed cross-wise, before a card was handed to us by a
young Englishman travelling in the same vehicle, who
most modestly and respectfully requested he might thus
introduce himself. The name on the card was Sorell.
He said he did not speak German, was quite alone, and

had taken the liberty of securing his place in this carriage
that he might have the advantage of being near us.  He
too was going to Prague.  Had he been a coarse, vulgar
man, this would have been offensive; but he was so
gentle and unobtrusive in his manner, that we cheerfully acquiesced.  He was a most amiable young man,
from India, and continued with us on our tour for some
distance beyond Prague.

Our other fellow-travellers—for there were various
vehicles—were chiefly queer men of a Jewish and Oriental type.  They were in fur caps, fur cloaks, or in furred
and frogged jackets.  It was to me quite awful, in the
morning, after the long night-journey, to see these strange,
wild, barbaric-looking men washing their faces in the
same bucket of water, and wiping them on one towel.

It was at Znaim, I think, where we arrived the first
night, that we could obtain no fresh relay of horses.
Great was the consternation.  They were required, we
were told, for M. Thiers, whom my husband saw quietly
seated asleep in his carriage, at the inn-door.

How strangely unvaried was the scenery through which
we passed!  My companions often slept.  I generally
kept awake, and studied the dreary, solitary character of
the landscape; and one afternoon, in so doing, I saw a
house on fire, situated at about a quarter of a mile from
the road, on one of the immense plains.  There was
little smoke, but a mass of burning fire, which looked
colourless in the hot sun.  I woke my party, but our
exclamations of surprise and sympathy produced no
response in the postillions or remaining passengers;
the latter were doubtless asleep, and the officials were
indifferent to the spectacle of fire and the misery it
implied.

Prague, of course, interested us greatly. Then on we journeyed to Dresden, where we vastly enjoyed the opera. From the Saxon capital we went to Herrnhut. I was much pleased with this peaceful settlement of Moravians—the clean, cheerful exterior of the houses, the well-kept streets, the pleasant gardens. Herrnhut lies high and bleak. The night of our arrival was intensely chilly; we were driving in an open carriage, and all took cold. The next morning there was a strong frost. The dahlias and the potatoes were frozen. But the sky was clear and the sun bright. We walked about and saw all that was to be seen. We were greatly interested by our conversation with the meek, quiet people, who all seemed so good. The healthy men had cheerful, serene countenances; the mild-looking women wore caps of snowy linen, tied with ribbons of various colours, denoting the wearer to be maiden, wife, or widow. We heard music of a soft, devotional character through open windows, intimating either worship or social enjoyment. Herrnhut seemed a haven of peace. The piety of these Moravians struck us forcibly, after the very little religious belief which we had met with amongst the Lutherans, whom we found full of sentiment and human affection, yet very cold in their love of Christ and His holy faith. They had, in fact, become philosophised out of their religion. The Rationalists had gained ground especially among the students, and Strauss, in his "Life of Christ," was believed by his numerous disciples to have undermined for ever the entire fabric of Scriptural revelation.

Of the Catholics we knew but little. I had, however, from our first arrival in Germany, been much touched by the wayside shrines and crucifixes; they seemed to me like religious thoughts on the highway—true guide-posts to heaven. The Catholic character of the valley of Petersthal, near Heidelberg, had likewise a charm for me. There were little images of the Virgin in niches on the front of the cottages, which, although wretched plaster figures gaudily coloured, indicated much devotion. At the end of the valley was a small chapel of a most simple and ancient appearance, sur-rounded by solemn woods. Every object in the edifice bespoke poverty and was of the most primitive con-struction, forming the greatest contrast to the magnifi-cent interior of Cologne Cathedral, for instance; and yet in both reigned the same spirit of sanctity and of prayer.

And let me now say, what I regard as one of the most important and marvellous circumstances of my life, but of which I certainly was not conscious for the greater part of it, that through periods of forgetfulness, wilful error, experiments of faith, doubt and despondency, I was never utterly forsaken by the Holy Spirit. I attri-bute this watchful, undying fidelity of Divine Love as greatly due to the sincere, heartfelt prayers of my ex-cellent parents, and their having, to the best of their knowledge, committed their children to the Divine Guide, the Enlightener.

To proceed with our travels. We returned to Dresden, and a glimpse of our doings can best be given in the words of my daughter, Anna Mary, who thus writes to a correspondent, September 22, 1841 :—

"As you are, like ourselves, an extreme admirer of Moritz Retzsch, I am employing my first spare five minutes to send you an account of him. You already know that he lives a few miles out of Dresden, in a small

country-house at the foot of the Weinberg, in the village
of Lösnitz. We took a carriage and drove thither. It
seemed an out-of-the-world sort of a place, a chain
of low hills covered with vineyards; at the foot a few
scattered white houses, with green shutters and red roofs;
in the foreground a bad road and two or three desolate
gardens. This was the scene of Retzsch's home, and
with a blue sky and plenty of autumn colouring, the
place did not want for picturesque effect. The house
in itself is very humble, the rooms small and badly
furnished, and nowhere I remarked even a single engraving or painting on the walls. There was, however, a
very handsome piano and plenty of music lying about,
for his wife is passionately fond of music. While we
were making these hasty observations, a stout man of
middle size, with an abundance of wild grey hair, stood
before us. This was Moritz Retzsch.

"Although he was outwardly polite, we could see he
did not recognise in our name that of the admirer of
his works, who, two years since, had sent him a flattering
letter and a book of poems from England. At length
a mist seemed to vanish from his eyes, and stretching
across the table, he seized mamma's hand with both his,
and began shaking it until his very arms must have
ached. Five minutes later, his whole face beaming with
pleasure, did he again begin violently with both hands
the same process; but this time it was papa's and my
turn.

"Now we must eat some of his grapes; must go to
his painting-room upstairs; must see his wife's album.
Through several very narrow passages, up a very small
flight of steps, and through one or two little bedrooms did
he conduct us, until we fairly entered his 'working-room,'

as he called a tiny chamber.  It contained a sofa, three
chairs, a what-not, an easel, and a little table, on which
he had made his drawings for many years.  He pointed
out from the window all the points of interest in his
vineyard, which stretched up the hillside opposite.  Then
he opened the table-drawer, and exhibited to us mamma's
letter carefully folded up among a heap of lead-pencils,
sketch-books, indiarubber, and penknives.  Then from
under a heap of papers on the what-not he drew forth his
wife's album.  It would be impossible to mention a tenth
of the gems which we saw as we turned over the leaves
of this remarkably rich book.  Suffice it to say that it
contains at least half-a-dozen designs equal to his 'Chess-
players.'  There were many drawings revealing some
exquisite sentiment or half-hidden moral.  One particularly pleased us.  It was his portrait, just a sketch of
his head and face, with an exquisite border of fanciful
and poetical figures—a perfect swarm, and imaging forth,
as he said, his own mind.

" While we were turning over the pages of the album,
he read to us his own explanations of these sketches,
every now and then breaking off into half-moralising,
half-sentimental and poetical remarks, quite in the spirit
of his 'Fancies.'  We went with the intention of
spending half-an-hour with him, when behold, as we
closed the book, the call had already lasted two hours!
In another hour's time we must be ready to start for
Leipzig; and thus, in spite of all his great kindness,
and his offer to show us still more of his drawings,
we were obliged to hasten away.

" He and an amiable young girl, whom we imagine to
be his niece, accompanied us to the gate, and as long
as we could keep sight of them did we see them still

gazing after us, good, kind Retzsch waving his cap in token of adieu.

"It is needless to say how unspeakably delighted were we with the face of the Madonna del Sisto and the little Jesus, in the Dresden Gallery, or how we wandered through the rooms in an amazement and enjoyment, until we were almost dazzled with Raphaels, Correggios, Titians, and Paul Veroneses. Yet beautiful as is this Dresden collection, we equally enjoyed the Belvedere Gallery in Vienna, of which very little is said. The Dresden Gallery is quite the fashionable lounge, and we met so many acquaintances, and were introduced to so many people, that we found it impossible properly to study the pictures."

We proceeded from Leipzig, where my daughter wrote the above extract, to Berlin. It was very different from the present magnificent capital. Along every street and before every house, even in the finest parts of the city and in the neighbourhood of the King's palace, was a stagnant sink, which filled the whole air with its rank odour. The inhabitants told us that it was impossible to drain the city, as it stood on a dead flat. Into one of these sinks we saw a little boy of about five years plunged headlong, as he was playing on the causeway, by a rough fellow who was going carelessly along. Nobody seemed to care. He was left to scramble out, and after cleaning his face and mouth in some degree from the filth, began to cry piteously. We asked the boy where he lived, and he showed us a little girl about his own age who was standing by and quietly knitting. With the utmost difficulty we compelled her to take her brother home, and were aided by a good man, who

seized her sternly by the arm and forced her to go on
with the boy, who all the time was weeping.

King Frederick William IV., who had recently ascended the throne, was embellishing his city, and in the
portico of the Museum opposite to the palace we observed Cornelius at work, adorning it with frescoes.
Schelling, the brothers Grimm, Humboldt, Savigny,
Rückert, Rauch, Schinkel, the Tiecks, poet and sculptor,
with other famous men, had been drawn to Berlin by the
sovereign, who wished to render his reign illustrious by
science and art.

On Tieck, the poet, His Majesty had bestowed a
pension, on the condition that he spent three months in
the year with him.   We had the pleasure of visiting
this oldest veteran of German literature in his charming
house just below the palace of Sans Souci at Potsdam,
given him for his use by the King.

After leaving Berlin, we saw Magdeburg and the wild
scenery of the Harz mountains ; and stayed in the beautiful Selke valley at Alexisbad.   Owing to its being late
autumn, the guests were all gone, and the place was considered closed for the season.   How astonished, therefore,
were we, and a young Englishman travelling with us, the
son of Dr. Southwood Smith, to hear in an adjacent apartment the most brilliant performance on the piano!  It
reminded our fellow-traveller of the music in "Robert le
Diable" and "Les Huguenots;" and we learnt from the
waiter that it was actually the great composer himself.
He was staying on at the bath to secure quiet and leisure
for the composition of a new opera.   The next morning,
as we were dressing, we saw our young companion paying
his respects in the garden to Meyerbeer, and then walking about with him.   The opera thus being composed at

solitary Alexisbad was "Le Prophète," which, although shortly afterwards finished, was first performed some eight years later.

We visited Luther's cell at Erfurt, and his retreat in the Wartburg. In Weimar we were most kindly received by Wolfgang von Goethe's mother, then in delicate health. She showed us many interesting mementoes of her great father-in-law; and also the common little table that Schiller had bequeathed to his friend Goethe, and which showed the simple life of those renowned geniuses.

I thus address my sister Anna, from Heidelberg, October 19, 1841 :—

"Thy kind and most deeply interesting letter I found here on our return from our long journey, the day before yesterday. I cannot tell thee the deep sentiment of love which it awakened. I truly hope and trust that the little stranger will live and grow to be the comfort of your old age. The children of one's later life are little desired; yet what a want of faith is it after all, for one's own daily experience proves, that often these younger children are given as positive blessings, to stand by their parents when their elder brothers and sisters are engrossed in their own cares and worldly concerns. I trust it will be so with your Agnes and this dear new-comer, and with our little Meggie."

"*Heidelberg, December* 9, 1841.—I have been waiting day after day in the greatest anxiety to hear from thee. The dear baby too, I hardly dare to ask after it, but hoping all is well, I must tell how I have rejoiced in its being a girl. I wish thou could have a peep at our little old-fashioned Marjory, in a brown merino frock with tight sleeves to the elbow. She has brown hair and red cheeks, and is withal so prim and demure; dressing herself up in any shawl she can find, 'to go,' as she says, 'into the city.' I am sure Red Riding Hood must have been such a child, and so must Goody-Two-Shoes.

"Did I tell thee that, while we were on our journey, a daughter of our relative, Richard Fryer, of Wolverhampton, came to this place with her four, children for their education. She is a very interesting woman, and has gone through unknown sorrows. People that have known tribulation always come recommended to my heart. High talent or a chastened spirit is in my eyes far nobler, far more winning, than high birth or worldly riches.

"We are leading such a quiet life here this winter that we might almost be hermits."


"*Heidelberg, Feb.* 13, 1842.—Thy letter came to us, dearest sister, in a dark time; and it cast a ray of sunshine round us that gladdened us for days. Now, I know that thou art impatient to learn what has troubled us. Do not agitate thyself, however; we are unscathed in life and limb, although, like the poor man going down to Jericho, we have fallen into the hands of thieves, and have had the most sorrowful revelation of human nature. We have even in this house been surrounded by much plotting and cunning; we have taken, therefore, a floor in another house, to which we go at Easter. We shall be at the other end of the city and have new views from our windows, and the rooms are of quite another character. It has been recently built; we shall be the first dwellers, and we hope, as soon as we get into it, to shake off all the lingering recollections of the persons who have deceived and cheated us."

·The residence to which I have just alluded was erected
by a ladies' tailor, who had made money in Russia; we
rented the highest floor.  The *Anlage*, or public walk
leading to the station—for the railway had been brought
to Heidelberg—ran along on the front side of the house,
which is now enlarged and converted into the Victoria

OUR SECOND HOME AT HEIDELBERG.

Hotel.  I wonder whether the summer-house, roofed
with silvered iron and painted inside with gold stars on
a blue ground, still remains in the vineyard !

It was delightful on a beautiful summer morning to
sit among the vines, with the Rhine-plain stretching
out before us, the distant mountains rising heaven-
wards, and the Rhine glancing in the sunny horizon,
our agreeable new home lying at our feet, and the

green, round, vine-covered, familiar Heidelberg hills rising behind us.

From this new home I write to my sister Anna, July 4, 1842 :—

"I, for my part, cannot help beginning to think with some despondency of our return to England. If we could only command an income here, how gladly would I yet spend ten years at least in Germany!  I like the country, and, above all, the quiet, regular, simple, and inexpensive mode of life.  We have, moreover, only recently learnt how best to live in Germany.  We had at first native servants, who could speak English.  They had all the views of English domestics, and, what was worse, they cheated us in a hundred ways, misled and kept us in the dark.  By degrees our eyes were opened ; we sent our fine servants away, and engaged in their stead a regular German maid for half the wages, and who is satisfied with a tenth of the indulgence ; and we find our pocket saved and our comfort increased every way.  We shall just begin to understand the true mode of living in Germany when we leave it.

"The German paper that William reads contains the most doleful accounts from England.  You, of course, know all—the people starving, the manufactures sinking, and Sir Robert Peel laying on an income-tax to cure all!  How dark and fearful seems the future!  I do not wonder at Harrison and Emma determining to leave England.  Although of this I am sure, that if they go to America with Utopian notions of finding human nature much better there than in England, they will be mistaken.  But this I can well believe : they will live calmer, and be surrounded by better subjects of contem-dlation.  They will find the perfect simplicity of life congenial to them, and will have the pleasure of seeing their children growing up healthy, hopeful-minded men and women. All is struggle, fever, and delirium in England. There is no room for the coming-up generation.

"I have been very busy translating the first volume of a charming work by Fredrika Bremer, a Swedish writer; and if any publisher will give me encouragement to go on with it, I will soon complete the work. It is one of a series of stories of every-day life in Sweden—a beautiful book, full of the noblest moral lessons for every man and woman. I hope it may be printed in England, and that it may be liked."


"*Oct.* 12, 1842.—The boys are just going to school, after their long holidays, which is a great comfort; for though they have been remarkably good at home, and, in fact, all the time of their papa's absence in England, I never like children to be at a loose end. Alfred is very much admired; he grows handsome, and carries himself well. Claude is a wild, harum-scarum, out-at-the-elbow fellow, with torn knees and dirty hands, but some way or other everybody likes him. He is the naughtiest of all, and yet the most gifted. He learns anything at a glance. Claude is born to be fortunate; he is one that will make the family distinguished in the next generation. He has an extraordinary faculty for telling stories, either of his own invention or of what he reads. He never for one quarter of a second hesitates for a word either in English or German.

"Thou canst imagine, dear sister, our delight at having William back again, after an absence of three months. We all feel as if we did not know how to make enough of him.

"We have had a splendid summer; its equal has not been known in Germany for fifty years. The vintage has been glorious. We all, old and young, great and small, turned out on the first day of the vintage at this house, and worked. It was like something Arcadian— the tubs and baskets piled up with most lovely, enormous clusters, the men and women carrying them away on their heads and on their backs to the place where they were being crushed; the laughing, the merriment, the feasting, the firing—for they make as much noise as they can—the shouting, the beautiful day: altogether it was delightful, to say nothing of the masquerading and dancing in the evening, which we saw, though we did not take part in it."

On November 19, 1842, I write to our friend, Miss Bowles, then Mrs. Southey, and whose wedded bliss had been almost immediately blighted by Southey becoming imbecile :—

"You did us justice when you gave us credit for caring to hear about you. We knew how painfully occupied was your mind as well as your time by your dear husband's grievous infirmities, and we saw sufficient reason for your silence.

"Our residence in Germany now approaches its close. In the spring we return to England; though we leave our elder boys behind us at their school, and our daughter in a French family. Greatly as I have enjoyed our German residence, I begin to have a longing for England, a sort of enthusiasm growing up for my native land, which I was glad enough to let sleep while it was convenient or desirable for us to live out of it. We have attained, I think, our present object in coming.

We have given our daughter opportunities of accomplishing herself which we had not in England; and we have made ourselves well acquainted with the establishment in which the boys will be placed. We regret extremely not having been able to reach Italy this autumn, which was our original intention. The project is delayed, but by no means abandoned.

" After Easter we shall be in England, and then I need not say that if my husband in any way can serve you, he will be most happy to be commanded by you. Of our exact whereabouts I cannot at present speak, as we do not intend to return to our former residence at Esher."

The journey back to England was carried out as proposed; its chief and most agreeable feature being the pleasant halt made at St. Goar, on the Rhine, to visit Ferdinand Freiligrath. He was a young lyric poet, and a great admirer of English poetry. .His renderings of Coleridge, Burns, Southey, Scott, and other authors read as originals. He liked my productions, and had introduced specimens to his countrymen. His accomplished wife, Ida, daughter of Professor Melos, of Weimar, and Goethe's god-daughter, was then, or perhaps a little later, engaged with her husband in the translation of the " Forest Sanctuary," and some of the minor poems of Felicia Hemans.

END OF VOL. I.

PRINTED BY BALLANTYNE, HANSON AND CO.<br>EDINBURGH AND LONDON.